CW01665710

The Boy at Willows End

The Boy at Willows End

Growing up in the Fens in 1940

Illustrated by the author

Frank Wrigley

FOR
China, Chippy, Podge and 'the Windmill Girl' -
not forgetting the 'Vacagees'

The Larks Press

Published by the Larks Press
Ordnance Farmhouse
Guist Bottom, Dereham NR20 5PF
01328 829207

October 1999

Printed by The Lanceni Press
Garrood Drive, Fakenham

British Library Cataloguing-in-Publication-Data
A Catalogue record for this book is available at the British Library

ISBN 0 948400 80 3

CONTENTS

'I did not consider publishing this manuscript...It was simply a pastime whilst bed-ridden...However...'

Foreword

If the reader takes a map of the Fens and draws a triangle through Wisbech, Downham Market and Ely, he will not find Willows End. He will, however, find a profusion of 'lodes', for a lode denotes a waterway linking villages to the main 'cuts' and rivers, so lending anonymity to its actual whereabouts.

Within this triangle during those between-the-war years lived many 'Boer Roberts', ex-Royal Horse Artillery or Cavalry Regiment regulars, returned home at the end of their service life to take their place as horsemen or teamsters on the farms. Many also were the officers' wives who found temporary accommodation in the fen villages to be near their husbands as the units reorganised following Dunkirk. It will be purely coincidental if one of the many happened to be christened 'Olivia'. 'Ferret' is representative of every indigenous Fenland girl who, at the age of fourteen, is wise in the lore and skills passed down from time immemorial, with a sagacity far beyond the 'book larnin' of her urban sisters.

Every Fen village held its veteran R.S.M.Kingshott, duly retired to take on a new lease of life in his sweet and tobacco shop, although it has been known for such a one to become the landlord of an inn. China, Chippy and Podge are typical of we Willows End boys of the 1930s.

Now, sixty years on, Willows End will have changed. Photographs, television and the written word all show a very different 'Fens', a Fenland almost unrecognisable to an ageing exile who, between the wars, grew up in an environment dominated by lonely roads reaching outwards between dykes of emerald reeds beneath cloudless blue summer skies, where tumbrils and waggons rumbled and swayed, pulled by glossy shires. Smart cobs pulling high-wheeled gigs passed by at a spanking trot, and antiquated lorries loaded with fruit, heading towards Wisbech, raised a miasma of peaty dust.

There were always larks singing, spring, summer and autumn. Flowers in swathes of colour bordered the roadside verges. Cool grey-green willow leaves drooped, during the dog-days of high summer, over glassy water. Partridges bathed with impunity in the roadside dust. Then came the 'thrashin' days', when the huge steam traction engines rumbled from farm to farm and rats ran the gauntlet of screaming boys with sticks and yapping terriers, while sagacious lurchers watched, silent and aloof, guarding their masters' 'docky bags' of cold tea and beef-dripping sandwiches. And always there were the lines of 'singlin', sugar-beet-choppin', pea-pullin' and tato-pickin' women.

Imbued with this wistful melancholy, I have relived my 1940 'Goodbye to the Fen'. Faces, long-forgotten, have materialised, wraith-like, vaporous as Fen distances from the past.

It is possible that a seventy-one-year-old 'Ferret' may still think back to a November night's 'partridge-nettin' under a moon with a duffer boy, while a spry 'Captain's Lady' of eighty-four may allow herself a nostalgic smile recalling 'Adlertag' and the 'Secret Fen'!

Glaspwll
Mid-Wales
October 1997

June 6th, 1940

A boy walked slowly across the village square disturbing a flock of white ducks who were preening on a patch of sun-warmed gravel at the edge of the pond. A heady scent of lime hung in the still air, drifting like the perfume of an elegant woman across the path of the boy. The simile went unnoticed for he had yet to become aware of the perfume of an elegant woman. He was acquainted only with the old forgotten men squatting on their haunches beneath the row of lime trees bordering the churchyard wall, and gauche wind-sculpted girls in Wellington boots immutably wedded to their hoes. Perhaps if her ladyship from the Hall had walked across the village square he would have been enlightened, but she came infrequently and always passed in a closed limousine whose fragrance was a well-bred miasma of exhaust gas.

It was the morning of the 6th of June 1940. Soft clouds glided slowly across a blue sky. The old men spat accurately in the pollen-sweet dust by the War Memorial and argued asthmatically about past glories. In his hand the boy clasped a Players' cigarette packet containing a Lime Hawk moth. Newly emerged from its chrysalis, it was a perfect specimen, a living likeness to a delicately-marbled young lime leaf, an emerald to be set in the crown of his collection of butterflies and moths.

Peace reigned in the Fenland village. The ducks waddled the few yards to enter the calm water of the pond. The old men followed the movements of the boy through rheumy eyes. Then, seeing the Postmaster's wife cycling over the hump-back bridge at the head of the pond, swivelled their heads to refocus on her fluttering cotton skirt.

But the peace of Willow's End was not reflected within the mind of the boy, for every muted rasping movement against the silver paper lining the cigarette packet caused his pulse to miss a beat as he imagined the pristine scales being dusted from the moth's wings before the fumes from the cyanide killing-jar could still its vibrant soul. Does an insect possess a soul? Frank Dutton was just sixteen years old and could not respond to the complexities of the soul, only to the compulsive urge of possession and the glories of the carefully-regimented rows of stiff insects in the mahogany cabinets which stood in his late father's study. Nor was he aware that elsewhere, beyond the bounds of the English Fens, a Dante's inferno to be labelled 'Dunkirk' was raging, and further away still others were being netted in their hundreds to be transported towards a holocaust of Semitic souls in greater chambers of cyanide gas.

The 'Square' was the hub around which Willow's End revolved, observed by the old men beneath the churchyard limes, recorded in the annals of their memory and replayed during the evening in the Snug-Bar of the Ship Inn. Tall weeping willows encircled two sides of the pond where a footpath wound between three red-pantiled cottages, the Wesleyan Chapel and the Post Office. There the willow boughs drooped to meet the water in a maze of secret leafy arbours for the ducks. From the Post Office the Square's boundary continued by the school railings towards the War Memorial along the church wall to the lych-gate, overhung by dark ragged yews. Here the church wall turned into the 'Street' which ran east to west forming the fourth side of the Square. Eastward the Street ran alongside the pond opposite the Ship Inn and the straggling ochre-washed, wisteria-clad home of the boy, and westwards by a row of terraced cottages to the village shop and bakery.

The boy paused below the blue mass of wisteria blossom framing the porch before quietly opening the front door to enter a cool, stone-flagged passage, purpled with shadows. Ignoring the hushed voices coming from the living room, he turned right and entered the door to his father's study to sit on the lid of the coffin, watched by a twittering flock of zebra finches and Java sparrows, green lovebirds and cockatiels.

Thomas Dutton had been an ornithologist researching the cranial sensory nervous system of birds. He had loved to be surrounded by birds and the indoor aviary took up a third of his large study which housed a brass microscope, prepared slides, books and his paintings of birds. Now these were overshadowed by the oak coffin which lay in the centre of the available floorspace. Frank gave a cursory glance at the black letters 'THOMAS DUTTON 1883-1940' incised on the polished brass plate before unscrewing the killing-jar lid with its lethal crystals of cyanide encased in plaster of Paris.

He tapped the Players' packet gently with a forefinger above the open jar, allowing the fluttering moth freedom to fall on the white plaster as a slow stream of golden ova oozed from its abdomen in a final bid for immortality.

The boy spilled the dead insect on to the coffin and carefully replaced the lid of the jar. Only the thickness of the oak plank lay between the insect and the scientist's unseeing eyes. Perhaps in death they were all-seeing and only the boy alien.

A drawer in the mahogany butterfly cabinet had been left half open and one butterfly stood out among the row of *Pieridae*. Frank, kneeling on the coffin in order to close the drawer, remembered. He was reminded of his father with long white hair, peering through his microscope...Welney, Lake's End, Three Holes, Outwell, Upwell....orderly rows of apple blossom in the spring...thunder rolling sullenly in the distance over the peaty black soil with blue trees on the wide horizon behind translucent mists. 'Hurry, Father, Swallowtail!' The sulphur-yellow insect, striped with black, gliding low above the drove-side blossoms of milk parsley ...flick the muslin net...'I've got her!...I've got her! Quick!'...kneeling together...crushed scent of mint...'*Papilio machaon*. Feltwell Fen June 8th 1937' carefully scribed with Indian ink and mapping pen beneath the stiff insect pinned in the cabinet drawer.

The sun was rising on the 7th June 1940, and a heavy fragrance drifted across the Square from the church-wall limes. Sparrows were noisy in the eaves and swifts dived screeching to their nests in the church tower.

Frank woke to the muted clip-clop of the farm horses passing below the window as the horseman led them to the pond to drink. He could see them through the bedroom window silhouetted against the soft mist that shrouded the pond. Beyond the Wesleyan Chapel the sun rose, casting long shadows from the willows across the Post Office roof. Girls crossed the Square wearing summer plimsolls and print frocks, their hair covered by bright headscarves, chattering like a flock of finches as they hurried towards the pea-picking field behind the stackyard. Their voices ricocheted back and forth as they teased 'Boer' Roberts.

Boer, as old as memory, bowed of back and legs, gnarled as a blackthorn after two wars with a cavalry regiment, was sitting like an Ely gargoyle on a Suffolk punch standing fetlock-deep in the pond surrounded by his team of heavy shires.

Movement sounded from the kitchen as Frank lingered in his other-world of loneliness. Lying in his narrow bed, he heard the farm horses as they returned to the stables to be curry-combed and brushed in preparation for the day's work. Then he heard old Boer's footsteps as he went home to his cottage up the street for his own breakfast before 'collerin' up'. It was just 6 o'clock, an hour before the shires would return with a clatter of chains and creak of stiff leather as they 'turned out'. Frank turned over and tried to sleep.

'Frank,' his mother was calling, the brittle words spiralling up the narrow staircase to shatter on his ceiling. 'Frank,' she repeated impatiently, 'get up!' She was standing at the foot of the stairs, pale and tight-lipped. For the first time in his life his mother appeared to be unsure of herself. 'Go and wash...There is so much to be done,' she added vaguely.

Mrs Dutton was the one person who had controlled the eccentric scientist's family. Now, with the unnatural emanation of death pervading the house, she seemed inwardly insecure and forlorn. He wanted to fling his arms around her and sob, but such weakness was unforgivable. She blocked the morning sunlight streaming in through the passage window between the hollyhock leaves, standing before him haughty and expressionless, her greying hair twisted in a puritanical bun. No wonder he was unsure of himself when any outward expression of love was repelled by her.

Frank followed her into the kitchen where the stout, comforting body of Ma Shipham hovered placidly in the background preparing breakfast.

'Come you on bor,' handing him a large black kettle of boiling water, 'and see you wash ahind your ears!' Ma Shipham was an ally. He felt he could kiss her, hug her; she alone was sane in a house of grey marionettes.

Mrs Dutton passed absent-mindedly through the kitchen to pick up a duster and disappear into the parlour, already saturated with the bouquet of Mansion polish and Windolene. Ma Shipham shook her head as the parlour door closed. 'She's a-taking it a lot harder than them what lets their feelin's go,' she murmured, twisting a dishcloth and methodically wringing out the warm soapsuds. 'Your Ma's a real Lady, that's a fact, but no one can talk to her an she's her own worst enemy.' She threw the dishcloth at the boy. 'Go you on and get washed!'

Standing in the murky light of the wash-house, Frank stared listlessly at the chipped enamel bowl standing in the stone sink below the pump and assisted a large spider to escape up its slippery side before pouring in the hot water and splashing a few droplets around his eyes with the tips of his fingers. He reminded himself that China, Chippy and Podge, in fact any of his village companions would go home after a day spent scrambling about the dykes, ratting or bird-nesting, with their faces streaked with mud, to reappear on the following morning with it still proudly in place. It gave them 'character'. He gazed at his own insipid, pale countenance staring back from his father's shaving mirror, feeling himself to be an utter stranger, an exile among his own kind.

His ablutions quickly over, he slipped unnoticed into the study to feed the birds. The coffin had been removed, leaving a space between the aviary and the desk, and he seated himself on the chair below the microscope. It was an unusually high bentwood chair, a backed stool rather than a chair, with a round cane seat. Sitting on the chair the first sobs came, slowly and spaced, like the first heavy drops of summer rain that fall silently, almost unseen, before the storm breaks.

Frank's sixteen-year-old world lapsed into nothingness as the finches watched expectantly in sociable chatterings. Everything in the study was suddenly bereft of meaning. The guns over the fireplace, the fishing rods standing idle in their brown cotton covers, the butterfly nets and the setting blocks, and the companionship of a white-haired, blue-eyed eccentric who had never grown up, ceased to exist.

The storm of overwhelming grief burst, stilling the birds into unnatural silence, but the storm passed quickly and the study took on a new brilliance as he fed the birds. The tiny African wren flooded the room with song, the finches twittered and the cockatiels began to chirrup as the lovebirds danced along the perch. As he closed the door and walked towards the porch he noticed that the stray dog had finally left.

A huge black dog, like a Newfoundland with the muzzle of a black bear, had lain, nose on forepaws, outside the back door during the time that the coffin rested in the study. Tradesmen visiting the house stepped round it warily and crossed their fingers. Boer took the longer path through the furthest stackyard when he watered the horses. And nobody seemed to know where it had come from.... or mentioned it. Once Frank had stroked its collarless shaggy neck as it gazed up at him with mesmeric eyes, but it refused food, nor would it move away from the doorstep. 'It must have left during the night,' he reasoned to himself, 'and that explains why Boer brought the horses past the house.'

It was twenty minutes past eleven by the clock on the church tower when the two ladies emerged from the house to cross the street to the church. By now the sun had climbed high above the Fen in a cloudless blue sky. Larks were singing above the peafield and the village square was bathed in unbroken sunlight, the lime leaves humming with foraging bees. The old men were early at their time-honoured posts, squatting below the church wall. Only the bees, droning through the morning heat appeared to be working. Jeremiah Shipham, wearing his Sunday grey suit with a black armband, stood propped by his crutches like a priestly heron beside his daughter Madge who was waiting with the vicar's wife and the postmistress as Mrs Dutton and Ma Shipham approached the lych gate.

Frank followed slowly, closing the front door and bending to stroke the ginger cat stretched upon the warm tarmac of the street. He glanced up to see the group of mourners waiting in the shade of the lych gate yew. He suppressed a smile, wondering what his father would have thought of the Headmaster, the Postmaster and the prosperous cattle-dealer, each standing uneasily aloof within his own aura of mothballs and Lifebuoy soap, wearing black coats, black suits and Homburg hats.

Thomas Dutton's eyes would have danced roguishly at the sight. Drawing freely from his store of satirical imagery, they would have become black Churchyard beetles presiding over the interment of a shrew by a solitary Sexton beetle. By mischievous whimsy the cattle-dealer would become the orange-and-black-banded Sexton beetle for he sported a pair of non-conforming boots whose brilliant ox-blood shine gleamed below the black serge of his trouser bottoms.

His father had refused to accept the asinine distinctions between religions while his Methodist wife calmly whitewashed over his eccentricities by referring to him as a 'free thinker'. To the Vicar he appeared as a stray lamb returned to the fold, for his widow had resurrected proof of his baptism into the Church of England fifty-six years and two months before.

At the arrival of the widowed lady the mourners regrouped and wound their way slowly along the gravel path between the yews towards the south porch of the Norman church. The funeral shrouds of the ladies' tightly-fitting dresses told all, shattering Frank's cocoon of disbelief. Reality filtered through and, as he passed the threshold, his eyes lit upon a drowned nestling starling floating in the holy water stoup, its naked pink belly and gaping yellow mouth floating below the message 'Let everything that hath breath praise the Lord' carved deep in an aged panel of oak.

Kneeling on a hassock in the nave, Frank closed his eyes and allowed his mind to slip back into a sanctuary from reality. Vaguely he heard the organ dirge followed by a blur of ritualistic responses to the Vicar's sonorous voice circling with the motes of dust in the shafts of sunlight as they drifted down to rest on the coffin. He opened one eye to see a spider carefully descend from the carved pew end on to the floor beside him.

Finally, with a shuffling of feet and suppressed coughs, the service ended and the small congregation passed from the cool of the church into the sudden glare of sunlight. Life returned to normal, the scent of lime continuing to flood the air about the old men dozing beside the lych gate. The coffin was being lifted on to the bier to be drawn to the cemetery by Sedge Farm's black cob.

Frank walked behind his mother in the small cortège as it passed slowly along the Street to the rhythmic clip-clop of the black cob's hooves. His mind wandered out into the Fen to become lost in the mists of *Morte D'Arthur.* Resurrected from snippets of fifth-form English the funeral became a dream-passage of Arthur drifting through the misty Fens in the black barge towards the apple orchards of Avalon with his three queens beside him, Ma Shipham, his mother and the Vicar's wife. He grinned outwardly at the thought of his father in the guise of the Arthurian king. Madge Shipham caught his eye and grinned back. Flaxen-haired, freckle-faced and just sixteen....'You should not be here,' Frank thought, 'you and I have no concern with death.'

She was wearing a lime-green cotton frock, the only spot of colour among the funeral shrouds, a dance-stepping greenfinch wearing white plimsolls surrounded by a flock of starlings. Her one concession to convention was to wear a grey square of chiffon over her bobbed hair.

The cortège was passing the 'Gospel Tree', standing in shadow beside the village shop, when the black dog returned to take up its position behind the bier, leading the mourners. The cob snorted and strained forwards as it quickened its pace breasting the slight rise which overlooked the cemetery and the wide expanse of Fen beyond. Jeremiah Shipham had fallen by the way, to be left swinging along on his crutches a full hundred yards behind, as ten mourners and a great, shaggy, black dog finally followed the bier into the cemetery gateway. The district nurse and her daughter joined the procession at the cross roads together with the 'Moocher' who had been on his way to the Ship Inn after a successful morning's molecatching.

Whenever the Moocher was in the village he became either 'cheerily drunk' or 'fighting drunk'. Cheerily drunk he was a hilarious character who added an extra *bonne bouche* of jollity to the Ship Inn. Fighting drunk he returned to the brave independence of his ancestors who had fought like tigers to defend the Fen from the onslaught of the Duke of Bedford's 'Adventurers' three hundred years earlier, and was left severely alone. Although completely illiterate, he was arguably the most learned sage of the remoter parts of the Fen which he shared with the wild creatures. He thought like his quarry and could conjure up any living or growing thing on demand...if he so wished, but this was only when the craving for ale and shag tobacco was upon him, or, as in the 'Birdman's' case, if he 'wholly took to you!'

If the ornithologist needed a certain rarity the Moocher would disappear back into the Fen, and within a few days the family would awake to find the specimen hanging behind the porch door, with perhaps a brace of 'Norfick sparrers' for Mrs Dutton's pantry hanging behind a scrap of sacking.

The Moocher never asked for payment and refused to do any manual labour on the farms. His living was made by selling plovers eggs, eels and wildfowl. Frogs he sold by the hundreds to the budding biologists of the Universities, and he did mole-catching and rabbiting for the landowners. He also possessed an extremely retentive memory and was an expert on Fenland caterpillars and insects. Frank's collection increased out of all bounds with the Moocher's help, although the names he bestowed on them would have floored any professor of etymology, wonderful archaic names, perhaps more readily understood by Chaucer and Langland.

At the graveside the mourners stood staring through downcast eyes at the coffin as it was lowered into the dark earth.A kestrel hovered with wide fanned tail and beating wings above the vicar as he began to read the burial service. A white butterfly danced between the gravestones, navigating a maze of poppies, side-slipping between the Vicar's flowing cassock and the Postmaster's wife, waltzing hither and thither to settle finally on the glinting varnish of the coffin.

The words of the service drifted towards the Fen, stretching away to the purple-grey horizon and Ely. The words passed over Frank. They were intangible. He glanced into the far distance to where the cathedral rose above the Fenlands. His mother stood in the foreground, aloof in her loneliness in the countryside she had never understood. She was a graduate of history, withdrawn into a self-imposed exile in her academic past. Beside her was Ma Shipham, the very soul of the Fen. The matriarchal dynasty of the Schippes had stood four-square on the raised land since they arrived with Vermuyden, three centuries ago, to cut the Old Bedford River. She was reality.

Maybe only the Moocher in his moleskin cords and jacket of nefarious pockets, skin weathered to the texture of bog oak, and Madge with her budding joy of life, and the imperturbable Ma Shipham were reality.

The black dog turned to pad soundlessly away down the green-drove towards the hidden heart of the Fen as the first handful of earth rattled down on the coffin.

'*Black Shuck'* whispered Ma Shipham portentously. 'He's a-leading your Dad home.' She nudged Frank in the ribs. 'Your Dad must have been something special for old Shuck to come for him.' As she followed his mother through the cemetery gate he could see that her fingers were crossed. He also noticed the Moocher ambling away in the opposite direction.

'I wonder,' Frank thought, as the black dog vanished into the sere reeds of the Fen, 'where is home?'

Friday June 14th 1940
Local Defence Volunteers

Boer Roberts, sitting sidesaddle behind the hames of an eighteen-hand shire, was leading his team homewards to the stables behind the house as Frank stepped down from the school bus.

'Are you a-coming to the Ship after tea, bor?' shouted Boer as the horses clatters by leaving a warm wake of sweat. 'Meetin' about defendin' the village or something '

Frank paused in the porch, below the wisteria. The Ship! To enter the *Ship*! He caught his breath in disbelief at the words. The Ship, that den of iniquity strictly designated a prohibited area by his Methodist mother.......

'Bout eight o'clock, bor, if you're a-comin'.'

Frank entered the kitchen where his mother was preparing their tea.

'There's to be a meeting in the Ship after tea,' Frank announced casually, flinging his school satchel towards the wide window ledge and disturbing the ginger cat who had been sleeping on a pile of his *Popular Flying* magazines. 'Something about Home Defence.'

Mrs Dutton glanced up with tired grey eyes at the dreaded words 'The Ship'. 'You will *not* .....'

'But it will only be a meeting, Ma, and a jolly important one too!'

His mother crossed the room to sit in her high Windsor chair and folded her arms. 'Really? And I suppose the next thing you will be telling me is that the Vicar will be there!'

'Actually, yes. And your friend the Headmaster,' Frank replied with a mischievous grin.

'Oh, well, if the Vicar is to be there it must be of some importance....not that he is a stranger to its door.' The tight corners of her mouth lifted into the semblance of a smile and Frank realised that he had won.

Mrs Dutton glanced towards the clock and crossed the passage into the living room to switch on the wireless. Frank paused on his way to the study in time to hear a quiet cultured voice announce, 'Here is the six o'clock news, and this is Alvar Liddell reading it. A small number of enemy aircraft crossed the channel during the night. They were repulsed with the loss of one enemy aircraft. The Royal Air Force has continued its attacks on the Channel ports by day. Lord Beaverbrook, visiting an aircraft factory, said....'

'What's on the wireless tonight, Ma?' Frank called through the open door.

'Your favourite, Much Binding in the Marsh, but you will miss it if you go to the meeting.'

'I must go. It's important...there's a war on you know!' he teased.

But apart from sporadic bursts of activity from the surrounding airfields nothing much had changed in normal village life. Only three people owned motor cars, so petrol-rationing had little effect, and the clothing policy of the villagers had always been 'make-do-and-mend' which made clothing coupons superfluous.

'Oh, yes, there will be a war going on,' she answered, 'but not yet. The Germans will consolidate and subdue the French first.' Mrs Dutton returned to the kitchen and began to pour two cups of tea. 'No doubt it will wait for you, ' she added bitterly.

'There's two more years before I can join up,' Frank mumbled. He had forgotten that his mother had been a historian, and wars and the strategy of wars were an open book to her.

Punctually at eight o'clock Frank gave the Bar door of the Ship Inn a tentative push and entered the banned domain of the landlord, Sam Rowsell. He descended a couple of steps on to fresh sawdust sprinkled over a red brick floor. Spittoons of highly-polished brass were placed at strategic positions beside aged oak settles and trestle tables. A huge stuffed pike stared malevolently from its glass case over the mantel at a case of bream swimming for eternity through faded rushes on the opposite wall, caught beyond doubt by the old men of the church-wall limes in the summers of their youth. Pewter pots glinted in rows hanging on wooden pegs from low beams, and the narrow strip of plaster wall between the high tops of the settles and the beams was hung with sporting prints of fighting cocks, the glass of their frames so encrusted with a patina of tobacco smoke and fly specks as to be barely transparent.

'Welcome aboard, bor!'

Frank started visibly as a stentorian voice filled his ears and Sam Rowsell loomed large behind the bar, a portly figure with his shirt sleeves rolled up to his elbows, bald, florid-cheeked with a small ginger moustache and lively blue eyes.

'Now what do you want, young gentleman?' He winked and passed a cloth across his brow. 'Do your Ma know you're in the old Ship, bor? For if she don't you'll get me hung drawed an' quartered...that's a fact!' He indicated the Vicar who was sitting on a settle below the pike. 'It's free beer with the Vicar's complements.'

'Dandelion and burdock, please, Mr Rowsell.'

The landlord thumped the bar with his fist. 'It's Sam, bor..*Sam.* We don't pay no regard to ceremony in the old Ship, do we vicar?' Frank glanced sideways towards the Vicar and missed the landlord's slow wink as he pushed a foaming pint towards him. 'One dandelion and burdock, bor.'

Frank made his way towards the nearest settle where his crony, Chippy, made room for him by shuffling along the seat, causing a domino effect by pushing Daggy Flegg and the Griggs family towards the vicar.

A strange pregnant silence hung over the nine men and boys, each with a pint pot in his hand, staring fixedly at the floor, conversing in muted monosyllables. It was reminiscent of the restive silence in church before the service begins. Lurchers and terriers lay, nose on paws, staring at each other in silence. Bella, Boer's seventeen-year-old retired racing greyhound, lay stretched in a warm patch of sunlight on the sanded floor, her aged lips curled in a perpetual sardonic smile. The fluttering wings of a trapped tortoiseshell butterfly rasped noisily between net curtain and window. So this was the rumbustious, disorderly bar of the Ship on a Friday evening! For as long as he could remember Frank had been led to believe that this was a den of iniquity whose door was to be given a wide berth as if the arch-fiend was ever waiting there to lure passing innocents to their doom. He gazed at the sleeping dogs and heard the soothing murmur of low voices in disbelief.

The landlord's wife materialised from beyond a heavy velvet curtain to satisfy her curiosity at the unusual silence. She was dark-eyed and Spanish with high cheek bones and sensual full-blooded lips. Rumour held that she was once a professional dancer on the stage, a rumour heightened by the fact that on special occasions the 'snug' furniture would be cleared, the gramophone wound up, and she would sing and dance proud moody flamenco before a packed house of well-oiled appreciative Fenmen.

Chippy's face appeared from behind his tankard. 'I dare say old King Kong will be a-comin'. What do you say, bor? I don't rightly know what this 'ere meetin's about, do you?' His face vanished again as he tipped his tankard up to drain the last dregs. 'Good old excuse for a pint though, isn't it?' Frank readily agreed with him. Chippy Roberts was two years his junior and grandson of Boer.

Frank ventured a long swig from his glass. This dandelion and burdock tasted strangely different from his usual bottle of Corona. It was frothy and had an unusual bitter taste which Frank supposed had something to do with it coming from one of the wooden-handled pumps that lined the bar. The Vicar caught his eye and smiled benevolently as he raised his own tankard to his lips. Humour lurked in his puckish blue eyes, half hidden below shaggy eyebrows sprouting like islands of sedge from a wrinkled face burnt by three score and ten years of Fenland wind and sun. A keen snipe-shot, naturalist and skater, the Vicar was a typical Edwardian country parson. In his youth he was renowned for his exploits at the skating matches held on the Washes. The old men still called him 'Patten Parson' and boasted of the sweepstakes he had won for them on the Welney Washes. They grinned toothlessly and chuckled at the memories of moonlit skating parties gliding up the river to the Feltwell Anchor, and skating the girls home through the early morning starlight to the hiss of their pattens cutting the freshly-frosted ice. On to Brandon Creek they had skated, then up the Ouse to Littleport and Ely.

Daggy Flegg leaned across Chippy to remark to Frank, 'Pity your Dad ain't here, 'cause I found somethin' down the Lode what would have wholly interested him.'

'What is it, Daggy?'

'Well now, I don't rightly know, but she's one of them there rusty old iron things what your Dad used to write about, Ancient Artefacts.' Daggy grinned. 'I got her in my 'tato shed waitin' for him then, damn me, the next thing I hear was that the Birdman had been buried!'

Daggy Flegg lived alone in a tarred wooden shack far out in the wilderness of the Fen, hidden by dense thickets of reeds. His half acre of land was surrounded on three sides by deep dykes with the fourth side running parallel to the slow-moving waters of a main drain. Access to this bastion was by a narrow plank, and whenever Daggy's peace of mind was threatened by unwelcome guests in the form of 'officials' he would lift his plank and remain the undisputed master of his own domain.

Mr Dutton had called Daggy and the Moocher 'The Last of the Fen Tigers'. Unlike the Moocher, Daggy never got fighting drunk; after a binge he could only be described as 'beatifically drunk' before falling asleep, looking much as a plump Abbey monk must have looked after a surfeit of mead. He had earned the title 'Daggy' on account of his fame as an expert ratter for the local farmers. His profession was usually practised along the banks of dykes near to potato or sugar-beet clamps where legions of rats lived in long underground networks of tunnels. Here Daggy would put one of his small white ferrets in the nearest hole and expertly 'dag' the rats as they bolted.

These rat-dags were three or four-pronged barbed tridents on a long-handle made by the village blacksmith. In the hands of a professional they were a very efficient and cheap way of dealing with rats. Daggy's technique was to block the holes in an area of bank, leaving six open within the range of his dag. The ferret was put in and, as the rats emerged, Daggy's speed and accuracy, together with his silence, beat a .410 gun hollow. Out of half a dozen rats bolting simultaneously, he had been known to spear five and get the sixth as it scampered up the bank by hurling his dag at it like a javelin..

For a boy to visit Daggy Flegg's shack on a warm afternoon during St Luke's summer was to enter a shangri-la of unforgettable peace. Sheltered by willows and tall reeds, holding the stifling hot scent of tar mingling with marsh gas, it was a kaleidoscopic riot of colour. It was a world where a brindled lurcher dozed in the sunlight above a dyke reflecting the cobalt of the sky against the warm ochre of the tip-tufted reeds, where red dragonflies and blue-banded damselflies hawked back and forth over shoals of young roach flickering in the deep, dark water below the plank, and ducks dabbled amongst the bright yellow-green scum that blanketed the still water, while every leaf vibrated with the somnolent drone of insects and the flutter of butterflies over heavy drifts of Michaelmas daisies.

Inside the shack, after one's eyes had become accustomed to the dim light from one small pane of glass, a low truckle bed, piled high with discarded clothes and blankets gradually materialised, followed by a table and plank seat grouped around a coke stove, whose chimney-pipe disappeared through the corrugated iron roof. A cast-iron cooking pot usually bubbled like a witch's cauldron on the stove. It contained a perpetually steaming stew of root vegetables, to which was added from time to time rabbit, hare, partridge, pheasant, wild duck, waterhen or any other edible fur or feather that came his way.

Whereas the outside of Daggy's shack was redolent of marsh gas and tar, inside one was instantly enveloped in a powerful fug of gamy stew, shag tobacco and beer, acting as a foil to the array of roughly-darned, sweaty seaboot stockings which hung above the stove pipe. During high summer, however, the gentler gastronomic delights of fresh strawberries and raspberries, stewed gooseberries, pike cutlets and stewed eels, together with the milk from his nanny goats, graced his board. Daggy Flegg lived well...'off the land'!

Looking through the Ship window, Frank could see Nelson Tydd's five milking cows wandering across the Square, returning to their field beside the Lode bank. They ambled slowly, turning their mournful faces frequently to look back at Nelson sitting on his almost stationary bicycle supported by his stick, shouting at an old roan shorthorn until she decided to move. Old Nelson, who got around on his one-pedal bicycle as well as most with two, was a cripple with a club foot, tenant of Church Farm which stood hidden behind the yews at the far side of the Church.

Passing between Old Nelson and the rump of the cow strode the

Headmaster, aglow with his own importance, but nearer, just passing the Ship window, came 'King Kong'.

Chippy Roberts gave Frank a sly dig in the ribs. 'Keep your head down, bor...Here comes King Kong!' And Chippy disappeared behind his tankard as the brilliant sun outside was eclipsed by the silhouette of ex-Regimental Sergeant Major Kingshott, Boer War, Indian Army, World War I, wearing a triple row of campaign medals.

Mr Kingshott resided in his small tobacco and sweet shop, the last cottage in the terrace forming the north side of the street. He lived alone in the back room of this two-up-two-down cottage, screened from the shop by a curtain of dusty red velvet through which he emerged at the jangle of the coil-spring bell above the shop door. Ex-R.S.M.Kingshott took it upon himself to discipline the village youth, looming menacingly, a full six foot four, above the glass jars of bullseyes, pear drops, jelly babies, liquorice and Sherbet Delights. Any man, woman or child failing to say 'please and thank you' would not be served, and their hasty retreat, followed by King Kong's full-throated roar, always had the effect of shaming the miscreants in the eyes of passers-by. Boys with hair grown long to the eyes of Mr Kingshott would ease themselves furtively out of the shop door to be followed by 'Get your father to put a puddin' basin over your head before you come here again!' The effect of this was that boys in our village were identifiable by their immaculate pudding-basin haircuts. He was a large florid man of military stature with silvery-white hair and a magnificent moustache whose waxed ends swept upwards with a flourish to reach the corners of his steely-blue eyes.

It had only been since the showing of the film 'King Kong' at the Downham Market Regal cinema that ex-R.S.M.Kingshott had become 'King Kong'. 'King Kong, King Kong, biggest monkey in the Fens!' chanted the brave handful of village children on the darkest nights, safe in the anonymity of the 'black-out'. 'King Kong...King Kong...' Their youthful voices rang along the village street in a carillon of glee. If this brought no response, the more daring of the boys would creep silently to tie a length of binder-twine to his door latch and the other end to stout Bertha Pope's latch next door, the remaining group standing breathless with excitement ready to flee as the doors were knocked simultaneously. Girls giggled nervously and made false dashes across the street to tremble in the shadows of the churchyard yews. Suddenly both doors would begin to bang. Windows would rattle and dogs bark as twenty-stone 'Big Bertha' and Mr Kingshott began a tug of war to the accompanment of alternately slamming doors. At last the binder-twine would snap, depositing Big Bertha flat on her living room floor, and Mr Kingshott would burst out flailing a broad leather belt.

'King Kong, King Kong....' echoed through the shadowy branches of the Gospel Tree as the children scattered screaming into the darkness, chased by Mr Kingshott bellowing like an enraged bull.

'What's he a doin' of?' whispered Chippy, as Mr Kingshott strode towards the bar to grasp a foaming tankard which appeared miraculously before him. His free hand reached over the bar and in one movement he swung the landlord's heavy stool to his side of the bar.

'Evenin' all' He proceeded to sit with his back to the bar, eyeing the group in silence before taking a steady draught from his tankard and wiping the froth slowly from his moustache.

'Evenin' Vicar.' He cast his eyes slowly round the nine silent men and took a heavy pocket watch from his waistcoat pocket. 'This 'ere meeting were called for eight fifteen, and it is now eight twenty-one.' His resonant voice filled the low-ceilinged room, bouncing from pike to bream and entering the nine pairs of ears like bees to their hive in a thunderstorm. '*Where is he?*'

Nine pairs of dry lips were spared the answer as the bar door swung open to admit the Schoolmaster, nattily dressed in his tweed plus-fours and diamond-check pullover,carrying a cardboard box under his arm. His face was flushed with exertion.

'Good evening men,' he began in a high falsetto voice, stopped, cleared his throat, polished his spectacles and started again three octaves lower.

'Blast, he look hot!' whispered Fancy Griggs.

'Buy 'im a drink,' chuckled the Moocher.

The Schoolmaster gave a short cough. 'Men,' he began, 'following Anthony Eden's speech on the fourteenth of May, I have been requested by the Ministry of Defence to organise what are to be known as 'Local Defence Volunteers' who will protect our land, our King and our loved ones in the event of enemy forces landing.' He paused for breath and took up a melodramatic stance with his back to the bar, shoulders squared and arms held rigidly to his side in front of a faded photograph of the skating team of 1889 at Welney Wash.

Young Chippy Roberts sat staring at the Schoolmaster. 'Bet he's goin' to go on about Hereward the Wake...' King Kong's eagle eyes silenced him.

'As you may know, the Poles, the Belgians, and now the French have been overrun by Germany's armoured divisions. Even now their invasion fleet is being assembled in the Netherlands. And we, in the flat lands of East Anglia, are in the front line.' The Schoolmaster drew another breath and mopped his perspiring brow. 'Therefore we must be prepared, and by being prepared I mean we must *study strategy.* For only through a masterly application of strategy are wars to be won. Remember how you learnt in our village school the masterly strategy of Hereward the Wake?' Frank felt a sharp dig in the ribs from Chippy. '...Drake and his intrepid defeat of the Spanish Armada...the peerless armies of England who built an Empire-upon-which-the-sun-never-sets! Well, men, now we are to organise Willows End into a fighting platoon. I am to resume my last war rank of Captain, and I suggest that our friend Mr Kingshott, whom we all admire as an outstanding non-commissioned officer, takes charge of the platoon as Sergeant, with Mr Boer Roberts, another old campaigner, as Corporal.'

The Schoolmaster glanced benevolently at the three boys and ventured one of his end-of-term Parents' Day smiles. 'I note that we have some rather youthful recruits to whom we must not disclose our strategy. Careless talk costs lives, you know! But doubtless they will carry out useful supporting roles, carrying messages and so forth....Any questions before I carry on?'

King Kong snorted. He rose to his full height, a mighty colossus with steely eyes set in a florid face, and began to speak in a measured voice, glaring at the Schoolmaster. A wide grin spread itself slowly across Podge's face and muffled gurgles exploded from behind Chippy's raised pot.

'Strategy!' The waxed ends of King Kong's moustache quivered ominously. *'Strategy is balls!'*

Silence fell instantly upon the bar. Even the trapped tortoiseshell ceased to vibrate its wings against the window-pane. Harnser's left hand, holding his pint, froze on its journey between bench and lips....

'Discipline is all that matters. Battles are lost or won on *discipline*. When I or Corporal Roberts say "jump", you *jump* and do what we tell you *instantly*.' Slowly his head swung in a half circle scanning his newly-press-ganged bunch of imbeciles, while Harnser's hand completed its journey to his lips.

'If them there Jarmans come droppin' parachutists on the Fen and start blowin' up Denver Sluice and creatin' havoc, you won't have time to bugger about with strategy. These 'ere men will have to do what they are told like clockwork, an' these here boys will have to grow up mighty fast and do the same job as the rest.' Mr Kingshott grinned. 'If the Jarmans come they are going to come very soon, afore the Regulars get re-equipped and sorted out, so I want you all on the Square tomorrow night at seven thirty, with a hoe handle each to drill with, and any weapons you have so's we can see what we can muster to fight an invading force with.' He turned to his self-appointed Commanding Officer. 'I suppose, sir, that we will be issued with arms eventually?'

'Coo!' breathed Chippy. 'Do that mean we'll get a rifle with a bayonet and some bullets? Better than the Scouts!'

'Well..um...armbands anyway,' replied the Schoolmaster, fussily untying the cardboard box and spilling its contents of khaki armbands with L.D.V. in large letters stencilled on them. 'One each to be worn on the right arm.'

Sergeant Kingshott rolled his eyes heavenwards seeking deliverance from the unenlightened. 'Well, in that case, sir, I suggest you also become Quartermaster, seeing as you were in that line of business during the last war,' he retorted, pointedly referring to the Schoolmaster's wartime duty as a Pay Corps subaltern in Blighty.

'Daggy,' said the Vicar in the ensuing silence. You must bring the old bank-gun out. Wonderful old gun that. It was you father's father's, made in the year of Waterloo.'

'I never did see it,' answered Daggy stiffly.

'Daggy!' The Vicar looked him in the eye accusingly. '*Daggy!*'

Daggy shuffled his feet. 'Must have been afore my time....Come to think of it I have an idea she were lost in the '61 drown.'

'Go you on, bor,' the Moocher broke in, 'I heard the old bugger go off many a time when the peewits were thick on the Wash... an that weren't a hundred years ago!'. He winked at the Vicar. 'I do recollect peewits are worth a bob each nowadays!'

'Maybe if I were to describe the gun to you, Daggy, you might possibly remember seeing it around your shack...an eight foot Spanish barrel of twisted Damascus steel,' said the Vicar helpfully, 'originally a flintlock, but converted to a percussion action by your father, 'Fowler' Flegg. She threw a pound of shot, and you and your father were brought up on what she shot. When I was a young man your father used to take me out on the Washes. I've helped sledge the old gun across the ice during freezes, floated her across the floods in his punt and lashed her to posts on the Bank. Glorious old days!

The Vicar rose to his feet and made his way between the sleeping dogs to the bar. 'How about another pint, Daggy, to help your memory?'

'I'll have a look for it, Vicar, but I can't wholly recollect what happened to her.'

'You have a good look ahind them there straw bales at the back of your 'tato shed. There's a lot of funny old things hid there,' said Harnser knowingly.

Daggy glared at his brother. 'I don't know nothing' about that, but I do know you seem to have a lot of long-tail sparrers hangin' round your backus every Christmas, an' they don't drop dead out of the reeds like old starlings in the frost, do they now?' Harnser, suitably silenced, glanced innocently upwards to stare at the stuffed pike.

'A small prayer before we go!' announced the Vicar, but before the last word had left his lips, Boer's Bella had lifted her sleepy head from the floor, Mrs Rowsell had retreated like a wraith behind the velvet curtain, and nine newly fledged Local Defence Volunteers had dived towards the bar door to bear home to their loved ones the proud tidings that England was to be saved.

Saturday 15th June, 1940
The Weapons of War

The clatter of a pony and trap passing across the village square caused Frank to glance through the living room window. He was seated on the wide window-seat surrounded by the reek of Rangoon oil and cotton rags as he cleaned his late father's ten-bore goose-gun in preparation for the proposed 7.30 meeting of the Local Defence Volunteers.

His eyes settled briefly upon the pony and trap. It was Sedge Farm's dog-cart being driven by Harnser Flegg. His portly elder brother, Daggy, was squatting over a mysterious object wrapped in tattered potato sacks protruding a good yard beyond the back flap of the dog-cart.

The old men on the church wall bench chuckled, and winked knowingly as the Flegg brothers dragged the weighty load from the cart and laid it reverently on the gravel beside the War Memorial before hitching the pony to the lych gate in the cool shade of the yews.

Frank raised his eyes upwards to the church clock. 7.25. It was time to make his way to the momentous first gathering of the Willows End defence force, that 'happy band of brothers' which was ordained to become the nucleus of Fenland's Home Guard. And so, with his heart pounding high in his chest, Frank gave a final polish to the burnished walnut of the old Tolley's stock, buckled his father's cartridge belt with its gleam of twenty-five 'deep shell'

Remington waterproof cartridges around his skinny waist and slipped quietly out of the house.

Seven men and three boys who had drifted towards the Square during the past ten minutes stood in a self-conscious group below the marble cross of the War Memorial. Each was wearing a pristine L.D.V. armband, and each carried a hoe handle and his own interpretation of a personal weapon. The Vicar arrived, free-wheeling to a halt beside the old men on his sit-up-and-beg bicycle. In the blue shade from the limes the old men continued to chuckle as the Vicar stooped to remove his cycle clips and unroll his trouser bottoms. Children playing tig around the gravestones in the churchyard stopped their play. Prams being heaved by elder sisters over the rutted surface of sun-baked pondside mud in their attempt to shake insomniac infants to sleep came to a halt below the hump-back bridge as Mr Kingshott marched briskly on to the Square.

The vision of ex-Regimental Sergeant-Major Kingshott striding across the idyllic Fenland village square was enough to send a surge of patriotic emotion through the onlookers' hearts. Who could doubt the invincibility of the British Empire? High overhead gentle clouds formed a mackerel sky. The Norman church stood firm surrounded by its aged yews, in whose safe shade the ten modern yeomen of England waited below the monument to the fallen in past battles...It was a green and pleasant land.

Sergeant (L.D.V.) Kingshott came to a halt smartly at the foot of the War Memorial. A triple row of campaign medals arched across his breast, a swagger-cane was held at the precise angle of ninety degrees by his left elbow, his twirled moustache-tips quivered and his eyes glinted like those of an old warhorse scenting battle.

'Squ...a...a...d!'

The words rolled round the village square breaking the awesome silence.

'On par...a...a...d...e!'

Jackdaws fled from their crannies in the church tower to spiral noisily above the gilded weathercock. The elder sisters rocked their prams feverishly as the 'nearly asleep' infants began to bawl, and the ten recruits glanced uneasily about them, anxiously wondering what they were expected to do as they squatted alongside their elders below the church wall.

Boer, wearing a rainbow of campaign medals, equal to those of Mr Kingshott, pinned to his Sunday jacket, rose laboriously to his feet.

'Get felled in together,' he murmured, watching Mr Kingshott out of the corner of his one good eye. 'In two ranks of five.' He glanced at the names of the previous war dead incised in the cold marble of the War Memorial as if to find inspiration. 'An' you'd better bring your hoes an' leave them guns agin the wall.'

Eventually, after a great deal of sheepish giggles and pithy asides to their elders, the six men formed themselves into a fair semblance of a line, with the four boys finding themselves pushed into the first rank alongside old Daggy.

Slowly the pond railings opposite the Ship Inn were being lined by an increasing audience of wives and mothers, the corporal in charge of the Lode searchlight battery, and a passing group of travelling Diddicoys, lurchers, piebald ponies, a donkey, and wild, black-haired young girls peering from brightly-painted wagons.

Ex-R.S.M. Kingshott's steely eyes swept peremptorily over the square, passing along the War Memorial railings, along the length of the church wall, where the Vicar and the patriarchs squatted in the cool of the lime trees, sweeping round to pass over the pond with its solitary mute swan and flotilla of white ducks, to settle finally upon the appreciative audience outside the Ship Inn.

He lowered his eyes, bringing into focus the ten recruits. As at the moment when the conductor raises his baton, a tense and electric silence fell upon the village.

'First,' he commanded, 'I want to inspect your weapons. When I give the order I want you to break ranks, collect your weapons, and place them in a single line on the ground with each of you standing "at ease" behind your weapon...Platoon! Stand by your arms!'

The Vicar, the patriarchs, the diddycoys, wives, mothers and girls, all watched Police Constable Fox stolidly wending his way across the Square during the period of confusion which followed until the platoon was uneasily standing 'at ease' behind a row of weapons that lay nakedly exposed to the light of day.

'Right!' said 'Sergeant' Kingshott to 'Corporal' Boer Roberts. 'What have we got here?'

Boer bent down to pick up his old single-barrel 12-bore which normally spent its days in the bottom of one of the tumbrils, or in the tool box of the hay-cutter, whence it was occasionally resurrected to shoot the odd rabbit or crow.

Sergeant Kingshott passed on to 'Ten-Mile' Griggs, who presented an old brown-barrelled 10-bore percussion muzzle-loader, whose nipples had been cleared of chaff and the dust of ages by one of his wife's hatpins, and oiled with a chicken feather dipped in paraffin. Sergeant Kingshott rolled his eyes heavenwards in silent prayer before moving on to 'Runner' Roberts, who had brought his 8-bore under-lever goose gun whose double barrel and stock had been heavily painted a dull battleship-grey.

'What is the killing range of this 'ere, Private Roberts?'

Runner Roberts never looked anybody full in the face. He glanced sideways towards the Wesleyan Chapel, and drew his sleeve across his lips.

'She killed a great old goose at nigh on ninety yards once. Dead as a turnip!'

Next in line stood young 'Podge' Griggs, disclosing for the first time his ownership of an old Remington 12-bore with a sawn-off barrel, that had illegally seen the demise of various varieties of fur and feather during Podge's clandestine wanderings around the neighbourhood. Immediately he raised the weapon from the ground a dark shadow fell over him and P.C. Fox materialised. Police Constable James Fox faced Ex-Regimental Sergeant Major Clive Kingshott.

'Hold you on a minute Mister Kingshott. I want to have a word with this 'ere boy!' Speaking sweetly, ignoring at his peril the dazzling display of medals, P.C. Fox turned to young Podge, who wilted visibly beneath his silent gaze, and proceeded to take his notebook from his breast pocket.

'How old are you an' do that gun belong to you?'

Podge stared miserably at the hole in his left plimsoll. 'Thirteen come August,' he mumbled.

Slowly P.C. Fox returned his little black book to its pocket and took the gun from Podge. 'Shortened barrel too,' he remarked smugly, before glancing along the line towards Chippy and China. 'Right everybody. Where are your gun licences?'

A broad grin spread over P.C. Fox's face. At last he had concrete evidence against the four boys who had been the bane of his life, and as slippery as eels to hold. At long last he had them, together with every gun-licenceless poacher in Willows End. He smirked at his cleverness.

In the meantime Sergeant Kingshott stood glowering with anger at this action against his authority, unprecedented in a lifetime of parades held on the holiest of holy barrack squares.

'Constable!' he thundered, so that all the spectators could be in no doubt as to what he was to impart to this blundering simpleton. '*One*...These weapons have been requisitioned by the War Office! *Two*...These are enlisted men carrying out orders under *my* command by direct order of the War Office. *Three*...Under War Office Regulations in Time Of War I order you to return that requisitioned weapon to Private Griggs!'

P.C. James Fox looked distinctly put out. Young Podge grinned from ear to ear as he was handed back his weapon by his arch enemy, and a hearty cheer from the spectators followed 'Old Foxie' as he began an ignominious retreat across the Square to his bicycle.

'Right...Where were we?' Sergeant Kingshott turned happily towards the next in line who happened to be old Daggy Flegg. He stared at the blank area of tarmac in front of Daggy's Wellington boots. 'No weapon, Daggy! Not even a rat-dag?' he inquired flippantly.

'Well, I can't lug 'er around on me own, that's a fact,' replied Daggy dourly. 'You can walk over to see 'er, or you can tell Harnser to give me a lift an' bring 'er to you...It's wholly up to you bor!'

'Fall out, Private Flegg, to assist Private Flegg,' barked Sergeant Kingshott, following correct barrack-square tradition. The two brothers ambled away towards the church wall where Daggy's miraculously-rediscovered weapon lay shrouded in sacking, guarded by the Vicar and the patriarchs.

They returned swaying drunkenly from side to side beneath the weight of the Flegg family heirloom, the eight-foot barrel of the aged punt-cum-bank gun that had clothed and fed three generations of Fleggs, beside providing hampers of wildfowl for city markets, trailing its heavy breeching ropes like fat pythons through the dusty tarmac to lie at Sergeant Kingshott's feet. He regarded this piece of heavy artillery musingly for a few seconds.

'Will it shoot?'

'Shoot!' Daggy lovingly pulled back the huge dog's-leg hammer which had been made by the village blacksmith at the time that the old flint-lock was converted to percussion. 'Course it'll shoot.' His wrinkled face glowed with an inner reverence. 'All she want is a pound o' black powder poured into her, rammed down with a wad of hay followed by a pound o' shot an' another little wad, put a cap on her nipple an' blast bor...she'll go off as sweet as a thrush. But you have to remember to let her cool down afore you put any more powder into her!...Do she'll blow your head off, bor!'

First in line along the second rank was Harnser with his spanking new Thomas Wild 'Wildfowler' magnum 12-bore, which had cost the enormous sum of twelve guineas, spoil from a successful foray in the pheasant coverts of a certain North West Norfolk estate. Standing beside him was China's father, 'Fancy' Griggs, who sported an equally new B.S.A. hammerless 12-bore also earned in the same foray. 'Chippy' Roberts had his 1904 model B.S.A. air rifle, and 'China'...Frank could not believe his eyes...China had produced a classic! For there, lying on the tarmac between China's plimsolls lay a beautiful German Merkel hammerless 16-bore, its sideplates deeply engraved with a brace of spaniels springing a woodcock in a woodland scene, and every inch of its action deeply chased with scrolls and leaves. Frank stared at this unbelievable treasure. Not once, even to his closest of cronies, had China even hinted at the existence of such an exquisite gun whose walnut stock gleamed with the sheen of a freshly-opened conker.

But, in common with many of the villagers' heirlooms, the gun had a history, a history that went back to the year 1898, when a party of adventurous undergraduates stocked a boat with beer, fishing tackle, guns, camping gear and frolicsome young ladies, and sailed down the Ouse from Cambridge to the Fens to spend four weeks of unbridled joy. It was July. They lazed beneath perpetually blue skies. The silver roach, the slab-sided bream, the perch and golden rudd provided sport during the long peaceful evenings and, for those whose hangovers and girlfriends allowed, in the misty light of pearly dawns. They shot out-of-season mallard, scrumped vegetables from the fields, purchased milk and eggs from riverside smallholdings, made eyes at the Fenland daughters, and lived like young lords, which some of them were!

One day they ventured up the Little Ouse to the Feltwell Anchor Inn where the whole party disembarked to descend upon the tap room and treat the 'regulars' to free beer, which started a jolly evening of singing and drinking until the early hours of the morning.

Meanwhile China's grandfather, drifting downstream in his punt after collecting ten bundles of ready-peeled white willows from his brother-in-law's isolated smallholding in Hockwold Fen, saw the gun lying on the river bank beside the vessel's mooring post. He also noted the boisterous din of noisy merrymaking coming from the crowded tap room, and, like the loyal Fenman that he was, he realised the danger in leaving a firearm lying around. So, quickly landing, he pushed the offending object beneath the load of withies and took it home to be condemned to nocturnal wanderings among the haunts of mallard and marsh pheasant in the loneliest of the outlying Fens.

So, in this vital hour of need, with our armies driven back from Dunkirk, the Chapman family decided to resurrect the gun to stem the expected flood of its Germanic makers. This proved to be exceptionally sound thinking on Sarah Chapman's part, for the War Office requisition of the gun would absolve the Chapman family from any come-back if anyone discovered how it had first come into their hands.

'Right!' exclaimed Sergeant Kingshott, mentally rubbing his hands with glee. 'Let's 'ave you with your hoe handles in the centre o' the Square.'

Interest revived alongside the pond rails. The searchlight corporal ceased his Cockney banter with the prettiest of the diddicoy girls. The steady flow of gossip between waiting wives and mothers subsided, and the children who had resumed their game of tig among the gravestones froze into delightful Peter Pan statues as Sergeant Kingshott shouted:

'Squ...aaaaa...ad!'

For the next hour the village was made to realise the hidden talents of 'King Kong'. They saw him for the first time in a new light. At the end of the hour even Harnser Flegg had learned the meaning of the verb 'to jump', and the watching womenfolk, even if they hitherto had been dubious as to the parentage of their husbands and lovers, had by the end of the hour certainly been enlightened as to this and much else besides.

The ten raw recruits had marched, trotted, and run a mileage equivalent to a month's leisured amble between their homesteads and the Ship Inn. They had 'presented' hoe handles, 'ordered' hoe handles, 'sloped' hoe handles, dropped hoe handles, and cursed hoe handles, while Sergeant Kingshott had stood before them like a living waxwork model of Kitchener of Khartoum, his voice, modulated to a pitch to command a regiment, shattering the peaceful evening air until, by the end of the session, every duck had disappeared from the pond to skulk beneath the weeping willows.

At last the church clock was heard to strike nine and the order came for the ten exhausted Local Defence Volunteers to 'stand at ease' to watch a demonstration of how rifle drill should be done by Sergeant Kingshott using Chippy's air rifle for the benefit of his audience. The final 'Squaaad dis...*miss!*' sent the squad rushing to collect their weapons before making a beeline for the cool sanctuary of the Ship's bar, leaving old Daggy to enlist the Vicar's help in getting the punt gun safely stowed in Sedge Farm's dogcart before they too disappeared through the Ship's doorway.

Frank wearily began to walk the few yards towards his home opposite the lych gate carrying the 10-bore, by now weighing like a sack of bricks but which lightened miraculously as he perceived Joy Rowsell approaching.

The Landlord of the Ship Inn had the two prettiest daughters in the village, Joy, who was thirteen, and Veronica who was fifteen. They were the prettiest girls in the neighbourhood because they were the only girls in the village to have new clothes purchased specially for them. They seemed to change their frocks almost every day, whereas most of the other girls would start off with a jumble sale frock or jumper that reached their ankles and wear it until they grew out of it. Veronica and Joy had faces as fresh as apple blossom. They exhaled an aroma of scented soap, and did not carry the peaty marsh-gas, potato-sweet smell of the land which followed in the wake of the village girls. It was even whispered from the shrewd calculations of the boys that they wore 'drawers', even in the summertime! Be that as it may, the two Rowsell girls were being brought up to be a cut above the rest of the village youth, attending Thetford Grammar School for Girls and returning home in their father's taxi each Friday for the weekend.

Beyond the occasional supercilious 'Hello', neither of the sisters had shown any special awareness of Frank's existence. Yet here was Joy coming smiling towards him.

'Hello,' she said. 'You looked jolly brave out there...and the very smartest!' She fell into step beside him as he crossed the road. 'Will you really be fighting the Germans if they invade? I was listening to Mr Kingshott last night when you were at the meeting in the bar.' She giggled. 'I can hear everything that goes on in the bar when Mummy leaves the living room door open!' she said knowingly.

Frank, lost for words, managed to mumble a tremulous 'Oh.'

'I think you are jolly brave,' she reiterated.

'Not especially,' he replied. 'Bit of fun really.' He kicked a pebble self-consciously.

'There's a lovely film on at the Regal next week,' Joy continued. 'Will you come with me?' She executed a little dancing step and kicked the pebble back to him. 'It really is a good film...Bob Hope and Shirley Ross in "Thanks for the memory".'

The suddenness of this invitation rocked Frank's equilibrium. Not in the wildest of his dreams had he contemplated taking a girl to the pictures, especially one of Landlord Rowsell's closely-guarded daughters.

'Your Mum will never let you go to the pictures with a boy!' he gasped.

'Of course she wouldn't.' Joy chuckled. 'But she won't know! Oh, do say you will take me, Frank.'

'How on earth can I?' Frank realised that he had no money.

She laughed, a roguish silvery laugh, and tossed her blonde curls precociously.

'Mummy thinks Veronica and I are going to the cinema together for next Saturday's matinée, but Veronica has arranged to meet her soldier from the searchlight down the Lode. So if you and I go to see the film we can meet up with Veronica on the way home and tell her what the film was about...So Mum will never know, will she?'

Frank looked dubious. But Joy pouted her lips, and made a grimace.

'I haven't any money for the tickets!' he said, frantically looking for an escape. 'It's one and sixpence in the back stalls.'

'Shoot a couple of nice rabbits and bring them round to the back door. Mummy will pay you ninepence each. Anyway I get in half price 'cause I'm under fourteen, and Dad will give me half-a-crown to spend,' she said brightly. 'Oh, really, Frank, *you must come.*'

She waved her chiffon scarf gaily towards her mother who was standing at the door of the Ship looking for her.

'See you Friday when I get home from school,' she whispered hurriedly, before running dutifully homewards, leaving Frank to turn into his front door porch.

Wednesday June 19th
The Army Arrives

Towards mid-morning a long convoy of army vehicles approached Willows End from the north-east, appearing suddenly through the screen of willow trees flanking the Wisbech road, led by three Bren carriers, which clattered noisily across the tarmac scattering the ducks before coming to a halt in the centre of the Square. The rest of the convoy, canvas-tilted transports with two 25-pounder guns in tow, parked in a straggling line along the main road between the Ship Inn and 'Old Money Box's' bungalow.

The children, enjoying their mid-morning playtime, rushed excitedly to gawp through the school railings at this unprecedented invasion of khaki-clad soldiers descending from covered transports and flooding the air with their raucous voices. The old men, dozing in the morning sunlight below the lime trees, awoke slowly to find themselves hemmed in between the church wall and the hot, oily fumes and mud-caked tracks of the Bren carriers. Sunburnt, bedraggled soldiers wearily made their way towards the cool waters of the pond, where they lounged on the grassy bank in the shade of the willows.

The school children, listening to the cacophony of strange tongues, hung back defiantly after Miss Lacy had blown her whistle three times.The seven times table could not compete with the spell-binding magic of these tribal tongues from distant lands...Glaswegian, Liverpuddlian, Geordie, sing-song Welsh, and the soft burr of Somerset.

Presently the Headmaster appeared, striding authoritatively towards a young captain and a senior N.C.O. who were dismounting stiffly from a small open scout car, no doubt to offer them refreshment. He ushered them through the ranks of speechless pupils to disappear through the front door of School House.

At four-thirty, as Frank stepped off the school bus, he was met by China, Chippy, and Podge.

'There's been a right old carry-on here today, bor,' greeted Chippy, dragging his lurcher in his wake on a length of binder-twine. 'The Army's here!...Great Old lorries...Bren-gun carriers...two great old guns...motor bikes...an' sergeants all a-yelling and a shouting like King Kong gone mad!'

'Don't be daft, bor,' said Frank, looking towards the deserted Square where the old men were dozing as ever by the church wall. 'I bet there's not a detachment of soldiers within a hundred miles.'

'Ar...that's all you know about it bor,' chimed in China. 'They've took over the Old Hall and are hid up there.'

'And you can't see nothing of them, 'cause of that great old wall and bushes what have growed up round it,' said Podge sorrowfully.

'Well! I won't believe it unless I see them with my own eyes...Big guns and armoured vehicles in Willows End!' said Frank flippantly, as he began to cross the road towards his front door. 'You haven't seen a big gun in your life!'

'Do you hold on bor...I have a brainwave.' China threw his cap high into the air, making Chippy's lurcher set off for a retrieve, causing Chippy to fall over backwards as the binder-twine leash encircled his ankles. 'You be here together about seven o'clock an' I know how we can see them.'

Mrs Dutton was setting the table in readiness for their evening meal when Frank entered the living room. He picked up the *Radio Times* and glanced hurriedly at the evening's entertainment. 'Band Wagon' was on at eight o'clock, with Arthur Askey. Frank liked Arthur Askey and Dickie Murdock, and quickly decided that listening to them would be preferable to falling for his cronies' fantasy of an army unit covertly hidden behind the Old Hall's nine foot wall.

'Lots of excitement on the Square this morning,' said his mother. 'A detachment of Royal Artillery spent the morning there.'

Frank dropped the *Radio Times* and pricked up his ears.

'Headmaster tells me that they are taking over the Old Hall in the process of regrouping...just returned from France.' She finished stroking a thin layer of potted meat on the bread and margarine sandwiches, and turned to lift the kettle from the stove. 'The men looked terribly exhausted...By the way I wish you would go and shoot a rabbit or a pigeon to help with the meat ration.'

'Tomorrow,' he replied hurriedly. 'I'm off to see the big guns after tea!' Listening to Big Hearted Arthur could wait another week.

Promptly at seven o'clock the four boys met beside the pond rails. Chippy stared dejectedly down into the muddy water and flung a pebble peevishly at the swan. 'I been down to the Hall and there's no way of seeing over that old wall. And there's two sentries with rifles and bayonets against the gates...So how are we expected to see anythin'?'

'I know how to make a simple periscope,' Frank suggested. 'You get two mirrors and...'

'No time to go messing about makin' things,' broke in China. 'Cause I have a masterful way...Chippy do you run to see if Boer is settled in the Ship!'

'Why?' mumbled Chippy, flinging another pebble after the departing swan.

China treated them to one of his special grins. 'Well now. If old Boer is there we can go and get Samson out and watch in comfort. Can't we bor?'

Chippy's expressive brown eyes widened in admiration for such a simple solution to what had seemed an impossible problem, and he hurried across the road to peer through the window of the Ship Inn where his grandfather was seated in his time-honoured place playing dominoes with Daggy.

The four boys slipped silently past the back door of Frank's home towards the stables where a row of carthorses were placidly munching their evening meal. At the far end of the row, in a loose box, stood Samson, a magnificent Clydesdale who stood eighteen hands high and was by far the largest horse in the area. Samson slowly swung his head round towards the intruders and eyed them suspiciously. Podge shot out of the stall.

'He ain't used to being disturbed after coming in from work,' said Chippy, speedily following Podge and pulling the bottom half of the stall door shut behind him.

'Don't you be frit, bor. He'll settle time I get a halter on 'im,' panted China, clambering precariously along the manger in order to slip a rope halter round the massive neck.

'You watch 'im!' shrieked Chippy. ' He's showing the whites of his eyes!'

With the halter finally in place, Samson patiently followed China towards the granary steps where the three boys dropped on to the Clydesdale's broad back, and with China leading Samson by the halter they proceeded by a round-about route through Back Lane to cross the 'twenty acre' to the Old Hall.

Reaching the high brick wall, overshadowed by laurel and rhododendrons, the boys scrambled from the Clydesdale's back to crouch on its parapet and peer down through a latticework of laurel leaves at the one-time stableyard and mews where many of the vehicles had been parked.

'Coo...look at them there!' whispered Podge, gazing mesmerised at the two field guns.

'What are they a-doing of?' whispered Chippy hoarsely, as half a dozen soldiers began to manhandle heavy boxes from one of the transports and carry them out of sight behind the double doors of the coach house.

'What about me?' bleated China from nine feet below. 'Get me up!'

'Can't,' panted Chippy, after hanging head down from the wall with outstretched hands, held by his feet by the other three boys. 'Can't reach.'

'Bugger!' swore China. 'I'll have to take the halter off Samson so's you can pull me up.'

'Do you do that old Samson'll run off home for his supper,' whispered Chippy urgently. 'Leavin' us perched up here like old hens...You'll have to think of something else.'

China seated himself at the foot of the wall and stared glumly into the far distance with Samson grazing grass contentedly beside him. Suddenly an engine backfired noisily, and the sound of tracks clattering over the cobbled yard sounded from beyond the wall. In desperation China took a flying leap for Samson's mane as he cropped the grass, clawing himself up one of the slippery forelegs by hanging on to mane and halter, to hang across the glossy broad back on his stomach. Samson broke into a steady trot circling the field, watched anxiously from the wall by his three cronies.

Feeling China securely seated on his withers Samson settled down to a walk, responding to the gentle twitching of the halter rope which steered him back to stand beside the wall. Podge held out his hand to take the halter rope while China joined them on the wall.

China's eyes widened as he surveyed the scene before him. Large transport trucks were parked in orderly lines on the overgrown tennis courts and vegetable gardens, with a scout car and several utility vans beneath the wide canopy of a cedar of Lebanon which grew in the centre of the front lawn. Nearer to the boys, the cobbled yard of the mews was a hive of activity as stores were being unloaded from a three-ton Bedford lorry, and for the first time in two decades smoke began to spiral from the kitchen chimneys.

'Look at that old Lewis gun!' gasped China, pointing towards a machine-gun mounted on the Bren-carrier which had just moved in order to command an open view of the sky away from the building.

'That's in case of being strafed by enemy bombers,' Frank replied.

'Coo 'eck! Do you think them old Jerries know they're here, then?' queried Podge with gleaming eyes. 'P'raps they'll send some of them there Stuka's to dive-bomb with screaming sirens like on the News at the Pictures when they bombed them old Poles.'

Their attention switched towards the main drive as a dispatch rider roared up to the front door on a Norton side-valve motor-cycle carrying a square canvas dispatch case slung round his shoulder.

'Bet he's got a message that the Jarmans are a-landing,' Chippy whispered with bated breath. 'I wish old King Kong would hurry up and get us issued with rifles an' bayonets,' whispered Podge melodramatically.

'Don't be daft!' answered Frank. 'They have wireless and field telephones for that.'

'Hie!... You there!'

Samson slowly raised a quizzical head from peacefully browsing the lush grass which grew in the shelter of the wall.

'You boys!'

'Bloody 'ell!' gasped China. 'They've seed us!'

They dropped nimbly on to Samson's broad back like water-voles plopping into a dyke and headed out across the 'twenty acre', leaving the source of the mystery voice hidden beyond the nine-foot wall. Samson broke into a steady trot, as he headed homewards to his supper with the four boys perched precariously on his back.

'I hope...you shut the...stable...door...Podge?' China panted shrilly. 'Do we'll have wholly bad skull aches when the silly old devil go through it!' This resulted in all four boys abandoning ship just before Samson streaked into his stall.

On the following evening Frank was about to set off to shoot a couple of rabbits for Joy Rowsell's mother, and hopefully one for his mother, when an official-sounding knock rattled the front door. He opened the door to find an army captain standing in the porch, an extremely stern-looking, impeccably-dressed officer, the mirror image of Ronald Colman in the 'Bengal Lancers'. Frank's heart plummeted, as his mind raced backwards. So they had been seen spying on the Army, and identified! Maybe he was to be taken and interrogated, together with his three friends. Spies in time of war were automatically shot at dawn!

He then became aware that he was holding his 12-bore, and that it was pointed directly at the officer's kneecap.

'Ah!' exclaimed the captain to the small boy with a large gun in his hands. 'I would like to have a word with Mrs Dutton if I may.'

Frank retreated backwards along the dark passage to the living room. 'Ma,' he announced. 'There is an army officer to see you.'

'Good gracious!' she answered, hurriedly closing the book she had been reading. 'I wonder what he wants. You had better ask him in,' adding, as Frank turned to leave the room, 'You have'nt been up to any mischief up at the Hall, I hope?'

After closing the sitting room door behind the captain he paused to listen at the keyhole, hoping to be forewarned of any dire consequences arising from the visit.

'Mrs Dutton?'

She looked him up and down and nodded her head.

'Captain Richard Vernon.'

He spoke with the crispest of military accents, and removed his gloves. 'How do you do?'

'How do you do?' Mrs Dutton replied, keeping a watchful eye on him.

'Earlier today I approached the Vicar with a very special request and straight away he advised me to have a chat with you.' Captain Vernon glanced towards the Windsor chair which had been hastily vacated by the ginger cat on his arrival. 'May I sit down?'

'Please do,' Frank heard his mother reply, very formally.

'Perhaps you may have heard that my company has been billeted in the Old Hall after our unfortunate return from the B.E.F.?'

Mrs Dutton nodded. 'I have heard that soldiers have taken over the Hall.' Her manner was defensive.

'In all probability we shall be here for a few weeks at least,' continued the Captain. 'And in these unsettled circumstances I would like to find somewhere for my wife to stay in the village. Nothing elaborate. Just a simple room and cooking facilities.' He flashed her a reassuring smile, a smile of such charm that any female of normal feminine response would instantly be overwhelmed by it. But Mrs Dutton was made of sterner stuff. She appeared hesitant.

'I don't know,' she replied at length. 'I have never considered letting a room.'

'I'm sure that Olivia would be no trouble to you. Possibly you might enjoy her company.' He leaned confidentially across the arm of the Windsor chair. 'The Vicar rather stressed the fact that you have lately become widowed and this is rather a large house. And of course, I can arrange for extra coal. And my cookhouse sergeant will look after you with extra rations...Unofficially, of course!'

Mrs Dutton still appeared dubious.

'Fifteen guineas a month rent,' he insisted. 'In advance!'

Mrs Dutton capitulated with alacrity.

'I have the front bedroom.' She allowed him one of her transient well-bred smiles. 'Perhaps your wife would like that as a bed-sitting room if I put a table and easy chair in it. Of course we have no modern conveniences. An earth lavatory at the end of the garden, and water from the well.'

Frank faded silently away from the keyhole at the sound of their approaching footsteps as his mother led Captain Vernon towards the front staircase.

'My goodness! This is absolutely splendid,' enthused the Officer, obviously surprised as he gazed down from one of the three large windows at the village square and the church with its massive yew trees. 'Olivia will love it here. Such a perfect view, with the willow trees leaning over the pond with its white ducks...even a swan!...and the lych gate. Oh, Mrs Dutton, it is absolutely perfect. And such a large, pleasant room.'

Mrs Dutton turned away from the window with her head averted, remembering happier times.

'May I bring Olivia next Friday?' he said, with the impetuous enthusiasm of a small boy. 'She has been staying with her parents in Chelsea. If I send her a telegram she'll be able to arrange to travel by train to Downham Market and I shall meet her there.'

'Of course,' Mrs Dutton smiled.

From his vantage point in the shadow of the yews Frank watched the beaming young officer go striding away up the village street swinging his swagger cane in a most unmilitary manner passing a glowering ex-R.S.M. Kingshott who happened to be standing in his shop doorway.

China, Podge, and Chippy were lounging with glum expressions on their faces beside the War Memorial steps.

'What did that old Captain want with you bor?' began China.

'Are we in trouble bor?' wavered Podge.

'Did he recognise you?' groaned Chippy.

'No. Of course not. In fact he wants to sort of live with me and my Ma!' boasted Frank. 'We have let him our front bedroom!'

'Coooo!' they gasped in unison. 'P'raps if we get in with him we'll get some rides in them Bren carriers!' said Chippy.

'And he'll let us have a shot with a rifle,' suggested Podge.

'Pull the lanyard on a twenty-five pounder!' continued Chippy.

'There's just one snag,' said Frank glumly. 'His stuffy old wife will be coming to live with us too! Someone from London!'

'She mightn't be too bad,' replied Chippy optimistically. 'Them old vacagees aren't so bad for a laugh once you've trained 'em...'specially the girls!'

'Anyway I've got to shoot my Ma a couple of rabbits,' Frank announced, picking up his gun and edging away towards Back Lane. 'And I'm going alone so that I can sit quietly and be sure of getting them,' he added quickly as the other three began to rise from the steps.

Frank left the road to follow a rough drove leading to the western boundary of the carr where a raised bank of tangled sedges and willow herb covered an extensive rabbit bury above a field of sugar beet. He seated himself within a clump of sedge thirty paces down-wind of the bury, and settled down to wait for the rabbits to emerge into the open headland to feed. He heard the distant chime of the church clock striking nine o'clock. Wood-pigeons cooed soothingly from the overgrown willows of the ancient carr, and waterhens clucked amongst the bright green duckweed in the ditches.

The clock chimed a quarter past nine. A pigeon settled with a startling clatter of wings in the willow above Frank's head. He watched the anxious movements of its head and the restless pale primrose eyes through the canopy of leaves. Faintly, above the song of the midges, the voices of the Lode searchlight crew drifted across the Fen. Then suddenly the first rabbit appeared, to sit, ears pricked and watchful, at the edge of the bank.

She was a 'milky' doe, huge and pregnant. Frank stilled his breathing and watched her as she sat without moving for a couple of minutes before disappearing back into the bury.

A little later a baby rabbit appeared, soon to be joined by five others, who began to pluck experimentally at the groundsel and chickweed between a row of beet.

At last a three-quarter-grown buck and doe skipped into view to chase each other recklessly around the beet plants, frisking and playing in the open, stopping now and again to sit with their ears flicked forward to listen. Frank waited until they were well away from the bury and sitting up on their back legs during one of their pauses and slowly raised his gun.

He was 'shooting for the pot' so he had no qualms about shooting the sleek young doe as she washed her whiskers, or the buck on his short dash for the safety of the bank. With the double shot the pigeons clattered up from the willows to circle the carr. Reloading hastily, Frank waited until one of the birds passed overhead and brought it down with another shot from his 12-bore. The sky, darkening in the dusk above the willow carr, suddenly became criss-crossed with bemused pigeons disturbed from their roosts, and another shot made certain of a couple of plump pigeons for his mother, two prime young rabbits for Mrs Rowsell, and the price of a ticket to watch 'Thanks For The Memory' at the Regal Cinema.

'I have something to tell you,' announced his mother as he flung the two pigeons down on the kitchen table, after collecting one and sixpence and a free bottle of Corona from Mrs Rowsell. 'We are going to have a lodger. The young captain's wife, a Mrs Vernon.'

'Oh,' answered Frank innocently. 'I wondered why he called to see you.'

Saturday 22nd of June
'Thanks for the Memory'

Saturday morning was marred by dark clouds as if a storm were about to break up the spell of fine weather. But by half past twelve, when Frank wheeled his bicycle away from the village towards the trysting place where the Lode Drove met the main Downham Market road, the clouds had broken and brilliant sunlight bathed the Fen through ever-widening patches of blue sky. He arrived early to sit on the roadside verge hugging his knees and staring compulsively back along the empty stretch of road which ran back through the screen of Lombardy poplars to the village. He felt physically sick with nervous anticipation. The minutes passed slowly. A solitary bicycle appeared in the distance, stopping his heart beat as his eyes followed its progress towards him until he could recognise the slender figure of the postmaster's wife. The feeling of nausea returned to the pit of his stomach. He had never before imagined that 'going to the Pictures with a girl' could entail so many hazards. For none of the imaginary pleasures could possibly make amends for the agony of mind and body caused by this wavering suspense.

A bank vole scurried across the dusty road and vanished into a maze of yellow silverweed beneath his raised knees. Lapwings circled and dived above a stretch of fallow ground, calling distractedly to their chicks at some fancied danger. The church clock chimed a quarter past one. A Handley-Page Harrow transport droned monotonously as it laboured across the sky heading for

Feltwell. Two figures suddenly materialized against the dark green backcloth of the poplars, white and ethereal like moths dancing over a dusk meadow, as they veered from side to side of the road, speeding outwards from the village.

Frank leapt to his feet, dragging his bicycle from the flattened silverweed as they skidded to a breathless standstill beside him. His heart began to soar to meet the larks carolling high above the reeds.

'Hello Frank.'

Veronica smiled in the condescending manner of an elder sister, as she ran her bicycle down the far side of the dyke and let it fall, hidden beneath a tangle of rushes and cow parsley, before disappearing herself behind a screen of reeds clutching to her bosom a tightly-rolled yellow oilskin cycling cape.

Joy turned to look back at Frank as she sat on her bicycle with one foot on the ground. It was a modern Sports Tourer with a Sturmey-Archer three speed, much superior to the usual village 'sit-up-and-beg' models with complicated dress-guards of cord laced around the back mudguards.

'I hope you haven't been waiting long,' she said.

'Oh no. I've only just arrived,' answered Frank, trying to sound nonchalant in spite of his racing heart.

'I'm so glad,' she smiled sweetly. 'Because I watched you pass the Ship nearly an hour ago.'

'Oh!...I had to take a message from Ma Shipham to Marsh Farm first,' he stammered huskily and blushing.

'I worried a little about you having to wait so long. But Mummy wouldn't let us leave until after luncheon,' Joy continued, teasingly, like a cat teases a tiny shrew.

'Make certain you are back here by a quarter past six,' came a breathless voice from within the green fastnesses of the reedbed.

'Quarter past six,' reiterated Joy, beginning to pedal away. 'Not a second before!'

'Make sure you pay attention and watch the film carefully, so that you can prime me about the programme when Mummy asks!' came the voice from the reedbed, where the reeds were now beginning to shake and tremble.

'We mightn't see much,' shouted Joy archly. 'We'll watch the best parts perhaps!'

'I'll murder you if you don't!' drifted sweetly back through the gyrating reeds.

'Give my love to Leon,' retorted Joy, bubbling with laughter.

'What on earth is Veronica doing in that reedbed?' asked Frank, intrigued by the covert rustlings behind the rushes.

'She's going to make herself look beautiful before Leon arrives. He's supposed to meet her here at a quarter past one. So she has only ten minutes to do it in!'

'But...Why on earth has she to do that?'

'Because Mummy won't let her dress up or wear lipstick or put her hair up. Leon comes from London so it is absolutely essential for her to make herself beautiful to compete with the sort of girls he is used to taking out!'

Joy tossed her head roguishly. 'Of course I don't believe it, but Leon told Veronica that his father is a master tailor who makes clothes for lords and ladies from his home in Whitechapel...of course soldiers will tell you anything. Won't they?...Especially Searchlight privates!'

They relapsed into silence as they cycled side by side overwhelmed by the enormity of being alone together. Joy was wearing a white cotton blouse, a dirndl skirt, and plimsolls and, apart from the addition of a wide leather belt, Veronica had been wearing the same outfit, which made her appear much younger than her approaching sixteenth year.

'Did Mum pay you for the rabbits?' Joy asked, breaking the silence and lifting her eye from the road ahead to glance momentarily at Frank. She had her father's vivid blue eyes and fair hair, unlike her sister who had inherited their mother's dark eyes and raven-black hair. Veronica was going to be a ravishing beauty, like her proud, flamenco-dancing mother.

'Dad slipped me half a crown without Mum knowing. And Mum gave me ninepence for the pictures, and threepence for sweets.' Joy flung another transitory glance towards Frank, swerving until their handlebars almost touched.

'I've got my usual Saturday sixpence, and the one and six from your mother for the rabbits.'

Frank's soul was in bliss. 'We're rich! I can buy you a box of Black Magic for sixpence.'

'Or a packet of Park Drive and a tuppenny bar of Cadbury's,' she replied daringly, with a brazen glint in her eye.

Frank gave a little chuckle, catching the eager abandonment and exquisite freedom of the moment. Suddenly the Downham Market road became exquisitely, glowingly, beautiful beneath the cycle tyres, sighing smoothly along the grey, metalled surface, raising trails of sweet-scented Fenland dust.

'Leon's O.K.,' he said defensively. 'He's one of the best down the Searchlight. Jolly clever at poker and gin rummy!'

'The Searchlight' referred to the corporal and eight privates who spent a contented and undisciplined life in a wooden army hut tucked into a thick whitethorn hedge at the end of the Lode Drove. Here they lived in comfortable seclusion with their searchlight, its generator trailer, a World War 1 Lewis gun mounted on a post, and a rickety path of duckboards, which led between the living hut, a lean-to camp kitchen, and a primitive latrine. Their only link to the world outside was a crank-up field telephone and the weekly truck which brought their mail and rations, together with coke for their stove and fuel for the generator. Far less regular were the spot-checks on their efficiency by the Unit Officer.

'Down the Searchlight' during the autumn and winter nights of the 'phoney-war' the platoon's hut became open house to the boys and the older girls of Willows End. It was a secret oasis of light, warmth, and adventure, fastness of the Fen. Outside, a sentry wrapped in his great coat with its collar turned up, a balaclava covering his nose, and a tin hat on his head, would huddle against the generator trailer for warmth, while inside the hut, bathed in the amber light from a couple of hurricane lamps, the Tortoise stove would be stoked high until its round top glowed cherry red.

Here, behind the blackout shutters, tales were told to the young initiates sitting owl-eyed round the glowing stove on rickety deck chairs, or lounging on the rough grey blankets of truckle beds. Curing like kippers in a fug of paraffin, nicotine and drying washing, they played Ludo, Snakes and Ladders, and Monopoly at a narrow trestle table. They learnt to gamble at Nap and Gin Rummy, Poker and Cribbage, while many of the more daring girls learnt other, more secret and joyful, skills beneath the rough hairy blankets.

But an even more piquant sense of excitement was experienced following the sentries' urgent banging on the side of the hut at the arrival of a Unit Officer for a spot-check. In a flash the lamps would be snuffed out to facilitate a frenzied dash through the far door of the hut as boys and girls fled outwards into the pitch-black night, to crouch shivering in the lee of the hedge. Then followed a stealthy return to the Drove by a circuitous route, feeling their way across invisible planks over deep dykes until they felt the solid surface of the roadway beneath their feet. Once safely on the road they would march joyously homewards, with starry eyes and glowing cheeks, singing lusty choruses of 'We're going to hang out the washing on the Siegfried Line' and 'Arm in arm together' and wistful renderings of 'Ol' Faithful' and 'Roll along covered wagon'.

'I hate to think what Mummy would say if she found out that Veronica was seeing a soldier,' Joy mused, with a giggle. 'But I think it's absolutely spiffing. I can do practically anything I like with her now! If she starts trying to be bossy I have only to say 'Leon' and she shuts up. So I shall blackmail her into covering for us from now on.'

The high-pitched rattling hum of an overtaking motor car sounded.

'Oh crikey! What if it's someone who knows us?' groaned Frank in a panic-stricken voice.

'Can't be,' she answered coolly. 'Dad's car is in the garage, Mr Barrett always spends every Saturday afternoon in the bar. And those uppish snobs at the 'Grange' wouldn't look at us anyway. Nobody else owns a car.'

'Your dad might have an urgent fare to Downham station.'

'Oh, don't worry.' She laughed aloud. 'Anyway Dad isn't as bad as Mummy. He never tells me off.'

With a rush of wind a diminutive Austin Seven open tourer, driven by a grossly overweight man, with a slim young woman wearing a red tam o' shanter beside him, scuttled fussily past like a maroon-coloured beetle.

'Huh! I'd like to know where he gets his petrol coupons from,' said Frank resentfully. 'Bet he is going to the Pictures. And that isn't an essential journey.'

'Oh, but it *is*...It's jolly essential! It's to see Bob Hope and Shirley Ross!'

'I bet Sir John Anderson wouldn't agree.'

'Don't be beastly!'

They were approaching a shack of thickly-tarred planks with tiny square windows on each side of a rough plank door. Only the pantiled roof was visible from the road, rising above tall reeds and overgrown sallow willows. The reeds parted to make a narrow gap leading to a plank over the roadside dyke which led to the shack door. A line of five tethered goats were grazing the rough herbage of the nearside bank, and languorous chickens bathed and scratched in the roadside dust.

It appeared to be an idyllic pastoral scene filled with sunlight, the epitome of tranquillity beneath the wide Fenland sky, with a patchwork of fields stretching away towards a blue horizon.

The furthermost goat, a shaggy-coated old billy with horns like an Abyssinian ibex and yellow eyes of demoniacal malevolence, lifted his head.

'Crikey! Nebuchadnezzar!' cried Frank, instantly lifting his bottom from his bicycle's saddle, wobbling alarmingly as his knees pumped up and down like pistons as he sprinted ahead. 'Hold your breath and pedal like fury!'

'Nebu...What?' shrieked Joy, above the clamour from a flock of truculent geese. 'Nebu...What?' she reiterated breathlessly, as they settled back on their saddles and resumed cruising speed.

'Did you get a whiff? That was Nebuchadnezzar. The stinkiest old billy-goat in the world! He pongs so much that he stinks out the school bus as it goes by.'

They had reached the iron bridge spanning the wide river Ouse to join a stream of people from the outlying villages biking steadily towards the 'Pictures', along with delivery vans, horses and traps, and the occasional motor car.

'I hope we are early,' Joy remarked, putting on speed as they passed by the corn mill and railway station, only to be forced to slow down again by the Saturday afternoon influx of traffic in Bridge Street.

'Oh goodness. Look at the time. It's ten to two already. Stop dawdling.'

But Frank was casting a longing glance towards Fells, whose windows displayed an array of bicycles, Hornby train sets, and Meccano and Trix outfits, together with less exciting ironmongery. Noticing a beautiful 2-6-4 L.M.S. locomotive next to an apple-green L.N.E.R. 4-6-0 Express he braked, and by the time his eyes returned to the road Joy had disappeared to their left at the clock tower into High Street, where a double queue of rowdy children waited outside the door to the Regent Cinema.

After hastily lifting the front wheels of their bicycles into the slots of the cinema's bicycle shed Frank led the way towards the end of the queue.

'Sweets,' pronounced Joy firmly. 'We must buy some sweets.'

'We'll lose our place in the queue.'

Joy wrinkled her nose. 'Poo! That lot will be going in the thruppennies. *We're* going in the ninepennies. At least I am because I'm under fourteen. You'll have to pay one and six!'

Her eyes danced and she tossed her hair with a disdainful flourish as she took his hand to drag him across the street towards a small sweet and tobacconist's shop, inwardly comparing the lasting qualities of a quarter of a pound of chocolate caramels to the transient luxury of two Whipped Cream Walnut Whirls.

A tiny white-moustached man appeared behind the counter to eye them soulfully from behind a row of glass jars filled with boiled sweets, bullseyes, humbugs, jelly babies, and chocolate caramels, with a patchwork display of chocolate bars, and more exotic delights including Whipped Cream Walnut Whirls nestling in foil cups.

'Two ounces of humbugs, please,' said Frank.

Joy dithered, while the man methodically weighed two ounces of brown striped humbugs on a brass scale before tipping them into a paper bag. 'I'll have...' began Joy indecisively... 'one Whipped Cream Walnut Whirl...a quarter of chocolate caramels...and a stick of liquorice.' She giggled. 'Mmm...I hope they never ration sweets!'

'They've just halved the meat ration,' replied the man mournfully. 'And one ounce of cheese isn't enough for Mickey Mouse, is it now?' He reached across the counter to take a Walnut Whirl from its nest and drop it into a bag. 'But there you are. We just have to do the best we can, don't we, my little old beauty?'

Frank, waiting at the shop door, had second thoughts. Realising that a girl in the 'Pictures' might not be too enthralled to be offered humbugs, he stepped back to the counter. 'And a quarter of Turkish Delight,' he said magnanimously, colouring to the roots of his hair as he looked into Joy's blue eyes.

The queue outside the cinema had vanished, allowing them to enter the empty vestibule to pay for their tickets and pass through heavily-curtained doors into the auditorium, to be greeted by a bedlam of screeching children competing with the soulful crooning of Cole Porter's 'Begin the Beguine'. An usherette appeared from the shadows, but before she reached them Joy had made a beeline towards the back row of the stalls, where a dozen couples were sitting bolt upright in their seats, peering self-consciously ahead at the curtained screen.

'Begin the Beguine' drifted imperceptibly away as the lights dimmed and the heavy plush curtains drew apart to reveal the screen.

A notice in large white letters flashed upon the screen:

IN THE EVENT OF AN AIR RAID ALERT PATRONS WILL BE INFORMED.

'Hooray!' shrieked the 'patrons', stamping their feet and tossing up sweet papers that descended like zigzagging bombers caught in the searchlight beams of the projector. The message vanished.

'COLONY PICTURES PRESENT...Ken Maynard and Fay McKenzie in... "DEATH RIDES THE RANGE"'

'Whoopeeeeee! Yahoo! Injuns!' howled the stamping children.

Veiled in the voluptuous darkness of the back row the lovers divested themselves of cardigans and jackets, surreptitiously draping them over strategic areas of their anatomy, before snuggling close together and abandoning themselves to the magic of thrill-seeking touch in the heavy shadows.

'Oh my giddy aunt...*cowboys!*' breathed Joy in feigned disgust. 'I'm going to sleep through this.' She proceeded to unbutton the top three buttons of her blouse and drape Frank's school blazer over their knees. 'Wake me when it's over.' And laying her head on his chest, she sleepily guided his left arm across their laps to rest on her knee beneath the blazer.

Frank continued to sit bolt upright, fearful to move, as he gazed uneasily towards his left and his right over Joy's head at the shadowy couples. She lay heavily against his shoulder. His right arm, wedged uncomfortably between her shoulder blade and the back of the seat, was rapidly becoming numb. The screen was only partly visible through a halo of wavy hair, as if he were a reconnoitring Indian scout peering through swaying prairie grass. The actors on the screen appeared and disappeared through the wisps of her curls while, with every breath, the fine hairs tickled his nose until the urge to scratch it became unbearable.

Joy lay in Frank's arms relaxed in utter bliss with closed eyes.

'Mmmm,' she murmured at last without opening her eyes. 'Mmmmm,' languorously lifting his hitherto immobile left hand from her knee to press it lightly against her bosom. Frank held his breath. 'Mmmmm,' she sighed, pulling the blazer higher, covering them within an enclave of eau-de-Cologne .'Mmm...'s nice!' as he gingerly let his hand slip through the open buttons to touch the soft resilience of warm skin.

From this moment the full-blooded roar of excitement coming from the 'thruppennies' which followed every staccato volley of shots from the cowboy's six-shooters blurred into a dream sequence as the torrid back row of the stalls drifted into a magical world of its own, swept by a dreamy mistral of voluptuous 'Oooo's' and 'Oh's' interrupted by some unexpectedly vehement 'Stop its'.

An hour later, after Fay McKenzie had been rescued from the renegade, Charles King, by her hero Ken Maynard, and the embracing couple had finally ridden out across the lonely prairie towards the setting sun......the lights came on.

In the back row of the stalls a frantic exodus from Utopia coincided with a frenzied buttoning up of buttons, tugging of zips and plucking down of skirt hems, the lovers finally regaining their composure to sit gazing down in wide-eyed innocence at the rowdy 'thruppennies'. Chocolate bars were unwrapped and sweet bags rustled. There was genteel conversation between the girls and short monosyllabic utterances between the boys. These were barely heard above the further confusion as small children packed the aisles on their way back and forth to the lavatories, helped on their way by the lively tempo of 'Run Rabbit Run'.

Joy's reaction to the lights being switched had been instantaneous. In a flash she had risen from her slumber on Frank's chest to sit demurely at the far side of her seat studying the audience.

'There they are!' She nudged Frank, indicating the middle-aged obese man wearing a flashy chalk-striped brown suit and the slim girl in a Tam o' shanter, who had previously overtaken them in the Austin Seven.

Frank raised his eyes while trying to extricate a squashed bag of Turkish Delight from the pocket of his crumpled blazer.

'I know him! He's a seed salesman from Wisbech. And she's the new parlour maid from the Garth.'

'How do you know?'

'He's often in the Ship for his lunch when he is travelling around the farms...always making eyes at Mum when Dad's in the tap room.'

She declined his proffered squashed Turkish Delight and retrieved her bag of chocolate caramels and Walnut Whirl from beneath her seat.

'Have a chocolate caramel,' she said, handing him the bag. before blissfully peeling the silver foil from her Walnut Whirl.

Frank sat uneasily on the edge of his seat watching her bite the top off the miniature Mount Etna, revealing a crater oozing white lava which she licked with the delicacy of a honey bear guzzling a wild bee's nest.

'Yummy,' she murmured, licking her fingers. 'I'll have a Turkish Delight now!' She treated him to a happy glance from beneath long lashes as the lights dimmed to announce the coming attractions.

Errol Flynn, Brenda Marshall, and Claude Rains in 'The Sea Hawk'... Barbara Stanwyck and Fred MacMurray in 'Remember the Night'...

A zestful fanfare proceeded the Pathe News...

'Mussolini declares war on the allies...'

'Booo,' hissed the crowd.

'Beaverbrook appeals to housewives for aluminium...Your pots and pans will help make Spitfires, Blenheims, Hurricanes, and Wellingtons...'

'Women's Land Army Girls show how they can handle tractors equal to our men. In the hayfield, or with the plough. Our Land Girls are on the job.'

Glamorous shots of curvaceous blondes posing in velveteen breeches perched upon the steel seat pans of Fordson tractors caused a standing ovation in the 'thruppennies'. Large boys and small boys jostled and stamped to exuberant whistles and falsetto shouts of 'Send them here...Send them here...Up the Land Girls!' until the Manager, accompanied by the very stout ticket-office lady, marched up and down the aisles with dire threats of eternal banishment to all who did not immediately *'Shut up!'*

Cloaked once more in sensual shadows the back row couples now sat back in their seats to watch the 'big film'. They became withdrawn from their partners as they entered a world in which they assumed the personalities of the film stars. The girls dreamily took on the role of Shirley Ross, while the young men, wrapped up in wishful thoughts, took on the reflected glamour of Bob Hope. They held hands, but lifelessly now, until they unconsciously drew apart allowing their hands to slip back on to their laps.

Joy leaned across the arm of her seat and laid her hand in his as the darkness closed in upon them.

'Remember. We must concentrate on watching the film now,' she whispered pertly, straightening her skirt.

Without answering, Frank pinched her thigh with a devil-may-care laugh.

'Shush!' Her fingers intertwined gently with his, and the credits started scrolling upwards across the screen.

The final curtain had closed. All the lights had returned with a brilliance that dazzled the audience, and after standing rigidly to attention for the National Anthem they had streamed through the vestibule with tear-streaked cheeks and lumps in their throats out into the afternoon sunlight.

Joy's power of speech returned as they wheeled their bicycles away into the bustle of High Street. 'Wasn't it a lovely film?' she said huskily, as if her throat were half-closed. 'Wasn't it sad?'

Frank hastily turned his face away.

'You've been crying too!' she exclaimed with a tender little smile, which made him blush. 'I heard you sniffing when Shirley Ross left Bob Hope writing that book!' She started to hum 'Two Sleepy People'. 'But it was nice when they sang that together, wasn't it?'

Return journeys always appear to be shorter than the outward one, and before long they had safely negotiated Nebuchadnezzar and his harem and were cycling across the open fen, watching the cloud shadows drift slowly over the patchwork of fields, along the road which ran as straight as an arrow's flight between dykes. They sang snatches of the songs from the film, 'Thanks for the Memory' and 'Two Sleepy People', until soon they were turning off the main road towards the willow-crowned island of reeds which marked the beginning of the Lode Drove.

Joy hurriedly flung her bicycle into the dykeside reeds and scrambled up the steep bank of the main drain to run towards a bullock-flattened area of grass beneath a polled willow tree.

'Hurry up,' she called flopping down with adolescent gaucheness and smoothing her skirt before patting the grass with her hand. 'Veronica will be here soon.'

Frank crimsoned.

'Didn't they kiss beautifully,' she remarked dreamily, turning towards him as he lowered himself gingerly to lie stiffly beside her looking up into the leaves of the willow.

'Aren't you going to kiss me, like Bob Hope kissed Shirley Ross?'

Frank coloured again as she nestled towards him. She seemed so frail, in the ivory-fleshed, pastel-cheeked manner of the Royal Doulton shepherdess who stood on the chiffonier at home, that Frank scarcely dared to touch her. She frowned. Putting her arm round his neck she forced his head down to crush his mouth to her mouth in a long kiss that left him flushed and half-suffocated.

'That's much better!' she cried impulsively. 'Now I'll show you how to French kiss.'

'Coooo-eeeee.'

'Damn!' said Joy fiercely. 'Veronica.'

Frank's gradual escape from the labyrinth of the kiss was hastened by a glimpse of an illusionary Fata Morgana rising out of the heat-haze above the reeds.

'Coo-eeee...It's only me!' Veronica paused unsteadily on top of the bank, before scrambling down in high heels to totter across the rough grass towards them carrying her rolled-up oilskin cape.

Frank stared hard at Veronica, a completely new Veronica, a Veronica who had undergone a metamorphosis from schoolgirl to glamorous *femme fatale* like one of his Puss moths from *pupa* to *imago* in less than four hours.

Her black hair fell about her shoulders in a soft glossy roll. Her dark eyes seemed larger, her lips dewy, reddened to a luscious deep coral with lipstick. Her modest white blouse and cotton skirt had gone. In their place she wore a light crêpe-de-Chine floral dress of bright colours, sheer stockings with black seams, and high-heeled court shoes.

'Quick,' she said urgently, kicking off her shoes and flopping down beside them to lean forward rolling down her stockings. 'We've no time to waste!'

She unrolled the cycle cape to reveal her discarded change of raiment.

'Here,' she said to Frank giving him a face-flannel. 'Go and wet this in the dyke for me.' She raised her arms, stretching them above her head as she started to remove her dress. 'Go on!' she said sharply as he dawdled.

He blushed and made his way to the side of the dyke, disturbing a metallic blue damselfly from a floating patch of duckweed. As he bent to dip the flannel in the water, sticklebacks flickered in and out of a pale silvery forest of water violet roots, and bronze flashes gleamed through the deeper water as small roach fled from the swirl caused by the sinking flannel.

Frank handed Veronica the damp face-flannel. The *femme fatale* had changed back into a naïve and innocent schoolgirl by donning her white blouse and dirndl skirt. 'Thanks.' She scooped her dress, stockings, shoes, and a silky black slip into a heap. 'You can roll these up in my bike cape.'

She smiled faintly as he picked them up and carried them a little way along the bank where the grass was shorter. Joy was kneeling behind her sister hastily plaiting her hair.

'Oh, do hurry up!' Veronica snapped petulantly. 'I've got to scrub my face yet.'

Frank began to fold the clothes into a bundle. In a home devoid of femininity he was fascinated by the sensuality of the black satin and crêpe-de-Chine which held the musky odour of body warmth. He felt an unknown involuntary ache for a 'mother', the archetypal mother who represents 'love' as opposed to 'duty'.

'Right, gal. You're finished!' Joy stretched a couple of rubber bands round the plaits and rejoined Frank below the willow tree, kissing him ardently in brazen defiance of the world.

Veronica scrubbed the remains of lipstick and mascara from her face with the flannel.

'You two have done enough of that surely. Tell me quickly about the film.' She glanced at her last birthday's wrist-watch.

'First film...Ken Maynard in "Death Rides the Range".'

'Mussolini declares war,' added Frank.

'Trailer for next week's big film?' asked Veronica.

'Errol Flynn in "The Sea Wolf".'

Veronica stood up and straightened her skirt. 'Tell me about the big film.'

'Bob Hope was a penniless writer just married to Shirley Ross...She was forced to go out to work to keep him...They quarrelled and she left him...' began Joy, pausing for breath.

'It was awfully sad,' continued Frank. 'After they had parted he lived alone in a slummy room with hardly any food to eat.'

'And he finally wrote a very successful book and became rich...but couldn't find Shirley Ross ever again,' Joy finished gaily. 'It was a lovely film. We both cried!'

'Jolly good,' Veronica said gaily, with a mischievous grin that suited her schoolgirl plaits. 'I shall walk into the house singing 'Two Sleepy People' and Mummy won't suspect a thing! By the way, did anyone who matters see you?'

'Only that horrid fat salesman from Wisbech. And he daren't breathe a word because he had that new parlour-maid from the Grange with him. He knows jolly well that we know that he's married, and she probably doesn't!'

Running easily up the high bank of the main drain in their plimsolls the two girls lifted their bicycles from the rushes, removed a tangle of angelica and willow-herb from the spokes, and pedalled away towards the village, leaving Frank to follow, keeping a respectable distance behind in order to confuse the village gossips.

Tuesday 25th June
The Captain's Wife Arrives

In Fenland villages outstanding events were few and far apart, and the most singular excitements were the clandestine 'goings on', imaginary or otherwise, of flighty young grass-widows with the airmen stationed at nearby airfields; and the careful scanning of the Births, Deaths and Marriages column in the *Cambridge Evening News* on a Thursday evening. But now the impending visit of an Army Officer's wife had become the main topic wherever whispering wives congregated. It held sway over all other matters at the Thursday evening Women's Institute meeting, to be continued on the following days in the village shop, the post office, and behind closed doors over cups to tea and digestive biscuits. Meanwhile the male fraternity outwardly remained aloof from such thoughts, although inwardly they cogitated as they walked the land, slodged ditches, or rode the creaking tumbrils back and forth between the pea fields and the packing sheds.

Everyone held his or her secret vision of what the Captain's wife would be like, but it was generally conceded that she would be fashioned in the mode of the late Colonel's wife who had owned the 'Old Hall' during the early post-war years, a very angular, tweedy female; sensibly shod and inclined to heavy hunters, small dogs, and her own interpretation for the social welfare of the indigenous villagers.

Ex-R.S.M. Kingshott behind his red velvet curtain was outwardly above such prognostications. Nevertheless there lurked in his memory jolly recollections of lively young wives of elderly staff officers dancing the Black Bottom and Charleston in faraway places. Ma Shipham standing in her wash-house thoughtfully thumping her dolly up and down in the tub fondly remembered past young mistresses of 'quality' from her days in service.

Even Daggy Flegg was not immune. from the distemper that had taken its grip upon the villagers. Sitting alone on his truckle bed in his shack, it had struck him down in a morbid way, causing him to be haunted by memories of the Colonel's philanthropic wife, who had publicly denounced him for using what he called 'good old humus' spread liberally on his strawberry plants and ostracized him for what she termed 'the wrongful dumping of night soil'.

Two hours after sundown every Friday evening in gale, rain, snow, or on the balmy nights of high-summer, Daggy's piebald cob would be heard clip-clopping around the village drawing a rusty steel tank on wheels accompanied by the rattle of a bucket. This was 'Sweet Violets'...Daggy's alias when wearing the hat of the 'Council contracted collector of night soil'.

The aged piebald cob would stop outside each village residence and stand with lowered head allowing Daggy time to trudge up each garden path to empty the closet pails. Most of the Willows End privies were purpose-designed with a trap-door flap which opened from the outside giving easy access to remove the pail. Every so often some unfortunate soul, not remembering that it was a Friday, would be disturbed, as he sat on a scrubbed pine seat by candlelight, by having the trap-door opened for a hand to whisk the pail away while a blast of icy wind anæsthetised his naked posterior.

During the past weekend covert movements by the troops billeted in the Old Hall had been observed by the villagers. The bush telegraph worked overtime. Wives watched in hushed expectancy behind twitching curtains along the length of the street's terraced cottages. Listening children loitered on strategic corners. Only the white ducks sleeping in the shade of the weeping willows seemed unruffled, and unaware of the electric tension that held the villagers all agog.

Late on the Saturday evening an army truck was seen to back furtively along the narrow alley leading to the 'Birdman's backus', followed by suppressed whispers and the shuffle of boots on the gravel path, with the unmistakable lumping sound of heavy sacks being dragged along the ground.

During the daytime when the wives were out 'pea-pulling' and the listening children were in school, the old men, huddled beneath the church wall limes, took over. They recorded the visits back and forth of Captain Vernon and the cookhouse sergeant in a canvas-tilted utility truck to the

'Birdman's' house, squinting through rheumy eyes at the various boxes and bags that were being hustled between the tailboard of the truck and the porch of the house.

It was all very exciting, far, far more exciting in fact than the War, which supposedly was still in progress. Of late the six o'clock News seemed to have nothing very exciting to report, just that 'France is thought to be seeking an armistice with Germany, and an enemy aircraft had been brought down by a nightfighter off the Scottish coast'. Nothing was said about the fact that a 'furriner' was soon to descend upon Willows End.

At last the fateful Tuesday the 25th of June 1940 arrived.

A chattering of 'pea-pulling' ladies sat in a corner of the pea field having their 'docky' in the mid-morning sunshine. Their weathered faces glowed below brightly-coloured head-scarves, and their usual heavy, sacking aprons and Wellington boots had been discarded for light cotton dresses and plimsolls.

'That old Army Captain's old woman is comin' today, isn't she?' remarked Rosie Flegg to get them going. 'I feel wholly sorry for that old teacher having someone like that living with her. She'll drive her out of her mind...that's a fact.'

'If she thinks she's a-going to run the Women's Institute she have another think coming!' said Miss Judd. 'That old Colonel's wife driv me mad when she were a-running of it!'

'And I'm certainly not making my kids trousers out of her rough old skirts neither. Proper old fools they looked... enough to make you laugh,' Molly Griggs enjoined contemptuously.

'She weren't so bad at getting the young uns to Sunday School though,' reflected Sarah Chapman as she hitched up her skirt to bare her knees to the sunlight. 'That give me a rare old treat with my old man on a Sunday afternoon...And don't you forget she started the Brownies and the Guides on Thursday nights. So the old gal weren't all that bad when you come to think on it!'

'That old gal even driv the parson to start the Scouts, poor old bugger!' giggled Big Bertha. 'And she stopped old Daggy Flegg polluting of the air by tipping Sweet Violets all over his strawberries!'

'Ar, but remember this gal. You have to admit that Daggy's strawberries have never been so marvellous since...Have they now?' Rosie answered. 'Sweet as honey...Come to think on it, isn't there somethin' in the Bible about that?... "Out of filth there cometh honey"?'

Young Madge, lying on her back between two furrows, crumbling the dry earth between tanned fingers, giggled.

'Don't you be daft...You been reading what it say on Golden Syrup tins about a stinking old lion what some bees swarmed in.'

She trickled a little pile of earth through her hand on to a patch of white clover and pimpernels. 'Anyway the old gal might be nice. That there Captain is wholly nice. Speak like a filum star he do!...And he always give me a lovely smile!'

All eyes of the ladies instantly swivelled to stare at Madge. Already they were setting the type for tomorrow's *News of the World* headlines 'Married Army Officer Seduces Sixteen-year-old Country Girl'...

Madge blushed beneath her golden-brown tan.

'Well...She might be nice,' she repeated truculently.

'*What!* An army officer's old woman?...Pigs might fly gal!...She'll be a right old devil. Doin' good and "do this an' do that, get your kids' hair washed, buy a dickie comb". Gawd help us,' snorted Selena Roberts, standing up to dust fish-paste sandwich crumbs from her skirt. 'I'm gettin' back pulling afore the worry drives me mad.'

'Come you on gals,' said Rosie, suddenly jumping up on to her feet. 'I'm goin' to knock off at half past three to give me time to get Harnser an' the kids their dinner so's I can see the old gal arrive...Molly Shipham say she's a-comin' on the six o'clock train from London...So she ought to be here by twenty past.'

One by one the gang of 'pea-pullers' followed suit, young Madge being left to help portly Bertha up from a nest of pea-straw between two furrows.

The morning sun rose towards its zenith to hang above the unshaded Fens. Its heat, beating back from the parched earth, carried with it the pungent scents of shrivelled pea-straw and clover. Larks sang above the brightly-coloured scarves and dresses as the women filled their sacks with peas.

It was six-twenty p.m. Outwardly the village was enjoying the peace of an early evening in high summer. The pea-picking women had long since cycled homeward. The old men dozed below the church wall. House martins and swallows swooped above the pond harvesting the clouds of gnats hanging above the brilliant green scum. The ducks slept above their perfect reflections in channels of clear water. Swifts dashed screaming to and fro between their nests in the church tower and the blue sky.

But inwardly Willows End was tense. Cottage curtains twitched, as if in the throes of the fenland ague. The postmistress hung her CLOSED notice in the Post Office window and disappeared into the house. Gradually the two benches outside the Ship Inn's doorway were being taken up by the 'regulars'. Mrs Rowsell had decided to sit in the fresh evening air on a wickerwork chair taken from the snug and her husband had taken a sudden interest in waterfowl, for he could be seen leaning over the pond rails feeding the swan and ducks with stale bread. Boer was sitting sideways on Samson's back as he watered the team of shires standing hock-deep in the pond an hour past their usual time, while Frank, China, Chippy, and Podge sat on the War Memorial plinth with their 'weapons' discussing the coming Home Guard drill.

An assortment of articles of uniform had been received by the Headmaster-cum-Captain of various shapes and sizes. Forage hats had been fairly good fits for the Willows End heads, but tunics, trousers, great-coats and boots tended to be of two sizes, 'Large' and 'Small'. Frank, having been lucky in the issue of a 'Small' tunic which was a passable tight fit, was presented with a 'Large' pair of trousers, which fitted like fishing waders up to his armpits, and were just as ungainly to move in. However he had managed to swop with Harnser whose six-foot gangling figure had been issued with 'Small' trousers, 5' 2" to 5' 5", and in the circumstances Frank was quite presentable. He had also been issued with a service gas mask and steel helmet, a webbing belt, and a pair of boots and gaiters.

China's mother, being a dab hand at altering jumble sale clothes, had cut China's oversize tunic and trousers down to size and re-stitched them on her treadle sewing machine; and Chippy's mum had done some undisclosed deal with the searchlight sergeant who had managed to have the whole of her son's uniform exchanged for a smaller size by the regimental company stores.

The one thing that was absent in each case was a rifle, but, as Headmaster-cum-Captain explained, they were coming!

Judging by the sudden swing of faces towards the east by the 'regulars' sitting outside the Ship Inn, something else was also coming. All eyes focused on the long straight stretch of the Wisbech road beyond the windbreak poplars, where a fast-travelling vehicle was to be seen approaching the village.

It was on this homely pastoral scene that Mrs Olivia Vernon, arriving in an Army truck, first set her eyes: the village Inn's landlord feeding a flotilla of ducks beside the village pond opposite his inn, where a group of jolly countrymen sat on benches with pewter tankards in their hands beside a handsome gipsy-like woman; a score of octogenarian sages dozing in the sunlight below the wall of a grey Norman church half-hidden by dark yew trees; a vicar lolling on its lych-gate smoking a pipe beside a tall angular lady while, standing fiercely to attention at the foot of a memorial cross to the fallen of the Great War was a beribboned non-commissioned officer with four schoolboys wearing battledress. Five glossy shire horses drinking far out in the water of the pond beneath a weeping willow, watched over by an old horseman smoking a clay pipe sitting on a large bay Clydesdale, completed this tableau vivant.

All the heads swung towards the west as the truck stopped outside Jubilee House, this being the grand title of Frank's home.

The Captain emerged from the driver's door to rush round the truck to open the passenger-side door.

A faint susurrus of movement sped through the air as curtains twitched and doors were slowly eased ajar. The postmistress appeared from her front door to pick up a strategically-placed watering-can and began to water the sweet peas bordering her garden path, and pint mugs froze during their passage up or down from the Ship Inn regulars' lips as the 'Captain's old woman's' lizard-skin court shoe appeared from the truck, to be followed by the rest of her as her husband gallantly lifted her down from the high vehicle.

Never in living memory had the people of Willows End suffered such a communal shock. A young woman stood on the tarmac with one gloved hand resting elegantly on the wing of the truck. She was as tall and slender as a Fen reed. Her classic fine wool suit was dove-grey over a white blouse. Her legs were sheathed in sheer silk and her fair hair was swept up beneath a tiny matching grey pillbox hat whose smoky veil gave mystique to a perfectly made-up face. It was as if a screen goddess had suddenly stepped out from the Downham Market Regal's silver screen.

The unexpected materialization of this vision instantly conjured up long lost responses in all who saw her. To the Headmaster peering through his opera-glasses from the School House window, the slender dove-grey wraith of a girl brought memories of Pavlova dancing Giselle at Covent Garden in 1925, whereas Boer, sitting puffing his clay pipe on Samson, was spirited back to Lottie Collins singing 'Ta-ra-ra-boom-de-ay' forty-five years before. The old men allowed their minds to rumble backward to the divine Gibson Girls of the 'nineties. To the Postmaster she was Mary Pickford, or maybe Greta Garbo. To young Madge, sitting on her new bike, she was nothing less than a genuine screen goddess incognito, perhaps Jean Harlow or Veronica Lake!

The vicar's sister, from her vantage point within the lych-gate, eyed her as possible material for the Women's Institute, while R.S.M. Kingshott fondly recalled the young ladies of India, not the dyed-in-the-wool memsahibs of the Raj, but their daughters newly returned from schooldays in Blighty. She had the same look of willowy demureness which personified the daughters of the Raj. R.S.M. Kingshott twirled the waxed ends to his moustache and turned to face the four boys, who were not at all impressed by the youthful look of the lady, seeing in her an obstacle to their high hopes of 'Getting in with that there Captain!' The Postmistress, overcome by the sight of such elegance, sprinkled her skirt with water which trickled unnoticed down her bare legs, filling her shoes.

With her luggage unloaded the trio disappeared through the front door, from which the soldier reappeared to drive the truck back to the Old Hall, leaving Captain and Mrs Vernon away from the eyes of the general public in Mrs Dutton's parlour.

Mrs Vernon dropped thankfully into a chintz-covered fireside chair on entering their room.

'Oh!' she sighed blissfully. 'This is so comfortable!'

'This really is a pleasant room, don't you think?' murmured her husband, turning towards one of the three tall windows overlooking the Square.

She rose from the chair to join him where he stood with his hands clasped behind his back looking down upon the village square and the pond. She was tall and graceful, silhouetted against the strong evening sunlight, with the heavy green of the yew trees opposite heightening the white of her blouse.

'Yes, I'm sure I'll be very happy here,' she answered, glancing towards Mrs Dutton who was standing in the doorway. 'So utterly peaceful after the bustle of London, although of course, Cheyne Row is quite a peaceful backwater. By the way, Mrs Dutton, where does one take a bath?'

'Bath?' Mrs Dutton looked pointedly towards the washstand with its pink rosebud-decorated jug and basin. 'One washes up as far as possible, and down as far as possible,' she replied primly.

'And what about poor possible?' replied Mrs Vernon with a droll grin, flinging her hat on the bed.

'The accepted procedure in the village is for the copper fire to be kept alight after the weekly wash, and one bathes in a tin bath during the evening in the wash-house,' said Mrs Dutton stiffly. 'Our washing is done by Mrs Shipham who takes in washing. Therefore our wash-house is never used!'

'Ah! The wash-house!' the Captain interjected hastily, after a heavy silence. 'Must hold possibilities!'

He smiled disarmingly. 'If Mrs Dutton has no objection, I will send a couple of my chaps to see what can be done. Very inventive lot. Performed miracles of improvisation for our ablutions in France!'

'Well, I will leave you to settle in,' said Mrs Dutton after another silence. She gave a last glance at the table where a meal prepared by Mrs Shipham had been left beneath one of her best linen tablecloths. 'Please let me know should you require anything.'

The couple turned away from the window and Mrs Vernon lifted the cloth to expose a green salad tastefully arranged in a shallow wooden bowl edged by a ring of hard-boiled eggs, cucumber slices, tomato quarters, and garnished with radish roses; a plate of the baker's crusty bread, thinly sliced and buttered with farm butter; a small jug of fresh cream and a bowl of raspberries, all laid out on a round table with two table mats and Mrs Dutton's family silver.

'But how lovely!' she exclaimed, unaware of what it had cost in favour, bribery and intrigue, to produce.

It had taken all the native finesse of Ma Shipham to coax a half pound of farm butter from Violet Judd, who very unexpectedly 'for such a tight old gal' had presented a jug of cream. The eggs for the mayonnaise and salad had been donated by Granna Fallows, whose nephew kept a flock of Rhode Island Reds at the bottom of her garden. The raspberries had been given by the

Postmaster from his market garden, together with lettuces, spring onions, tomatoes from his greenhouse, radishes and half a cucumber, while old Daggy Flegg, grumbling at the thought of the coming of another in the cast of the late 'Colonel's old woman' gave a panful of freshly dug new potatoes, and a sprig of mint from his salubrious soil. Last but not least, the Moocher had arrived with a bunch of watercress from a clear-flowing backwater of the Main Drain and a bunch of yellow flags with three bulrush spikes which had been arranged in a tall Wedgwood blue vase standing on the centre window-ledge.

All this unbeknown to Mrs Dutton who was kept sublimely unaware of her 'help's' duplicity, for by keeping the tin of corned beef (Army issue), which had been on the original menu, for Madge's 'docky' bag, and tinned peaches (Army issue) with tinned evaporated milk (under-the-counter Village shop issue) for her own 'Sunday tea treat', all had been happily catered for. Ma Shipham had not spent her formative years 'downstairs' in service to gentry in vain!

As Mrs Dutton left the room the buxom body of a beaming Ma Shipham entered, wearing a frilly apron tied round her ample waist and bearing a steaming tureen which she placed in the centre of the round table.

'There you are Ma'am,' she announced, lifting the lid of the tureen to reveal Daggy's peerless pigeon-egg-size potatoes, glistening with farm butter, garnished with a sprig of parsley, and redolent of mint. ' 'Tain't much.That's a rare old job to get to know what to get to cook these days, on account of this here rationing,' Mrs Shipham beamed at her two diners, folding her steam-reddened arms across her bosom. 'Still, we have to do the best we can, don't we Ma'am?'

'Thank you. It looks delicious! By the way, I take it that you must be Mrs Shipham?'

'That's right Ma'am. I do a bit of cleanin' and the teacher's washin' for her. Do your washin' if you want. Water's the problem round here. We haven't any taps a-bringin' it to you. Have to crank it up in buckets from the well. And them there are deep old wells. Come hard on them what are used to just turnin' a tap on!'

The corners of her mouth lifted into a wry smile. 'Mrs Dutton havent cranked a bucket up a well in her life! She leave it to that poor little old boy of hers when he come home from school!'

'She has a son?'

'That's right. Poor little old soul. She let him run around the Fen catchin' butterflies, shootin' things what he didn't oughter like ole patridges and long-tails, babbin' in the Drain, and comin' home with his clothes plastered with muck for me to wash and get dry. Nice little ole bor though! Ain't frit of nothing.' She lowered her voice. 'Beween you and me, Ma'am, I think she is wholly disappointed 'cause he didn't turn out brainy like his old dad! He don't take to school at all, that he don't.'

Ma Shipham gave a large sigh and unfolded her arms.

'Gawd, I'm a-mardling on. Stopping you getting your tea, aren't I now?'

'Not at all. It is so pleasant to meet you, Mrs Shipham. I'm sure we will find lots to talk about during my stay here. What a sweet person,' said Mrs Vernon as she handed the serving spoon to her husband, sliding the tureen towards him to help himself to some potatoes.

'At last...We are alone!' murmured the Captain, taking her hand in his, before dipping the spoon in the buttery tureen. 'Absolutely marvellous! Shades of the "Blue Cockatoo",' he whispered.

'Squa...a...a...d!'

Captain Vernon, totally unprepared for the explosive quality of Regimental Sergeant Major Kingshott's lungs, dropped the serving spoon, dripping melted butter with a horrifying 'splot!' on Mrs Dutton's Irish linen table-cloth as he rushed to the window.

After fifteen evenings consisting of two hourly periods of drill, Sergeant Kingshott had performed miracles with his Willows End Army. The Fenman's tireless slouching gait, developed over centuries of holding his head bent forward facing windswept acres of cloying mud, had gone. They had developed an alacrity of brain and limb which was little short of miraculous. Backs had straightened. Eyes were alert. Ears twitched, eager for commands. Even old Daggy's figure had been fined down by the loss of his sagging beer-belly, and the four boys lived in a seventh heaven in which they identified themselves with their heroes in *The Champion, The Hotspur,* and the *Boy's Own Paper.*

Mrs Vernon joined him at the window to look down upon a squad of six men and four boys drawn up in two ranks before a white-haired non-commissioned officer. Simultaneously both realised that they were witnessing the invincibility of the British people! The loss of an army in France and Belgium paled into insignificance. As Winston Churchill so aptly said: 'We shall fight on the beaches', to which he ought to have added, 'and in the Fen!' for tanks, 88 mm guns, stormtroopers, and all else that Germany could muster might come to England, the Fen had its answer with shotgun and hoe-handle, and would prevail. Had not the Captain-cum-Headmaster during one of his parade-night pep talks told them, 'The last little corporal who tried to invade had retreated from ladies waiting on the cliff tops wearing red skirts.'

The Captain sighed, remembering the last few days of the retreat through the Lowlands to the sand dunes of Dunkirk. The memories returned as a physical pain, momentarily taking away the joy of being with Olivia.

'What are you thinking of?' she asked, as she rested her head against his shoulder looking out of the window.

For a moment his spirit ignored her.

'The futility of all that,' he answered bitterly, turning away from the window to return to the table.

‘They are “doing their bit”,’ she said, running her finger-tips lightly across his face as she reached for the salad bowl.

Her husband made a hopeless gesture.

‘They have no guns, no equipment...’

Meanwhile the crisp staccato commands of R.S.M. Kingshott drilling his corps d’elite filtered through the net curtains, gently reminding Olivia of her childhood in the Raj.

Sunday July 7th 1940
The Vicar's Secret

The four boys were sitting on the pond railings with their bicycles beside them staring moodily at the ducks.

'How are you doin' about gettin' in with that old Captain?' asked China, breaking a long silence.

Frank continued to glare gloomily at a dragonfly resting on a raft of scum.

'I never get a chance to talk to him. He's upstairs with *her* all day. Even when he does come down she's always with him!'

'Can't you get him wholly interested in something?' murmured Chippy. 'Like showing you how to shoot a Lewis gun, or drive one of them Bren Carriers. Then you could put in a good word for us comin' along too!'

'Or ask him to come for a bike ride with us. That would get him talkin'. Say we'll take him to see the Wellingtons at Feltwell,' suggested China.

'Tell him we know how to get close to them when they are being bombed-up without being seed!' interjected Podge brightly.

'He wouldn't think much of that!' said Frank disconsolately. 'The Army and the Air Force don't get on just now. Anyway he can't think much of planes or he would have joined the Air Force in the first place!'

Frank scowled at the swan who had sailed gracefully across the pond in the hope of a titbit. Podge threw a pebble at it making it hiss. 'Bugger off,' growled China.

A cob swan who has been told to 'bugger off' reacts curiously. He raises his wings and advances with the battle cry of a thousand snakes and a particularly evil glint in his beady eyes.

The four boys, now safely sitting on the plinth of the War Memorial, turned their attention to the sight of the Vicar who was cycling along the street on his sit-up-and-beg bicycle. They watched him raise his shovel hat respectfully to Mrs Rowsell before raising his left hand from the handlebars to give the boys a cheery wave as he pedalled quickly across the Square.

'That's a rummun! I seed the old Parson going up the street and then down the Lode every night for a week. He must be up to something,' said China thoughtfully.

'What is there for him to be doing down there?' inquired Chippy. 'Nothing down the Lode that I know of!'

'He's meetin' thet new gal what works down The Garth,' giggled Podge triumphantly.

'The old devil,' breathed China, wide-eyed with admiration.

'That he ain't!' interjected Ferret, who had silently joined them. 'She's going with some fat old feller in a little old car. I see them every night down the side of the bank on that bend where the pussy willows grow. She don't want an old Parson on a bike when she's got someone with a suit and tie and a little old car. That's a fact!'

'Let's follow him and find out who he's meeting,' said Frank.

All eyes sparkled deliriously at the thought of finding their beloved old Vicar in a compromising situation with a young parlour maid. Or, even if The Garth's new parlour-maid was out of the running, at least there was a chance that the Vicar might be with one of the two Land Girls who had been inflicted upon Nelson Barratt's Mile End Farm.

Joyfully they leapt on their bikes and sped down the street following in the wake of the philandering parson.

'He have to be up to somethin' goin' down there alone every night,' Podge panted hopefully, as his knees flashed up and down so fast on his 'Junior' size bike, trying to keep up with Frank on his Raleigh sports, that his legs became a human fly-wheel. China followed, riding his sister's tall sit-up-and-beg machine, leaving Chippy to bring up the rear on his ex-errand boy's 'Sunbeam' with its enormous parcel carrier which rattled alarmingly at speed.

They turned down the Lode road just in time to see the Vicar drop his bicycle out of sight behind a clump of hogweed and scramble furtively up the side of the Lode bank to disappear over the top where a row of crack willows grew beside the water's edge.

'Hurry up!' China called, standing hard on the pedals of his bicycle forcing it into an extra burst of speed. 'The old Parson's up to something. That's a fact!'

They dropped their own machines in a bed of hemlock thirty yards beyond the Vicar's hidden bicycle and rushed headlong up the bank, where they lay peeping through a frieze of rough grass.

‘There ‘e is,’ whispered Podge, trembling with suppressed excitement.

The Vicar was kneeling on the grass beneath a gnarled old willow trunk at the water’s edge, with his back towards them, rocking rhythmically backwards and forwards.

‘Crikey! He’s saying his prayers!’ breathed Frank.

‘Don’t be daft bor. He’s got a gal a-stretched out there!’ said China as he gazed at the rocking Vicar’s back transfixed.

Chippy contemplated the Vicar solemnly. ‘Let’s get the other side of them. So’s we can see better,’ he suggested.

‘Blast, bor. This is better’n the Pictures, isn’t it!’ Podge stammered to Frank as they retreated hastily down the bank to scramble back up it twenty yards further along.

With hearts thudding high in their chests, the four peered down from their new vantage point. Stretched out on the flattened sedge between the Vicar’s knees was no parlour maid or jolly Land girl, but an old white pillowcase from which some objects had been taken and were now being hidden, like sixpences in a Christmas pudding, in a ball of Fenland blue clay.

‘What's ‘e a-doin’ of now?’ gasped Podge, as the Vicar raised himself laboriously from his knees to hurl the ball of clay dead centre into a bay of clear water to one side of a vast bed of waterlilies. Then he carefully rinsed his hands at the water’s edge, folded up the pillowcase, stowing it out of sight beneath his clerical dicky, before glancing furtively in every direction and returning to his hidden bicycle.

‘Eureka!’ Frank shouted as they watched the Vicar pedal soberly homewards towards the village.

‘Now I know how to get in with the Captain! *Really well in!* So well in that he will do *anything* for us!’

His cronies stared at him with wide open mouths in amazement.

‘Was that Eureka thing what ‘e chucked in the Lode?’ asked Chippy finally, after a long silence.

‘I know!’ said Podge brightly. 'He must have been frit that the police might find out that ‘e ‘ad one!’

‘And you’re goin’ to tell the Captain so’s he can arrest 'im an’ get a reward!’ chuckled China, with the return of his irrepressible grin.

‘Eureka,’ Frank explained slowly, with penetrating authority, ‘simply means that I have discovered the answer to a difficult problem. Worms. Lots of lovely chopped up lobworms and boiled potatoes and old crusts of bread!’

Their jaws dropped again, and the grin faded slowly from China’s face like the last rays from the setting sun as it slipped below the Bedford Levels.

‘Worms?’

‘Yes...Worms. Wriggly things you ‘bab’ with. Things that live in muck-heaps. What greedy hens peck at!’ sang Frank light-heartedly, executing a little war-dance on the bank top.

'Have you gone right shanny, bor?' groaned China, his high hopes of one day riding in one of the Bren-gun carriers being dashed to the ground.

'Well, I'll tell you the Plan,' answered Frank, flopping down in the long grass. 'When Mother showed the Captain and Mrs Vernon the birds in Dad's study he became jolly interested in the fishing rods. He actually started talking to me while she was looking at the birds and told me that he used to spend his school holidays with his father coarse fishing the Irish lakes. So...use your brains. *Think!* Worms...Fishing...!

'You know what the Vicar is up to. He has been ground-baiting his secret bream hole at the same time every evening for ages. Then he will arrive one evening with his tackle to find a shoal of over-confident bream waiting to guzzle a nice fat lobworm on a hook. He'll have a wonderful evening's sport. But only one, for they won't be there on the second night after being disturbed. So we must make sure that the *Captain* gets there first.'

'Coo!' they all breathed in unison, as they joined him, sprawling full length on the grassy bank.

Frank smiled benignly at the gang, and continued with mock pomposity.. 'We must first do as the Headmaster always says we must do, "outline our strategy"! Today is Saturday which means that tomorrow will be Sunday and the Vicar will be taking evening prayers, and anyway the Vicar never fishes on a Sunday. So I shall invite the Captain for a guaranteed good evening with the bream. I will make sure that he makes a real 'red letter day' catch, probably by catching the largest grand-daddy of the shoal who by now will be used to taking the choicest morsel. This will be a specially toughened lively red lobworm from the stableyard muck-heap sinking gently down to the bottom of the hole on the Captain's hook! Then, when he is all excited and in a good mood, I can ask him to show us all the guns and things at the Hall and take us out in a Brengun carrier. He simply can't refuse, can he?'

'That'll do it!' chortled Podge, rolling over and over down the bank to the road in glee.

'Good old bor!' China reiterated, as they collected their bicycles from a tangle of willow herb. 'Let's go on down to Sedge Farm's willow carr and see if we can catch that new Garth gal shywanickin' like Ferret says. I have a mind that I see'd that little old Austin parked down there with no one in it!'

Frank had placed himself strategically on a kitchen chair in the porch with an open wicker fishing creel blocking the front doorway. It was Sunday morning and the east-facing porch, surrounded by tall yellow hollyhocks, was bathed in sunlight. The ginger cat slept with the pale honey-coloured fur of her belly turned towards the sun, her whiskers twitching in her sleep as the warmth released stale fishy scents from the basket. His father's favourite tench and bream rod, an Avon-style eleven-footer, consisting of split cane top and middle section with a whole cane butt to steady the action, was leaning against the porch, above a cigar box containing a feast of floats. Here Frank waited, sitting like the earth-closet spider for the Captain to enter his web.

He did not have long to wait. Promptly at ten o'clock the camouflaged staff car drew up outside the house and the Captain came rushing along the gravel path, to come to a sudden halt at the tackle-blocked threshold.

'Morning Frank,' he said breezily.

'Good morning, sir,' answered Frank, politely. 'Sorry about all the mess.' He made to remove the cat, the creel, and the coil of Father's best silk line that looped from his chair-back to a wisteria twig as he loaded it on to a reel.

'Going fishing?'

'Yes, sir.' Frank began to reel in the line. 'Sir, would you like to fish my special bream-swim this evening?' he said, gazing guilelessly at the Captain. 'I have been ground-baiting it for a couple of weeks and there will be a shoal of huge ones - six, perhaps eight-pounders on the feed. Usually big bream are hard fish to find round here. You can fish for a whole season and never get one over a pound!'

'So I believe,' murmured the Captain, beginning to look interested. He stooped to take a dark green cork float from the cigar box, idly turning it over in his hand.

'They swim in large shoals like flocks of sheep,' Frank continued. 'The shoals of little half-pounders aren't very hard to find, but the real bream are as elusive as the Loch Ness Monster...and nearly as big! Father's best one weighed just over eleven pounds. There's a painting of it in his study. The trouble is, even after baiting a hole, you only get one chance. Fish it today and they'll be gone tomorrow.'

'You say you would take me,' said the Captain, glancing upwards towards the open window above them.

'An hour before the sun sets,' Frank answered.

The Captain gave another furtive glance upwards towards the open window of his wife's room.

'Marvellous!' he said in a hoarse whisper. 'I'll meet you at half past nine.'

Frank kicked the creel to one side. The ginger cat shot off in a huff. The Captain ducked beneath the fishing line and ran up the front staircase to his unsuspecting wife. The bream-baited trap had been sprung.

The four boys were once again sitting on the War Memorial plinth in the evening sunlight. At the far side of the pond the cob swan patrolled his territorial waters beneath the weeping willows. Evening Prayers had just finished, and the Vicar, wearing his flowing cassock could be seen standing outside the South Porch chatting earnestly with the Captain and his wife as the rest of the congregation streamed out through the lych-gate.

'Heck!' Frank exclaimed suddenly, noticing that they were deep in animated conversation. 'Blooming heck! I hope he's not telling the Vicar that I'm taking him to a ground-baited bream hole tonight!'

'Cooo!' breathed Chippy, filled with consternation at the thought. 'Do 'e'll be scuttling off down the Lode like a broody old hen!'

'Blast! That's a fact,' said Podge nodding his head in agreement. 'You can't fool the old Parson. I daren't tell 'im nothing that's not wholly right. He always seem to know what your thinkin'. Like an old goat!'

China, who sat silently ruminating as he watched an overloaded bumblebee crash-land between his feet, regarded Frank gravely.

'You'll have to find out what he's been telling the Parson afore you go,' he said finally, bringing his left plimsoll firmly down on the bumblebee as it started to walk along its ley line to the hive.

'What if he *has* told him?' said Frank dolefully.

'Well, in that case, you'll have to take him down the Hundred Foot to that old stretch where them fences are stickin' up. He'll get some little old bream there for certain!'

'Yes, I know. Tiddling little half-pounders if he's lucky!' said Frank sarcastically. 'We'll never get in with him if I let him down. I promised him a specimen fish, not half a dozen little perch!'

'Well, bor, you can always have a sudden terrible belly-ache an' be sick,' Podge advised, in his usual helpful way. 'Push your fingers down your throat an' bring your tea back up. That'll fool him.'

'Do he do that we'll have to think of somethin' else!' groaned Chippy.

Silently they watched the Captain and his willowy wife walk arm in arm across the Square to disappear through the portals of Jubilee House.

'What time are you a-goin'?' Chippy asked.

'About half past nine.'

'Have he got a bike, bor?' said Chippy. 'Cause I can lend him mine if he haven't. Good old bike! an' he can carry that great old fish in the basket!'

'Pooh! He will take me in the Army truck, of course,' Frank replied grandly. 'What on earth would King Kong think if he saw a captain of the regulars riding a tradesman's bicycle up the street!'

'Bloody good bike. Better'n yourn,' answered an aggrieved Chippy. 'I'd like to see your bike carrying a sack of tatos, or carry three people on it!'

'My Raleigh is designed for speed, not carting sacks of potatoes!' replied Frank haughtily, bringing the subject swiftly to a close by standing up and straightening his jacket. 'Let's go to the stableyard muck-heap to dig some worms to chop up for ground-bait.'

They ambled slowly across the Square towards the stableyard where they collected a dung fork, a bucket, and a rusty biscuit tin. China took possession of the fork and led the way to the dung heap to turn over the mass of dank humid straw, while three pairs of hands hovered over each forkful ready to snatch the head-end of escaping worms.

'That's enough,' said China, resting on the fork as he peered into the bucket, whose base was covered in lively red worms tying themselves into writhing knots, while others were slithering up the sides.

Replacing the fork in its proper place within the cartshed to avoid Boer's wrath, the four boys repaired to the tack room, collecting a sack on the way from a rotting pile which lay abandoned on the cartshed floor. Here, on the lid of the galvanised feed-bin, they began the unsavoury task of chopping the worms into very short, still squirming portions.

'What you goin' to do about 'tatos?' China remarked. 'You have to have boiled 'tatos for baitin' bream!'

'No you don't,' said Frank, 'because we don't want to ground-bait. The Vicar's done that for us. We just want to make a splash and scent the water with tiny scraps of worms and dusty chaff drifting through the rotten sacking!'

'Ar. That's right. That's what old Daggy do!' agreed Podge. An' I'll tell you somethin' else bor. You have to make the splash at exactly the same time as you've been doin' afore, do you'll frit the buggers off for ever!'

'My dad was a good bream-fisher,' said Frank disdainfully. 'You can't teach me anything about catching them!'

'Huh! You ain't much of a scholar at babbin' anyways. That you aren't!' snapped Podge in a flash of pique, as he followed the others across the yard to the granary to tip a shovelful of dusty floor sweepings into the sack.

'That's everything,' said Frank turning towards the house. 'I've got a bag of lovely tough lobs ready for the Captain, and some bread paste for myself. I shall let him think what an expert fisherman he is by catching nothing but small roach while he gets nothing but huge bream. He won't know that I shall be fishing just below the surface with tiny bits of paste while he will be on the bottom with a lob-worm. That will be sure to make him happy!'

'That's right! And don't forget to larn him about waitin' till them old fish start feedin' afore he chucks his line in!' advised China. 'They're like old pigs a-splashin' when they get there afore they settle down.'

'Blast!' exclaimed Chippy suddenly. 'I hope he don't take *her* with him! Do she'll frit every fish in the Lode.'

'Blast!' reiterated Podge, being struck with the awful possibility of the female 'furriner' sending shoals of startled fish stampeding down the length of the Lode to its parent river.

'Course she won't. She'd be frit to death if she see'd a worm...an' I bet she's never wore any water-boots in her life...bloomin' Londoner. Them evacuees are as bad. Without a word of a lie them's frit of everythin'!'

It was one of those idyllic evenings in midsummer when, at nine-thirty, the Captain descended from his room to greet Frank who was sitting on the front doorstep surrounded by fishing tackle.

The sun was gilding the church weathervane cock, hanging low in a yellowing sky above the western horizon. Bees worked feverishly in the hollyhocks filling their pollen baskets before bumbling away, their furry bodies dusted with yellow pollen. The screams of the swifts intermingled with the high-pitched hum of midges as they floated high in the upper air to sleep the night on the wing.

Frank gazed awestruck at the camouflaged staff car which was parked outside the house. In all of his sixteen years he had only once ridden in a motor car, this being when he was convalescing after septicæmia caused by gashing his wrist on a barbed wire fence. Mr Barratt, the cattle dealer, had taken him to a sale of Irish bullocks in Bury St Edmunds, a long run in his spanking new Rover 14 with its long black bonnet, walnut fascia, and enamelled Viking galley on the radiator. He had often ridden in the baker's 'Trojan' van, helping on the bread round, and sometimes to Wissington factory in one of the sugarbeet lorries, otherwise his only experience of 'motoring' had been the daily ride in the school bus and the once-a-year trip by charabanc to Skegness or Hunstanton on the Sunday School Outing.

The Rover 14 was not quite the only private car in the village. The *nouveau riche* master of the Manor owned an obtrusive Rolls Royce and a rarely-seen and equally pretentious yellow and black, chauffeur-driven Lagonda, bearing a lady shrouded in mystery (a lady whose background even the most ingenious Willows Enders had failed to penetrate). The remaining car was Landlord Sam Rowsell's 1937 Vauxhall 12 which doubled as the village taxi. Old Granny Farrow's nephew owned a 350 B.S.A. 'hand-change' motor cycle, whose gears were worked through a 'gate' on the side of the petrol tank by a wooden grip the size of a golf ball. Lastly there was the Headmaster's pride and joy, which was a 1938 Morgan two-seater three-wheeler. Everyone else rode push-bikes. The farmers drove gigs and traps pulled by smart 'Norfolk Trotters' and the rest walked.

The Headmaster's Morgan, with its Matchless V-twin, water-cooled engine mounted on the front, was his one and only love. Teetotal and non-smoker, the little Morgan was the escape route for his subliminal desires. Its 'British Racing Green' body was kept polished to perfection, while the engine, exposed naked to all eyes without the protection of a bonnet, gleamed with the combined efforts of Brasso, oily rags, and the Headmaster's undying love.

On high days and holidays, and always on a rain-free Sunday, the Headmaster would manhandle the Morgan, which had no reverse gear, out from the schoolyard bike shed. He would then walk round it, flick a duster over the paintwork, check the oil-level, and kick the two front tyres. He had imitated this professional way of testing the tyre pressures after watching

Raymond Mays kick his E.R.A. prior to the start at Brooklands on the Pathé Newsreel. Then, after giving a last glance towards the heavens, he would return indoors for luncheon. At one-thirty he would reappear wearing an ankle-length, brown leather flying coat, a white silk scarf flung nonchalantly round his neck, a pair of ex-R.A.F. Mk.IV goggles pushed up over a peaked cloth cap worn back to front, then, with the twin 500 c.c. engine started and running evenly, its exhaust purring, he would await the coming of the 'Little Woman'.

Invariably she would be wearing a gaberdine trench-coat buttoned high up to her neck, with a chiffon scarf tied tightly beneath her chin holding down a cloche hat. Then they would be away, silk scarf fluttering like a pennant in the wind, goggles pulled down to keep the flying dust and kamikaze bees from his eyes, chin thrust aggressively forward in the Headmaster's re-run of Brooklands Grand Prix at thirty-five miles per hour along the village street. Meanwhile the 'Little Woman' would have slid down in her bucket seat until only the tip of her hat could be seen above the twin windscreens.

Although they always drove off looking immaculate, not so the home-coming. The Headmaster's face, white scarf, and any part of the polished paintwork with which his hands had come in contact would be smudged with black, greasy, gooey oil. This confirmed to those who were well versed in such matters that 'the drive chain had come off'. If the Headmaster's assessment of the weather conditions had been faulty, they would arrive back half drowned. The chiffon scarf would have taken on the look of a limp piece of Skegness seaweed, and they would extricate themselves from bucket seats which, true to their name, were half full of water. In the event of a passer-by politely commiserating with their bedraggled appearance before they reached the sanctuary of their front door, the Little Woman would give a wan smile and the Headmaster would brusquely reply: 'An exhilarating run! An exhilarating run! Now for a hot bath!'. Whereupon the passer-by, seeing no smoke rising from the Schoolhouse chimney, would give a knowing grin and answer: 'Nothing like a hot bath, is there now? I'd put some of that old mustard in it. Wholly good for the poomonia!'

China, Chippy and Podge watched enviously from their vantage point beneath the churchyard yew tree as the Captain held the passenger side door open for Frank to load the fishing tackle on the back seat.

'Which way?' he inquired, slamming the door after Frank had settled himself on the front seat.

'Up the street, and then down the Lode road for about a mile.'

Three heads, unseen in the shadows of the great yew, followed the car's progress up the street until it disappeared from their sight.

'I daren't think what the old Parson would do if he took it into his mind to have a look down the Lode tonight!' China said with a huge grin.

'Be a right old laugh,' giggled Podge, swinging merrily on the lych-gate.

'Anyways we aren't to know he were baitin' that there hole, are we now?' said Chippy piously.

At that moment their fears were being received telepathically by Frank as he sat beside the relaxed and whistling Captain.

'I hope you didn't mention that we are going fishing to the Vicar, sir,' said Frank breathlessly. 'He gets so annoyed with people who fish on a Sunday!'

'Of course not,' he grinned. 'I happen to have a cleric for an uncle. Dashed funny people clerics!'

'Well, actually, Vicar's a jolly good sort, but he thinks every bream-hole in the Lode is his own private property. So it's always best not to tell him.'

The Captain gave him a conspiratorial grin.

'Call me Dick. Save the 'sir' for when you are in uniform,' he chuckled, apparently transformed by the magic of going fishing. 'You will have to salute me then, *and* get a better polish on your boots!' He swung the car round to follow the cinder track running alongside the high bank of the Lode. 'By the way, who is the sergeant I have seen drilling you? Jolly pukka sort of chap. Ex-Guardsman without a doubt!'

Frank, recovering from the enormity of being allowed to call a captain of the regulars by his christian name, swallowed hard.

'That's R.S.M. Kingshott. He's top-hole. He fought in the Boer War, the Great War, then out in India. Now he's our sergeant in the L.D.V - I mean the Home Guard!' Frank paused for breath. 'He's jolly strict, and makes every boy in the village get his hair cut before he will serve him anything from his shop. Old 'Boer' Roberts - he's the farm's horseman - served in the second

Boer War in the Royal Horse Artillery and in the Great War, and Mr Rowsell went out to fight in Spain four years ago. But he only lasted a year! Got shot in the knee and that's why he limps. His wife is Spanish, and she ran The Ship while he was away. He was a Navy man during the last war and that's how he met her. Headmaster was a captain and...'

'Oh yes! I know all about the Headmaster!' the Captain interjected with a wink. 'Jolly good at organising I believe.'

Frank threw a hurried glance through the windscreen, suddenly noticing that they were opposite the clump of hogweed marking the spot where the Vicar had hidden his bicycle.

'Stop!' he said, grabbing the dashboard as the car bumped to a standstill on the rutted grass verge.

The yellow sky was changing to a pale apple-green as the sun dipped towards the horizon, casting long shadows, as Frank climbed the steep side of the Lode bank. The water beneath the crack willows was motionless, reflecting the last golden glow of the sky, and the water-lilies took on the look of translucent fine-china gilded at the edges.

Frank led the way down the bank to the water's edge, where he placed the fishing-basket against the trunk of the willow for the Captain to sit on while he prepared the ground-bait by emptying the mess of chopped worms into the rotten sack on top of the granary sweepings, before adding wet clay from the shallows and a half-brick he had brought with him from home. Meanwhile his companion had already untied the cotton rod-case and was busily assembling the rod, fitting an 'Aerial' reel to the butt, and threading the line through the rod rings to await further instruction from 'the expert'.

He watched the boy lob the sack out into the centre of the clear water to one side of the lily-bed where it quickly sank, to lie on the bottom of the hole emitting a turbid cloud of husk particles, laced with the scent of worms, and allowing the occasional worm morsel to escape from the rotten sack.

Frank turned towards the Captain's tackle, threading a quill float on the line above a drilled ledger-weight to run freely up and down the line to a single split shot pinched on where the line joined the gut-cast and hook.

'Ah!' exclaimed the Captain airing his knowledge in piscatorial matters. 'I see we're to use a float ledger. I do like to see a float. Don't you?'

He stood up and reached for the tin of specially toughened lobworms.

'Hang on!' gasped Frank, suddenly realizing that his carefully constructed plans were at the point of being dashed. 'There are no fish here yet. We have to wait for them to arrive.'

He made himself comfortable by leaning back against the willow and the Captain lit his pipe to deter the clouds of midges that began to emerge from the reedbeds.

For half an hour nothing happened. The surface of the placid water became dimpled by small fry as they began to feed on hatching gnat larvæ. A water-vole plopped into the water a few yards further along the bank, causing a V-shaped ripple as it swam toward a clump of flags. The smell of rotting vegetation mingled with crushed water-mint and a pot-pourri of sedges, meadow-sweet and hemlock, began to infuse the warm evening air as gnats rose in clouds of droning females. A heron cried 'Kra-a-ark'. Waterhens scolded, and a mallard duck, closely followed by a drake, flew low along the centre of the Lode.

'Don't you think we had better start fishing now?' remarked the Captain, looking anxiously, first at the sky and then at the water.

'They will be here very soon,' whispered Frank, staring intently downstream beyond the lily-bed.

The whole arch of the sky flamed rose-pink above a narrowing band of yellow. Against it the willow twigs and slender leaves became crisp silhouettes and the evening suddenly became alive with pipistrelle bats swooping and diving above the water, taking the emerging moths. Above, huge noctules patrolled up and down in straight lines.

At the first distinct splash Frank's pulse quickened. He touched the Captain's knee and pointed downstream where the glassy surface of the water was suddenly being broken by intermittent swirls as a shoal of large bream approached, surfacing with a lazy rolling of broad backs, their dorsal fins and forked tails breaking the surface as they dived.

'Sh!' whispered Frank, as the Captain moved excitedly to take up his rod. 'Not yet! Wait until I tell you!'

The shoal was within twenty feet of the water-lily bed when all movement disappeared. The fretted water returned to its glassy stillness and the excitement faded from the Captain's eyes.

They sat on for a few more minutes, while the Captain's hands stopped their trembling and he inwardly denounced his foolishness in listening to the advice of a schoolboy when he knew that he ought to have rushed to cast his bait to the feeding fish!

He was about to communicate his displeasure when Frank tapped his knee again. 'Sh!'

Trails of bubbles were rising from the water-lily bed at their feet and muddied water clouded the shallows as the fish worked their way upstream towards the baited hole.

The Captain's hand dropped towards the rod.

'Not yet!'

Frank, not moving his eyes from the surface of the water, laid his hand over the Captain's as the lily-pads stopped swaying. Then a few moments later strings of bubbles started to break surface directly above the ground-baited hole followed by a turbulence of dusty grain husks.

'Now lob your worm out so that it falls where the bubbles are rising,' Frank said, 'and then leave it alone!'

Heart in mouth, the Captain gazed at the float sitting nicely cocked above the bream-hole. Five long minutes passed. Then without warning it trembled and moved sideways before sliding purposefully out of sight beneath the surface. The Captain struck and he was into a fish.

The supple rod bent as the fish made a half-hearted dash towards the lily-bed before the Captain turned it and brought it in over the landing-net. Re-baiting hurriedly he cast out again and within a few minutes the sequence was repeated and another bream of identical size was landed.

'Rare sport this!' chuckled the Captain as the fifth slab-sided fish rolled on to its side to join its companions in the keep-net. 'Never caught such large fish in my life.' He threaded another large lob worm on the hook. 'Why don't you bait up your rod and join in the fun?'

'No sir, um, Dick, I want you to get a good fish,' Frank replied artfully. 'These are only about two-and-a-half-pounders and middle-sized bream are not very good fighters.'

'They are jolly big against the sort of fish I usually catch,' the Captain replied warmly. 'Ten-ounce roach are my normal limit! Can't say that I've ever seen a coarse fish over two pounds.'

'You might tonight!' answered Frank brightly, inwardly crossing his fingers and looking at the sentinel float.

The warm-scented night air was closing around them. A swathe of white mist hung above the water and it became difficult to make out the float as they sat silently staring at it with heightened expectancy.

After a while the float trembled, sending widening circles of iridescent ripples fluttering across the still surface to break against a reed. A little later it vanished and the line became taut as a fish took the worm in its mouth and moved out towards the centre of the Lode.

The Captain lifted the rod and struck expecting the fish to follow the pattern of the previous five bream by making a half-hearted dash for the lily-bed followed by a passive surrender. But this time an irresistible force was bending the rod slowly into a half-circle, following the wake of the line which was heading towards the far bank.

'Crikey!' gasped Frank. 'You've hooked one!'

The rod began to straighten as the Captain gave the fish line.

'Don't do that! Hold him from the reed-bed or you'll lose him. Keep your rod up and get him upstream in the clear water.'

'B-b-but the rod?' stammered the Captain, as it arched over again into a bow. 'It'll break!'

'No, it won't,' answered the boy. 'But the cast will if you don't let the rod work.'

He picked up the landing-net and sank it in the shelving water. It was his father's grilse net, designed for fish far larger than the usual coarse fish.

The Captain managed to turn the fish and bring it in towards the boy holding the sunken net. It was then that he saw the fish, a fleeting glimpse as it turned on its side, just a split-second impression of a dark, flattened shape under the rod tip, before it was off again, boring deep towards the lily-roots.

'Hold him!' Frank groaned, catching his breath as the tight line moved purposely within the lily-pads.

The Captain desperately applied more pressure, forcing the fish to surface in a welter of splashes and broken stems in the centre of the lily-pads.

'You can bring him in now,' said Frank confidently, as the fish rolled slowly on to its side. 'Bream aren't very good fighters!'

The last of the afterglow reflected back from the bronze scales of the bream as it lay on the bank at their feet. The Captain's fingers trembled and his knees shook as he gazed spellbound at the fish in silence.

'What a whacking great fish,' he said at last in a voice that was husky with emotion, 'ten pounds?...twelve?...fifteen?' His hands were shaking so much that Frank had to drop on to his knees and remove the hook from the bream's jaw for him.

'Oh, about seven, maybe eight,' answered Frank laconically, as if the catching of a specimen bream was all in a day's work. 'Jolly good fish for the Lode though!' he added diplomatically.

'By Jingo, it's a corker. It's like a portmanteau!' The Captain leaned close to Frank and tapped his arm confidentially. 'I shall have this one set up!'

He relit his pipe and stood leaning against the willow in a trance of utter content watching the boy release the five bream from the keep-net before gathering the tackle together.

'Eight pounds,' he mused dreamily. 'You say the others were about two and a half? That means a bag of twenty and a half pounds! Never have I had such a red letter day. Deuced good of you, Frank, to invite me.'

Inwardly Frank was grinning with anticipatory delight, the delight the closet spider must feel at the successful entanglement of a fat bluebottle in her gauzy web.

'How can I repay you, Frank?' continued the Captain warmly as they struggled up the steep side of the bank making their way back to the car. 'I have noticed that you are a Hornby railway enthusiast. Anything I can get you? A new locomotive perhaps? Or more track for a new branch line?'

This was the moment to execute the *coup de grace.* Frank took a deep breath and blurted out the fateful words that had been circling uneasily in the back of his mind all evening.

'Could you show me and my three friends the Bren-carrier and the guns and things sometime please?'

The Captain paused as he was about to open the car door. 'Is that *all?'* he asked incredulously. 'To visit the Unit?'

The easy opening loosened Frank's tongue.

'Oh, yes, sir. China, Chippy, Podge, and I haven't even seen a rifle close to...or a Lewis...or a Bren...or anything! We've been promised a rifle and a bayonet each, but they haven't come through yet.'

'Know how to prime a Mills bomb?' said the Captain, entering into the spirit of the conversation. 'Load a Vicker's belt or Lewis pan? Know how to fit a 'body-locking pin' in the dark?'

Within the closed sympathetic darkness of the car the boy's eyes widened in stunned amazement as the Captain continued to utter promises.

'Whenever you decide to come I'll get my armourer sergeant to put the four of you through it. Drilling with weapons is not much use if you don't know how they work!'

'Really! We'll be allowed inside the gates?'

'Of course,' he answered as the car glided to a halt outside Jubilee House. 'Only you had all better wear your uniforms. Just to make it official. Mustn't have civilians firing off machine-guns!'

'Crikey!' Frank gasped incredulously as he rushed towards the porch carrying the tackle, followed by the Captain proudly bearing the great fish in the grilse net.

The ladies were sitting quietly reading in the parlour when the two anglers burst in through the door, startling the ginger cat, which fled through the open window. Mrs Vernon, curled in one of the easy chairs, dropped the magazine she had been reading and glanced up at her husband's face, which was strangely flushed.

'Wait!' he cried, turning smartly on his heels and dashing out of the room.

Mrs Dutton looked over the top of her reading-glasses and carefully placed a bookmark between the pages of her novel before placing it on the table, and the Captain's wife raised her eyebrows questioningly towards Frank.

'Does this mean that Dickie has actually *caught* something?' she murmured with a smile.

A moth flew in through the wide-open casement to circle within the pool of light cast by the Aladdin lamp. Frank glanced at the moth, a dingy-coloured noctua, then towards Mrs Vernon, lowering his eyes and blushing when she smiled. Meanwhile bursts of Gilbert and Sullivan choruses filtered along the stone-flagged passage leading from the dairy, reaching a crescendo outside the parlour door with the arrival of the Captain carrying a candle.

'Come!' he announced, throwing his arms wide in a majestic gesture. 'Come to see my catch of a lifetime!'

Mrs Vernon stood up, straightening her dress. 'Sounds beastly,' she said, holding out her hand to assist Frank's mother to rise from her chair. 'What d'you say, Mrs Dutton?'

Mrs Dutton simply grimaced, well versed in the vagaries of fishermen.

'Where are you taking us? Back to the river?' Mrs Vernon giggled, as they followed the fluttering candlelight in single file along the passage.

He paused inside the dairy doorway and took a deep breath in anticipation, like an artist about to present his *piéce de résistance.*

'What do you think of *this?'*

Laid out on the cool slate slab was the bream in all its deep-bellied, glory. The candlelight gave a soft lambent lustre to the large bronze scales along its flank and a sheen of old-gold to its gill-covers. The Captain put his arm over Olivia's shoulder in glee and pointed to the fish.

For a moment she eyed the fish in silence.

'Hum!' she said slowly. 'It looks enormous. Is it edible?'

'Of course not. I shall have it set up! Seven pounds twelve ounces. I've just weighed it!'

Mrs Dutton's eyes lit instantly upon her prized kitchen scales that had obviously been commandeered by the military from her kitchen cupboard. Noting the thick sludge of fishy slime she gave a supercilious sniff and her 'Christian Martyr' look manifested itself with the tightening of her lips.

'Must find a good taxidermist!' exclaimed the Captain. 'Do you know of one in the district, Frank?'

'There's a jolly good one in Littleport who does nothing but set up fish. Father always said he was a real artist at it because he knows his fish.'

'Wonderful. We can go tomorrow, and you can show us the way.'

Mrs Vernon's interjection left Frank floundering and before he could reply his mother had replied for him. *'School,'* she said with determination.

'Never mind. You can give us directions,' Mrs Vernon said. Then, catching the boy's disappointed eyes, she added, 'We have planned to spend Saturday visiting Ely. Perhaps you would like to come and show us around.'

'Gosh!' Immediately his spirits lifted. 'Father used to take me to see the cathedral. Are you going to see the cathedral?'

'I can think of nothing I'd like better!' she exclaimed, tenderly.

'I can take you along the riverside to Cherry Hill Park, where we used to picnic on the grass of the old castle mound...and show you the painted ceilings in the cathedral...and Oliver Cromwell's house...'

His chatter drifted down the passage as Mrs Dutton led the way back towards the parlour carrying her scales, followed by Mrs Vernon and the Captain bearing the candle, whose flickers cast sepulchral shadows on the ceiling of the narrow passage.

Frank closed the dairy door on the cadaver, stiffening in state on the cold slate slab.

Tuesday 30th July
Blenheims at Bodney

For the past three weeks the army unit had been the main topic of conversation and the cause of many diverse hives of activity among the residents of Willows End.

On Sunday afternoons, the 'big-girls', dressed in their best floral dresses, arm-in-arm in giggling pairs, took to leisurely walks which took them past the sentry-guarded gates of the Old Hall. They flashed demure glances towards the younger gunners, neglecting the searchlight privates who were left to languish out of sight and mind down the Fen.

Friday evenings in The Ship's snug became even more rumbustious. The Junoesque landlady performed her flamboyant flamenco dance to an even more appreciative audience, and the landlord hurriedly trebled his order for kegs of Best Bitter and crates of Worthington E. Harnser Flegg negotiated a deal with the cookhouse sergeant for the swill from the unit to feed his sow and her twelve piglets, while old Daggy supplied the unit with choice fresh vegetables in return for slabs of cheese, which were worth their weight in gold on the black market. (The civilian ration had been cut to one ounce a week). Nelson Jarvis's cows worked overtime providing fresh milk, and Ma Shipham looked after the Captain's washing. Even young Podge's latent business acumen showed in his clandestine sixpenny introductions to his pretty elder sister Lucy, the sultry Willows End *femme fatale.*

A close bond had developed between the four boys and the soldiers. Every available moment after school and at weekends they lived, ate, and if it had been possible would have slept in the Old Hall. It was the ultimate height of their patriotic ambition to share a world of weapons, vehicles, Blanco, Brasso, and camaraderie with men newly returned from battle.

They lined up with their aluminium dixies, tin plates, and cutlery to receive generous helpings of piping hot stew, meat and three veg, or 'bangers and mash', followed by rice pudding laced with a dollop of strawberry jam, or spotted Dick, washed down by lip-scalding tin mugs of strong tea, an unheard-of diet compared with their usual meat-paste and margarine sandwiches, and Norfolk dumpling and Oxo gravy on Sundays.

This camaraderie spread to include the Home Guard Captain and Captain Vernon who together hatched up an impromptu 'Night Exercise' in which the Home Guard was to defend the perimeter of the village from attack by the regulars.

As the Willows End Home Guard had not yet been issued with rifles it was agreed that Sergeant Kingshott, Corporal Boer Roberts, Harnser, Fancy, and Runner Roberts would each be issued with 'thunder-flashes', which were to be thrown when, or if, the attacking force came under fire. Alternatively, if the attacking force was in a position to surprise the defence, then they would use small-arms firing blank ammunition.

It had been a long night, as black as pitch, its silence broken only by the infrequent harsh warning notes of the night-birds. Contrary to Sergeant Kingshott's advice, the Headmaster had deployed the platoon to man the four hastily-constructed pill-boxes which had been set in the Lode bank to command the Lode road and had told 'Boer' to take Frank as runner and take up a position in a ditch three hundred yards ahead to give advance warning of the expected attack.

Midnight came with the distant clangour of the church clock booming like a bittern across the Fen... one o'clock.... two a.m. came and the night became colder as the retained sun-heat died in the soil. By three a.m. Frank was heavy-eyed and drowsy, and his limbs were cramped from lying on the hard clay of the dyke-side peering through a fringe of sedge towards a horizon of nebulous gloom.

'Bugger this!' Boer whispered truculently. 'That's a load of old squit us a-lying out here for nothin'...Silly old fools might have gone home without a-telling of us!'

He gave Frank a nudge.

'Go on back to the bank and see what they're a-doing of.'

Frank crawled out of the dyke and started to cross the rough hummocky grass of no-man's-land, which happened to be one of Nelson Barratt's pastures. In the pre-dawn darkness no light reflected back from the stars. All that was visible was the darker blackness of the land against the darkness of the sky with the damp misty night air softening away sound.

Unseen hummocks caused him to stumble and grope his way blindly in the direction of the far side of the pasture. He had safely accomplished two

-thirds of the three hundred yard stretch when he took a header on a hummock that for a few moments pitched and tossed in a series of seismic tremors before it lumbered into flight. Instantly, in a chain reaction, hummocks began leaping to their feet as Nelson's latest consignment of Irish bullocks went careering towards the pill-boxes, leaving Frank lying flat on his face in bovine ordure.

Comfortably ensconced in the concrete pill-boxes behind six imaginary rifles, two imaginary Lewis guns, and the Headmaster's recently disinterred World War I Webley and Scott service revolver, the defenders of the village awaited the attacking force.

'That'll be wholly a miracle if them there lot come afore dawn!' exclaimed Runner Roberts, settling back and lighting a Woodbine, safe in the knowledge that Sergeant Kingshott was in the adjoining pill-box a quarter of a mile away. 'I reckon they'll come like the old geese...just as it's gettin' light.'

Throughout the night at hourly intervals the Headmaster, with China as his runner, surreptitiously patrolled the mile of Loke road between the four pill-boxes to check the alertness of his troops, bestowing upon them such gems of encouragement as 'Stand firm lads'... 'Backs to the wall boys'... 'Hold back the flow of the Hun.'

'Do a sight better to blow a great hole in the bank,' Old Daggy pithily remarked, as he receded into the darkness. 'Bring back that old nineteen fifteen 'drown'. That'd larn 'em without a word of a lie!'

As the Headmaster, with his runner close on his heels, headed back to his base in the centre pill-box, his long-sublimated id was having a holiday. He found himself cast in the role of Henry V on the eve of Agincourt passing the lonely night vigil, giving hope and courage to his merry band of brothers. No insignificant Pay Corps Subaltern ever before could have been given such a monumental task!

He stood in the centre pill-box peering out into the murky night and began to give rein to his imagination in fanciful thoughts of Fenland battles to be fought and won, as imaginary as the pipe-dreams of the German generals standing staring out at the inviting white cliffs of Dover. He conjured up a vision in his mind's eye, a vision that out in the gloom of the darkened fen the offensive had begun, as charging troops, with bayonets fixed, were bearing down upon them.

Suddenly he realised that this was no cosy figment of the imagination, for a very tangible attack had erupted in a typical Hun advance.

His nervously high-pitched 'Fire!' was followed by the first thunderflash forming a meteoric parabola across the Lode road to explode on the pasture side of the dyke at the bullocks' feet.

A couple of dozen thunderflashes covering a three-quarters-of-a-mile stretch of open pasture was more than sufficient to upset fifty Irish bullocks who were already suffering from the trauma of a sea passage and a long rail journey. Reaching the edge of the wide dyke they about-turned, regrouped into a solid phalanx, and careered off towards the centre of the pasture.

The pounding of their hooves as they bore down upon Frank lying out in no-man's-land brought instant recollection of a passage from his favourite Zane Grey novel *The Thundering Herd*, where the stampeding buffalo destroyed everything in their path. But fifty Irish bullocks in a large expanse of rough fen pasture missed flattening a small boy in a tin hat by a hair's breadth and he made his way back to Boer who was chuckling at the fiasco.

'Bloody hell!' gasped Harnser. 'I always heard that them there regulars were mad. Come at us like a lot of old bulls they did!'

'Never you mind, bor. Them's a-runnin' away like a lot of frit old hens,' began Fancy. 'Just you hear them go bor! They...'

A couple of heads appeared simultaneously above the bank top and quietly lobbed two thunderflashes which dropped fizzing on the floor of the bunker between the feet of the two defenders, who bolted, like rats before one of Daggy's ferrets, only to look up into the muzzles of Sten guns held by half a dozen grinning soldiers standing on the bank top in the first grey light of a depressing dawn.

'I warned you to look after your flank, sir!' said Sergeant Kingshott smugly to a deflated Headmaster as they all marched home in single file along the top of the Lode bank. 'You ought to have thought how easy it were for them regulars to crawl along the side of the Lode and sit there all night ahind our backs making fools of us!'

'Yes, yes!' answered the Captain hurriedly. Then, having a bright thought: 'Still, Sergeant, that's what these exercises are meant to demonstrate - weaknesses in the defence! I should say that this has been a very instructive exercise, wouldn't you?'

Instructive or not militarily, Frank had learned by experience that it was going to take all of Ma Shipham's expertise to remove the bullock-pats from his khaki battledress in time for the next parade.

The heady feeling that they had entered into a fantastic dream ended abruptly for the four boys when orders arrived for the unit to rejoin the regiment at an undisclosed destination on Monday the 29th of July.

The 'big-girls' walked openly arm in arm with the young gunners on that last Sunday afternoon, oblivious to gossiping wives as they wandered love-lorn and tearful, absorbed only in each other, to disappear among the golden kingcups within the swathes of swaying reeds lining the Loke Drove.

Ma Shipham laundered the Captain's shirts on her kitchen table, paying special regard to the starching of collar and cuffs. Harnser Flegg's nursing sow guzzled the last of the free swill. Daggy carefully hoarded the last hunk of army cheese out of sight in the back of the beer-crate which was his 'larder', and the four boys sorrowfully tucked into what was to be their last helping of spotted dick.

It was mid-morning on that fateful Monday when the convoy moved out through the gates of the Old Hall to head westwards. The schoolchildren, out at play, rushed screaming to the school railings to jump up and down yelling as the leading Bren-gun-carrier clattered across the Square, followed by a transport towing a field gun. Podge, Chippy, and China, dodging Miss Lacy who had come out to see what all the commotion was about, rushed through the school gate to line the pond railings, to be followed by mutinous 'Juniors' and skipping 'Infants'. After Miss Lacy had successfully herded her flock of infants back through the school gates, the Headmaster capitalized on the situation by setting the 'Seniors' and 'Juniors' the task of writing an essay 'Why I admire the British Armed Forces', leaving Miss Lacy to organize her over-excited class into drawing their impressions with chalk on the Infant Room blackboard.

Mrs Rowsell appeared at the open doorway of The Ship, wearing a poppy-red full skirt and black bolero over a long-sleeved white blouse, to receive an ovation of exuberant whistles from the departing gunners, which continued until the last vehicle had passed the screen of poplars to head out into the Fen, where girls working in the fields stopped their labours to wave, standing to watch the convoy cross the flat landscape, until it appeared nothing more than a dark, undulating caterpillar crawling slowly above the ripening wheat to merge finally and be lost in the blue haze.

Frank had risen early and was leaning against the porch in the morning sunshine. School had broken up for the summer holidays and he stood idly gazing at three Blenheims as they droned over the Fen towards Ely .

Mrs Vernon came downstairs to join him. 'What are you watching, Frankie?' she asked, shading her eyes from the sun with her hand, and looking across the Fen to where the Blenheims were disappearing into the distance.

'Blenheims. Probably 82 Squadron back from France. Nicky says they are based at Bodney, which is a satellite field for Watton.'

'It's going to be another absolutely glorious day,' she remarked, lowering her hand and breathing in the scent coming from the limes and hollyhocks.

Frank flashed a glance towards his 'Golden Arrow' bicycle leaning against the side of the porch.

'I think I'll go for a long bike ride,' he said, downcast at his recurring thoughts of the Hall reverting to its previous dereliction. 'Or perhaps I'll go down to the Old Bedford fishing.'

'How far is Bodney?' asked Mrs Vernon suddenly.

'Oh, about twenty-five...thirty miles.'

'Is that what you call a "long bike ride"?'

'Middlin',' he grinned, boastfully.

'It's such a beautiful day, Frank. What do you say to biking to Bodney to see the Blenheims?'

He stared at her, speechless.

'What...with you!' he answered brusquely, with a flush of contempt.

'Why, yes! That is if I can borrow a decent bike.'

He contemplated her solemnly for a moment.

'Madge Shipham's got a new Hercules tourer,' he said at last. 'All the rest are "sit-up-and-begs". Are you sure you want to bike all that way?'

'Good gracious, yes. Of course I do.' She laughed at the idea. 'I'm very tough, ex-captain of the hockey team I'll have you know. Strenuous exercise is what we need to take our minds off the Unit leaving us. Now, you run along and ask if I may borrow Madge's bike while I pack a picnic lunch.'

Frank made his way to the first terraced cottage on the street where Ma Shipham was lustily plunging the dolly up and down in her tub, scattering soap-suds and bubbles on to her wash-house floor. She stopped plunging to turn towards Frank.

'I haven't finished your Ma's washin' yet...If that's what you've come for,' she said. 'You're too early.'

'It's not the washing, Mrs Shipham. I've come to ask you if I may borrow Madge's bike for the day,' he began brightly.

'No, that you can't!' Mrs Shipham folded plump arms, scarlet to the elbow from the steaming water, and glared at him.

'I aren't having the gal lend that to anyone. Poor old mawther, she's 'tato-picked, singled beet, pulled peas, gathered daffodils, and gawd know what to get that bike! What's wrong with yourn anyway...have you broke it?'

'Oh, no, Mrs Shipham. It's not for me. Mrs Vernon would like to borrow it to go for a bike ride.' He glanced up at her with wide innocent eyes. 'She's feeling upset because the Captain has had to leave, so I'm taking her for a longish ride to get her mind off it!'

'The Captain's lady!' Mrs Shipham's expression softened into a conspiratorial smile. 'That's different bor.'

She wiped her hands on her frilly pinafore and led the way towards the shed where the blue frame and spotless white celluloid mudguards of Madge's new Hercules could be seen leaning against a sack of potatoes, surrounded by a tumbled arrangement of shallots, a tin travelling trunk, and a huddle of potato baskets.

'There you are, bor. You get it out time I get somethin' for her.'

Ma Shipham darted back into the house, to reappear carrying a lettuce and a bunch of spring onions. 'I dare say she can make some docky out of these to take with you,' she said, dropping them in the cycle bag.

Leaning the bicycle against the porch Frank went in to meet Mrs Vernon coming down the stairs swinging an army haversack in her hand.

'Oh, topping!' she exclaimed, noticing the bicycle. 'You've managed to borrow one. I've packed a bottle of lemonade and some fish paste sand-sandwiches...wish we had a couple of hard-boiled eggs!'

'There's a fresh lettuce and onions on the kitchen table,' he replied. 'Ma Shipham sent them for you.'

'How kind of her.' She laughed with pleasure and turned hurriedly towards the kitchen to make some more sandwiches. Immediately Frank's spirits lifted. Perhaps there were compensations to be found for the troops leaving their billet. The loss of his father's companionship began to weigh less heavily as this new friendship grew.

The church clock was striking nine as they mounted their bicycles and pedalled away up the village street and past the poplars towards the Fen, where the low-lying mist was still loitering above the dykes. The air was still cool, with a hint of dew on the roadside grass, as they cycled side by side along the straight flat road skirting the Methwold Fens towards Feltwell. A marsh harrier flew above a dyke in an easy glide, suddenly to swerve and drop upon some unsuspecting waterhen or frog.

'Father would have loved to have seen that!' exclaimed Frank. 'Harriers aren't at all common.'

'I thought it was a kite!'

'Crikey! Kites are almost extinct, only about three pairs left...and they're in Wales!' he said, disdainful of her 'Townie' ignorance.

'Well...they were as common as pigeons in Trafalgar Square when I was a little girl in India...horrid scavengers!' she replied laughing at his pomposity.

'There is nowhere quite like this in the world,' she remarked softly as she glanced around at the vast emptiness, with the road stretching ahead, narrowing to a pin-point in the distance. 'It's like sailing across a becalmed ocean of brilliant green seaweed. It's the Sargasso Sea, Frankie, and we are becalmed. We don't seem to be moving at all!'

White clouds in full sail drifted across a blue sky. Fields like oversized allotments made chequer-board squares, some of black soil ridged between potatoes, others green with sugar-beet, criss-crossed by a grid of metallic blue lines where the sky was reflected in freshly-dredged dykes. An occasional tradesman's van passed. Otherwise the road was deserted and silent apart from the soft sigh of an almost non-existent breeze that, like the ceaseless singing of larks, is seldom absent from the open Fen.

'Bet we're doing ten miles an hour,' said Frank cheerfully. 'Feltwell isn't far now.'

'Let's make it fifteen,' Mrs Vernon answered, pressing down hard on her pedals and surging ahead. 'E.T.A. Bodney eleven thirty.' She slowed down breathless after a few minutes. 'On second thoughts, let's make it twelve miles an hour!' she gasped.

They had just left the village of Feltwell, heading towards the rising ground beyond Northwold when a 37 squadron Wellington suddenly roared low over their heads, its undercarriage retracting as it climbed away.

'There used to be Harrows based at Feltwell,' Frank remarked. 'They've now re-equipped with 'Wimpies'. I remember two Harrows colliding near Wissington beet factory a couple of years ago. I biked over with China straight away and we managed to get some bits! One fell into the river and the other crashed on the Fen...and the crew were all burnt to death!' he added cheerfully.

'Oh Frankie! Why are you so crazy about æroplanes?' She had noticed his expression of pure rapture whenever an æroplane appeared in the sky, and the pile of *Popular Flying, The Aeroplane, Aero Modeller* and *Flying* magazines that littered the living-room window-sills.

'I have always loved 'planes,' he said dreamily, 'but especially after going to see Sir Alan Cobham's Flying Circus at Wisbech when I was eleven.'

It had been during the last week in August 1935 that posters had appeared in the surrounding Fenland villages portraying a flying-helmeted pilot gazing as forcefully as Lord Kitchener had done twenty years earlier recruiting young men to the trenches. 'Fly with Sir Alan Cobham' invited this hero of the post-war skies.

'Frank,' Mr Dutton had announced on his return from King Kong's shop, 'I shall take you to see an exhibition of flying.' At which Mrs Dutton had given a sniff of displeasure as he sought refuge in the sanctuary of his study to light one of his newly-purchased Will's Whiffs.

The morning of September 3rd, 1935, saw Mr Dutton and Frank cycling along the road passing through Three Holes, Upwell, Outwell, and Emneth, towards Wisbech and the venue of the 'Flying Circus'. Little Austin 7 open tourers fussed by, bearing the families of the better off, Father sporting a trilby hat, with Mother sitting bolt upright beside him wearing her best cloche bonnet, and the children in the 'dicky'. Every now and again a bright red M.G. two-seater sports sped past allowing a fleeting glimpse of a girl in a saucy Tam-o'-shanter and fluttering chiffon scarf driven by a young man wearing Prince of Wales check sports coat and pale yellow pullover.

But the distractions of passing cars were few and far between. Redadmiral, peacock, and comma butterflies sunned themselves on over-ripe Victoria plums and rotting windfall apples in the roadside orchards. Families of tits see-sawed among the heavy leaves, and spotted flycatcher feasted upon the drugged butterflies, swooping from their perches and neatly scissoring wings from bodies. The air was heavy with bee-hum and dragonfly-whirr.

They came at last to an arrow-shaped sign which directed them along a lane between overgrown thick-set hedges to a gate which bore the message: 'Admission 1/3d, Child 6d, Cars 1/-'. They joined an excited crowd of spectators who jostled and chattered behind a roped-off section of a large grass field.

Frank's enthusiasm wilted. A faded yellow windsock hung limply in the still air. A gull glided overhead then disappeared over the hedge. A girl passed among the crowd selling programmes. There was not an æroplane in sight. For days he had dreamed of actually seeing on the ground one of those fabulous machines, which flew above the Fen like silver specks in the sunlight. But apart from a group of men wearing grubby white overalls chatting near a petrol bowser parked in the shade of the hedge, and a caravan beyond the roped-off section, the field was empty.

Suddenly a tannoy crackled into life welcoming 'the people of Wisbech to witness an outstanding display of airmanship...If you look to the sky on your left you will observe the Circus approaching.'

A sea of pink faces about-turned as from the distance came the combined roar of a fleet of aeroplanes flying in Vic-formation, led by a three-engined biplane. Behind flew a medley of Avros, Moths, a tiny Planette, and a Cerva Autogiro.

Spellbound with awe, Frank held his breath, as one by one the aeroplanes circled the field to land, blipping their throttles as they taxied towards the crowd. Supermen, as distant as the gods, climbed down from the flimsy little biplanes. A young woman, jumping down from her Tiger Moth, only became a woman when she released her flying helmet, allowing a cascade of light brown hair to spread itself over the shoulders of her leather flying jacket.

Dixieland Jazz began to play over the loudspeakers as the show got under way, until the scene became a kaleidoscope of colour and sound. Gaily-painted old Avros and Moths, pilots in riding breeches and leather jackets with silk scarves flung carelessly around their necks below goggles and helmet, the rhythmic throb from idling engines and babble of voices on the green grass beneath a vast expanse of cobalt sky, it was like Frith's 'Derby Day' in the Tate Gallery. Beautiful engines smothered in hot Castrol 'R', the incense of racing fuels and glycol mixed with the sweetness of crushed grass and burning rubber. It had been Frank's initiation into the world of Biggles.

The tannoy began its stream of announcements as aeroplanes took off and landed in a continuous display of ærobatics. It seemed to Frank that all his idealized heroes of *Popular Flying Magazine* were here in the flesh. He watched Flt Lt Geoffrey Tyson, whose photograph graced his bedroom wall, speed upwards towards the sun, glinting high above the crowd as he turned to dive towards the ground. He finished with a barrel roll, skimming the length of the field upside down with the Tiger Moth's rudder tip almost parting the tallest grass stems, then a flick roll, and round in a wide vertical bank to swoop like a swallow and lift a handkerchief from the grass with a wingtip hook. No sooner was he down and trundling back towards the line of parked aircraft than all eyes lifted to see an old Avro 504 with Martin Hearn doing his wing-walking act, finishing a spectacular finale by sitting on the Avro's skid while it looped the loop. Meanwhile Joan Meakin was being towed up in her scarlet glider, rising in an ascending spiral high above the field until the tug released her and fell away, leaving the glider, a silent, moving speck against the blue of the sky.

The crowd who were craning their necks trying to follow the glider were suddenly diverted by the sound of another biplane climbing away from the field with a figure standing midway along one of its lower wings. They watched it head out over the surrounding countryside, before all eyes swivelled to see the glider float like thistledown along the length of the field to land accurately between two marker flags. Heads jerked skywards again as the biplane reappeared overhead in time to see the figure fall backwards off the wing, plucked by a parachute which was streaming in the slipstream.

'That's Naomi Heron-Maxwell!' gasped Frank. 'She releases her parachute and lets it pull her backwards off the wing. It's jolly dangerous because she has to miss getting caught up by the tail. Crikey! Look at that, Pa!'

At the far side of the field the three-engined Ferry was rumbling heavily across the grass bearing its first cargo of four-shilling passengers, to thunder over the spectators' heads and head out towards Wiggenhall.

The afternoon's programme was by now well under way. The 'Airliner' continued to take off and land from the far side of the field bearing its full load of passengers, whose white faces could be seen pressed against the celluloid panels in the fuselage sides. After every landing the last passengers to alight came staggering off distinctly green about the gills, heading erratically towards the nearest hedgerow.

The tannoy crackled into life offering a 'Free flight' to whoever came nearest to guessing the correct speed of an aircraft.

'Write your estimate on your programme, with your name and hand it in to the Officials in the control van. The aircraft will be the Avro 504 now taking off, and it will appear from your left in five minutes.'

Frank pressed his programme into Mr Dutton's hand with a silent invocatory prayer, and hurriedly pulled a pencil from his blazer pocket.

Conjure up in your mind the classic picture of an 'eccentric professor' and you have a picture of Mr Thomas Dutton. He stood out among the good people of the Fens just as Prince 'I-gotta-horse' Monolulu stood out wearing his full Zulu tribal regalia on Newmarket racecourse. Although Mr Dutton did not run to ostrich plumes and silken robes, he did have long silver-white hair brushed straight back from his forehead to fall upon the collar of his long black overcoat - almost a frock coat - which he wore summer and winter over a shirt with a winged collar and loosely-knotted necktie. His face was gaunt, with brilliant violet-blue eyes beneath scraggy white eyebrows, giving him the look of an ecclesiastical 'Denchman' (which is what we in West Norfolk used to call the Hooded Crow).

The old Avro, flying at one hundred feet and about a hundred yards from the spectators, burst over the hedge with a roar and a rush of wind from its slipstream, seeming to flash past at a terrific rate of knots. Flinging up his arms, Mr Dutton took imaginary aim with his ten-bore goose-gun - for he was an inveterate wildfowler - and followed the rapidly disappearing machine as it swept across the field, almost knocking the flower from the hat of a very stout lady in the process.

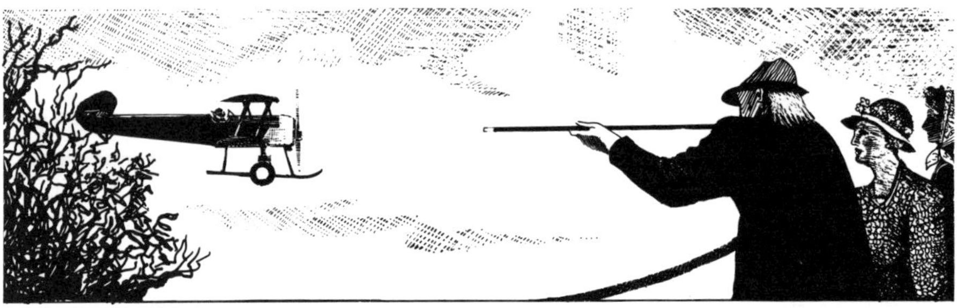

All around them, from behind and either side, estimates were being tossed like straws in the wind.

'She be a-goin' like the wind. What do you say, bor?' one said.

'I dunno,' came the answer. 'She be goin' a sight faster than the old Cambridge train anyhow. And she do nigh on eighty.'

'A hundred and twenty,' someone hedged.

'Silly old fools,' another voice quavered imperiously. 'That there chap a-flying of it couldn't get his breath at that speed. Blow his lungs inside out. That's a fact.'

The very stout lady, having righted her capsized hat, stopped glaring at Mr Dutton and turned towards her comparatively skinny companion.

'What do you say, gal? Shall we have a go?'

'If you were to win, gal, you couldn't get in one of them there little holes what they're a-sitting in,' her companion replied smugly.

'Don't you be too sure of that. There's plenty of squeeze in me,' she giggled, squeezing her hips where they bulged beneath a silky dress.

'I'm going to put down my age for luck. I reckon that were flying at thirty-eight miles an hour.'

At this the stout one burst into peals of laughter.

'Do you know what gal? Do you put your proper age and you ought to win,' was her brilliant repartee. 'That were doing gettin' on for fifty.'

'What do you think, Pa?' Frank asked anxiously. 'Top speed of a 504 is only eighty,' he added in a hushed voice lest he should be overheard.

Mr Dutton paused before giving his customary considered response to problems.

'Well, with the wind behind it a goose would be travelling at roughly forty miles an hour. So, with the forward allowance I had to give I calculate it to have been plus times half, which gives a speed of between sixty and sixty-five miles per hour. Let's say sixty-three miles an hour.'

Clutching his programme Frank elbowed his way through the crowd to hand it to a young woman wearing a brown leather flying coat who was standing on the van steps collecting the entries. Wide-eyed and inarticulate he thrust the entry into the outstretched hand of....Naomi Heron-Maxwell!...the flesh-and-blood hand that barely half an hour ago had grasped the interplane struts of a climbing æroplane while she stood on the wing facing the icy blast from the propeller before allowing her parachute to pluck her backwards in a death-defying stunt high above the crowd!

The mid-afternoon air became heavy with the reek of hot engine oil and petrol fumes. Necks sagged from watching loops and bunts, spins and rolls. Ears, used to the indigenous silence of the Fens, were shattered by the snarl from exhausts and chatter of the tappets of aged engines.

At long last the tannoy came on with the eagerly awaited result for the 'Free Flight'.

'From the many attempts submitted no one has come up with the correct answer,' announced the anonymous voice, which was greeted by a subdued moan. 'However, I am sure you will realise from the wide area of your guesses that it is extremely difficult to calculate the speed of an aircraft which appears suddenly from behind, flying low and parallel to the ground close to you.'

The voice paused to allow the noise of the 'Airliner' taking off over their heads to diminish. 'Now,' he chuckled, 'if the highest speed submitted had been correct, all I can say is that our pilot would have captured the world speed record from the American, Lieut. Doolittle. Not bad, folks, in a 1913-designed anti-Zeppelin fighter. By the way Lieut. Doolittle achieved two hundred and thirty-two miles an hour. Our pilot has been credited with two hundred and fifty miles an hour!'

The happy crowd cheered and hooted enthusiastically.

'At the other end we found the speeds submitted to be just thirty-eight miles an hour, although we have a suspicion that the contestant was confused by the marker car rushing across the field at the same time. Well done, sir or madam, the car was doing forty! Well, the winning speed lies between the two.'

'There! What did I tell you now?' came the self-righteous voice of the slimmer of the two ladies. 'If you hadn't been so proud and put down your proper age you might have won. Thirty-eight! Don't you forget I were at school with you so you can't fool me, gal.'

'...The exact speed was held at sixty-one miles per hour and the nearest entry is for sixty-three miles an hour. If the winning lady or gentleman will kindly come to the control van he, or she, will have a breathtaking flight in one of our modern two-seaters.'

The tannoy switched off with a crackle of static and Frank was dragging his father through a milling crowd towards the Control caravan, where a tall sandy-haired man lounging on a camp-chair beside the caravan stood up as they approached.

'Congratulations!' he exclaimed. 'I take it the young fellow will be the one to go up?' He pointed towards a silver and blue Avro Tutor which stood parked alongside the caravan. 'First the formality of a Parent's Responsibility form to sign.'

Mr Dutton's face blanched, and he glanced uneasily towards the frightening bulk of the aeroplane realising the enormity of his sin should anything untoward happen to his son and heir.

But Frank was already heading towards the waiting pilot who stood chatting to one of the petrol bowser men.

'Come on son!' The pilot gave him a comradely wink. 'Help me give her a pre-flight inspection. Rule number one. Never take a kite up without giving it the once-over!'

Frank followed bewitched as the pilot twanged bracing wires, rocked control surfaces, and kicked the tyres, before heaving him up into the front cockpit of the two-seat trainer and handing him a leather helmet and goggles.

Frank was in heaven from the moment he sat in the cockpit, grasped the padded leather cockpit coaming, and settled his feet next to the disconnected rudder pedals. This wasn't the world of Biggles. He *was* Biggles with a joystick between his knees, even though a disconnected joystick! A quick glance at the instruments, and the petrol bowser man was swinging the propeller. The engine coughed, fired, the varnished wooden propeller disappeared in a shimmering wheel of light, and they were bumping away towards the far edge of the field giving Frank a last glimpse of his father standing alone with his fears on the caravan step.

The Avro turned to face the length of the field, the engine roared and the whole machine vibrated as it sped swiftly over the grass until suddenly Frank was aware that the bouncing had ceased and they were climbing gently away, leaving behind a pocket-handkerchief-sized field surrounded by Dinky toy cars.

They flew above the River Nene, following it northwards above golden stubble fields and regimented lines of orchards. Ahead were the salt-marshes, purple with sea-lavender, and dappled by blue tide-pools and winding gullies leading to marram-topped sandhills where mile after mile of brilliant white beaches stretched away towards the far distant purple haze of Lincolnshire beyond the deep ultramarine of the North Sea.

They left the Nene at Sutton Bridge, banking sharply round to circle westwards, then south, dropping the port wings as the pilot banked steeply above the Whaplode cross-roads, continuing the far-flung circle south-east to pick up the Nene at Guyhirn and follow it northwards back to the flying field.

The spectators, now becoming quite blasé to aircraft coming in to land, scarcely turned their heads as the Tutor made its final turn and levelled off for the touch-down. It was gliding gently above the boundary hedge with the runway stretching out before it when without warning the pilot gunned the engine, pulled back the joystick, and the little machine went up and up, higher and higher, in an almost vertical climb to go into a loop high above the crowd. Frank's stomach, which had been left somewhere on the way up, fell back into place as he looked up at the spinning earth and down at the sky as they looped, only to lose it again in a rapid series of bunts and barrel rolls. Then they were bumping across the grass towards the control van to be greeted by a visibly distressed Mr Dutton expecting to see an equally green-about-the-gills son, who emerged from the cockpit to clutch an undercarriage strut for support before staggering drunkenly towards his parent.

'Crikey!' was all he could say.

But his inebriety was not that of the orchard butterflies disorientated in their drunken worship of Bacchus. His coming down to earth was that of a neophyte after his initiation by the Goddesses of Air.

'Crikey!' he reiterated, looking round in a dazed sort of way and noting for the first time the worried countenance of his father, who had placed an arm round his shoulder and was easing him away from the Avro's silver leg.

'If your mother ever gets to know that I allowed you to go up in an aeroplane - especially one that rolled upside down - my life wouldn't be worth living, so I don't think you had better let on.'

'I know,' sighed Frank happily. 'Anyway I will fly myself one day. I'm going to join the Royal Air Force.'

'You will have to do much better at school for that!' answered his father tersely, thinking some good might possibly have come from the experience.

They made their way towards their parked bicycles and cycled down the lane towards the main road as the 'Airliner' was taking off with its last load of passengers. Ahead the sun hung low above the Bedford Levels, while following them, drifting through the ragged hedge, came a boisterous jazzy melody...

'Amy...Wonderful Amy...You Can't Blame Me for Loving You'...

'By this time next year I shall be in the R.A.F. as a fighter pilot,' Frank continued.

'Not a bomber pilot?' Olivia grinned.

'Well, actually, I did once want to. But not any more.' For Frank had become disenchanted with his previous fantasy of sitting high above the ground between the unleashed thunder of twin Bristol Hercules radials in a Wellington Bomber, giving a nonchalant 'thumbs up' to the erks to pull the chocks away, pushing the throttles forward, and roaring across the airfield to lift gently and climb upwards into the night sky.

'Being a single-seat fighter pilot is more fun!'

They left the black flat earth of the Fens behind as they cycled through the little village of Northwold and crossed the main Thetford to King's Lynn road leading towards the higher ground of the Brecks, to pedal between verges bright with dog-daisies and scarlet poppies and hedges fragrant with honeysuckle, festooned with large white convolvulus blooms. The few isolated farm cottages shimmered as the sunlight glanced off their flint walls and there were trees, oaks and elms with ivy-clad trunks bordering pastures with shorthorn cows and calves lying in lush grass. They cycled beside small fields of ripening barley, rustling with heat, and a hayfield where a horse was drawing a mower around a centre square of still-standing grass leaving it tossed in swathes to dry in the sun.

A few miles on, the lush fields began to give way to sandy heath. For the first time in Frank's life he saw heather, with isolated clumps of tall Scots pines, and delicate silver birch trees growing out of sand carpeted with yellow ragwort and rabbit-cropped turf.

Crossing another main road running towards Fakenham from Thetford, they entered the valley of the Wissey to cross over the stream by a hump-back bridge.

'Do you know where we are?' Olivia said gaily. 'I don't think you do!' she added with a laugh.

'Not really!' he answered helpfully. 'Nicky said that the airfield is next to the Watton road, and the aircrew are billeted about three miles away in Claremont Hall.'

'I can see a church,' Olivia exclaimed, 'and a farm house.' She pointed towards the narrow river winding beneath an arch of leafy trees below a small Saxon church half-hidden by its churchyard elms. 'This must be Bodney.'

An old man was cutting the roadside hedge parsley and long grass with a scythe.

'Excuse me, are we on the right road for the airfield?' Frank asked after dismounting from his bicycle.

The man ceased swinging the scythe to give them a suspicious stare before taking a stone from his trouser pocket and beginning to stroke the blade in silence.

'Keep a-goin' and you'll see it bor. That's on this old Watton road anyway. What d'you want to know for? Rum old lot up there.' He looked sideways at Olivia. 'Get a bloomin' sight more furriners around these parts since they brought them there aeroplanes out of Watton. I whòlly wonder what they had to do that for. They were out of the way down at Watton!'

'Thanks,' answered Frank starting to pedal away, with Olivia following him along the quiet road after giving a pleasant smile to the old man.

'Fare thee well, bor,' the man mumbled as he returned to his task of decapitating the heads of moon-daisies and vetches to fall in frothy white waves of hedge-parsley beneath the hiss of the blade.

'Tally-ho! Tally-ho!...'

Four young airmen on bicycles, pedalling furiously, caught up with them to draw alongside Olivia, whistling and giggling like schoolboys let loose from class.

'Escort duty, Ma'am. Exceedingly dangerous area for a pretty woman!' said one of the four. He spoke in a Hollywood version of a dashing English milord-cum-aviator voice Frank, who had been jostled and boxed in on the outside of the bunch, scowled. Olivia giggled.

'Clive of India, I presume?' she asked with a quizzical raising of her eyebrows.

'Flying Officer Muldownie...and may I introduce Flying Officers Kite, Johnson, and 'Ginger' McIver, just back from pranging the Hun's invasion fleet!' His blue eyes danced and his bicycle wobbled as he lifted one hand from the handlebars to stroke an almost non-existent ginger moustache. 'And you are...?'

'You're from 82 Squadron?' she asked, with a disarming smile. 'Oh, I'm so glad. You can show me the way to Claremont Hall. I'm your Station Commander's wife.' For a second the airman's jaw sagged. 'It really is typical of him to send me an escort of gallant Flying Officers,' she added, with another smile.

'You're not!'

'I am.'

'No! Really?'

'Oh no? Well, I am not an 'erk', that's a sure thing, *Aircraftsman* Muldownie,' she answered with mock authority.

At this his three companions roared with laughter, rang their bicycle bells, hooted and whistled gleefully.

'You've been shot down in flames this time, Paddy my boy. To be sure an' all!' they mimicked. 'Ye'll be found in the bog wi' the banshees!'

'Shoo!' Olivia cried, waving her arms as if at a flock of cheeky starlings on a bird table, and a rather deflated 'Flying Officer' Muldownie followed his companions as they pedalled merrily away up the road, allowing Frank to regain his position beside her.

By now they had reached the side of the landing ground with a series of notices placed at regular intervals printed in large red letters on a grey ground

'NO LOITERING. MINISTRY OF DEFENCE.'

'Phew! We're here!' Olivia gave an exaggerated sigh of relief as she laid Madge's bicycle gently down on a clump of camomile. 'Let's have a long drink of lemonade.'

But Frank was gazing wistfully at three Bristol Blenheims parked facing away from the road about a quarter of a mile away. Their perspex canopies gleamed in the sunlight above the delicate duck-egg green under-surfaces, presenting to Frank the perfection of form that a flawless body might present to Rodin.

'Not much of an airfield,' Olivia remarked looking around her. 'No runways, just a few wooden huts each side of the field.' She flopped down on the soft camomile to lie on her back looking up at the sky. Frank took his late father's field glasses from his bicycle bag. 'There's a Church Army canteen van parked under a clump of trees,' he observed after making a hurried sweep of the area through the glasses. Gosh! And a Hampden near the huts.

He lowered the glasses, before turning towards Olivia.

'That oughtn't to be here... K.M....44 Squadron from Waddington.'

'Oh Frankie! You and your squadron letters. Where on earth do you get all this 'restricted information' from? By the way you had better keep those glasses out of sight or else you will get us arrested for spying.'

'Nicky's dad is a pilot flying Wimpies from Marham. He gives me all the gen at school.'

She rolled over on to her stomach and dragged the haversack towards her. 'Gosh! I'm hungry!' she said, beginning to unwrap the sandwiches. 'And hot! Take your eyes off those aeroplanes for a minute and pour me out an apéritif of fizzy lemonade.'

Her blue eyes twinkled as she spread a little white cloth on the short grass before holding out a bakelite mug to be filled from the Corona bottle. Scarlet poppies with delicate petals, drooping in the heat, trembled beneath the weight of tiny leaf-beetles, and from some overhead telephone wires a cock stonechat chattered noisily, disturbed from its noon siesta by the approach of a creaking bicycle carrying a red-faced and perspiring police constable.

Olivia quickly grabbed the field glasses and pushed them out of sight under her skirt.

'Mornin' Miss.' The large fat policeman descended from his bicycle and lifted his helmet to mop his brow. 'Lovely weather, Miss, isn't it? Do you know this is a restricted area. No loitering!'

'It's a gorgeous day, Constable.' She flashed him a smile. 'We're notloitering. We're picnicking. Have a sandwich and a mug of lemonade. You look dreadfully hot!'

The policeman dropped his heavy bicycle on the ground, removed his cycle clips from the bottom of his thick serge trousers and sat down beside them.

'Come to see the bombers, bor?' He turned to Frank. 'Not allowed!'

'Oh, Frank here is suffering from a terrible affliction....in fact an epidemic, for the whole of his form at school is suffering from it.'

'He look wholly well to me, Miss. But then, looks aren't everything, are they now? What's he got?'

'Well, along with the rest of the fifth form, he has got this overpowering craving to be a pilot in the Royal Air Force...and it has gone to their heads!'

'Ar that's right. I have the same problem with my gal. My old Missus worked, an' I worked overtime to send her to Thetford Grammar School so's she could be a teacher. Got herself a scholarship to University an' all. And what have she done? She broke my Missus's heart by going in the W.A.A.F.'

He finished his mug of lemonade with a sigh, and held out his hand for another sandwich.

'You know, Miss?' he said slowly with a wide grin suddenly appearing on his face. 'You can take them old glasses out what your a-sittin' on. They show up a treat under that thin skirt of yours! And that poor little bor won't see much if you keep them hid up there!'

He turned towards Frank as Olivia gave a suppressed giggle.

'Come to think on it, I just been talking to them at the Guard hut and they tell me there's a Hampden down what come in last night, out of petrol. She's goin' home anytime now. So if you keep sittin' here she'll come up right over your heads.'

He slowly replaced his helmet on his head and methodically folded his trouser-bottoms before replacing the cycle clips.

'Do you keep sittin' quiet so's them Airforce police don't see you. Do they'll be up here after you like a shot. Bored, that's their trouble. Nothing for them to do out here!' And with a conspiratorial slow wink he pedalled philosophically away up the road.

Olivia bent forward to take another sandwich from the haversack.

'England!' she exclaimed, after a moment of silence. 'There is nowhere else in the world like it! Where else would an officer of the law sit down and share lemonade and sandwiches with two law-breakers sitting underneath a warning notice and then go away telling them not to get caught?'

'Oh, he knew we were alright,' Frank answered confidently. 'We don't look like spies.'

She glanced musingly at her bare foot, rotating the ankle.

'I could be a beautiful spy,' she murmured, pouting her red lips provocatively and fluttering her eyelashes, causing Frank to flush like a young girl.

'Not much to discover here anyway.' He shrugged and gazed at her over the rim of his cup of lemonade. 'I don't suppose it would be critical for Nazi intelligence to hear that one of our bombers had run out of fuel on the way home.'

As he finished speaking a steely whine suddenly came from the Hampden as its engines were run up ready for take off, and slowly it began to move forward away from the huts and their shadowing trees.

'It's a strange looking æroplane,' Olivia remarked, raising her head to peer through the coils of barbed wire lining the hedge. 'Reminds me of that funny fish Dickie caught. Deep and narrow in the body, with wide wings.'

'That's how it gets its nickname "Flying suitcase",' Frank said, airing his knowledge as usual, as the bomber's wheels left the ground fifty yards from the road and thundered like a great black crow over their heads, eclipsing the sun.

Olivia took her hands away from her ears and glanced at her wristwatch before stroking the creases out of her rumpled skirt.

'Half past three, Frankie! Hadn't we better head for home?'

Frank sighed and cast a last lingering glance towards the slumbering Blenheims. The Hampden was banking in the distance as it circled before passing over their heads to the north.

'How about going to spy on Marham next?' Olivia smiled, indulgently as though to a child.

He gave her a grateful grin, sensing an end to the frightening sense of loneliness which gripped him when he thought of his father.

Olivia was kneeling down, packing the haversack.

'I'd love to see a fighter station next,' Frank said hesitantly. 'There's Spitfires, Hurricanes, and Blenheim Mk Is at Wittering, and Hurricanes at Bircham Newton. Trouble is they are a long way away from Willows End!'

'Heavens! *Surely* not further than Bodney?'

She burst out laughing as she raised Madge's bicycle from the roadside and sat astride waiting for Frank to hide the field glasses in his bicycle bag.

'Much further!' He leapt on his bicycle and started pedalling happily homewards. 'Bircham's beyond King's Lynn...and Wittering's beyond Peterborough...almost at Stamford!'

'Crikey!' she exclaimed, adopting Frank's favourite expletive. 'I consider this to have been a long ride...and we're still thirty miles from home!'

Thursday 15th August 1940
The Secret Pool

After three days of heavy grey cloud Thursday dawned clear, and by seven o'clock when Boer led the horses past the porch there was not a cloud in the sky.

'Have you any stale bread to spare, Ma?' Frank was standing beside the front door, where a shaft of sunlight filtering through the broad leaves of the hollyhocks warmed the ginger tom-cat's outstretched body. 'I think I will go fishing.'

Glancing up at the sky he decided to get away into the depths of the Fen and spend the day searching around the 'Secret pool' for caterpillars. He needed a series of Sallow Kittens for his collection, and would search the sallows for their caterpillars; also he could take a rod and hope for a tench. It would be far too brassy a day for the fish to bite, although later, as the sun set, the large golden-sided rudd would begin to feed among the water-lilies.

Mrs Dutton was about to fry yesterday's left-overs of cabbage and mash in the cast-iron frying pan on the scullery oilstove.

'No!' she answered. 'Go and dig some worms.'

'Worms will be too deep to find in this dry weather. I'll ask Mrs Vernon. She's sure to have some stale bread.'

'Your breakfast is nearly ready.' He heard the irritable clatter of a fork against the iron pan. 'You mustn't ask Mrs Vernon for anything.'

'She doesn't mind, Ma,' he answered happily. 'She would probably like to see Pa's 'Secret pool' anyway.'

Mrs Dutton's hot flushed face appeared in the doorway.

'You certainly must not mention it to her. I do not like you traipsing about the countryside with a soldier's wife. Eat your breakfast and get off...By yourself!'

She glanced towards the clock, and sighed.

'If I could ride a bicycle I would come with you. But you know that I have no sense of balance.'

'You could have overcome that years ago if you had really wanted to come out with Pa and me.' His mother retreated back into the scullery fug. 'It has never stopped you doing everything else,' he added bitterly. 'The trouble is that you have never wanted me to have friends. China, Chippy, Podge, Ferret, and the rest you say are not *'our class'*. Now you say Mrs Vernon isn't suitable. Who *can* I have for a friend now that Pa is dead?'

'You don't care for my company,' she replied, sullenly. 'You never take me out with you.'

Inwardly Frank shrank from her. She seemed pathetically inert and vulnerable, standing with the black frying-pan in her hand and her greying auburn hair scrimped back in an untidy bun.

'Mrs Vernon at least isn't common. She was educated at a very exclusive boarding school. And she isn't 'stuck up', even though her parents belong to your precious Raj that you are always talking about. Her father was a colonel in the Indian Army, and now he is working as one of the top brass at the War Office. And Dickie is a captain in the Artillery. You should be pleased she takes an interest in me.'

Frank went across to the scullery door. 'I suppose the only way Mrs Vernon would suit you would be for her to stay in her room and ignore me!'

Mrs Dutton clenched her jaw, drawing her lips into a bloodless shrewish line, and banged the scullery door in his face.

The living room door opened and Olivia entered the room. Immediately the atmosphere brightened as she smiled at Frank before glancing at her reflection in the fireplace mirror.

'Anything the matter?' she asked, raising an eyebrow towards the scullery.

'Not really. Just Ma in a mood.'

'Because of me? Perhaps it would be better for me to go back to mother in Cheyne Row?' She glanced again towards the scullery door. 'Your mother probably resents having another woman in her home. I expect I would feel the same if I had my own home and had to put up with another female using my things,' she said generously.

'Oh no. It's not because of you! She simply doesn't want me to go fishing in the "Secret pool". That's all.'

'Why ever not?'

'She thinks I might fall in. Have you any stale bread to spare?'

'Bread?' She looked puzzled.

‘To make bait for fishing,’ he explained.

‘Oh...for fishing! I can give you some bread. What’s this about a “Secret pool”?’

Before he could reply the scullery door opened and his mother gusted in like an oppressive sirocco wind bearing two plates of bubble and squeak.

‘You had better eat this quickly and be off before it rains,’ she said, turning to Frank.

‘I’ll put some bread to soak for bait while you eat your breakfast,’ Olivia murmured, half-rising from her chair.

‘Please do not trouble. Bread is rationed. He can dig some worms.’

‘Tell me more about this “Secret pool”,’ Olivia whispered as Mrs Dutton returned to the scullery. ‘Is it very far?’

The boy pulled his chair closer to her.

‘Pa and I discovered it a couple of years ago when we were biking down the Loke.' He told Olivia how they had followed an overgrown drove which took them to an unclaimed part of the Old Fen. As they biked along the bumpy drove they noticed the tip of a tall willow and a crescent-shaped row of alders standing above acres and acres of thick reed-beds. His father thought it might be possible for a colony of Large Copper butterflies to be surviving seeing that they were common there during the 1820s. The Large Copper was considered to be extinct in Britain, and so his father became really excited at finding this original bit of Fen and insisted that they must find a way to it through the reed-beds.

'We found a half-sunken plank crossing the drove dyke and tunnelled our way through the reeds on Quaking Fen until we eventually came to the pool. It was simply unbelievable. A lost pool of about five acres completely hidden from the rest of the world. There was a great trunk of bog-oak rising from the water surrounded by water-lilies, and basking on the trunk a large, snaky-necked turtle, which dived instantly into the water and vanished.'

His father had gasped. 'Did you see what I *thought* I saw?’

‘I thought I saw a huge tortoise as quick as a lizard!' Frank had replied. 'Whatever was it?'

‘The only thing I can think of is a European Pond Turtle,' said his father, 'although it seemed to have more of a Terrapin’s beaked jaw and agility.’

‘We named it “The Secret pool” and often went there to fish. It holds immense pike and tench, lots of perch and rudd, and enormous eels. Father made a drawing of the "Terrapin" from life and wrote a letter to *The Field,* then thought better of it and didn’t post it, in case it brought an invasion of naturalists to spoil our secret fen.’

Olivia laughed. ‘Oh Frankie! A fabulous beast lurking in an English fen! I’d love to see it, although I’m sure you are pulling my leg.’

‘Honest. You will see it if you come with me,’ he whispered, anxiously eyeing the scullery door in case his mother had heard her burst of laughter.

Olivia glanced at the closed door. 'I know, Frankie. I'll pack some sandwiches and we shall have a picnic at your "Secret pool".' She reached for her purse which lay on the dresser and took out half-a-crown. 'Run up to Mr Kingshott's and buy a large bottle of pop, while I make the sandwiches and borrow Madge's bike.'

Frank took the coin and dashed towards the door. 'Oh, see if he has a couple of Lyons Individual Fruit Pies as well,' she added, raising her voice as he passed by the open window.

He was waiting a short distance from the house with his fishing bag and rod when Olivia appeared wheeling Madge's blue Hercules. She had changed into plimsolls and a light skirt and blouse of gauzy Indian cotton and carried a haversack holding the picnic slung over the bicycle's handlebar.

'It's going to be another scorcher today,' she exclaimed. 'I'd change into shorts and leave that pullover off!' She laughed at his thick grey flannel trousers, woollen shirt, jumper and tie. 'You will be absolutely boiled in those.'

'Ma wouldn't like it...I have to always wear a jumper and tie,' he answered with a rueful grimace.

'How far is it?' she asked, as they left the village street and turned down a narrow road leading to the Fen.

'Oh, about seven miles,' he replied amiably, as he ripped the black tie off with one hand and steered with the other. 'We follow the Loke as far as the Main Drain. Then we have to keep our eyes open for the beginning of the derelict drove running towards the Old Fen.'

They cycled easily across the flat land, following the Loke road which ran straight between dykes and narrow verges frothing with meadow-sweet and cow parsley to converge beyond the haze of heat shimmering on the horizon. Barley was being harvested on a distant field, where high-loaded wagons lurched hull-down on the horizon across ochre stubbles, drawn by teams of heavy shires on the way to the stackyards.

'China said Sedge Farm were cutting today,' Frank remarked. 'We could have gone and helped. It's good fun riding the trace horses back and forth from the field to the yard. Pitching is the hardest job, but the men do that.'

'I expect it would be terribly hot work loading the sheaves on a day like this,' said Olivia, looking across the intervening fields towards the faint clank of the cutter which was going round the last square of standing corn drawn by a blue tractor.

They caught up with a skinny girl riding a large shire horse slowly along the roadside verge.

'Wotcher bor!' she called. 'What are you a doin'?'

'Going fishing down the Cut,' he lied. 'What are you doing with Samson, Ferret?'

'Them silly devils cartin' for Sedge Farm have a wagon stuck in a dyke. So they sent me to lend old Samson to get it out!'

She twitched the end of the rope halter and looked down at them, lounging side-saddle on its glossy bare back with one hand nonchalantly holding a collar hame as the horse stopped.

Olivia stared disbelievingly at the skinny young girl perched on a horse that appeared as tall and as round as an elephant.

'How on earth did you manage to get up there?' she said, looking up to meet a pair of green eyes, speckled grey like blackbird eggs, below a bush of black curls.

'Oh, I just got up the granary steps an' dropped on, Miss. I dursent get off him on the Loke 'cause there's no willow trees to get up to get on him again.'

'But he is huge. Do you feel safe up there?'

'Old Samson is the biggest hoss on the Fen as sure as I sit here.' She wiped her nose on the sleeve of her dress and kicked the horse into a steady walk. 'You mind you don't fall in the Cut together,' she giggled as Samson carried her through the cow parsley on feet as large as dinner-plates. 'Fishin'!'

'Is that girl safe out alone on that huge animal?' said Olivia after they had remounted. 'She has no reins or saddle, and it must weigh a ton.'

Frank laughed. 'That was Ferret. Ferret can do anything. She's one of the gang. There's China, Chippy, Podge and Ferret. And she beats us all.'

'Isn't Ferret rather an unusual name for a girl? She could be very pretty with that mop of curly hair if she looked after it.'

'Ferret is the champion ratter amongst us. That's how she got her name. Ferret's uncle Daggy is the real expert with a rat-dag...That's a sort of pronged trident made for spearing rats.'

'We live and learn,' Olivia murmured with mock humility. 'Would I make a good ratter?'

'I don't think so,' he chuckled.

After another mile they came to the wagon on its side in the ditch surrounded by its scattered load of sheaves. Two Suffolk Punches stood, lathered in sweat, tied to the gateway leading on to the Loke Drove, while a labourer lay on his back among the sedges staring blankly up at the sky.

'Have you see'd that mawther, Ferret, with Samson, bor?' he shouted. 'She's been gone an hour already!'

'Yes. She's almost here. If you stood up you could see her coming,' Frank answered cheekily.

The man laughed. 'Do you know what I believe in bor? Never run when you can walk...never walk when you can stand...an' never stand when you can

sit...or sit when you can lie. An' that's what I'm a doin' now.'

Olivia was gazing abstractedly at a line of women shocking the sheaves ready to load in the wagons.

'This is so perfect,' she said, as if to herself. 'It is like stepping backwards into the world of the nineteenth-century painters. The women are the women of Millet...Lepage...Jules Breton. Nothing seems to have changed. Look at their headscarves and long cotton skirts and sacking aprons. That girl on the shire horse could have been a girl from any age. Do you know what Baudelaire once said, Frankie? "Natural things exist only a little; reality lies only in dreams". These harvest fens are like a dream.'

'Who was Baudelaire?' asked the boy, beginning to cycle away.

'You haven't yet come across Baudelaire?' she teased, pedalling quickly after him. 'Shame on you!

La Nature est un temple ou de vivants piliers
Laissent parfois sortir des confuses paroles;
L'homme y passe a travers des forêts de symboles
Qui l'observent avec de regards familiers...'

She stopped pedalling, laughing, and short of breath. 'How's that, Frankie?'

He slowed down, and they continued to ride side by side between verges of meadowsweet and the tall spikes of bullrushes lining the dykes.

'Nature is a temple where living pillars sometimes allow confused words to escape. Man passes there through forests of symbols that watch him with familiar glances.' Frankie translated. 'How's that Mrs Vernon? That was easy.' His blue eyes danced with an air of unsophisticated intelligence.

'Jolly good, Frankie! You have actually progressed beyond the chanting of verbs,' she replied. 'You told me that you were absolutely hopeless at school!'

'But I am hopeless at everything else. It's simply that I like French because of Mam'selle. She's so different from the other teachers. She doesn't wear a gown and mortarboard. Instead she wears pretty clothes and pointed shoes. And her hair is like a ballet dancer's, parted in the centre and tied up in a net behind. She's a spiffing sport too!'

'Better not tell your Ma why you like French lessons, Frankie. Why don't you ask your Mam'selle about Baudelaire? Then she might show special interest in you.'

He blushed and sped ahead to hide his confusion. Olivia quickly drew level again. 'Don't worry about Maths or the memorization of irrelevant facts...reality dies. The poets and the artists are the only true visionaries. You must study them, Frankie, especially the French, Verlaine, Rimbaud, Mallarmé and my Baudelaire.'

'We've arrived!' Frank announced. 'That's the willow above the Secret pool.' He pointed across an expanse of original fen to where Olivia could see the ochre wilderness of reeds broken by the tip of a grey-green tree.

A curious excitement surged through Olivia as she helped Frank lift the two bicycles over the raised bank and hide them beneath a trellis of bindweed and angelica before parting some reeds to reveal a half-sunken plank.

'You can't possibly suggest that we have to go through this!' she exclaimed, looking up at the towering reeds from the level of the plank. 'Frank, these reeds must be ten feet tall.'

'Oh...there's a sort of track. It's a bit shaky underneath but it's safe enough if you don't step sideways off it,' he replied. 'Just follow in my footsteps.'

Olivia followed him blindly through the reeds. 'Where's this fabulous beast?' she whispered as she became confident that she was not about to disappear for ever beneath the quaking peat.

'There,' he whispered, slowly parting a wall of sedge so that she could see a large expanse of sky-blue water glinting between rafts of water-lilies 'On the log to your left. He's there basking, just as I said he would be.'

'Frankie...*it actually exists!* It is not one of your fantasies...But *how?*'

At the sound of her voice the terrapin's neck shot up and its head swivelled in their direction before diving off the log into the water.

'Father came to the conclusion that some eccentric naturalist must have secretly re-introduced a few and this is the only survivor. Or perhaps it is an escapee from a private zoo, or a pet that has travelled along a network of rivers and settled in the Fen. At any rate we thought it must have been here for a long time.' He picked up his fishing rod and turned towards the side of the pool. 'Let's go and sit beneath the willow. It will be shady there and I can cast out into the open bay.'

'You know,' she said wistfully, after Frank had assembled his tackle and they were sitting together below the willow watching a red-tipped cork float. 'I feel so guilty lazing day after day in the sunshine, writing during the evenings to Dickie, and simply waiting negatively. For what?'

She turned impulsively towards him. 'We're both in the same boat, Frankie! You want to leave school so that you can volunteer for the R.A.F. and I want to join the W.R.A.C. and belong to an anti-aircraft battery...or drive an ambulance...*anything!*'

'You're lucky. At least you are old enough to join up!'

'I am *old* enough, but Dickie won't hear of it. Officers' wives are nothing but glorified camp-followers, left to rot in hotels or lodgings every time the regiment moves, waiting for the next telegram to move to other rooms, other hotels.' Olivia pouted petulantly. 'What *can* I do? Knit socks and balaclavas? I can't even knit!' she giggled. 'I want to do something *exciting!*'

'How about becoming a spy? The Mata Hari of 1940!'

'But I would end up by being shot! And it's far more pleasant to lie here in the sun than to be a martyr.'

'Florence Nightingale?'

'Don't like blood.' She rolled over to lie on her back and study the sky. 'I think I would much prefer to ride a grey charger at the head of an army returning to France - Jeanne d'Arc and Henry the Fifth in one - and roll the German armies back from Dunkirk in revenge for what they did to Dickie's lot!'

'And may I be your escort in a Spitfire?'

'Of course. So long as you don't make my grey shire bolt.'

'And Ferret? Will you take Ferret on Samson with her rat-dag?'

'Yes,' she smiled, gazing at her ankle where a reed had left a red mark. 'I think I would enjoy that.'

She lay back on the soft mosses between the gnarled roots of the willow with her hands beneath her head looking up into the sky. A heron flew leisurely overhead, before planing down out of sight beyond the perimeter of tufted reeds. She closed her eyes. The sun's heat, beating back from the rushes, burned through the thin cotton of her skirt. Reed warblers sang, their staccato bursts drifting drowsily from the dense fortress of reeds to mingle with the soporific drone of insects.

Frank looked at her, furtively, through half-closed eyes, as he sat leaning against the willow trunk. She moved, to curl fœtus-like in the cleft of the willow roots with her breasts falling heavily against her blouse as she turned. He glanced hurriedly away to stare at the red tip of the float mirrored motionless above its reflection in the still water. A pair of damselflies mated, their metallic blue bodies arched end to end on a lily-pad. He ached to place his head on the softness of her blouse which rose and fell as she breathed.

Presently Olivia stirred. She rolled on to her stomach, cupping her face between her hands, watching the boy through eyes shaded with long lashes. The stifling heat of the enclosing thickets of reeds created an atmosphere of other-worldliness, allowing her to escape into a world of fantasy, in which the lodestone was Desire.

Frank sensed her eyes watching him. Olivia smiled, lazily, like a cat.

'It is probably too hot for the fish to bite,' he explained. 'I suppose this must be a bit boring for you, Mrs Vernon. You should have brought a book to read.'

'Not at all, Frankie. At the moment I am a nymph in the rushes with my Pan. And you should be lulling me with your pipes!' she teased.

The terrapin raised its snaky neck, turning its head towards the sudden sound of her voice, and a sedge warbler burst into its territorial song.

'There are your pipes.'

Frank was feeling content, warm, and utterly at peace with the world in a way that he had never before experienced.

'That is a bird,' she whispered. 'I want Pan to play to me.'

'Then...You are the nymph Syrinx?'

'I didn't say that I was!' she answered, with raised eyebrows, giving him a quizzical glance.

Frank broke off a brittle reed stem. 'That didn't hurt?'

She burst out laughing. 'You are showing off!'

He snapped another reed...then another...and another, prancing about, sending the sleeping caddis flies bumbling from their siesta in the reeds.

'Oh, stop.' Olivia was convulsed with laughter. 'Oh, stop...stop...stop,' she cried, acting her part of a mortally stricken maiden between giggles. 'You are tearing me apart! You are cutting my throat!'

'Then...You are Syrinx!'

'And you are Pan?'

'If I am Pan...Surely I can hold you to my lips, and play magical notes?'

Olivia giggled with obvious delight.

'But only in the form of a reed...Remember, I have escaped your frolicking for ever!'

She flung herself down on the cool reeds beneath the willow's shade. 'You are a very strange child,' she remarked tenderly. 'How is it that you know so much about Syrinx and Pan?'

'I am alone a lot,' he mumbled. 'Father owned so many books, and all there was to do was read.'

The terrapin slipped silently from its log to disappear beneath a dense mat of duckweed. Concentric ripples rocked the spidery filaments of water -millfoil below the clear channels. Olivia closed her eyes.

'He has not yet awakened,' she thought. 'He is still in the awakening stage of childhood, like a butterfly newly emerged from the shard of a chrysalis.' And she felt saddened, overwhelmed by a desire to share in the awakening.

'Shall we have lunch now?'

She reached for the haversack and took out a lettuce and tomato sandwich, forcing herself to ignore the quickening of her desire.

He took it shyly, feeling her desire flowing out towards him, but not knowing what it was. He was aware only of his ache to be close to the warmth and softness of her. Frank ate his sandwich as he gazed at the float. He ate mechanically as if in a trance, sitting some distance from Olivia within a green enclave of saw-sedge. The dull ache had become a physical pain. A kingfisher flashed past, a scintillating streak of turquoise, to perch upon an alder twig above the terrapin's log. But he did not notice the bird. He was sinking deep into an abyss of self-hate that would obliterate everything conceived in his dreams about her. He suffered death in his sixteen-year-old soul with mute yearning. Looking into the calm waters of the 'Secret pool' he realised that he could never betray his true feelings to her.

Olivia stirred, raising her knee so that her skirt fell back exposing a bewilderment of thigh.

'Frankie!' she exclaimed teasingly. 'You have gone awfully quiet. Come and finish off these sandwiches with me. At least I'm hungry if the fish aren't.'

He did not answer, sitting motionless within his redan of reeds holding his fishing rod.

'Frank!' She flung a clod of dried clay at him. 'Put that rod down and come here. Holding that rod won't make the silly fish bite!'

She raised her voice, being irritated by his silence, but wavered as she sensed the callow wretchedness in him, feeling in its place a compelling tenderness as she watched him press a forked twig from an alder in the soft mud for a rod rest, and uncoil a few inches of line from the reel, before joining her beside the picnic cloth.

'Are we going to catch anything today?' she asked brightly, handing him an apple and blackberry pie.

'Fish hardly ever bite in the middle of the day,' he answered dully, avoiding her eyes.

'Then why bother to come fishing at all?' she exclaimed petulantly. 'Why didn't I sit in the garden all day...or wash my hair?'

'I thought you might enjoy a day by the Secret pool,' he faltered, tortured by the nearness of her breasts.

'Oh yes...I like your Secret pool...I like the blue sky, and the reeds, and the birds, even that ghoulish reptile. I might even like *you* if you were a little more sociable.'

She flung herself on her back and stretched out her arms, staring bitterly upwards at the sun. The sun blazed down upon the wide open Fen. Emperor dragonflies hawked, flying backwards and forwards over the blue water. Frank stole a quick glance at her as she lay cruciform amidst the soft wild-mint and emerald burr-reeds. If only she knew the treachery of his heart, and duplicity of his desires! There was no hope for him. He would worship her for ever! And she would never know.

Olivia sat up with a start. 'There's a lot of activity going on up there.' She pointed upwards beyond the willow's topmost leaves at the azure sky where the white trails of high-flying aircraft streaked southwards.

'Fighters!' Frank leapt to his feet. 'Heck, a dozen of them.'

'Ours?'

'Can't tell. They are in 'finger-four' formation, same as the German 'schwarm'. Must be ours because we're out of the range of German fighters!'

Very faintly the thunder of their engines droned through the sunshine, resounding from the reed beds making the reed warblers burst into song.

He knelt beside her as they watched the trails drift into broad white ribbons. Olivia returned to lie in the dappled shade from the willow drowsily hovering between consciousness and sleep.

'It's so hard to believe that there is a war on,' she said softly. 'I wonder what's in the minds of those boys up there? They are all so young, and desperately brave.'

'I'd give anything to be up there with them,' Frank answered, a quickening upsurge of patriotism sweeping his despair away. 'Just imagine. Another whole year before I can leave school. Do you know, I read somewhere that the R.F.C. took boys of sixteen for pilot training during the last war!'

'And where are they now?' she replied with gentle irony.

He gazed at her blankly, unable to grasp the implication.

'They will be Squadron leaders and Wing Commanders,' he said brightly with youthful conviction.

She smiled wistfully, remembering the day that Dickie sailed with the B.E.F. to France. He had the same small-boy patriotism dancing in his eyes and bright dreams of idealised battle. She also had been caught up in the hysteria of the prelude to war, the parties and the unreal laughter, the tea-dances and dinner-dances, foxtrots, quicksteps, last-waltzes, Joe Loss playing 'We're going to hang out the washing on the Siegfried Line' and 'Roll out the barrel', and Dickie so utterly happy and confident with his men.

Olivia watched the cloudless sky through half-closed eyes. The sun was directly above the willow, whose outline dwarfed the crescent of alders bordering the pool. She became aware only of the droning of bees among the silvery-green leaves, and the hum of flies blending with the gentle cooing of wood-pigeons. The sunlight blinded her to form. The Secret Pool became a tapestry of kaleidoscopic colour. The cobalt of the sky-reflecting water, the yellow of water-lilies, the lilac of water-violets... Away in the dense bed of irises a water-vole noisily nibbled a reed stem. Her thoughts drifted away to Dickie.....

'Frank!... The float!'

Olivia was brought back from her reverie by the gyrations of the float which had suddenly lifted high in the water, to fall flat on the surface before gliding swiftly across the clear channel between the lily-pads.

'Crikey!'

Frank half-fell over the haversack as he stumbled to take up the rod.

'A tench!' he gasped. 'That's a tench bite!' He raised the rod tip in a firm strike. 'And he's hooked!'

Olivia watched the rod bend to the pull of the fish, and the tuppenny eel-line thrummed through the water, cutting the stems of submerged lilies which rose to float free on the surface. She stood up as the boy dragged the fish to the surface, where it struggled far out in the centre of the water-lily bed scattering spray and duckweed with its powerful, broad tail.

There was no finesse, no artistic playing of the fish on light tackle, but the simple brutality of heaving it to the surface on tackle designed to hold anything from a submerged log to a cunning eel.

With a final effort the fish bored down into the spongy depths of the weed-beds, forcing its way through clinging tendrils of water-crowfoot, but the heavy line and stout eel-hook offered no sporting contest, and the fish came sluggishly on its side as the boy dragged it towards the bank and heaved it out of the water.

'Bet it weighs four pounds,' Frank shouted, easing the primitive black hook from the fleshy lips of the fish with trembling fingers. Olivia knelt beside him looking down at the creature which lay gasping among the pungent stems of dark green watermint. She marvelled at its thick-bodied powerful shape. It was deep bronze-green with blue-tinged rounded fins, a bejewelled, un-fishlike creature, that appeared to be sheathed in shot-silk instead of scales.

'Isn't it beautiful?' she breathed as they knelt with the fish between them.

He was aware of the silken caress of her hair falling forward to brush his cheek, but his thoughts were with the fish. Everything took second place to the fish as his world flooded with sunshine, rippling in waves along the opalescent flanks of the fish.

'Must be four pounds!'

'It is so beautiful. But awfully slimy,' she murmured tenderly.

'They call it the "physician of fish",' he replied. 'It's supposed to heal other fish with its slime.'

The fish stared back at them through tiny blood-red eyes, malevolently, like a basilisk, cold and snake-like, reminding Olivia of the brass ornaments the Burmese made of lizards set with small ruby brilliants for eyes.

'Frankie...Let's put him back. He is far too exquisite to kill.'

'I always return them,' he replied at length, but dreamily as if loth to part with the fish. 'I can't kill anything without a reason, except eels and pike which we can eat.'

Olivia bent forward to draw her finger along the golden skin and gently massaged slime on to the jagged tear made by the hook in the fleshy lip of the fish. The crimson eyes rolled in their sockets and a tremor rippled along its side as she continued to rub the damaged palpi.

'Quickly! Before the poor thing dies in this heat.'

She watched as he lowered the tench into the shelving water of the pool, steadying it between the palms of his hands until it recovered its senses, its white lips opening and closing, whilst the rest of its form blended into the dim shadows of flannel-weed.

'Physician heal thyself,' she murmured gravely as the boy released the fish, allowing the dark shape to sink deeper and deeper into the depths, until only the lips remained in sight.

Frank gave her a transient glance as he turned away to bait the hook. The magnetism of her nearness filled him with a burning that was beyond the simple joy of the capture of the fish. It was the intermingling of imageries and scents. It was scent of sap rising, and all the time the opposing polarity of self-distrust, which made him draw self-consciously away from her.

Olivia returned once more to her seat below the willow feeling an inner restlessness. 'Wouldn't it be gorgeous to go for a swim?' she said. 'How far is it to the nearest seaside?'

'Oh, about forty miles, I suppose,' he answered as he cast his tackle out beyond the water-lilies. 'Hunstanton is where we used to go before the war.'

'It is so hot,' she said. 'It's like an oven, sheltered by these walls of reeds.'

She watched him as he removed his shirt, followed by a wool vest exposing an unsunned white body. How pitifully thin he appeared! The hollows above his collar-bones and between each rib sent waves of maternal tenderness surging through her.

'I think I'll take my blouse off too,' she teased.

Frank panicked.

'Mrs Vernon...You can't do that!'

'Why ever not? If you can take your shirt off, surely I can take my blouse off!'

'Ladies are different,' he replied huskily in a cracked falsetto voice.

'Fiddlesticks! Nymphs and Fauns always go naked in the sun.'

She laughed inwardly at his panic, thinking of his possessive, puritanical mother. Prudishness would destroy him.

'I am going to be a nymph in the sun,' she announced, pulling her blouse over her head and releasing a filmy lace brassière, allowing her breasts to fall free. 'Come, let's explore your Secret Pool.'

Frank moved away as the provocative wisp of white lace fell to the ground. Olivia bent to untie her plimsolls, falling silent as she contemplated him solemnly, full of merriment and innocence, until he yielded and reluctantly turned to face her.

'Someone may see you,' he blurted out, avoiding her laughing eyes.

'Don't be silly! You told me that this is a Secret Pool.' She caught his hand and led him towards the nearest of the tall reed-tunnels whose windings and turnings reached outwards into a maze of wild fen. 'Anyway, what does it matter if anyone should see me...I am a nymph now!'

His heart beat wildly at the swing of her breasts above the waist-band of her skirt as he followed her along the flattened reeds of the path. She led the way beneath a screen of alders to enter a secret citadel where sunlight streamed in narrow shafts of golden light casting a mosaic of sunspots on the tawny floor.

He felt a new sense of freedom as he followed her. The spontaneous exposure of her breasts banished all the erotic fantasies engendered by the nudes in *Men Only,* those dog-eared copies of titillating photographs taken against the light in shadowy silhouette, leaving detail to be heightened by the imagination in guilt-ridden urgency behind locked doors. All that had gone. It had passed away at the shedding of a cotton blouse.

With the absence of a breeze the sun's heat lay heavily like a blanket over the Fen. Pollen drifted slowly down from the reed-plumes to hang suspended in the turbid air. Within the heart of the reed-bed nothing moved. Great Red Sedgeflies slept clinging to the stiff reed-stems. Even the aggressive hordes of gnats remained hidden beneath the flaccid leaves waiting for the sun to set.

Another wave of aircraft droned overhead, dreamy and distant and of another world. Below them the great phalanx of reeds faced the sky with a multitude of spears and slept. Spasmodic bursts of machine-gun fire sounded faintly from the distance, the sound drifting between the reed-stems as innocently as the popping of wine-corks.

'There seems to be a great deal going on up there,' Olivia remarked, pausing to peer upwards to where the vapour-trails crossed and re-crossed the narrow ribbon of sky between the reed-tips.

'Yesterday's low cloud and drizzle must have kept them grounded. I suppose the Jerries will make the best of today's clear sky,' answered Frank off-handedly. 'Anyway the R.A.F. did jolly well on Monday by shooting down thirty-nine Jerries for the loss of only nine fighters. I bet those are 12 Group Hurricanes on patrol!' He parted a clump of saw-sedge clearing a way through a tangled thicket for Olivia to follow. She found herself at the edge of the pool beside the terrapin's log whose fossilised bark was emblazoned with brilliant green moss and speckled with the yellow and blue of tormentil and speedwell.

Olivia turned to look at the boy, who was engrossed in searching the reeds as he waded amongst them along the edge of the pool.

'Mrs Vernon. Come and look.'

She followed him, wading through tepid knee-deep water feeling a glutinous mass of liquid mud and algæ ooze sensuously between her toes. A sedge warbler ran up a nearby reed to perch singing above her head, almost deafening her with its sudden burst of trills and erratic chatterings.

'Frankie!' Her feet started to slide apart through the shelving mud. 'Frankie...I'm *falling!*' She made a desperate grab for his shoulder, almost overbalancing them both as her feet continued to slide apart on slippery waterweed until they found purchase against the stout roots of a clump of irises. 'What have you found?'

'Baby reed warblers.'

She leaned against him with her arm across his shoulder as he parted some reeds to reveal a small nest of woven sedges decorated with reed flowers which was suspended between three reed stems.

'Baby birds? Where?' she whispered, peering into the nest.

'Here.' Frank held his hand above the nest and instantly five orange mouths gaped wide.

'Oh, how lovely! What do they eat?'

'Caterpillars...insects...grubs...'

Olivia lifted a small green caterpillar which was hanging by a thread from an overhanging sallow twig and held it over the nest. Promptly the mouths gaped and the nestlings clamoured noisily until she dropped the caterpillar into an orange target.

'They are absolutely adorable. May I hold one?'

Frank took one from the nest and placed it in the palm of her hand, where it squatted naked, blind, and utterly repulsive in its translucent pink skin. 'This must be a second brood, they should be feathered and have left the nest by now,' he remarked.

'Ugh!' She made a grimace. 'It's so *ugly!*'

She had expected a bird, soft-feathered and with bright bird eyes.

'Ugh...Put it back.'

The creature gave a heave, and with a Herculean effort shot a slimy white capsule on to her wrist.

Frank moved his hand over the nestling and immediately its mouth gaped wide. 'This is the in-basket. You've got the out-tray,' he chuckled as he dropped another caterpillar in its mouth.

'At least I know what it thinks of me,' she said gravely, splashing her wrist in the water.

'Come and sit with me on the terrapin's log,' Olivia said quietly, as she turned to wade to the bank. She clambered precariously along the trunk to lie amongst the yellow tormentil on the soft moss. Frank followed, easing himself past her along the trunk to crouch half-hidden by sedge above the point where the log arched into the deepest part of the pool.

The sedge warbler returned to sing its ascending notes from within the green shade of the sedges, a hesitant prelude, then the sudden wild beauty of its trill followed by a finale of harsh scolding chatter.

Olivia rolled on to her stomach with her arms pillowing her face, watching the boy. He appeared so lonely and wretched. She yearned to hold him close and banish the tension that lurked within his thin frame. Then, restraining herself, she turned her face away to peer down into the steeply shelving water. Below her was an underwater garden in which the palest of translucent green febrils undulated gently a foot below the surface. Deeper, below dark green wavy-edged leaves of pondweed and purplish reefs of submerged grasses, a shoal of small fish drifted, spotlighted by sunbeams against the dappled floor of the pool.

Lazily she watched large black water-beetles with bright orange margins to their wing-cases swimming between the weeds. Water-boatmen rowed themselves in jerks up to the surface to dive away carrying a silver bubble of air which glinted in the sunlight. Whirligigs whirled erratically in gangs on the surface. Pond-skaters skimmed between lily-pads. Everywhere there was movement, from the transparent shrimps and daphnia to the darting sticklebacks.

Vaguely she heard, as if from a great distance, another wave of aircraft passing overhead. Lost in her dreamy state of half-awareness, Olivia felt she was balanced precariously between two worlds.

'Look...A pike!'

Olivia started at his sudden loud whisper.

'There,' he continued, pointing. 'Just below you.'

She turned her eyes to stare into the water, where the small fish were still lazily drifting in circles below the fallen branch.

'There is nothing there,' she said. 'Only a sunken branch.'

'No. A pike,' he insisted.

Olivia looked intently for the outline of a fish.

'There is nothing there.'

'Look at the branch,' he said stubbornly. 'See? There! Don't you see it? Among the lily-roots.'

She inched forward, catching him looking at her breasts as she bent further over the edge of the log. All at once she became aware of a gentle movement of fins feathering the water, and gradually the 'branch' took the shape of an immense fish hanging motionless in the water.

'I can see it! It's huge! Quick, get your rod and catch it!' Her eyes danced. 'Daphnis...Catch me this fish!'

Her hair fell heavily forward in wavy tendrils as she bent her face closer to the water, its sudden shadow causing the small fish to scatter like silver sequins caught in the sun's rays. The pike exploded in a swirl of displaced water, shooting like a rocket towards the centre of the pool, leaving broken underwater stems of water-lilies slowly rising to the surface in a mælstrom of displaced mud.

'It's gone.' She stared at the broken lily-stems, transfixed. 'Oh Daphnis...it's gone!'

'Who *was* Daphnis?' he asked

'Oh, he was a handsome herdsboy.'

Frank laughed as she stood up and moved away from the log towards a group of sallows. She dragged her bare feet lazily through the drifts of willow-herb, feeling the sensual rasp of brittle sedge on her legs. She glanced upwards through a tracery of leaves at the sun, then at her wristwatch. The boy was still squatting at the far end of the terrapin's log above his mirrored reflection in the pool. 'He is a faun,' she thought. 'But a very mortal faun,' she added with bitter yearning.

'Frankie...it is almost four o'clock. Ought we to be moving?' she called.

'If you like,' he answered flatly, without feeling.

'Let's stay a little longer,' she suggested gently, making room for him on the flattened grass beside her. 'Come and talk to me for a little while.'

He sat down awkwardly a little way from her side and nervously toyed with a reed stem while she watched him.

'Could you have caught the pike for me if I had not frightened it?' she asked to break the heavy silence.

'Not with a rod in this heat. It was basking. I could have snared it if I'd had a rabbit wire with me.'

'I suppose faun-shepherds are experts at ensnaring fish...and straying nymphs?'

He blushed. 'I've only read about nymphs. They're pure fantasy. You can't hold a fantasy!' he mumbled, looking away from her.

Olivia giggled, and lay back lost in thought as she wove her imagery around a nymph whose supple white throat was encircled by a golden snare, set by a handsome Arcadian shepherd.

Frank turned to gather a dozen green rushes and began to weave a tiny basket as he sat beside her. Four tiny aeroplanes passed overhead.

'More planes Frankie. What are they?'

He raised his eyes from his weaving and squinted upwards.

'Too high to be certain. Could be Hurricanes.'

He lowered his eyes and continued with his weaving to still the intangible ache to place his head on the softness of her skirt and to sleep in the cool shadow below the sallows for ever.

'What are you making?'

'A basket for færies.'

He rolled on to his stomach and held it out towards her.

'Færies!' she laughed a gay tinkling laugh. 'You *are* a romantic! Are there really færies around the Secret Pool?'

'Of course! If there are nymphs and fauns, surely there are naiads and dryads, elves and pixies...'

Olivia reached out to pluck some petals from willow-herb and meadow-sweet, tormentil and eyebright. 'There! A floral libation,' she said with a wistful laugh, dropping the petals one by one into the basket.

As she lay back she guided his head to lie in the curve of her hip and idly caressed his tousled auburn hair with her hand.

Another wave of aircraft droned overhead, suddenly appearing between the leaves, lower, twin-engined, and sinister.

'They are Germans,' she murmured drowsily.

'I'll be up there to fight them some day,' he answered, loth to raise his head from the haven of her thigh.

'Wouldn't you be awfully scared?'

'Not up there. I would be terrified of being bombed in a town, or shot at on the ground. But up there it's different.'

'Don't be ridiculous! In the air, on the ground, everywhere in war you face death. It is simply ridiculous to say "it's different".'

'But it *is* different. It's a fair contest of skill. Fear of death does not come into it.'

'That is sheer romanticism. I don't imagine the pilots who are shot down would feel the same. Some are terribly burned and mutilated. They don't all die. What about the German boy you would be trying to kill? Would he feel the same?'

'Of course he would feel the same if he was a fighter pilot.'

Olivia's fingers pensively stroking his hair relaxed him, so that he continued to talk softly, without shyness.

'We held a discussion about it last term at school and came to the conclusion that fighter pilots are the only honourable combatants in modern warfare. We decided that it is between equally-matched single combatants, each in a thoroughbred machine of equal performance. It is purely a contest of skill in which death is never a disgrace, but an honour, like medieval knights seeking mortal combat.'

She laughed and rumpled his hair. 'You're a strange boy. You don't worry about taking the life of a pike or an eel, but you are sentimental towards a tench...and you think it honourable to lose your life as a fighter pilot. Daphnis dear, you really are an incorrigible romantic!'

Frank continued to gaze upwards through the green canopy of leaves as she leaned back against the smooth trunk still holding his head in her lap. The whiteness of his young body was gradually reddening from the sun. 'In a few days he will become a beautiful golden-brown,' she thought.

'You are safe in the Fen, Daphnis,' she whispered dreamily, 'where there are no cliffs...and hopefully no Chimera!'

Olivia smiled at his puzzled expression.

'Daphnis met his end by falling off a cliff. I suppose you could say that falling from a Spitfire could amount to the same thing. Stay in the Fen, Frankie, where you will be safe.'

'And what about the Chimera?' he asked, opening his eyes for a moment to look into her face.

'Chimera? She was a cruel princess whom Daphnis became infatuated with. There really isn't much chance of you meeting a Chimera here!'

For a split second their eyes met and from the dreamy expression on his face she felt less sure.

One of the caterpillars landed on Olivia's arm and she watched it arching its way through the fine hairs while her mind day-dreamed. She awoke to the sound of an aircraft approaching and sat up.

Suddenly a single aeroplane roared across the centre of the pool, missing the willow's tip by inches. Pandemonium had arrived as wild duck exploded from the sedges. Waterhens scuttled across the open water trailing their feet in flurries of spray.. A multitude of warblers sprang to the reed-tops to sway with a deafening cacophony of chattering, until every reed seemed to hold a small brown bird hurling abuse at the invader.

Frank leapt from her enclosing arms.

'H.B....205 squadron!' he shouted excitedly. 'A Hurricane from Wittering!'

As the Hurricane flashed past the willow they could see great rents in the canvas behind the cockpit decking, where the sky showed between its wooden framework. One undercarriage leg hung down, and the rudder fabric streamed back in the slipstream.

'Will it make it?'

The knuckles of Olivia's hand were white as she gripped the boy's shoulder. 'Wittering? Isn't that beyond Peterborough?' she said anxiously, as they watched it crossing the flat eternity of black earth which stretched beyond the Old Fen.

'It's not all that far to Wittering,' Frank replied confidently. 'He's heading for March and Peterborough. He'll be home in about seven minutes.'

Olivia shivered, feeling suddenly chilled.

'Let's go back now,' she suggested, turning towards the track leading back through the reed-beds. As she turned a sullen thud sounded from the Bedford Middle Level, followed by a towering pall of black smoke on the horizon.

A stillness like a wraith was rising within her, causing her to glance hesitantly back towards the column of smoke. She opened her mouth to speak, but could find no words as she scrambled through the tangled bindweed and sedge before striding silently back along the reed tunnel to put on her blouse.

The boy followed lost in thought. The magic of Arcady had evaporated. It was 'Adlertag' - 'Eagle Day', the fifteenth of August 1940.

Thursday 15th October 1940
Rattin'

The Downham Market bus bringing Frank home from school rattled itself to a standstill beside the churchyard wall.

'Are you comin' rattin' bor?'

China, wearing an oversized coat tied round his middle with a rope of fraying binder-twine and a ragged shock of hair like bleached dyke-reeds protruding from his rabbit-skin cap, was leaning against the lych-gate holding a brindled lurcher on a yard of clothesline.

'It's goin' to be moonlight an' Chippy an' Podge an' *Ferret* are comin'.' China's voice went up a decibel as he said 'Ferret'.

Frank took the sagacious lurcher's head between his hands.

'Are you sure that Ferret will come?'

'She always come...Can't keep old Ferret from rattin',' China grinned knowingly, 'specially if it's moonlight!'

Frank gazed into the lurcher's yellow-flecked eyes as his heart missed a beat. 'Alright...About half-past seven,' he replied offhandedly. 'The moon will have risen by then.'

Sauntering into the living room he flung his school satchel on the floor and proceeded to carry out his usual chores of trimming the oil-lamp wicks before fetching a couple of pails of water from the well. His mother was in the dimly-lit scullery peeling potatoes by the light from a candle stuck in the neck of an empty H.P. sauce bottle.

'How long before tea?' he called brightly. 'I want to go ratting with the boys at seven-thirty.'

'Oh, in about an hour,' she replied in an dull voice. 'In the meantime you had better take a bucket of coal up to Mrs Vernon's room. And make sure you check her blackout at the edges. You know how lackadaisical she is about putting it up. She will be getting us bombed, or fined!'

The words drifted depressingly around Frank as he climbed the stairs carrying a heavy coal scuttle. 'Good job too!' he murmured rebelliously.

Olivia was seated at the round table writing a letter. She always seemed to be writing, since Captain Vernon had left. Frank wondered what on earth she found to write about, sitting alone in her room all day with her poetry books and hardly ever leaving the house while he was at school, except to walk across the Square to the post office.

She smiled at him, and laid her pen on the red velvet tablecloth as he began to make up the fire in the small grate.

'How was school today?'

'Alright.'

He turned on his heels to face her as he crouched before the fire. 'That wick needs trimming,' he observed, as the fire began to blaze.

'It's not very good, is it?' she agreed.

Frank turned the lamp out allowing the bright firelight to flicker across the ceiling. He carefully removed the glass chimney from the lamp and laid it on her bed while he trimmed the double wick. The room was aglow with firelight and enchantment, scented with expensive perfume and sandlewood. A satin petticoat, flung carelessly over a chair, shimmered in the dancing light. It was a world completely alien to Willows End.

Olivia lifted her head and looked thoughtfully across the table. 'Thank you, Frankie.'

He finished polishing the lamp-glass with a rolled-up wad from the *Eastern Daily Press* and relit the lamp, which burned brightly, bringing the room back to normality. He could not bring himself to look into her calm blue eyes, and felt the blood rushing to his face at the nearness of the satin petticoat.

She laughed, then removed the petticoat, folding it carefully, smoothing its filligree lace border pensively before laying it on the pillow of her bed.

'Come and sit down and talk to me for a little while.' She leant over him as he knelt before the grate. 'I suppose school was pretty horrid...Or did you have French with Mam'selle?'

Frank sat on the edge of her bed avoiding the petticoat, aware only of her face reflecting the golden light, and her eyes dark and moist in shadow.

'I'm going ratting tonight!' he blurted out, in a cracked reedy voice. 'With China, Chippy, Podge, and Ferret!'

'The pretty girl on the massive horse? But surely, it will be dark outside. What is "ratting"?'

He avoided meeting her eyes, but felt more on his home ground.

'We go out to the corn stacks and hit the rats with sticks as they move through their runs. It's jolly good fun. Then we hang the dead rats on a fence for the farmer to see. And for every rat we get a "nick", which is a mark cut on your ratting-stick. Ferret's the champion!'

'Pretty *horrid* fun, I would say,' she murmured. 'You say the pretty girl is the champion? Isn't there anything better to do in the evening than killing rats?'

'Crikey, yes!' he said enthusiastically. 'We go rabbiting, rooking, sparrow-netting, snaring, shooting pigeons roosting in the moonlight and play billiards in the hut!' Frank had diplomatically substituted 'pigeons' for 'pheasants'.

'Gawd 'elp us!' Olivia teased, bouncing on the bed. 'Whatever have I missed!'

'Olivia.' He whispered lest his mother should hear. 'I could take you ratting sometime.' Then, looking at her high-heeled strappy sandals, added, 'Course, you would have to borrow Madge's wellies as the rats are liable to bite your legs as they drop!'

'No thanks!'

Frank went crimson.

'But I will come to the 'Wings for Victory Dance' with you on Friday evening,' she said with a devil-may-care grin.

He stared at her transfixed. 'But I can't dance,' he groaned.

'Well, old boy...I shall just have to teach you. It is frightfully important for a young man to be able to dance.'

He held his breath in a thrill of dread mingled with excitement.

'You will? Honest?'

'Of course...I shall dress up especially for you!'

Ferret and the three boys were waiting at half past seven beside the churchyard wall as Frank left the house with his 'rattin' stick'. The hunter's moon was just rising above the Wesleyan chapel willows, casting long black shadows from the yews, its saffron orb reflected in the placid water of the pond.

'Got your rattin' stick, bor?' asked Podge as they formed a shadowy huddle against the War Memorial to examine each other's weapons.

'Ar...It'll do,' admitted Chippy grudgingly.

Frank was proud of his stick. It was five feet long, of seasoned ash, polished with linseed oil and tipped with two inches of lead pipe.

'Ain't got no nicks on it,' China jeered. 'Not much of a stick without nicks!'

'Idiot!' said Frank, snatching the stick from his grasp. 'It's my new one.'

'Better christen it then, bor,' suggested Ferret, wiping her nose on the sleeve of her tattered jumper and leading the way towards the carr stackyard.

Wood-owls called urgently to each other from the shadowy alders bordering the ancient osier carr where the corn stacks stood away from the greeny-blue night sky, silvered with moonlight, and rustling with rats. Half-way across the field a roosting covey of partridges whirred up from the stubble setting the peewits calling.

'Noisy old buggers! They'll frit the rats,' grumbled Chippy.

'Don't you be daft bor...They don't make half as much of a racket as you lot together!' snapped Ferret scornfully. 'I'm goin' to have that farthest stack to myself. You're all too bloomin' noisy.'

She glided away, silently.

'Chippy and me'll take the nearest stack. An' you and Podge can have the middle one,' decided China like a general commanding an army as they moved forward to the attack.

Frank waited mid-way along his side of the stack alert to a strange restive silence in which the faintest movement of a loose straw in the light breeze became magnified beyond recognition. Nothing stirred. He felt that he was being watched by an invisible army of eyes as he stood motionless, a yard back from the stack, with his stick held poised above his left shoulder. Suddenly, as if by some hidden command, the whole stack became alive with movement. Rats began to scamper joyously along their runways to test the night air for scents, appearing and disappearing along the edges of the stack in tiers, splashed by moonlight, like faces at portholes.

Fast and furious the sticks began hitting the stack sides. Thwack...Thwack...Thwack. Rats began falling like rain from the stacks, dislodged by the weighted sticks striking above the boys' heads. 'Bugger...Bugger...Bugger...Bugger,' chanted China, skipping and leaping like a dervish possessed as rats fell about his wellies. 'Got one! Got...Got one!' yelled Chippy. 'Got one! Thwack...Thwack...Bugger...Bloody 'ell...Got one!' echoed Podge. 'There's one in my boot!' shrieked China.

The tempo slowed, then stopped, as the rats retreated back to their innermost citadels. Podge appeared from behind the stack carrying three rats by their tails, to be joined by Chippy carrying two. China shortly materialised from the shadows carrying five, followed by Frank carrying one.

Warm and breathless they collapsed on a pile of loose straw and leant against the leeside of a stack. Ferret's stack was silent, apart from one or two desultory thwacks.

'What's that bloody mawther a-doing?' muttered China, rising to his feet so that he could see her stack.

'Dare you to go an' find out,' challenged Chippy.

'She'll think he's a rat and thack him with her stick!' giggled Podge, rolling over and over in the straw at his own wit.

'Go you and look,' began Chippy to Frank.

But Ferret was walking towards them trailing her stick.

'Have you lot together ever been to Wisbech Mart?' she asked sweetly, wiping her nose on her sleeve.

China sat down next to Podge. 'Course we have...Why?'

'Well...You buggers sound like the bloody Helter-Skelter, Dodgems, Caterpillar, an' Fat Lady Show all in one. How many have you got together?'

'Three,' said Chippy. 'Well, two, and a mouse.'

'Five,' grunted China, bending forward and swinging them by their tails in her face.

'Three,' said Podge.

'One,' Frank mumbled, apologetically.

'Oh...Your stick is a christened then bor,' Ferret replied, sitting herself down on the straw and leaning back with her stick across her knees. 'What did you want to hit that poor little mouse for, Chippy? Poor little old thing!'

'I never heared much of you anyhow, Ferret,' replied China defensively. 'Did you get any?'

Ferret slowly untied the binder-twine which was holding her mackintosh together, and hitched up her skirt exposing to the moonlight two bare knees above her Wellington boots.

'I might have done...Then again I might not,' she hinted with a demure lowering of her eyes. 'Anyways I didn't go a thrashin' and a shoutin' fritin' everythin' like you lot.'

China leant forward. 'What's that there you're wearin', Ferret...a sack?' He flicked the hem of her skirt with his stick. ' 'Cause if it's a sack old Boer will have it off you mighty quick fer a nosebag fer Samson!'

Ferret did not respond and China glanced at the three boys for moral support.

'Ferret...I got a little old rabbit wot wants a hole to go in!' he continued in a quavering, reedy voice.

'Have you really got a little old rabbit what wants a hole?' giggled Podge.

'Have you got a nice little hole fer China's rabbit?' reiterated Chippy coaxingly to Ferret.

The four boys stared at Ferret with bated breath, trembling with suspense in nervous anticipation as they awaited her answer.

Ferret gave a large sigh before taking off her mackintosh, hitching up her skirt, and leading the way into the warm, moonless space between the stacks.

'There!' she exclaimed triumphantly as they emerged from the shadows into a circle of brilliant moonlight. 'If any of you can beat me at rattin' then I'll show you a beautiful hole for your rabbit!' And she bent over a pile of very dead rats and methodically began to tie their tails to her binder-twine belt.

The boys counted up to eleven corpses before retracing their steps between the corn stacks in silence. Ferret picked up her old mac, gave another hitch to her skirt which set the dead rats swaying in a moonlit *danse macabre,* and strode off towards the village alone.

As Ferret disappeared into the night she began to sing. Her words drifted loud and clear above the witchery of owl cries across the stubbles.

'Ten fer a look... Twenty for a feel.

Tharty fer a ride on the bumpy wheel... Tra-la-la-la... Comin' rattin' tomorrow night together?'

'Not with her,' mumbled China. 'Silly old tease!'

Frank found Ferret sitting on the pond railings swinging her legs, waiting for her father to emerge from The Ship. 'Ferret,' he asked, 'how is it that you always beat us hollow at rattin'?'

'I ain't tellin' you!'

'Oh, come on, Ferret. Be a sport and tell me. I'll keep it a secret.'

'Have you got a cat?'

'Cat! What's a cat to do with it?'

She was silhouetted against a perfect reflection of the moon in the dark waters of the pond, appearing like Artemis with her hunting spear, the moonlight glinting on her hair while her face remained lost in shadow.

'Well, you watch your cat, bor. She'll larn you! She stands quiet, watchin' till a mouse gits near her... Then she pounces once... You got to be like an old cat bor. Not like them other silly buggers a thrashin' an' shoutin'.'

'Thanks, Ferret,' Frank said softly, 'I like you a lot!'

'Ar. I like you bor,' she replied with equal softness.

She took a heavy ex-army knife from her mackintosh pocket and proceeded to cut thirteen fresh nicks on her ratting stick.

'Good night bor. Do you keep what I larned you to yourself. Then you can beat all them other silly buggers! And you might even beat me some day!'

Frank could not sleep. He lay restlessly watching the high clouds drift like sheep across the face of the moon from his bedroom window, haunted by Ferret's pale knees above her Wellington boots, forming images of her wearing her flapping old mackintosh, standing like a scarecrow silhouetted against the hunter's moon, her hair a tangled mass of black curls, her 'rattin' stick' pointing towards Orion. In fantasy he showed her his pile of dead rats, comparing them to her smaller pile, imagined her astonishment and capitulation, then the thrill of leading her by the hand into the fecund darkness between the stacks where the sack skirt, magically not a sack, but the silky satin petticoat hanging on a chair back in the front bedroom, floated like thistledown towards the straw.

Friday 18th October 1940
'Wings for Victory Dance'

Frank leant against the corner of the chiffonier listening for the first sound of footsteps on the stairs. His mother was sitting bolt upright in her Windsor chair reading a historical novel beside the fire with her lips pursed in puritanical silence.

At last he heard the loose third step down from the landing creak, and a few seconds later Olivia entered the sitting room wearing a long-sleeved white chiffon blouse over a floral dirndl skirt and trailing expensive perfume. She appeared pure Hollywood, a close-up from the Ziegfield Follies, or Deanna Durbin in 'Spring Parade'!

Frank blushed crimson. Overcome by this beautiful vision he longed to run and hide. He trembled. For the first time in his life he felt the exquisite surge of love that floods the heart with pain.

'Hello, Frankie!' The vision did a skirt-swirling pirouette in front of him, almost causing a catastrophe to his mother's Dresden candelabra on the centre of the chiffonier.

'How do I look, Mrs Dutton?'

Mrs Dutton scarcely raised her eyes from her novel, but her grimace of displeasure conveyed the message that this young married woman had committed some impropriety under her roof.

'Oh, Mrs Dutton! You don't look terribly enthusiastic,' she said, with a laugh.

Mrs Dutton inspected her coldly.

'I have not been brought up to indulge in dances.'

She rose from her chair and pointedly removed her Dresden candelabra to the sanctuary of the mantelpiece.

Olivia did another pirouette.

'*Mrs Dutton!* Don't be so serious. Why not come with us? I'm sure you would enjoy yourself.' She spoke scoldingly, while looking at herself in the mirror.

Warm from the heat of the coal fire and the paraffin lamp, the room took on the heady essence of Olivia's perfume. It drifted head-high into the dark shadows beyond the glow of the lamp. Her gaiety was infectious, and Frank's earlier anguish of self-consciousness left him like mist from the river at the coming of the sun.

'Why, Frankie. You look positively dashing!' she exclaimed with a laugh. Then she frowned. 'My goodness! This won't do at all!'

Olivia was pouting as if she had suddenly become disenchanted with him. Frantically his thoughts back-tracked to where he had failed in his efforts to impress her. His best school flannels with their twenty-two-inch bottoms had been pressed to knife-edge creases beneath his mattress. Ma Shipham had carefully laundered his shirt and starched its collar. The boil on the back of his neck had burst, and his freckles were far less obvious in lamplight. He had painfully plucked his heavy eyebrows with a pair of pliers where they almost met above his nose (a sure sign of bad temper according to Joy Rowsell) and so he came to the agonising conclusion that his breath must smell, and stopped breathing out.

Olivia giggled and kicked off her high-heeled sandals descending with a bump to Frank's height in her stockinged feet.

'This is far better, isn't it? I shall have to change my shoes.'

Frank breathed out with an audible sigh of relief.

Mrs Dutton continued to read in hostile silence until Olivia returned, having changed her high heels for a pair of silver pumps, with a matching wide belt around her waist.

'Are you sure you wouldn't like to come with us?' she asked, taking her small evening bag from the chiffonnier.

Mrs Dutton drew herself with dignity from her chair and eyed them with a kind of pathetic forbearance.

'I shall wait up until you come home,' she replied. 'At least it is Friday so I shall not have to go out to teach tomorrow!'

Outside the porch door the wisteria twigs formed a filigree frame to the moon as it rose above a low bank of silver-washed clouds. Searchlights swung aimlessly around the sky above the Middle Level, and from the deep shadows beneath a clump of willows a cacophony of shrieks and laughter and stamping of feet on bare boards to desultory snatches of brassy music guided them towards the Village Hall.

An R.A.F. Utility truck parked outside the Village Hall, illuminated by the moon, showed the way to a heavily-curtained doorway, beyond which the Vicar's sister was standing holding out her hand for their two shillings.

Frank fumbled with the inner blackout curtain, holding it aside for Olivia to pass into the interior of a large 1914 ex-army hut lit by a galaxy of naked electric light bulbs, beneath which groups of young children were charging in mad confusion. At the far end of the Hall, on a makeshift stage, the visiting Royal Air Force bandsmen were trying to tune their instruments, while a blonde W.A.A.F. leant nonchalantly against the school piano, talking earnestly to a Brylcreemed young airman.

'My goodness, Frankie! Is *this* the dance?' Olivia whispered as they attempted to cross the floor through a colliding mass of tiny children which appeared to be made up from the entire Infant School. Little boys with flushed faces chased little girls in and out, shouting and stamping until the floor bounced. Bevies of toddlers competed by screaming as the bigger girls, their skinny legs flashing under fluttering skirts and their hair flying behind as they ran, bowled them over.

'My goodness, Frankie!' Olivia reiterated, as they reached the far side of the floor to join a group of mothers and elder daughters who were sitting gossiping on a row of wooden chairs. 'I feel we are slightly over-dressed!'

The gossiping ceased as the ladies turned to stare at Olivia as she sank thankfully into a bentwood chair. Ma Shipham, who happened to be standing guard in front of the curtained doorway to the Women's Institute refreshment tables, waved cheerily to Frank, and the ladies returned to their chatter.

Olivia was about to say something to Frank when the darting shoal of Infant School sticklebacks was split asunder as China, with Podge and Chippy in his wake, came skidding across the floor to slide to a standstill on hob-nailed boots beside her chair.

'Good old evenin' ain't it bor?' China was heavily flushed and bursting with *joie de vivre.*

'This is China, Mrs Vernon. And Chippy, and Podge.'

Frank introduced them hesitantly, fearful of revelations of his past.

'Hello, China...Chippy...Podge. I hear you are all champion ratters.'

'Ferret's the champion,' answered Podge.

'How do you like livin' in these parts, Miss?' said China very seriously.

'I think it very peaceful,' she replied, conscious of a new lull in the rhythm of the ladies' gossip.

'Ar that's right, Miss. Lots of things to do round these 'ere parts...How'd you like to come rattin'?' offered Chippy.

Olivia laughed. 'I have already been asked. But somehow I don't think I would enjoy ratting. Horrid creatures rats!'

'That's right,' Podge agreed. 'No money in rats. Babbin's better. You get paid for babbin' from old Gizzie the fish-hawker.'

'Babbing!' She raised an eyebrow. 'What on earth is "babbing"?'

China, Chippy, and Podge collected a chair each from the orderly row which had been neatly arranged around the room and formed a half-circle around her.

'You get a flashlamp and go out an' get a tin of worms,' said Podge.

'Big old worms,' Chippy broke in.

'Huge old worms,' said China.

'You see them crawled out on the grass with their tails in their holes,' continued Podge.

'An' you have to be very quick and 'ang on to their heads until they let go with their tails,' said China.

'No good you pulling 'cause their heads will break off in your hand,' added Chippy. 'Without a word of a lie, them there old worms is as obstinate as my old Granna!'

'I'm sure I wouldn't like worms any better than rats!' exclaimed Olivia with a shudder.

'Ar now. Just you a-listen, Miss,' said Podge. 'You can make a lot of money with babbin'. But you only get a nick on your stick rattin'.

'I'm listening,' she replied.

'Well now...You put them old worms in a bag of moss and sand to harden them. Then the next night you have to get a ball of wool from an old jumper and you sit and thread them old worms through their middle till you have a line of worms. Then you roll the wool back into a ball like a cricket ball with all them worms a-danglin' and a-squirmin'!'

'Tha's what you call a "bab",' explained China.

'I'm larnin' her. Not you,' growled Podge.

'When it go dark you go and sit on the middle of a plank over a drain an' dangle your bab in the water.'

'Don't forget the bucket, Podge,' murmured Chippy, as he sat holding his chin between his hands studiously gazing up into Olivia's face in rapt appreciation.

'Ar that's right, Miss. You have to have a bucket next to you. And when yew feel the eels a-nigglin' you have to lift your bab out of the water slowly with them old eels a-hangin' on to the worms and swing them over the bucket. Then you give the string a shake an' they fall in the bucket!'

China jumped excitedly from his chair.

'Moonlight tomorrow night. Do you want to come babbin' Miss? Old Daggy'll set us up with a bag of worms!'

Olivia smiled very sweetly at the three faces eagerly awaiting her reply.

'I honestly don't think I would make a good "babber". I'm not used to being out in desolate dark places. I would be frightened. Very frightened!'

'Nothin' to be frit about. We ain't frit!'

The twinkling stars faded from China's eyes.

'I'm frit of Willow Farm's old bull when I can't see it,' admitted Chippy.

'Ar, and I'm frit of that old headless monk. I see'd him once down the Lode, that I did, without a word of a lie!' said Podge. 'And I'm frit of that great old dog, Shuck!' His blue eyes widened. 'I dursen't go down the Fen o' nights without my mole's foot!'

'What about takin' Miss hinglin'? Then she won't have to go out in the dark,' suggested Chippy, after scratching his head thoughtfully.

China glared at him, giving him a furtive kick.

'Mustn't mention that...Hinglin's agin the law nowadays.'

Olivia chuckled at China's shocked expression.

'Now that *really* sounds exciting! Do tell me. What is "hingling"?'

But the boys had scattered like a shoal of startled roach through the integrated mass of Infant School sticklebacks, hiding their tracks.

Olivia frowned. 'This is the most bizarre dance I have ever seen. Does one ever actually dance? Anyway, Frankie, what does "hingling" entail? Why should it be illegal?'

'You'd absolutely hate it,' he replied, with an involuntary shudder. 'Father abhorred it! Thousands of small birds used to be caught on twigs smeared with bird-lime for sale in pet shops. Linnets and goldfinches were the most sought-after, and larks were snared or netted to provide Londoners with lark tongues. It still goes on, but one of the best things about the war is that it has lessened demand.'

Before Olivia could reply the band came to life with a resounding burst of swinging rhythm as the R.A.F. 'Seven Gremlins Swing Band' opened up with a thunderous rendering of 'It's a Hap, Hap, Happy Day.'

Protesting clumps of infants were rapidly dragged by their elder sisters to sit cross-legged on the floor beside the row of chairs, with dire threats of grievous bodily harm should they move. The suave Brylcreemed airman and the blonde W.A.A.F. took to the floor, gliding with practised ease into the fast rhythm. The bit-bigger-girls whooped and screamed, holding hands and cavorting excitedly around the floor, colliding unceremoniously with their elder sisters who were dancing together. The Postmaster strode self-consciously across the floor to drag the blushing Postmaster's wife hesitantly into the fray as the Vicar climbed on to the stage, to gaze down into the mêlée with puckish delight.

'Come, come! We must not be wallflowers!' he exclaimed, clapping his hands to the young wives who were sitting in a silent row looking down at their feet, or casting surreptitious glances towards the three off-duty privates who had arrived from the Lode searchlight battery. But his words went winnowing away like chaff in the wind, unheard above the beat of the traps.

Olivia leapt to her feet. 'Come on Frankie...I'll teach you the quickstep.'

Frank's heart sank. This was the dreaded moment of truth, and the palms of his hands started to sweat.

'It's easy.' She dragged him from the bentwood chair. 'You hold my right hand in your left...so. And slip your right arm round my waist.' He felt her other arm fall softly upon his shoulder.

'Now Frankie. You lead. Glide forward with your right foot...follow with your left foot. Now the chassé. Side, close, side. Slow, quick-quick, slow. Slow, quick-quick, slow...'

At last the music stopped, leaving Frank bathed in perspiration and disorientated.

'Mrs Vernon. I'm hopeless. I'll never learn to dance!'

Olivia pretended to limp painfully back towards their chairs suffering from crushed toes.

'Oh, I wouldn't say hopeless. You just appear to have a slight anatomical fault. Somehow you seem to have been born with two left feet! Just remember that when your foot is sliding forwards, mine is supposed to be sliding backwards!'

Frank writhed within himself, and his face turned beetroot as he noticed Madge Shipham grinning at him. The band began to play and the airman and the W.A.A.F. returned to the stage.

'This is a foxtrot,' Olivia confided. 'Let's sit this one out!' and she pulled a face and giggled while rubbing her ankle.

The Group settled into a regular swinging beat as they played 'Scatterbrain'. The W.A.A.F. began to sing, with the Brylcreemed airman joining her as a virtuoso saxophonist. The traps beat a compulsive rhythmic backing for the jazz guitar and the pair of trombonists. Frank's spirits soared to dizzy heights. This was living Hollywood! Broadway! It was Glenn Miller, Joe Loss, Harry Roy, celluloid in the flesh with Vera Lynn and Ann Shelton thrown in. He made up his mind. He *would* learn to dance.

The tempo slowed, changing into a softer, gliding movement like the slow dreamy flow of the Fenland rivers below sultry willows, and the airman began to croon 'Somewhere In France With You' into the microphone.

Olivia placed her handbag on her chair seat.

'This will be easier for you. It's a waltz.'

Frank, his heart beating fast, led the way on to the floor and held her with growing confidence.

'Now this is three beats to the bar. Forward right foot, left foot to the side. Right foot to the side of left foot...one...two...together. Rise on the balls of your feet, toes, one, two...together. Fine! Now the turn. Follow me...'

He lost all count of what his feet were doing and stumbled.

'Mrs Vernon...Let's sit down...I'm completely hopeless.'

'No. Keep going. You're doing fine.'

'I'll never learn.'

'Of course you will,' she said warmly.

'It's a thousand times worse than learning to skate!' he panted.

'Well, I have been told that you are a very good skater,' she said. 'The Vicar told me! He said that he watched you teach yourself by pushing a chair in front of you round and round the pond! So just pretend that I'm a chair and you will learn to dance!'

'You are nothing like a chair,' he replied gravely.

She grinned. 'Are you sure?' She glanced at her silver pumps which looked decidedly crushed. 'Anyway, Frankie, why have you suddenly started calling me "Mrs Vernon"? What's happened to "Olivia"?'

'Someone would be sure to tell Ma, and she would be awfully cross if she knew that I call you "Olivia".'

'And I might be awfully cross if you don't,' she replied, teasing. 'But, really, you must not allow her disillusionment to influence your outlook as you grow older. Always remember that life is for *living*. There is no time or place in it for embittered, puritanical nonsense.'

With the band now silent, the Vicar took the centre of the stage and raised both his arms for silence, waiting with a large gold hunter watch in his hand for the last child to skid to a standstill.

'Now,' he boomed in his best 'Sunday Sermon' voice. 'The time has come the Walrus said' - his eyes twinkled. 'The time has come for you patient wives and neglected sweethearts to cut across to The Ship and drive those menfolk of yours, who have been imbibing Dutch courage since opening-time, back here so that festivities may begin!'

Again he flung up both his arms for silence.

'A loaf of bread, the Walrus said, Is what we chiefly need.' He beamed at the Infants, the bit-bigger-girls, and the big-girls.

'Off you go to the Back Room for pop and cakes. Then off the floor, and on your chairs, for the rest of the evening!'

Stout and thin, tall and short, young and not so young, the motley bunch of Fenland womanhood advanced down the moonlit street towards the Ship Inn, reappearing five minutes later like Valkyrian maidens driving a 'high-spirited' band of singing men before them.

The Village Hall was suddenly filled to capacity. The band burst into life with the blonde W.A.A.F. and her soloist tenor-sax singing 'Somewhere Over The Rainbow'. The wooden floorboards reverberated and bounced to a thunder that could be heard from one end of Willows End to the other.

Harnser Flegg advanced towards Olivia grinning from ear to ear in a face as ruddy as a fifth of November mangel wurzel lit by a candle, although Harnser's inner-light was 'Special Occasion' brown ale laced with malt whisky.

'Evenin' bor...Wunnerful night!' He bowed like his heron name-sake towards Olivia. 'Will you trot round the floor with me, Ma'am?'

'You must introduce us, Frankie,' she said demurely.

'This is Mr Harnser Flegg, Mrs Vernon.'

'How do you do,' she smiled.

'Right well, Ma'am.'

The band switched into a rollicking rendering of 'Wish Me Luck As You Wave Me Goodbye' and Olivia was whirled away. Frank tried hard to watch Harnser's feet, hoping to learn something. But Harnser's feet were not doing anything like the 'quick-quick, slow' of Olivia's teaching. Harnser's dance pattern was more that of a frisky young carthorse let out to grass on a Sunday!

Madge appeared at Frank's side, looking very pretty in a green taffeta dress with her chestnut hair held in a pony tail by a black velvet bow.

'I never knew you could dance,' she said shyly.

'I can't,' he replied. 'But Mrs Vernon is trying to teach me.'

They sat side by side watching the now lively crowd stamping round with abandonment in a whirl of colour and cacophony of music.

'Oh, come you on. Let's have a go,' urged Madge, excitedly tugging his arm.

'I can't. Mrs Vernon says I've got two left feet!'

'Don't be frit. We can do what they're doing!'

She dragged him towards the dance floor where they joined the whirling mass of flying skirts and perspiring faces and soon they were spinning and colliding with the best of them. Olivia made a droll face at Frank as she spun around in the arms of old Daggy, who, in honour of this auspicious occasion, was wearing a maroon-coloured velvet smoking jacket, bequeathed to him by a visiting Cambridge don for services rendered among the secret bream swims. Madge blushed as Olivia passed.

'Mum says your Mrs Vernon is a real lady on account of...'

She stopped abruptly in mid-sentence. 'Whoops!' laughed the Vicar as he adroitly saved the Headmaster's wife from imminent collision.

'...on account of the washing she do for 'er. 'Quality' is never stuck-up. Tha's what Mum always say. Not like that jumped-up lot at the Manor!'

The tempo of the band slowed as the W.A.A.F. took the microphone stand in her hand and began to sing 'Only For Ever' and the couples drifted dreamily into a slow foxtrot.

'Don't she sing nice!' Madge sighed, as they returned to their seats.

'Do I want to be with you...As the days come and go...Only for ever if you care to know...' crooned the blonde.

'Don't you think she's just like Ann Shelton?' Frank breathed, gazing at the W.A.A.F. spellbound.

'Her hair's a different colour and she's skinnier!' replied Madge with down-to-earth factuality.

Her song ended, the W.A.A.F. handed the microphone to the Vicar, who once again held out his arms for silence, and again he had to defer his announcement until the last of the big-girls had made a dash across the floor to join her mates.

'We shall now entertain you with our local talent, while the orchestra takes a well-earned rest with a cup of tea and excellent home-made fare provided by the ladies of the Women's Institute.'

The 'orchestra' clambered stiffly across the planks of the stage to resounding claps and demure glances from the young women as they headed towards the lean-to where motherly matrons were waiting all a-tremble with importance. The children, meanwhile, were being herded by the young infant teacher to sit cross-legged on the floor in a half-circle in front of the stage, while the men sat on the chairs with their giggling partners on their laps. Anyone without either a chair or a lap sat on the floor. Just inside the doorway in front of the blackout curtain stood P.C. Fox, the A.R.P. warden, and the two Home Guards who had been detailed to guard the perimeter of Willows End for the night.

Harnser, who appeared to have deserted his wife, took over Olivia's chair mopping his perspiring brow with an enormous handkerchief.

'Come you on Ma'am. Do you come an' sit on my knee.'

Olivia laughed, and looked askance towards Frank.

'No good a-lookin' at him. Why, bless my soul, Ma'am, his little old knees wouldn't perch a sparrow!'

Harnser slapped his knees and grinned up at her.

'Do you know what my Rosie say? She say "When you wear them trousers, Harnser Flegg, you can charm the birds off the trees".'

Harnser glanced proudly at his legs. He was wearing his specially-tailored Sunday cords which had flared bottoms with a gusset of navy-blue velvet decorated with brass buttons tapering up on the outside of each leg as far as the knee.

'And do you know what I say to her? I say "A lot of thinkin' is wholly bad for you gal. It only makes your head ache!" That's what I say to her.'

He pulled Olivia down to sit on his lap laughing infectiously and as merry as a cricket, leaving Frank to sink to the floor with the boys and bit-bigger girls.

Harnser cast his eyes around the hall before bending forwards to speak to Frank, balancing Olivia on his lap with a protective arm round her waist and his hand on her knee as she began to slide forward.

'That's a rummun and no mistake bor. Look at them there lot standin' by the door. A.R.P. warden's supposed to be keepin' his eyes open for lights and a-listenin' for Downham siren. Old Foxie should be a-bed out of the way. An' them two silly buggers with tin hats on ought to be out down the Lode guarding the village an' lookin' out for Jarman parachutists! You tell me bor. What do you think would happen if them Jarman parachutists landed while we sit here enjoying ourselves? Rum old how-do-ye-do that would be. Wouldn't it now?'

Before Frank could think up an adequate answer a sudden crackle of static as the Vicar moved the microphone switched all thoughts towards the stage and the sight of R.S.M. Kingshott marching stiffly towards its centre.

'Gawd! Whatever's King Kong a-doin' of now?' gasped Harnser.

'Ladies and Gentlemen and Tiddlers,' announced the Vicar jovially. 'Sergeant Major Kingshott will open our short entertainment with a heroic soliloquy..."Mandalay".'

The background buzz of magpie chatter and giggles drifting from the girls curled in the laps of their lovers and the shrill bickering of infants, suddenly faded as Mr Kingshott, the crescent horns of his waxed moustache bristling against his pink cheeks, glared at the audience.

'By the old Moulmein Pagoda, lookin' lazy at the sea,
There's a Burma girl a-sittin', and I know she thinks of me;
For the wind is in the palm trees, and the temple bells they say;
Come back you British soldier; come you back to Mandalay.'

Five verses later he came to a thunderous finale. His voice which had crept up octave by octave, now fairly rebounded from ceiling to floor in a full-throated crescendo to give way suddenly to absolute silence.

Not a sound was uttered or a child moved until the Headmaster started to clap, and R.S.M. Kingshott saluted and marched briskly off the stage carrying an imaginary swagger-stick beneath his arm.

'And now,' said the Vicar reappearing from the opposite side of the stage, 'we have one of our young visitors evacuated from Stepney in the City of London, who will sing and tap-dance for us. Miss Linda Perks!'

Linda, who was billeted with old Granny Fallow, bounced on to the stage carrying a brass bird-cage with a cardboard canary wobbling on its perch. She was wearing one of Granny Fallow's 'Floradora' hats adorned with ostrich feathers, and a shawl over a long black silk skirt, from beneath which her matchstick-thin legs and tap-shoes appeared, while her pinched white cheeks were coloured by two large blobs of lipstick.

She peered at the audience over the top of a pair of gold pince-nez, from which both lenses were missing.

' 'Ow do,' she said with all the confidence and cheek of a London sparrow. 'I'm Miss Cherry Frost, warm wivin an' cold wivout an' I've come to you straight from the Palladium an' the 'ammersmith Palais.' She cocked her head on one side and winked confidentially. 'I oughter be dancin' at the Windmill tonight, "but my mum won't let me",' she sang.

The Junior Mistress struck an introductory bar with a flourish on the piano, and Linda trotted a few mincing steps across the stage before starting to sing:

'My Old Man says follow the van...an' don't dilly-dally on the way,' followed by a brief tap-dancing routine before carrying on, 'Orf went the van wiv me 'ome packed in it, I followed on wiv me old cock linnet...'

With the ending of her song, Linda went into an enthusiastic tattoo of taps, blew a kiss towards the audience, and ran off stage to rousing applause, followed by China, Chippy, and Podge leaping up and down yelling... 'Good old 'vacuee...Good old mawther!' while the shoal of Infant School Sticklebacks, not to be outdone, shrilled... 'Good old 'vacagee...Good old 'vacageeeee-eeeee--ee!'

Bedlam reigned until the Headmaster gallantly escorted the Postmaster's wife by the hand across the stage carrying a sheet of music which he handed to the Junior Mistress.

When calm was finally restored, and the last over-excited infant had been silenced, the Junior Mistress struck a single note on the piano. The Headmaster, immaculate in dinner jacket and bow tie, took up a melodramatic pose with one arm resting nonchalantly along the back of a chair on which was seated a sensational 'never-been-seen-before' Postmaster's wife, wearing a midnight-blue creation of layered taffeta and long, matching gloves.

A long 'Ooooo' swept down the length of the hall, like a zephyr through the reed beds.

'Mrs Caroline Howes and I would like to entertain you with a duet from "Maid of the Mountains".' He nodded to the Junior Mistress to begin. 'Thank you Miss Lacy... "The Indian Love-call".' And they were away, Headmaster's tenor and Caroline's soprano, rising and falling like cooing doves.

'Your mother ought to have come,' whispered Olivia leaning forward to give Frank's shoulder a squeeze. 'Look. Her favourite Nelson Eddy and Jeanette MacDonald in the flesh!'

'Never in all my born days have I seen that skinny old Postmistress lookin' like that!' gasped Harnser. 'Without a word of a lie, I'd never have-believed it if I hadn't seen it with my own eyes!' He regarded the lady in question with an intensely disbelieving expression while resting his chin on Olivia's shoulder.

'Why, she's all a-padded out. She ain't natural! Don't you agree Ma'am? She's...'

With an unearthly cry of anguish he suddenly leapt to his feet allowing Olivia to slide inelegantly to the floor.

'Oh my Gawd!' he cried hoarsely. 'You silly old devil!' and his pain-stricken eyes turned towards Olivia before he rushed towards the stage.

The 'Indian Love Call' had ended, and the duo were making a superbly dignified exit across the stage at the same time as old Daggy, well and truly lubricated after two hours in the Ship Inn, was attempting to clamber up the four steps at the other end.

On his third or fourth attempt he made it, and stood merrily in his maroon velvet smoking-jacket swaying dangerously near to the edge of the stage.

'Come you on down from there, you silly old fool,' yelled his brother approaching from the front.

'Now, now, Mr Flegg,' admonished the Vicar, forming a pincer-movement from the wings. 'This was not rehearsed, you know!'

Undeterred by the opposition, Daggy began.

'Parson, Ladies, and Gentlemen. I will tell you some good old-time yarns an' sing you some ditties!'

Daggy eyed the audience roguishly. 'Have you heared of "Cadilly of Cambridge"?' He commenced to sing in a shrill beery voice... 'Cadilly were pretty of the Little Rose Inn, had a boat on the river that...!'

But Harnser had him firmly by the jacket collar and smartly frog-marched him off the stage before he got to the stanza that told of high-jinks on her sailing boat the 'Willing Maid'.

Olivia regained her seat, convulsed by a fit of uncontrollable laughter.

'Oh Frankie!' she giggled. 'I can't think when I have ever enjoyed a dance so much! Joe Loss and the Savoy are nothing compared to this.' She smiled so sweetly at Daggy as he passed by, muttering darkly to himself, that he almost stumbled over a chair. Immediately his face blossomed into its usual screwed-up grin.

'Them lot don't appreciate a good old tale, Ma'am. Why, let me tell you a lot of them there high-up intellect'l professors come out all the way from Cambridge to hear my recollections and tales what my old Grandad tell me. Ain't that right bor?' He turned to Frank. 'Why your old Dad used to be mighty taken with the artefacts I dug up, drawed them and writ about them in books, didn't he now?'

Daggy paused for breath, for the stress to his bruised ego at having been prevented from doing his 'turn' had temporarily knocked the wind from his sails - but not for long. The band had returned to the stage, and the first blast of music set the feet tapping and signalled a stampede for partners.

Daggy made a grab for Olivia's waist. 'Come you on quick Ma'am, along o' me! Afore that old Schoolmaster gets his 'ands round you!'

'You must tell me lots of your tales some day, Mr Flegg,' Frank heard her whisper gently as old Daggy whirled her away.

Daggy steered Olivia along an unsteady course down the centre of the hall. 'I don't rightly know who this 'ere "Mr Flegg" be! I been called "Daggy" fer the last thirty years, and I'm wholly proud of it, that's a fact! Best man with a rat dag on the Fen. How'd you like to come rattin' with me one nice moonlight night?'

'Not you too, Daggy! It seems as if *everyone* wants to take me "rattin'".' Nevertheless she was starry-eyed and rosy-cheeked as he whirled her along in a style more reminiscent of the Gay Gordons than a quickstep.

Madge Shipham made her way towards Frank, edging herself round the crowded floor, in between the empty chairs, to join him beside the stage.

'Mum say you and Mrs Vernon have got to come for some sandwiches. Mum's been a-savin' some special spam and egg. And she's hid one of Granna Farrow's buttermilk cakes fer you.'

But strange things were happening to the dance. The band had swung into a new number with all the dancers following behind Harnser in a stamping, swaying, shouting, giggling line, arms round the waist of the person in front, like rats bewitched by the Pied Piper.

'*Conga!*' Madge gasped. 'Tag on behind as they pass and grab my middle.'

Elevated into a seventh heaven of lyrical delight, Harnser jerked his gangling body, stamped his feet, and wove the line in and out, this way and that way, to lead them finally through the blackout curtains and out into the cool moonlit night air.

'Parson!' a wag shouted hilariously. 'Old Harnser's a-takin' us to the Ship!'

'Keep that curtain closed!' bellowed the Air Raid Warden and P.C. Fox in unison. But enemy aircraft were of no consequence to Harnser Flegg on this 'Wings for Victory' night.

The Ship was not Harnser's destination; it was closed anyway. Instead he swung the line wildly round the trunk of an old willow, passing perilously close to the dark waters of the pond before leading the way back into the hall by its rear entrance and overturning one of the W.I. trestle tables. Instantly that gallant band of sisters of the W.I. defended their citadel of steaming tea-urns, sausage rolls and spam sandwiches by belabouring the backsides of the invaders with mops and broomsticks in a free-for-all which ended with the flushed ladies shaking their mops victoriously as the curtain fell behind the last invader.

Harnser's wife, Rosie, joined Frank sitting on the stage steps. Harnser had once again detached Olivia from the Headmaster's clutches and was dancing like a dervish, swirling her circular skirt thigh-high on the turns.

'You'll have to keep a strict eye on Harnser, Rosie!' Frank teased. 'Proper Fred and Adèle Astair they are together!'

Rosie's placid face was like a mellow Russet apple, with bright red cheeks warming a wind-tanned complexion.

'Oh, I don't have to worry about Harnser. He always know what's best for him. It's just that after a drop of beer he come over all of a warm glow and it make him as happy as the day is long,' she said proudly. 'Like a dog with two tails with her he is! He'll never stop mardlin' about dancin' with the Captain's lady after this! An' she look right merry too!'

Rosie flashed them a maternal smile as they kicked their legs high in the 'Palais Glide'. 'No "side" with her, that there ain't. She's a proper "Lady", and ain't frit to let the plums drop out of her mouth!'

Rosie's roving eye settled on the figure of her eldest daughter who was dancing with one of the searchlight unit soldiers. She frowned ominously.

'I haven't seen you dancin' with Ferret yet!'

She held a deep-rooted distrust of soldiers, for the genes of the Fenwomen have carried through the ages memories of persistent repression and revolt, stretching back to the Roman massacre of their menfolk when the Fenwomen were forced to build the road from Denver to Peterborough.

'Ferret rarely like you, bor,' Rosie continued. 'She say to me "That birdman's old bor is a-goin' the proper way to beat me at rattin"...and that's a right old thing for Ferret to admit!'

'There are so many people here, Rosie, I haven't seen her,' he replied, suddenly embarrassed.

'Well, there she be bor. Dancin' with one of them soldiers from down the Lode. Bloomin' old furriners! I don't hold to my Ferret bein' out a-nights with them. Go you on bor and get her away from him!'

But Frank was saved from rescuing the fair Ferret from a six-foot member of the forces by the Vicar taking his place on the stage, and by the sight of Ferret following the soldier quietly through the blackout curtain.

The Vicar cleared his throat. 'Ladies and gentlemen,' he said. 'The midnight hour approaches on this most auspicious occasion, the first "Wings for Victory Dance" in aid of the Pride of the Fens Spitfire.' He waved his hand towards the airmen and the W.A.A.F. and everyone clapped and stamped their feet in rollicking assent.

'You will be proud to hear that we have raised fifteen pounds five shillings from the sale of dance tickets. The W.I. ladies' contribution of an excellent refreshment room and the raffling of Granny Fallow's fruit cake makes an addition of five pounds threepence-halfpenny. Members of the parish have also sent truly generous donations. Ruth and her father of Church Farm, ten pounds; Mrs Judd of Willow End Farm, five pounds; and The Manor has made a contribution of twenty-five pounds.'

'That's a miracle...I don't believe it!' gasped Harnser to Olivia. 'Twen'y-five quid! Them lot never give nothin' for nothin'!'

'Maybe it's conscience-money,' breathed Olivia, softly, having noted during her stay in the village that the nouveau-riche master of The Manor appeared to be a fit young civilian of roughly Dickie's age.

'Mr and Mrs Box from "Dunroamin' " sent me a further five pounds,' continued the Vicar, 'making a grand total of sixty-five pounds and eightpence-halfpenny, to which I have the honour of bringing the grand total to seventy pounds by donating five pounds from the Church Funds!'

'One would have expected the local big-wig and his family to support the village war effort by their presence,' said Olivia, 'and twenty-five pounds seems an awfully measly amount for the owner of a Rolls-Royce.'

'That's right Ma'am,' Harnser answered, his eyes on the stage where the Headmaster and R.S.M. Kingshott could be seen deep in animated conversation, with much nodding of heads and serious smiles. After the passage of a few tense moments they appeared to have come to some momentous decision, and the Headmaster beckoned the Vicar, who joined them.

'Them's a hatchin' something...Like a flock of old hens,' observed Harnser. 'I dunno what though! Do you, gal?'

Olivia's blue eyes widened. She had never been called 'gal' before - well, not the Norfolk 'gal' which differed distinctly from the Raj-orientated 'gel'!

She was about to retaliate by calling Harnser 'bor', when the Vicar retraced his steps to the edge of the stage with his face wreathed in benevolence.

'Ladies and gentlemen, I have just been given the wonderful news that the Headmaster and R.S.M. Kingshott have between them decided to make the balance up to a magnificent grand total of one hundred pounds.' He beamed at the W.A.A.F., and cleared his throat.

'I now propose we...'

Whatever it might have been that the Vicar was about to propose was interrupted by old Daggy who had mounted the stage steps unseen and, not to be outdone by the largess of the Headmaster and King Kong, faced a cheering hall of flushed and tousled villagers.

'Parson...I have a feelin' to make a contribution by auctioning something towards a Spitfire fer these old boys in blue to fight in.'

Daggy swung his body round to face the band-leader. 'How much do one of them there Spitfires cost, bor?'

'A great deal of money, sir,' he replied, thinking to humour the old man.

'Right then! We'll begin. First bid fer a Mystery Bag of Feathers?'

The crowd gave Daggy a rousing cheer.

'What sort a bag o' feathers?' shouted a frivolous farm-wife.

'Why, bird feathers of course. What do you think...fish feathers?'

'Sixpence!' she shouted above the uproar.

'*Sixpence!*' answered Daggy. He turned to the band-leader again. 'How much of a Spitfire will sixpence buy?'

'I really can't say...a rivet perhaps.'

Daggy put on his doleful crestfallen look.

'A *rivet!*' That's not enough to give towards the Pride of the Fens Spitfire. Who'll give me ninepence?'

'I will,' giggled Ma Shipham.

'Do we get the pilot too?' asked Violet Judd in mock innocence. 'If we do, I'll give you a bob!'

Merrily between an ebb and flow of witticisms the bidding grew until it wavered at two shillings and sixpence.

'What have you got in a bag of feathers what make it worth half a crown?' cried one woman. 'I could buy a pillow for that!'

Daggy fixed her with a chilling stare.

'This here's in aid of the War Effort, not the Sunday School Outing to Hunst'on. And I said a Mystery bag of feathers, not nothin' about a pillow!'

P.C. Neville Fox, standing at the back of the hall, pricked up his ears suddenly like his namesake.

'Three bob,' he shouted, moving out of the shadows into the light.

'Three and six.'

'Four bob,' from P.C. Fox.

'Four and six.'

'Five bob.'

The unknown female voice in the crowd dropped out and P.C. Fox looked immeasurably pleased with himself. But Daggy, standing forlorn at the edge of the stage looked distinctly unhappy. Pale as a ghost he croaked, 'Who'll give me five an' threepence?'

But there were no takers.

'Five an' a penny?' Daggy gazed soulfully into a silent sea of despair.

'Six shillings.' All eyes swivelled upon Olivia.

'An' sixpence,' growled P.C. Fox.

'Seven shillings.'

Olivia swept the bidding along between herself and the now red-faced police constable until it wavered once more at nine shillings and sixpence.

'Ten shillings,' shouted the policeman desperately.

'Ten *pounds* towards the Pride of the Fen Spitfire!'

For the very first time in living memory Harnser Flegg was momentarily lost for words as he stared open-mouthed at Olivia.

'What ever have come over you, Ma'am. What ever did you want to do that for! Ten quid for a box of old feathers that like as not come off of that old stinkin' swan what got itself drownded in one of Daggy's eel lines...Gawd, gal! You must have gone clean out of your mind!'

But Olivia, flushed and elated, only laughed.

'Oh Mr Flegg, bor...I simply had to beat the constable,' she laughed, flinging her arms round Harnser's neck.

'He appeared to want Daggy's bag of feathers so much that I believe he must suspect that they conceal King John's treasure, or something equally exotic unearthed from the Fen!' Her eyes danced with glee. 'Did you notice the expression on his face when I bid ten pounds? Probably I shall be kept under strict surveillance for the rest of my days!'

'Go you on Ma'am. You're a real caution. That you are!' gasped Harnser admiringly, as she flashed a happy smile to Daggy.

'*Sold!*' shouted Daggy, emerging from a brief trance. 'Sold! to the Captain's lady.' And he burst into a joyous jig and tap-dance at the humiliating downfall of his arch-enemy.

The band-leader thankfully raised his baton and turned to face the audience. 'Ladies and gentlemen...'

'Don't he talk like a film-star,' murmured Madge, gazing up at him with a faraway look in her eyes. 'Just like David Niven when I saw him in "Raffles"!'

'Ladies and gentlemen. May I thank you on behalf of the Royal Air Force "Seven Gremlins Swing Band" for your wonderful support...and, let me add, for the many, many rivets this grand old gentleman has donated towards your very own Pride of the Fens Spitfire.' He paused for breath, and the W.A.A.F. smiled shyly, until the confusion of yells of 'Good old Daggy' coming from his three-sheets-in-the-wind cronies at the back of the hall subsided. 'May I also thank you once more on behalf of the "boys and girls in blue" for your hospitality.'

Softly, with muted percussion, the band drifted into the slow dream-like rhythm of 'Who's Taking You Home Tonight', which was the cue for all the wives to make bee-lines for their husbands. The W.A.A.F. began to sing, tapping her skirt with relaxed fingers as the lights went out one by one, until the hall was softly lit by a single amber-shaded bulb which cast a circling sea of shadows on the walls, the muted music accompanied by the swish of shoes on the floorboards.

Olivia slid her hand into Frank's and led him on to the floor. 'Hold me very close, Frankie,' she said in a strangely hushed voice, 'and follow me...slowly.'

He gave himself to the moment and to her arms as they became one with the languorous gliding sea of movement within an unreal world. He found his face crushed against her breasts where a faint intoxicating odour of her perfume made him long to be six feet tall. Even a few inches would make all the difference, so that it could be *her* face resting on *his* chest as the dancers drifted by.

Frank, with his head nestling exquisitely in the cool silk of her blouse, was oblivious to everything but its hidden warmth, until he suddenly realized that the band had stopped playing and the main lights had come on, shattering his dreams with their stark brilliance.

Olivia held his hand as they returned to their seats to retrieve her handbag and scarf.

'How did I do that time?' he asked.

She smiled, and as the band struck the opening bars of the National Anthem he noticed that her eyes were misted with tears, as every man, woman, tiddler, bit-bigger-girl, and big-girl stood patriotically to attention before making towards the doors as the last note died away.

The home-going crowd dispersed noisily along the village street shouting 'good nights', singing lusty snatches from the evening's medley of tunes, and bearing sleepy infants piggy-back on their shoulders home to bed.

'You aren't collering up in the mornin', are you Boer?' a voice called through the darkness beyond the pitch-black yews. 'Because I'm a-lyin' in.'

Boer's pithy answer was lost in Daggy's off-key rendering of the 'Indian Love Call'.

The bright orb of the hunter's moon had begun to dip towards the western horizon, and slim pencil-beams of searchlights swung restlessly about the sky, now and again to rush together to hold a homecoming bomber for a second before switching off to leave a darker backdrop of stars.

'Shall we walk home round the pond?' Olivia suggested tentatively.

A nebulous couple walked slowly hand in hand ahead of them, appearing and disappearing in the swathes of moonlight and deep shadows cast by the weeping willows. Olivia strolled very slowly along the narrow path to allow the couple to draw further ahead, stopping to lean against the pond railings to look down into the dark waters spangled with moonlight along ripples made by an inquisitive flotilla of ducks.

'I love to watch the moon in the water,' he murmured wistfully.

They were enclosed within a net of shadows. He placed his arm timidly round her waist, drawing nearer to her warmth, as she leant back against the railings above the glinting water.

'Frankie!' she exclaimed, quickly turning away from his adolescent fumbling as their noses bumped. *'Behave!'*

Trembling with trepidation he placed his hand closer to the warmth of her within her blouse.

'I can't be a nymph. Not here!'

She made a small sound of tenderness, like a small animal to its blind young. 'Moonlight is dangerous. It is the realm of the Moon Goddesses who provoke desire remorselessly and the macabre chimera who would overwhelm you mercilessly, especially you, for less sensitive souls might escape.'

She covered his hand over her breast with her own, trapping its movement within her unbuttoned blouse.

'I could never be a chimera to you, Frankie!'

He leant limply against her on the point of tears. Gently she eased his hand away from her breast and lightly kissed him on the cheek before turning to glance beyond the moon in the water to the moon-washed village street. Peals of laughter drifted faintly across the water from the deep shadows below the church yews. A few candles fluttered briefly behind bedroom windows before blackout curtains cloaked the village in darkness. Nearer, the ducks tucked their heads beneath their wings as they slept, rocking gently on tiny ripples raised by the night breeze. Suddenly the church clock shattered the moment as it began to chime half-past midnight.

Olivia started. 'Gawd!' she gasped, imitating Harnser Flegg. 'Your Ma will kill me, bor! Race you home. And, remember, keep clear of all chimeras,' she added as she ran lightly over the hump-back bridge.

They burst breathlessly into the living room to be confronted by Mrs Dutton sitting in her Windsor chair looking first at the clock and then at their flushed faces.

'I shall make supper now that you are home,' she said flatly, getting up to cross the room towards the kitchen.

'Oh, please don't trouble, Mrs Dutton. All I want is to take my shoes off and roll into bed!'

Olivia glanced at her disarranged hair in the over-mantle mirror. 'It really was a wonderful evening. Even a moving duet from 'Maid of the Mountains' by the Headmaster and Mrs Howes. And the Vicar was in top form as master-of-ceremonies!'

Mrs Dutton brushed past her as if she had not been in the room.

'Oh, was it?' she said ominously.

Olivia glanced at Frank and sighed, shaking her head in despair as she left the room to climb the wide stairs of the front staircase.

Saturday October 19th
Daggy Flegg's Shack

Frank!' His mother's voice came brusquely from the front porch. 'There is a strange parcel in the porch for Mrs Vernon.'

'Crikey!' he gasped, as his eyes focused upon a large rectangular box wrapped in sacking and sewn up with binder-twine. 'What on earth can it be?'

'Feathers!' she said wryly, as she handed him an envelope on which was written in carefully formed copper-plate capitals: 'MYSTERY BAG OF FEATHERS FOR THE CAPTAIN'S LADY.' 'You had better call her.'

Olivia came running barefoot down the stairs, hastily tying the belt of her flimsy dressing-gown.

'Oh Frankie, Daggy's box of feathers! How lovely. Open it for me.' He cut the twine and removed the sacking to reveal a wooden beer crate with its lid nailed firmly in place.

'The old devil!' he giggled. 'It's a full crate of beer!'

Mrs Dutton, hovering just beyond the passage door, burst upon them as the dreaded word entered her ears.

'Feathers indeed! Some ridiculous village prank.'

Olivia knelt in a circle of sunlight on the red brick floor. 'It simply says "Mystery parcel",' she murmured, her eyes dancing with anticipation. 'Take the lid off, bor!'

Lifting the lid revealed a covering of cool rhubarb leaves.

'Heavens! Pandora's box. What untold treasure lurks beneath?' she breathed.

'This is most probably George Flegg's idea of a joke - a grass snake or something equally revolting. Before going any further, Frank, take the box outside,' his mother advised, taking a hurried step towards the door.

Her advice fell upon deaf ears as he proceeded to toss the leaves on to the floor to uncover a layer of Daggy's peerless King Edwards on a folded page from the *Cambridge Evening News.*

'Spuds!'

'Golly!' cried Olivia. 'Potatoes!'

'Edible.' Mrs Dutton gave an eloquent shrug of her shoulders.

'Better than a grass snake,' Frank chuckled.

With the potatoes placed in a pile beside him a second layer emerged made up from a mixed assortment of carrots, onions, and a swede turnip on the centre pages of last week's *King's Lynn Advertiser.*

Olivia leant over the crate as the next layer of newspaper was removed. 'Heavens! What next?' She clasped her hands ecstatically, rocking back on her heels to grin at Mrs Dutton. 'I'm really enjoying this.'

Gingerly the last sheet of newspaper was lifted to expose *feathers* - feathers in the form of a cock pheasant lying breast uppermost in all its feathered brilliance with its feet piously crossed and a plump hen bird on either side, looking for all the world like the brightly painted marble effigy of some Norfolk knight with his two faithful wives beside him gracing the top of a tomb in one of the rich Fenland churches.

'Pheasants!' said Frank in a conspiratory whisper. 'No wonder Daggy went pale when old Foxie started to bid.'

'Pheasants? Oh the dear old man!' Olivia gave a gasp of pleasure. 'It really isn't the "stinking old swan" forecast by Harnser?'

'Pheasants! Poached, of course. Village men never send gifts to young women unless they have some ulterior motive. You should return it,' Mrs Dutton murmured through pursed lips, glaring at Olivia's dishabille.

'A whole dinner,' Frank chuckled, inwardly licking his lips at the thought of roast pheasant, roast potatoes, mashed swede, onion and bread sauce.

'Really, Mrs Dutton, you should not misjudge the villagers so unfairly,' Olivia quipped cuttingly. 'I'm sure Mr Flegg has a heart of gold.' The sudden movement as she stood increased her state of undress by allowing her dressing gown to flutter wide below the belt exposing her satin nightie. 'Frankie, you shall take me to his cottage immediately after luncheon.'

'Cottage!' He burst out laughing as he piled the vegetables back in the crate. 'I've never heard Daggy's place called a cottage.'

'Not a cottage?'

'Crikey, no. It's an absolutely spiffing place. More like a fur trapper's log cabin beside the Saskatchewan river. You'll love it.' He tossed the last onion into the crate and leant back on his heels. 'I can lend you a jolly exciting book about an old trapper working along the Saskatchewan river for the Hudson Bay Company nearly a hundred years ago.'

Olivia wrinkled her nose as she gathered up the sheets of newspaper.

'I'll save these for lighting my fires, so nothing will be wasted apart from the rhubarb leaves,' she said, following in the stormy wake of Mrs Dutton who was disappearing into the gloom of the passage.

'Oh, they can go in the pig-swill bucket,' he called after her as he carried the pheasants towards the pantry to hang them in the large perforated zinc meat safe.

After lunch Olivia found Frank in the stableyard. He was sitting on an upturned bucket with his back to the bottom half of the loose-box door. A Suffolk mare's head drooped from the open top half with her nose resting on his shoulder. The October sunlight reflected its heat upwards from the concrete stableyard. Hens lazily scratched amongst the straw of the muckheap. Swallow titter mingled with the chatter of sparrows drowsing on the pantiled roof and, for the last time before migrating south, young swallows lined the long wireless aerial strung from the granary to the gable end of the house.

'Do you realise what day it was yesterday?' she asked stroking the glossy neck of the mare.

'Friday?'

'No.'

'Your birthday?'

'No. Try again.'

She squatted beside him, rocking back on her heels as the mare nuzzled her hair.

'I don't know,' he answered peevishly. 'The cat had kittens.'

'Wrong again. It was Saint Luke's Feast day, and that is why the weather has changed into this glorious golden autumnal spell.' She jumped to her feet, passing her hand across her forehead to brush back her ruffled hair. 'So take me down to your wild fen to call on Daggy Flegg.'

'We'll have to walk,' he said, giving the bucket a parting kick. 'Because Madge always bikes to Downham on a Saturday afternoon to go to the matinée at the Regal. And it's over three miles to Daggy's place.'

'Good,' she replied. The thought of losing themselves in the wild sea of reeds delighted her. 'I feel like a long walk.'

'We must take Daggy a present,' she murmured thoughtfully as they walked up the street towards King Kong's shop. 'Any suggestions?'

'Baccy,' he said quickly. 'Daggy is always boasting that the only things he has to buy are baccy and beer, coke and candles.'

'Right!' she laughed. 'Baccy it is.'

He followed her into the dimly-lit shop where the clanging door-bell danced a merry jig on its coiled spring as the door opened.

Bullseyes, pear-drops, jelly-babies, dolly mixture, and chocolate caramels greeted them from large glass jars. Chocolate bars and boxes of England's Glory matches, pipe-cleaners and a selection of briar pipes, together with bottles of fizzy lemonade and Lyons fruit pies lined the cluttered counter in a hotch-potch below a framed photograph of King George and Queen Mary...but no King Kong.

A heavy silence descended upon the shop as the bell stilled, and Olivia glanced hesitantly towards Frank silently forming the words 'Is he closed for lunch?' with her lips.

Frank shrugged his shoulders in reply, and gave a polite cough.

From behind the heavy curtain came the booming roar of King Kong, that dread sound which had the effect of striking terror into the youth of Willows End.

'I'm havin' my dinner. You'll just have to wait.'

'It's quite alright, Mr Kingshott,' Olivia answered sweetly, raising an eyebrow to Frank. 'Please don't hurry.'

Instantly the curtain was flung aside with a slither of brass curtain rings and King Kong appeared framed in the opening.

'Mrs Vernon!' he exclaimed, wiping crumbs from his moustache with the back of his hand. 'Mrs Vernon, ma'am. I thought it were some little blighter who it would do a world of good to wait. They don't know nothin' about discipline, that they don't! And what can I get you together?'

'Well, I would like four packets of tobacco, please. That is if you can spare four packets,' she added diplomatically.

'Of course I can for *you*. What sort of tobacco would you like? I have a good selection of fine tobacco hid down here out of pryin' eyes!' he said, stooping behind the counter. 'Goin' to send the Captain a parcel?'

'Actually, Mr Kingshott, I need your help - in confidence of course,' she confessed apologetically with a girlish smile. 'I want a little present for Daggy Flegg, and I am sure that you will know the brand he likes to smoke.'

'Daggy!' King Kong's steely blue eyes regarded her with astonishment. 'For Daggy Flegg? Good gawd!'

'Yes, Mr Kingshott...*please,*' she put in quickly.

He cancelled his left hand's search for his stock of finest of fine tobaccos and took four packets off the shelf.

'You want rough old shag. That's what Daggy smokes. He wouldn't thank you for fine tobacco if you gave it to him. Wasted on 'im, Ma'am. Them old professors from Cambridge that he take down the Lode fishin' always send Daggy presents of fine tobacco an' after they've gone home he bring it to me to change for rough shag. That's how I manage to get a supply of good tobacco that I keep 'specially for them who appreciates the best!'

'Thank you, Mr Kingshott.' The expression on her face was one of sheer delight as she paid him. 'I knew that I could rely on your judgement.'

Olivia, clutching the small parcel wrapped in brown paper and neatly tied with string, glanced at Frank and giggled as they left the shop. 'You know, Frankie,' she murmured, 'I *adore* elderly men with waxed military moustaches!'

The words entered his ears as harbingers of doom, causing his heart to plummet to the depths of despair. Surely this was an encoded message referring to his callow, clodhopping, lack of manliness!'

'Do we follow the Lode,' said Olivia, 'or keep to the loke road?'

'As you wish,' he replied, without lifting his downcast eyes from the grass verge.

'On top of the bank, then,' she laughed, impetuously taking his hand and climbing joyously up through a riot of long grass to gain the sunbaked clay pathway that stretched away ahead of them along the top of the Lode bank. 'Isn't it glorious?'

To their right lay the flat blue waters of the Lode drifting many feet above the Loke track. Teazles and burrs plucked the hem of her cotton skirt, and flies rose in clouds from drifts of cow parsley, angelica and hogweed, flies whose bodies glinted with iridescent greens and blues, large grey and black flies, and lazy soldier beetles who settled quickly on the nearest surface.

Around them the panorama of fenland stretched away to infinity. There were infrequent standings of tall crack willows forming wind-breaks for cattle on the marshes at the edge of the unclaimed fen, and in the middle distance a straggling line of women chopping sugar-beet.

'See that willow?'

Frank pointed towards a gnarled old willow which leant over a tangle of sedge at the edge of the Lode. 'That's where I caught my first pike.' The memory of that epic struggle lifted his heart and his feeling of awkwardness vanished.

They were passing a clump of tall willows growing along the side of a dyke which ran at right angles to the dirt road below the bank. Shrill voices of children filtered through a screen of willow branches, through which the partly-obscured base of a derelict wind-pump could be seen below the skeleton timbers of its sails.

'Harnser's place,' Frank commented with a grin.

Olivia glanced downwards to see an area of trampled grass in front of a thickly-tarred weather-board cottage with a roof of red pantiles surrounded by an annexe of tarred huts with rusted corrugated-iron roofs and shelters constructed of potato sacking nailed around posts with reed-bundle roofs. But it was the open patch of grass between the dirt road and the cottage that held her attention. Like the vibrant hum of worker bees outside their hive magnified a thousand times, Harnser's place was alive with movement and sound. Hens clucked from coops surrounded by cheeping chicks. A flock of ponderous white geese cackled as they grazed. Nanny goats with kids wandered aimlessly in the shade of the willows browsing on trailing branches and a black lurcher bitch lay drowsing in the sunlight.

She heard children playing, and moved her head slightly to obtain a clear view through the screen of leaves. Five near-naked children romped with a litter of puppies and a goat kid, chasing half a dozen kittens in a whirlwind game of tag in and out of a labyrinth of paths within a wall of reeds, falling over bloated Muscovy ducks and puppies as they ran screaming with laughter in the wake of the kittens.

Suddenly the bitch became aware of the strangers and gave a sharp warning bark. In a flash all movement froze. Like young foxes disturbed at play the children, puppies, and the kid stopped dead in their tracks, while the kittens, taking advantage of this sudden truce, vanished beneath a pile of logs.

The silence lasted thirty seconds. Then, clutching puppies to their chests, the children made a mad dash into the cottage. They heard the slamming of the door and rattle of a massive bolt being shot home. The lurcher bitch slunk furtively through a hole beneath the brick foundation of the mill, and the geese closed ranks ready to attack.

Olivia's heart flew outwards to the children. 'This is how it once was,' she thought. She imagined that she was standing on the threshold to a Golden Age, an idealized world of Arcadian simplicity. Here were fauns and dryads sporting with goats. She searched wistfully for Pan, feeling his presence out there within the labyrinth of reeds. Then she sighed at the certainty that Pan, if he manifested, would be in the guise of Harnser Flegg.

'Goodness! Have I startled the children?' She turned to her companion. 'How about calling on Rosie now that we are here?'

'She'll be out chopping beet with Ferret on Marsh Farm until tea-time.'

'But those small children. Who will be caring for them?'

She plucked a grass stalk and pointed with it to where the edge of a net curtain drawn across a small window twitched to give a fleeting glimpse of two little heads peering out.

'They are the five-year-old twins, Rosie and Sam. Then there's two-year-old Mollie, Martha who's seven, and Charlie who's almost ten. Jenny is the eldest, two years older than Ferret. But she's away in service.'

The curtain fell back into place as another curtain shrouding a window on the opposite side of the door trembled.

'Goodness! I had not realised that Ferret had any brothers or sisters,' she murmured thoughtfully, flinging a lingering look back over her shoulder towards the now silent patch of trampled grass as they continued to walk along the top of the bank. 'I've not seen any of them in the village,' she added.

'And you won't, if they can help it! They probably think that you are the Dicky Nurse.'

For any form of officialdom was resented by the Fleggs, and thankfully its unwanted visits in the guise of School Attendance Officer, or Dicky Nurse, became further and further apart as the family increased. So the happy Flegg youth rarely appeared in school. When they did, it was usually at the start of winter, appearing like winter migrants in unsoled boots or holed plimsolls after walking the three miles along the slushy Loke drove, whereupon the schoolmistress, in accordance with her Methodist missionary's daughter ideals, presented each of them with a secondhand pair of footwear. Refurbished migrants would dutifully fly back to their fastness in the fen, where they would linger until cold feet, and the migratory urge, came upon them once again in twelve months' time.

Harnser, at forty-five, was head of a 'wholly independent family'. They lived 'off the land' in the traditional proud independence of the untamed 'Fen Tigers' of yore. They poached fish, flesh, and fowl. They caught eels, lifted their needs from potato, carrot, swede, pea, and bean fields - that is when what they grew on their own vegetable plot ran out. They shared the half acre of ground around the old wind-pump with goats, chickens, ducks, geese, and a wire-fronted bacon box which housed an exceptionally pugnacious jack ferret.

'Who, or what, is a Dicky Nurse?' Olivia asked curiously.

'Oh, the school nurse. She bends your head over a sheet of paper and drags a dicky comb through your hair so's the nits drop on the paper.'

'Sounds absolutely *horrid.*'

'Not as bad as the school dentist.'

He grabbed her hand to lead her in a wild scramble down the steep side of the bank to the loke drove where a cock-up bridge crossed the opposite dyke to the bullock marsh.

'Where are you taking me?' she screamed as they gathered momentum in their headlong tumbling descent through the long, soft grass. She was laughing, her hair laced with sprigs of angelica and her skirt fluttering thigh-high as she ran.

'Frankie!' she gasped, as they leant breathless and flushed against the rough timber of the bridge. 'That was fun.'

He grinned, and taking possession of her hand began to lead her across the bridge.

'Now where are you taking me?' she asked, petulantly.

'Across Mr Barratt's bullock marsh.'

He led her along a bullock track where the hoof-flattened mud had been baked hard by the sun. Ahead of them, goldfinches flitted amongst a clump of sow thistles sending tufts of thistledown floating slowly in the still air to tremble gently on the tussocky grass. A covey of red-legged partridges walked leisurely up the track ahead of them, and a hare broke from its form to weave its way swiftly across the marsh, dodging in and out of ragwort clumps with its ears flattened close to its back as it ran. The air on the marsh was heavy with autumnal sunlight that carried with it the rich bouquet of decomposing haulms of pea and potato and the dank mustiness rising from heaps of weeds left to rot on the dyke edge.

Olivia inhaled it deep into her lungs. The ruby and yellow flash of the goldfinches held her eye as they flitted twittering from thistle head to thistle head.

'Those little birds. What are they?'

He turned towards her and then quickly looked away. For here on the open fen she was more lovely than ever, no longer a grown woman, but a kindred spirit loving birds. He looked up at her, full of gratitude for her show of interest in his 'wild fen'. This was the turning point. Hitherto his father had been the source of knowledge; now he was to take on the role of mentor.

'King Harrys.'

'Oh...I'm sure they are not?'

'That's what we call them,' he answered teasingly.

'Fibber!'

She smiled with teasing complacency as her skirt swung sideways brushing a ragwort, disturbing a late gatekeeper butterfly which fluttered ahead before settling on a patch of red clover.

'Goldfinches, but round here we call them King Harrys. They are the hinglers' chief prize, together with linnets and other finches.'

Mr Barratt's Irish bullocks were trotting across the field in an extended line behind the couple. They were rough-coated and wild-looking, tossing shaggy necks that flung froth from snuffling muzzles. Olivia glanced over her shoulder and stared horror-struck.

'Don't look now.' Her fingers tightened on his wrist in a convulsive movement. 'We are being followed by a herd of bulls!'

He laughed at her fancy. 'Only bullocks.'

She ventured another glance over her shoulder to see the leading bullocks just a couple of yards away rolling the whites of their eyes and jostling each other as they trotted in her footsteps.

'I don't like them,' she cried, with a startled grimace.

'Shoo! Scram!' he shouted, breaking away from her to rush towards the nearest of the bunch sending them cavorting playfully in wide-ranging circles around them. 'See, they're nothing but a bunch of overgrown pail-calves.'

The pounding of her heart slowed, and she burst into a fit of giggles as they continued to head across the hummocky grass towards a line of reeds marking the furthermost headland. From the border of filmy reed-heads lining the headland a heron languidly lifted into flight, slender and plumed, with broad sail-like wings, barking his explosive cry.

'Wotcher bor!'

They had reached the headland of the bullock marsh which followed a broad dyke running as straight as a die through a limitless army of reeds dividing the reclaimed land from the wild fen.

'Wotcher bor.' Lying on his back in the sunlight regarding them through half-closed eyes, with his billy-cock hat tipped forward over his face, lay the Moocher in Daggy's gunning punt.

'Hello, Mr Fowler,' said Frank, peering downwards through a screen of rushes (nobody ever called him Moocher to his face). 'I'm bringing Mrs Vernon to see Daggy.'

'Are you now! Do Daggy know you're comin'?'

'Not really. It's to be a surprise,' laughed Olivia.

'Old Daggy don't welcome surprises like that,' he grunted, squinting up at her. 'Like to keep hisself to hisself like an old fox. Anyway do you come and sit here a minute, then I'll give you a ride to Daggy's place.'

Fretted water slapped soothingly against the steep sides of the dyke as she stepped gingerly into the shallow well of the punt to lean back against the forward decking with her legs stretched alongside the Moocher's body. Frank sat on the after-deck.

The air was hot and still below the level of the bank where the smooth wood of the punt gave off a scent of tar mixed with eel-slime and fish-scales. A ladybird landed softly on her skirt. Two larks spiralled upwards in a half-remembered springtime dance. Olivia shaded her eyes from the sun with her hand to watch them.

'You got a Bishy Barnabee on you. That's supposed to be lucky.'

'Ladybird,' Frank laughed.

The Moocher glanced hesitantly towards Olivia. 'I found somethin' really interestin' last week bor.'

'Oh, Mrs Vernon is alright. She won't split. What is it?'

'I don't rightly know bor.' He scratched his head and tipped his hat further forward. 'Nothing but a rusty old bit of iron, though you know that your dad thought things like that were marvellous...Didn't 'e now? He shew me a drawing once that he made of somethin' I dug up down the fen once, and it were printed in a newspaper.'

He treated Olivia to another suspicious look (for the Moocher held an inherent distrust of 'furriners') before rising slowly on to his feet to pole the punt towards its owner's shack.

A wren burst into song as they passed beneath an overhanging sallow.

'Listen, Frank. A nightingale.'

'Lor' no, ma'am. That's only a little old wren. Plenty of nightingales warblin' hereabouts in February,' Daggy grinned. 'Rare keep me awake they do.'

'February!' she said, hesitantly. 'Nightingales!'

'Fen-nightingales. Frogs. Thousands of croaking, splashing, spawning frogs in every dyke, the ones you send off to the University for the biology students to mess about with.'

'Ar bor.'

Between the steep banks of the dyke they could see nothing of the land. Above them the azure sky with teazles and thistles in stark silhouette, and tip-tufted reed heads quivering in the light air. Occasionally a willow's cascade of trailing branches brushed the deck of the punt, and water voles plopped into the water ahead. Brilliant dragonflies rustled on stiff gauze wings as they flashed overhead patrolling up and down through the drowsy afternoon sunshine.

A grass snake swam ahead of the punt leaving an undulating wake through the duckweed before vanishing into the tight mass of reed stems. Olivia gave an involuntary shudder, remembering the rat snakes that took the place of cats around the bungalow of her Indian childhood.

Presently they came to a plank crossing the dyke beneath a polled willow on the left bank and a makeshift fence of untrimmed osier poles on the opposite side.

'Daggy's place,' Frank cried enthusiastically as he scrambled up the slope of the bank. 'Come on up,' he added, pausing to hold out his hand to steady her as the punt rocked.

She looked over the parapet of Daggy's first line of defence to see a tarred wooden shack standing within a wind-break of tall reeds and impenetrable sallows, surrounded by a circular narrow dyke overgrown with giant water dock, bulrushes, and flags.

Daggy was taking his afternoon nap on a church pew that was standing beside the door of the shack. The aged pew had been, in Daggy's words, 'a divine gift,' an offering left high and dry on the drain bank within a stone's throw of his door after being tossed for many miles across the wild inland sea from St Peter's church during the 1915 drown.

Olivia's sudden appearance above the parapet brought a low growl from a lurcher, and the old fensman, slowly opened his eyes.

'My Gawd! I don't think I can believe my eyes!' he gasped, hastily ejecting a cat from its siesta on his knee and rushing down the trodden clay path to meet them, followed by a brindled lurcher, a disgruntled cat, and a particularly ugly Muscovy drake. 'Come you on together and sit you down.'

'Daggy, you dear,' she said, greeting him with a hug, 'I just had to come to thank you for your box of feathers. It was absolutely splendid!'

He blushed beneath the sun-tanned mahogany of his cheeks and grinned, while the Muscovy drake gave a malevolent hiss, raised its crest, and glowered viciously at her bare legs.

'Oh, go you on, Ma'am. It were nothin' spectacular.'

'Well,' she said, bending to stroke the cat, 'I think it was a really lovely surprise.'

'You rarely confused that old Schoolmaster and old Kingshott though. That you did, gal. 'Specially that there Constable Fox. Gawd know what he would have done if you hadn't saved my bacon!' His wicked little eyes twinkled, and she gave him another hug for good measure.

'You don't have to be in a hurry, do you now?' He indicated the pew placed between the open door of his shack and a water butt facing the south-westerly sun. 'Sit you down an' I'll get a bite of tea.'

'A cup of tea would be lovely, but you mustn't go to any trouble. I've come to see you,' she put in quickly.

'Don't you fret. That's a rare old treat to see you Ma'am. Just you sit there and have a good rest.'

Daggy rolled up his shirt-sleeves and lifted from the water butt a sack writhing with squirming movement, from which he took a large eel before retying the neck of the sack and dropping it back into the water.

Olivia was intrigued at the sight as the eel coiled around his wrist.

'Isn't that a lovely eel? You can't get one fresher than that, can you now?'

He hit the creature on the head with an iron bar, and again on its tail.

'Got two brains have an old eel. One at each end. Go on for ever they do. That's a fact!'

She glanced away as the eel, despite having suffered a severe bashing on both head and tail, continued to writhe with unabated strength around his arm. She then heard the hammering change to a metallic note and turned her head to see him nailing the eel to the doorpost by its head.

'Don't you worry Ma'am, he's as dead as this 'ere nail.' She gave an involuntary shudder as he circled the skin at the neck with his pocket-knife and drew it off downwards like a glove.

'There you are. I'll have to make you a garter with the skin to keep the agues away,' he said, disappearing within the shack carrying the skinned eel.

Olivia leant back against the wall of the shack, spreading her fingers out on her sun-warmed skirt.

'Isn't it peaceful here,' she murmured.

'I knew you would love it,' Frank answered.

She gazed drowsily through half-closed eyes at the scene before her. 'It is heavenly...a Peter Pan land where butterflies fly in October.'

For beneath the silvery-grey arbour of willow leaves a tangle of loosestrife and Michaelmas daisies, great water dock, and bindweed was alive with red admiral and peacock butterflies. A mixed flock of finches twittered as they searched for stray grains of corn with some chickens, and from a row of willow fencing posts that had rooted and sprouted a crown of slender shoots a yellowhammer sang monotonously. She leant forward impulsively to stroke the lurcher which had returned to lie stretched out in the sun at her feet, but it growled deep down in its throat and backed away to flop down heavily beyond the water butt.

Frank laughed. 'A good lurcher distrusts all strangers.'

'Like our friend the Moocher,' she smiled.

Frank left her to inspect an otter-skin stretched out to dry on the side of a nearby shed which revived his longing for a fur trapper's life by the Saskatchewan river. The shed, made of tarred planks and roofed with thick bundles of reeds, housed a diversity of rat-dags, eel-picks, wicker griggs and baskets that made up Daggy's stock in trade.

Smoke spiralled upwards from the chimney pipe as Daggy quickened the coke fire within the Tortoise stove with a rattle of poker followed by the dull clang of a heavy lid being dropped on a cast-iron pot.

'Let them boil for half an hour, time I sit down an' we'll have a good old mardle together.'

Daggy's voice roused her as he collapsed heavily on the pew beside her.

'Do you know, you're the only lady to visit me since that old Colonel's missus come aggravating about me spreadin' muck on my strawberries, an' that were years ago. Interferin' old gal she were! Sight for sore eyes you are!'

Daggy beamed like a benevolent gargoyle and placed his hand on her arm.

'And your mysterious box of feathers was a sight for sore eyes too, Daggy,' she added flippantly.

'Gawd bless you gal! You saved my life you did.' He lit his pipe and puffed noxious nicotine over a cloud of dancing gnats. 'I'll tell you some old tales, shall I, now we're together?'

'How about telling me the one about "Cadilly of Cambridge", the tale you were prevented from telling at the dance last night?'

'Right. My old dad told me tales about Cadilly what his old dad, who knowed her time she lived at Brandon Creek, used to tell - I suppose that would make it nigh on a hundred an' fifty years ago.'

Letting her eyes close, she listened to the incorrigible old fensman hold forth on his favourite subject, Cadilly the blithesome light o' love of the late eighteenth century undergraduates and local gentry and their boisterous romps in her sailing boat *'The Willing Maid'*.

Meanwhile Frank was wandering happily about the sheds and lean-to shelters that held a treasury of traps and tools embalmed in a heady incense of fish slime, tar, compost, and the reek of a shaggy old billy goat. Avoiding the goat which was tethered by a chain in the shade of some sallows, he discovered Daggy's small white ratting ferrets leaping excitedly against the wire mesh of their hutch with their bright albinic eyes riveted on him and their pink noses twitching expectantly as he approached. 'Wish Ma would let me keep a ferret,' he mused. 'Keep us supplied with cold rabbit and pickles and rabbit pies.'

Olivia awoke with a start and an awareness that the retelling of the legendary adventures of Miss Anna Maria Cadilly had ended and that Frank was calling her in for tea from the open doorway.

She stepped into the room to see the old man bent over a cast-iron frying pan wielding a large fork in his left hand. 'Come you on in,' he greeted her, giving the sizzling pan an energetic shake and sending an appetising scent wafting about the room.

Sunlight falling through a tiny window cast a bright rectangle of light on a table covered with red-checked American cloth. Sticks of celery arranged in a jam jar formed the centre piece, beside a plate of thickly-sliced bread, liberally spread with black-market butter, and a jug of milk.

'Sit you down together,' he beamed, indicating the one chair. 'And you'll have to sit on that old tub, bor.'

Olivia managed to squeeze alongside Daggy's bed and the stove to seat herself on the chair as Frank settled himself on an upturned sherry case.

'Oh, Mr Flegg!' she exclaimed. 'You shouldn't have gone to all this trouble.'

'It ain't no trouble, Ma'am. Do you pour out a cup of tea time this is a-cookin'.' He placed a blue enamel teapot and three enamel mugs on the table. 'That's goats' milk. Keeps you free of that old consumption it do.'

She poured out two cups and passed one to Frank.

'Don't you be frit of usin' the sugar. I got a good supply saved up from when them army lot left. Proper good they were to me. We had an understandin'. I kept them in eggs and vegetables and an old hen now and again, time they gave me cheese and sugar and tins of corned beef and tea. Worked out a treat it did!'

He gave her a woeful look. 'I do wish they hadn't been shifted. Same's as I suppose you wish they were still 'ere, seein' that the Captain were beginning to get settled in. But that's what this old war do to folk. Spread 'em all over the place it do.'

He gave the frying pan another energetic shake before placing it on one side and turning his attention to a saucepan that had been boiling merrily on a primus stove at the far side of the room. Olivia's thoughts drifted back to intimate pre-war supper parties in Chelsea's 'Blue Cockatoo', street lamps pooling hazy circles of amber light through the sulphur fog, and the grey silhouettes of ghostly barges passing up and down the Chelsea river seen through its window; Dicky walking her home along the watcrfront.....

Daggy presented her with a plate loaded with creamy white potatoes fragrant with mint and oozing butter, wild mushrooms, and eel cutlets on a bed of onion rings. 'Get that down you together,' he said, placing it before her with a flourish that would have done justice to a Parisian waiter.

'Why, Daggy! This is delicious,' she exclaimed, tasting the eel.

His face broke into a beatific grin.

'Do you know what, gal? It don't cost nothin' to live like one of them gentry. That's a fact.'

She raised one eyebrow disbelievingly.

'I got a dyke full o' eels, plenty of birds like duck an' partridges and pheasants, rabbits and hares and all the 'tatos and greens for the pickin' - fact I got everything bar beer and somethin' to smoke!'

'Tea, sugar...bread?' she queried.

'Ar. You have a point there. But I have the old goats for milk.'

After a second helping, Olivia pushed her plate to one side. Daggy glanced at her inquiringly. 'Have some more.'

'Oh, I simply couldn't.'

'How about you, bor?' He speared another couple of cutlets and dropped them on Frank's plate.

He watched the boy quickly down the last of the cutlets then he stood up. 'That's going to be a cold night after the sun go down. Frosty no doubt! So's you better soon be goin' home together.'

The large orb of the sun hung low above the horizon almost filling the frame of the small window, and a cool breeze entered the room.

'You ought to have brung a coat,' he said solicitously to Olivia eyeing her thin frock. 'I got a coat you can have.' He took a black frock coat from a peg behind the door. 'One that one of them professors give me.'

She eased herself back between the bed and the stove and stood in the doorway. 'I'll be fine, really. We'll run to keep warm,' she smiled happily. 'Thank you, Daggy, for a wonderful afternoon. I honestly cannot remember having a more enjoyable meal. It was simply perfect.'

Daggy's face creased in a wide grin and he roared with self-conscious laughter.

'Go you on home, gal. It weren't nothin' spectacular.'

They left him standing in the doorway of his weather-boarded shack surrounded by its moat and palisade of reeds. The cat, with the lurcher and the Muscovy drake who had silently drifted back to his side at the going of the 'furriners', watched them cross the plank and disappear from sight behind the willows.

A breeze began to sigh fitfully among the reed-stems, bringing magic to the dank-smelling dykes. The bright insects of the afternoon sunshine had vanished. The dykes were coming alive with furtive movement. Waterhens croaked, and mallard flew overhead in family teams with a sibilant whistle of wings as they flighted out towards the stubbles.

Soon the couple were crossing the bullock pasture with the Lode bank ahead and Marsh Farm's weather-vane cock ablaze with the last rays from the setting sun.

'Did you like Daggy's place?' Frank asked tentatively.

'Of course. It was fun. Especially the high tea!' She glanced at him with amused twinkling eyes. 'Killing the eel was pretty awful.'

'Tasted jolly good though.'

'Jolly good.' She placed her hand over his. To the boy, the gentle clasp was an embrace, leaving him flushed, and glowing with pleasure.

'You'll come with me to Daggy's place again?'

'Perhaps.'

A flock of starlings hurtled past with a rush of rapidly beating wings towards their roosts in the dense reed-beds.

'I love your fen, Frankie,' she murmured presently, as they left the dirt road of the loke and turned into the main road.

Thursday 7th November 1940
'Aren't them stars bootiful'

Ferret was leaning against the pond railings whittling a point on a willow stick with her clasp knife when Frank stepped off the school bus.

'Bor!' she called as he started to cross the road. 'Ar you comin' for a walk down the Lode with me?'

Frank stopped dead in his tracks. His heart missed a beat, before racing ahead at the wild suggestion. Within the hour it would be dark, and 'going for a walk in the dark' held only one meaning to the 'big-girls' of the village, exciting explorations in the warm intimacy of stack bottoms.

She followed him across the road, closing her knife with a metallic click.

'I got an idea how you and me can get up to something clever, if we keep our gobs shut after we done it!'

'W-what time?' he stuttered, blushing.

'Why, now, of course. While it's still light so's you know what to do time it's dark. Seein' as you ain't ever done it afore!' she added condescendingly.

Ferret spoke in a low, clandestine voice tinged with laughter as Frank hesitated. 'I'll wait round the corner time you take them old school books and things in.'

He dashed into the house, flinging his satchel and blazer on to the Windsor chair. 'Ma, I'm going to see China,' he called, grabbing his old shooting mack and Wellingtons. 'I won't be long!'

'Your tea is...' But the back door had already closed behind him.

Ferret was waiting for him beneath the Gospel Tree and they started to walk demurely along the village street before turning off to follow the green loke running alongside the Lode bank. The November air was damp with the beginning of a mist and there were splashes of water in the rutted cart tracks, reflecting a crimson sun hanging low above the bank top. Frank took possession of her free hand while Ferret absent-mindedly switched the dying heads of thistle and keck with her stick as they squelched through the puddles in silence.

His thoughts were dancing ahead, like a young spaniel let off the leash. In a few more minutes the girl would indicate a warm secluded nest among the tangle of keck and bents. But Ferret, as she flicked the heads of teazles and scattered the brittle seed-heads from the hemlock, had other thoughts fermenting beneath her raven curls.

'How much further are we going?' Frank asked as he glanced anxiously back towards the receding village. 'Nobody will see us here.'

'A bit further yet,' she replied chastely. 'Where the old bank begins to bend.'

A flock of plover appeared, wheeling over the bank with rounded wings, flashing white then black as they settled silently on the fallow field across the Lode. Ferret's hand was warm in Frank's. 'I like you, Ferret!' he murmured.

'Ar, I like you bor.' Ferret wiped her nose on the sleeve of her tattered mack. 'You have the sense to keep the things we do quiet. Not like them others what go yappin' and boastin' about what they've done!' Her hand tightened confidingly, and he could feel her finger nails digging into his sweating palm.

They had reached the start of a slight bend in the Lode bank, a place where hemlock and meadow-sweet tangled with the rough grasses formed a snug windbreak for gunners to command the icy bend of the Lode on winter nights.

'This'll do!' Ferret lowered herself carefully into a clump of dying meadow-sweet. 'Sit you down an' I'll show you something!'

Frank sat close to her with heightened expectancy, feeling the warmth of her flowing outwards through her layers of old jumpers, while Fenland scents drifted slowly around them in the evening air. Ferret did not move a muscle. She sat staring intently across the flat empty fields ahead as the November sun faded.

The minutes passed, infinitely slow, with nothing happening.

At a loss to know what was expected of him, Frank tentatively placed his hand on her bare knee above her Wellington.

'I like being with you, Ferret!'

'Ar,' she whispered, not moving her head from scanning the empty sky.

Black silhouetted shapes now stood against the greyness of the sky. Every reed stem and thistle head breaking the skyline of the bank above them stood stark against the grey. Ferret's head appeared as a black silhouette; her lips seemed to have been chiselled in marble, bewitchingly distant, their very coldness spurring him to risk a kiss. He was foiled as he leant towards her by the sudden rush of a covey of partridges whirring over the bank, before gliding on bowed wings to settle in the field opposite.

'There they are bor. That's what we come to see!'

Ferret gripped his shoulder excitedly. 'Keep your eyes on 'em where they lit!'

She rolled in the grass towards him. Frank's hand, escaping from her knee, got caught up in her Wellington bending his fingers back with excruciating pain.

'Hang on a minute!' he groaned.

But Ferret was worming her way up the steep bank on her stomach to plant her willow wand firmly against the skyline.

Out in the field below, the partridges were noisily settling themselves in their roosting circle, the plump little cocks happily 'jugging' as the last glimmer of light vanished.

'Them's about a hundred yards from the dyke on a line from my stick to that old willow at the end of the field. Do you remember that bor!'

Frank peered into the dusk until he was just able to make out the blur of a small polled willow in the distance.

'Why?' he snapped irritably, in disillusionment at his dashed hope of romance. 'I do happen to have seen a covey of partridges before!'

'Don't you be daft bor. We aren't here to *look* at the birds! Come you home to tea quick and then we'll get back about half past eight and get 'em!'

Ferret started to run back towards the village with her effortless loping strides, leaving Frank to follow squelching through the muddy puddles trying to keep up with her. They parted at the beginning of the street, where Frank paused breathless beneath the Gospel Tree to watch her dissolve into the shadowy darkness of Back Lane.

The six o'clock news was on when Frank arrived home late for his tea. The soft amber light from the oil-lamp and the cherry-red coals burning brightly in the grate made him blink, almost dazzling him after the darkness of the blackout.

'So, you're home!' His mother hovered in the doorway between kitchen and living room with a covered dinner plate in her hands. 'Where on earth have you been? Your meal has been in the oven for an hour, and it's probably ruined by now.' She placed the plate on the table removing the cover to expose two blackened dried-up sausages on a field of swede and potato mash... 'And I was fortunate to get half a pound of sausages today for a treat. Where have you been?'

'Sorry, Ma,' he answered meekly as he quietly slid into his chair at the table. 'China asked me to help him build his *Daily Express* glider...China's got no idea of cutting wing ribs accurately.'

'I remember hearing you tell your father two years ago that China had sent for a *Daily Express* glider,' she said suspiciously.

'Ah, yes, but China didn't start building it until today. He was only eleven when he had it, and it is quite complicated with all those wing ribs, spars, and tissue covering!'

Her suspicions suitably laid to rest, Mrs Dutton settled herself before the fire in her Windsor chair with a novel.

'By the way,' murmured Frank, 'I offered to go back about a quarter past eight to help finish off the tail. And his dad said something about giving you a bird for Sunday's lunch!'

'That would be nice,' she said pleasantly, not lifting her eyes from her book. 'You may stay there till ten o'clock if you want.'

At eight-thirty Ferret appeared, looming furtively from the shadows of the wisteria as Frank opened the front door. When his eyes had adjusted to the darkness he noticed that she had suddenly put on weight, with an unusually well-filled stomach bulging beneath a flapping mac held together by binder-twine.

'Where'd you tell your Mum your goin'?' she said seriously. 'It don't do to tell her anything about it, she being a teacher, I don't suppose she hold with selling birds!'

'I'm helping China build a non-existent glider,' he chuckled.

Frank repossessed her hand, and they went softly past the sitting room window to walk in silence down the deserted village street.

'You look jolly fat, Ferret,' he observed with unromantic candour as they passed the shuttered window of King Kong's shop. 'Are you feeling very cold?'

'Well, it ain't what your'e thinking, that's a fact,' she replied tartly.

They continued to walk in silence until they reached the cemetery.

'You can have a feel if you want!' Ferret giggled, breaking the silence to pause against the cemetery gate and place his hand on her chest, a chest which felt like a sack of peas.

'Old Daggy been larnin' me to knit my own jumpers. But it's a bit big. Come right down to my knees it do!'

A short distance further along the road they came to the drove where the puddles, gleaming silver in the starlight, marked their path. Above them the sky was darker than the surrounding land, where the mist lay in a starlit shroud, chest-high above the dykes softening the sound of the breeze in the reeds.

'Can you see the plank over the dyke?' whispered Ferret. 'It ought to be about here. Blast bor! There's my stick.' Ferret had lifted her eyes from the dyke to scan the skyline of the Lode bank behind her. 'We'll have to go back 'cause we've gone and passed it.'

As they retraced their steps the water grew lighter, reflecting the brilliance of the stars, until a shadowy plank appeared. Ferret led the way, crossing the plank quickly, disturbing a water-vole that rustled through the sedges to dive with a gentle plop into the water.

'Keep right quiet now bor,' she ordered in a whisper. 'Don't go a-fallin' over the furrows and disturbing the little buggers.'

Frank found himself in the field where, far out in the starlit furrows, a covey of little brown birds would be huddled together in a warm circle with their heads facing outwards as they slept. He followed her along the dykeside headland, moving like hunting cats as they followed the line of the Lode bank, crossing furrows newly turned and clear of brittle stems, looking for the marker stick.

It materialized suddenly, a slender wand stark against the sable sky. Ferret halted to remove her macintosh and unwind yards of light net that was wound around her body. A dog yapped from Marsh Farm, a mile away. A high-flying mallard quarked.

Ferret worked silently, unrolling the net until it lay stretched out on the ground in an invisible oblong thirty feet wide and fifteen deep. She turned to whisper to Frank.

'Where's that old tree bor? Can you see it?'

He moved in the shadow of the sedges to gaze across the field, his eyes following the ridges of the ploughland. 'I think I can make out Marsh Farm,' he whispered hesitantly, seeing a blur on the horizon.

Ferret wiped her nose on the sleeve of her jumper. 'That's no use. Them birds are down in the line of the stick and that old tree. So we have to see it!'

She lay flat on her stomach to make a rapid sweep along the skyline trying to penetrate the tenebrous line between earth and sky.

'I see it! Hold you on to this rope bor.' Frank caught a glimpse of the white oval of her face and felt the end of a rope being held out to him.

'And stand you there a minute 'cause we have to get the net another bit further along.'

He felt the net twitch as she rolled it up from the back, then slither over the furrows as she dragged it a few more yards along the headland.

Ferret reappeared, floating soundlessly across the furrows. The starlight transformed the ragamuffin-girl into a Swan Maiden...an Amazon...an Artemis! Forgotten was the skinny village girl with the perpetually runny nose. He stood in the starlight surrounded by the open fen experiencing intense bliss, with his heart thudding heavily with excitement.

'Ar you ready bor? You follow that furrow steady and don't get out of it.' She gave her instructions in a tense whisper. 'I'll jerk the rope if you go too fast. Keep it level. And drop it as soon as them birds jump so's they hit the net.'

Frank watched his Swan Maiden dematerialise again as she went to take up the other end of the net. Then a jerk on the rope and they were moving. His heart throbbed high in his chest with suppressed excitement. Every nerve was taut in the absolute silence broken only by the faint whisper of the net as it rose and fell over the sea of furrows.

Suddenly, with no warning, the earth seemed to erupt in a rush of thrashing wings as the covey exploded from their roost to crash against the meshes of the net as it slithered over them.

Frank dropped the rope, following the example of the Swan Maiden who by now was lying spread-eagled on top of the net expertly dislocating the necks of the prisoners between her finger and thumb.

'Grab 'em bor,' she hissed. 'Keep 'em down do they'll go scuttlin' along the furrow and get out.' He knelt on the net trying to follow her lead, while a bird, seeing its way clear down a furrow, ran out to whirr away noisily into the distance.

'Blast you, bor. Can't you wring a bird's neck yet?'

She clambered on to her knees and stood counting. Below them the pale breasts, with the chestnut horseshoe markings of partridges, jerked spasmodically on the dark earth, just visible in the starlight.

'Thirteen bor! Fourteen if you'd have been a bit quicker.'

Together they quickly rolled up the net containing the birds and set off towards the shadowy Lode bank. Twenty yards from the plank crossing the drove dyke Ferret dropped flat on her stomach in a furrow and peered into the dense shadows ahead.

'What on earth are you doing?' whispered Frank, anxious to get the birds away from the scene of the crime. 'Let's get back quick.'

She lay there for some moments before rising to her feet and continuing to walk towards the plank.

'Gawd! You might have a lot of book learning, bor, but I'll have to teach you how to get birds. You don't know nothing. Old Foxie could make a right fool of you if you ever try getting birds on your own!'

'Huh! What good does it do to lie down in the mud?' he retorted.

'I'll tell you what good it do. If there be anyone waiting, you got more chance to see them against the sky. And if there is someone and they been watching you comin', if you lay down, you suddenly vanish...and they get all confused wonderin' if they have see'd you or not. So they stand up and move trying to make you out. If they do, you can jump up and race them to the ligger like an old rabbit out of a clump of thistles. Gawd, I'll larn you a thing or two bor, that I will.'

They crossed the dyke by the ligger (plank) and regained the comforting

shadows of the Lode bank carrying the bundled net containing the birds between them.

'Better get over to the Lode side out of the way,' Ferret suggested, scrambling up the steep bank through the long grass dragging the net after her. Thankfully Frank flopped down among the mass of keck and sedge that covered the bank.

'How on earth are we going to smuggle this lot through the village?' he ventured nervously . 'Foxie will surely be out and about by now.'

His Swan Maiden was not listening. She was busily unrolling the net to remove the birds before rolling it up again tightly. Thirteen plump partridges lay in a tidy row, breast uppermost, beside her on the flattened grass. 'There! Three birds fer your Mum and the Captain's wife. And ten for old Gizzie when he come. He'll give me five bob each for them.'

Frank whistled incredulously. 'Ferret! That's a lot more than someone like Boer earns in a week. That's fifty shillings. The price of a posh suit!'

'That's right. Two quid for Mum and Dad, an' ten bob for the kids.'

'But what about you? Don't you want something for yourself?'

She lay back in the soft grass looking up at the sky.

'What I really like,' she answered, chuckling with childlike delight, 'is to have a tin of Nestlés milk in my docky bag all to myself when I'm choppin' beet. I'll have to get Mum to get me one out of her money.'

Frank eased himself a little closer.

'I can give you a tin of Nestlés milk if that is what you really want,' he murmured. But she rolled away from him to stoop over a clump of rushes growing out of the bank at the water's edge.

'I've hid the net and I'll come back for it in the morning,' she said, working the bundle beneath the matted roots and clay. 'I don't want to lose it. It took me a week to knit.'

She returned in the guise of the Swan Maiden to where he lay in the darker shadows of the tall keck, rubbing her chilled hands on her skirt before settling herself beside him.

'Aren't them stars bootiful,' she murmured, moving closer, so that her head rested against his shoulder as she looked up at the sky. 'That's the Hunter.' Ferret indicated the wide square of Orion. 'And if you follow them three stars on his belt they go to his dog. An' if you follow his belt the other way that orange star is the Bull. And above the Bull there's a flock of little old pigeons.'

Her tousled curls, dampened by droplets of mist brushed his cheek as she moved her head. 'The Hunter's got a little hare somewhere, but I can't see it.' She turned on her stomach to peer down at Frank, her warm breath fluttering on his face supported by her elbows.

'Do you know the stars bor?'

'All I know is that that group over there forms the Plough and it always points to the North Star,' he confessed, suffering a crick in his neck as he tried to turn his head towards the Middle Levels. 'I learnt that in the Scouts.'

'I'd have thought you'd have knowed all about the stars with all that schoolin'. Don't they larn you nothing at Downham?' she answered with a flicker of contempt.

'My uncle Daggy larned me to find my way with the stars. Old Daggy love the stars and say they always kept him company better than any woman when he were young and out gunning on the Washes. You always know where you are with the stars gal, that's what he used to say to me. They never change.'

She raised her head to listen as a flock of duck passed overhead with a crisp swish of air through stiff pinions.

'When I were little I used to go with Daggy in his punt when the eels were running. And after we had set the griggs we would lie there floating on the Hundred Foot and he would show me the stars and tell me stories of bootiful princesses...and fighting men up there in the sky, and swans who would come a-flighting through the sky to land on the Washes in the moonlight and change into bootiful yellow-headed gals. Lovely old tales what his grandfather telled him.'

'Don't you find it scary when you are out alone on the fen at night?' Frank murmured, dreamily contemplating the pale glimmer of her throat through the shadows.

'I aren't frit of nothing. 'Cept meeting old Shuck on the drove at night. Old Shuck's alright when he have two eyes and look like a great old dog. He'll come and shew you the way across the fen, and look after you. But if you see him at night with his one great eye flashing red in the middle of his head it mean you'll be dead within the week. Daggy warned me, if ever you hear anything padding and snuffling behind you don't you ever turn round. You got to run straight home without looking back because if you see that great old flaming eye you'll die.'

She gave one of her giggles. 'I nearly got killed through not turning to look back once. Marsh Farm went and turned a cantankerous old bull out on the bank without telling anyone, and when I were coming home in the dark I heard something huge come trotting and snuffling a'hind me. I dursent turn round thinking it were old Shuck. So I started running and old Shuck started running and snorting and I only got to the middle gate in time to jump it afore that great old dog stopped. My gawd bor, I were frit! I never knew till the next day that it were only a cantankerous old bull.'

'You are awfully clever, Ferret,' whispered Frank. 'I bet Headmaster was jolly sad when you stopped going to school.'

'I'll tell you what I larned at school bor. I larned to read a bit and write a bit. But I never did get the hang of doing sums. I suppose the best thing that I did was take the little kids to the lav. I were a real scholar at that. Your mum would send someone into the Top Class saying as she wanted some little old kid taking down the yard to the lav, and Miss Lacy would say "Doris Flegg, Infant Room". I always made it last out by saying "She took a long time Miss, 'cause she was all bunged up" or "She's got the runs, Miss, and every time I had her done, up she started again". I past a lot of time sitting side by side with some little old kid waiting for playtime!'

'You will make a wonderful wife for someone,' said Frank admiringly, filled with awe for a girl who could not only be the free provider of fish, flesh, fowl, and vegetables gleaned from the land, knit her own nets, strip willows with which to make skeps and eel griggs, cope with bunged-up and un-bunged infants, but would also be a companion for journeying amongst the stars with the Swan Maidens.

'Ar,' she said, after a moment's pause. 'Perhaps I would, and perhaps I wouldn't, though I'd still rather be out on the Fen with the stars. Like old Daggy say, "They never let you down".'

A slight breeze wafted cold on Frank's cheeks, and he could feel the keck crisping with frost. He moved closer to the girl within the shared warmth of the tangle of soft bents. A long way away the unsynchronised engines of bombers throbbed, coming in from the north-east, followed by the sudden clatter of the searchlight's generator starting up further along the Loke drove.

'Germans,' he murmured. 'Off to the Midlands again.'

Searchlights sprang into life along the distant horizon in pencil-slim beams circling and probing the sky, questing restlessly like hunting spaniels. Voices came drifting across the black land from the searchlight unit half a mile away, then the blinding brilliance as the beam came on, momentarily turning the leaden surface of the Lode into a silver mirror as it swung upward to be joined by beams from Ten Mile Bank and Southery Fen. A silver speck appeared suspended like a dust mote in a ray of sunlight caught by the Ten Mile Bank beam. It held it for a moment then lost it. Three beams leapt across the sky searching feverishly until they found the silver speck and held it steadily.

'Blast! They have got one lit up bor...like a little moth in a candle.'

As she spoke, every light was doused as if by the touch of a master switch, leaving the sky darker than ever as a new note crept slowly across the heavens.

'Night fighter!' Frank cried. 'Just listen to that V-twelve Merlin. Wouldn't you love to be up there, Ferret?'

'Silly buggers!' was her pithy comment, sitting forward and hugging her knees. 'Why didn't they keep the lights on that there German? So that he could see it. How's the feller supposed to see them Germans up there in the dark?'

'Carrots...Didn't you hear it announced on the wireless how night fighter pilots have to eat raw carrots? There is some special vitamin in carrots that gives you extraordinary night vision.'

'Do they really? We'd better start eating raw carrots then bor. See the long-tail birds when they're roosting better! Still I think they ought to have kept the lights on for him to shoot by.'

'That would have ruined his night sight. Nicky told me it has all been worked out. First the searchlights find out exactly where the target is and the fighter pilot is given its position by wireless. Then he approaches from behind and above, sees the enemy planes' exhausts glowing, and *Brrrrrroomph* another Heinkel bites the dust. Oh, Ferret, the war *must* go on long enough to give me the chance to join up. I'm going to be a fighter pilot in a couple of years!'

'Well you're rarely daft bor. It remind me of rattin'. If you get one you don't get nothing for it. Come to think on it bor, them Germans are like a lot of old rats scuttling after the corn in our towns. And them boys up there are the ones with sticks trying to hit 'em down. Don't see any sense in it at all.'

Seconds later a short burst of machine-gun fire sounded from the west, and two searchlights appeared on the horizon forming a stationary arch beyond the Middle Level. 'Those are Sandra lights to guide the fighter home,' said Frank knowingly. 'Probably a Hurricane from Wittering.'

As he spoke, the lights were switched off returning the night sky to the stars, and the fen to silence as the clatter of the searchlights' generator faded. Bicycle lamps appeared from the direction of the village, singly and in pairs, like glow-worms wavering homewards through the darkness.

'They're coming out of the Ship,' said Ferret, standing up to remove her mac before tying the heads of the partridges together in pairs with binder-twine and hanging five pairs spaced out around her waist like a farthingale.

'Help me get my coat on bor.'

He helped her struggle into her macintosh and giggled. Her hour-glass figure of the early evening had changed to a new look. She stood before him silhouetted against the night sky as slender as a willow wand, with swelling hips rising above voluptuous thighs hidden under a full skirt.

'Right, grab your three and put them in your pocket.'

They entered the village, walking hand in hand like lovers along the street meeting the convivial crowd of home-going men from the Ship. P. C. Fox glanced suspiciously at their silhouettes as he wheeled his bicycle across the square.

'Evenin',' he growled through the crisp frosty air.

'Beautiful night, isn't it, Mr Fox,' Frank answered gaily, conscious of the three corpses bumping his leg at every step as they nestled in the large poacher's pocket of his shooting jacket.

Harnser appeared among the last of the 'regulars' to roll unsteadily out of the bar door of the Ship.

'Dad,' Ferret called, 'I been waiting for you.'

Harnser stumbled across the road towards them temporarily blinded after leaving the brightly lit fug of the pub.

'What have you two been doing of then?' he said roguishly. 'Are you coming home yet, gal?'

'I been larning him about the stars. And he's been helping me to pay for your beer!' she giggled, leading him unsteadily towards two bicycles which were leaning against the Ship railings. 'And I wholly hope you have a battery in your lamp 'cause it won't do for old Foxie to stop us tonight.'

Frank kicked his Wellingtons off in the porch and felt his way gingerly through the blackout curtain and along the unlit passage to the living room carrying the three partridges by their legs.

'Sunday luncheon,' he announced proudly.

'How perfect! Partridges!' she exclaimed, with her face breaking into one of her rare smiles. 'I must get some Brussel sprouts from Mr Howes, and roast some potatoes and make bread sauce. Better put them to hang in the larder.'

'By the way, Ma,' he said confidentially, 'perhaps you had better not thank China's father for giving them to you. He gets very embarrassed because he can't afford to buy a game licence.'

'I understand perfectly,' she answered. 'Mum's the word. And you must certainly not let Mrs Vernon know where her Sunday luncheon came from!'

'Oh, no. Of course not,' he replied meekly.

Frank paused at the top of the stairs to knock softly on Olivia's door.

'Come in,' she called. He found her sitting on the goatskin rug before the fire reading an old magazine. 'What happened to you all evening? The house has been like a morgue. The wireless accumulator needs recharging. Your mother has had her nose in a book all evening and I have written two boring letters, and I am just going to get into bed. Now tell me about your exciting moments.'

'Well, for mother's edification I have been helping China build a non-existent model glider. But really I have been out with Ferret poaching our Sunday dinner.'

'Oh!' she exclaimed. 'Rosie said Ferret's father could charm the birds out of the trees with his blarney. Is that what you have been doing to poor Ferret among the straw stacks?'

'Not exactly. Ferret knitted herself a jumper which was miles too big. So she took it off down the Lode bank in the dark and we managed to catch a covey of partridges in it.'

'Liar!'

'Honest, we did.'

'I don't believe you.'

'Plump, lovely partridges.'

'Oh, go to bed!'

He dodged the pink mules she flung at him and escaped to collapse giggling on the landing lino, just as his mother's head appeared at the top of the stairs.

Thursday 14th of November
Bombs fall on the Village

At precisely 23.00 hours a gaggle of Heinkel bombers from Luftflotte 2 crossed the coast of the Wash at Sutton Bridge, where they altered course to follow the silver ribbon of the river Nene westwards.

Lieutenant Ernst Hoehmer, the pilot of one of the bombers in the third wave, and his bomb-aimer sitting on a folding seat beside him, were relaxed as they chatted in the glow from the instrument dials. Beyond the narrow gangway between the bomb bay bulkheads, the wireless operator was seated on his stool in front of his set monitoring the course between parallel Lorenz beams. The dorsal gunner was comfortably ensconced in his cradle seat lulled by the monotonous drone of the engines. Above him the sky was an opalescent blue-black star map revolving around Polaris, and from time to time the black elliptical wings of a following aircraft, flying slightly above and behind, would be silhouetted against the glow of the Milky Way.

The bomb-aimer leant sideways to take a canvas satchel from the side of the repeater compass, from which he produced a flask of coffee and a paper bag containing a dozen knackwurst sausages and crusty bread rolls liberally spread with Dutch butter.

Ahead, searchlights were probing the sky, fluttering on wisps of drifting cloud before switching off. The blitz was going well for the bomber crews, and it was relaxing to be drifting over the countryside with the dykes and rivers softly illuminated by the stars, and the comforting red glow from the shrouded exhausts on each side of them. It was good to fly thus in the calm anonymity of the night sky after the strain of daylight missions crossing and re-crossing the Channel to face the Spitfires and Hurricanes of August and September, and it was bliss to return from leave to sit chatting while the formation flew along a corridor beamed out by wireless waves leading them to an insignificant Midlands town, Coventry.

Ernst remembered visiting it once, when he and his wife visited their English friends at Stratford-on-Avon. 'Stratford!' His face mellowed as he recalled peaceful June days, and the first sight of Holy Trinity Church from the bankside meadows, golden with buttercups in lush grass.

Ernst sighed. 'If only the British had listened to the Führer when France capitulated there would have been no need for this offensive. The Führer had no wish to fight the English. The Third Reich would control Europe, while the British would keep their Empire. Together the Saxon cousins would dominate the world.'

He took the coffee from the bomb-aimer and settled back comfortably in his seat. The wireless operator appeared in the gangway to collect some bread rolls and sausages for the dorsal gunner and himself. He peered ahead through the glazed nose at the silvered grid of Fenland dykes.

'Better than crossing the Channel in daylight, Lieutenant!' he chuckled. 'No Spitfires!'

As he spoke the aircraft lurched violently as, unbelievably, a line of holes appeared running the length of the starboard wing, followed by a spent bullet ricocheting around the eight bombs standing upright behind the bulkhead.

Then complete silence, an uncanny silence apart from the regular thump-thump of the engines. Panic returned to Ernst. The silence was broken by the intercom crackling into life as the gunner, peering impotently into the night sky, shouted '*Nightfighter!*'.

Minutes later a cone of tracer bullets overtook them to converge in a cross ahead of its nose. His immediate reflex action was to drop the port wing and turn for home, losing height until he was well below the following bombers, then to follow the widening river Ouse towards the friendly North Sea and the airfield at Maarsen.

Three minutes later he glanced through the glazed side panels to see the parallel Old and New Bedford rivers glistening like tramlines in the rain and ordered the bomb-aimer to ditch the bombs, reasoning that if he flew a dog-leg course north then south-east he could use up time and fuel to enable his return to base to coincide with the returning formations to report 'Target Bombed' to the interrogating officer, thus escaping the *Gruppen Kommandeur's* wrath.

At 23.25 hours a lone German bomber passed over the Terrington Marshes to head out into the night above the glittering sea after having unwittingly toppled Big Ben, shattered the Lord Mayor's coach, and overturned H.M.S. Hood in one fell blow.

Mr Montague Box and his buxom wife Milly resided in the neat new bungalow 'Dunroamin', half a mile from the village beside the Wisbech road.

'Old Money-Box' was a retired railway engine-driver whose overriding passion, beyond 'fretwork', was to retire from the footplate in order to create his dream vegetable garden, and so, when the time arrived after riding forty-three years on the footplate latterly on a crack L.N.E.R. express hauling passengers between London and Edinburgh, he was duly presented with an ornate clock and a pension and Montague's dream came true.

He withdrew his lifetime savings and commissioned a local builder to build him a bungalow on a long narrow acre of fertile Fenland soil bordering the roadside dyke.

Here he set about the realisation of the dream that had held his thoughts over countless thousands of miles by planting a triple row of privet cuttings along the side of the dyke, which quickly grew into a thick hedge stretching the length of his property, leaving access through a neat white gate where the plank crossed the dyke.

Money Box's one concession to Milly, who loved cottage flowers, was to allow her a small patch of earth each side of the gravel path leading to the front door. The remainder of the rich Fenland soil was dedicated to the growing of vegetables, jealously guarded from all birds, insects, humans, and animals alike. No cat was allowed to use Old Money Box's asparagus mounds for an elevated toilet. No bird was allowed to sing on his wigwams of pea sticks, or perch on the willow arches above the runner beans. Potatoes were blissfully banked, lettuces lovingly bedded, strawberries strawed and raspberries caned.

At each end of his plot Montague had an armoury: a No. 3 garden-gun, with its cartridges kept handy in Milly's 'Present from Edinburgh' sugar bowl, ready to be used against any bird, mouse, or rat that dared to set foot on his seedbeds, a catapult for use against trespassing cats, and a selection of ball-bearings in the milk jug, 'A Present from Brighton', which told of Mrs Box's extensive travels on free railway warrants.

Likewise the potting shed, wreathed in an exuberance of honeysuckle at the opposite end of his plot, held a .410 shotgun and some rabbit snares, a sack of soot to combat the slugs, several mole traps and a Flit spray, together with a whole gamut of powders and contraptions guaranteed to bring an early demise to any living creature.

Adjoining the potting shed was the only Anderson Shelter in the village, for no sane person would waste time, money, and soil, installing a shelter in a land of sugar-beet clamps, ditches, and wide open spaces, which clearly confirmed the belief that 'Old Money Box' were 'daft'!

It was Milly who had insisted on having a shelter, but when it eventually arrived in four sections of corrugated iron on Gizzie's removal cart and was dumped on the roadside, 'where to put it' sparked off a heated discussion. Milly wanted it outside the back door where Montague's shallots were sprouting, while Montague insisted that it must go at the very end of the plot out of sight among the elephantine leaves of the rhubarb plants. And as usual Montague had his way.

Montague Box Esq. was a bit of an enigma to the indigenous population of Willows End. They were not themselves over-disposed to converse with 'furriners', but 'Old Money Box' was utterly dumb! He smiled. He was polite when accosted in the village street, but in the eyes of the locals he was 'verra deep'. Nonetheless the whole village knew his full history, the pedigree of his Whittlesea parents, his wife's March parents, and even a fictitious wayward daughter who had left home, and according to the better informed 'were one of them there in Piccadilly' and to the even better informed 'it were her what was sendin' the money to pay for that new bungalow! Old Money Box is rarely deep!'

In the evening, when the setting sun had finally slid away beyond the smudge of Ramsey, or during the times when gales forced him to retreat indoors and don the slippers beside the fire where Milly sat placidly pegging away at a fireside rug, a willow skep at her feet holding narrow strips of material cut from old clothes, Montague would carry a mug of cocoa with him into the scullery, where his Hobbies Al fret machine stood between Milly's dolly tub and her bicycle.

This was Montague's other dream-world, from which emerged a model of H.M.S. Hood sailing on a polished mahogany sea and displayed on the parlour mantelpiece. The Lord Mayor's coach, complete with horses and outriders, graced the top of Milly's highly polished chest of drawers in their bedroom, while one opened the front door to be confronted by a five-foot-high model of Big Ben standing in the tiny vestibule.

Neatly stacked copies of *Hobbies Weekly* stood on top of a tea-chest holding his stock of marquetry veneers with another tea-chest filled with plywood off-cuts and strips of hard wood. 'Dunroamin' was a pantheon to fretwork. Its walls were adorned with marquetry pictures. Milly's kitchen displayed teapot stands, an intricate letter rack, and a 'love-spoon' with interlaced ivy leaves and hearts along its handle, all vying with Milly's peg rugs on the floor and crochet-work mats beneath every vase and on every flat surface.

One might say that the sum of life for Montague and Mildred Box in their neat little box of a home would read:

Garden + Fretwork + Crochet-work + Pegging = Serenity

A large, rotund, silver-blue Persian cat, which *never* defiled a seedbed, or bruised a tender shoot, completed the picture.

At precisely 23.12 hours on Thursday the 14th of November Montague was standing in the middle of his vegetable patch smoking a last pipe before joining Milly in bed.

It was a beautiful starlit evening. Orion was brilliant in the south pointing towards the Dog Star in the velvety blackness of the night sky. A light breeze carried with it the tang of the dykes, and the faint cry of a disturbed heron drifted above the rustling of reeds. Searchlights wandered aimlessly above the Middle Levels.

Monty breathed deeply, savouring the crisp November air with its peaty potato-sweet bouquet. His Brussels sprouts were just reaching perfection. The tinge of frost would crisp their tight green whorls to an epicurean succulence unknown in 'field sprouts'. Montague was supremely content with life.

Engines throbbed soothingly below the stars. Montague knocked the ashes from his pipe and turned to walk back to the bungalow to nestle next to plump, warm Milly in the feather bed.

The first bomb fell in the sugar-beet field across the road from 'Dunroamin'. The second one rocked the bungalow, causing Big Ben to collapse across the vestibule floor, and by the time that the fourth and fifth were exploding Milly was out of bed following in the wake of the fat Persian cat in a mad rush towards the shelter.

'Monty! Monty! Where are you?' she shrieked as she took a short cut through the middle of the sprout patch. 'Monty where a...' Then the earth opened up, and like Persephone, Milly was dragged down into the depths of the earth amongst the remnants of the Brussels sprouts, not into the welcoming arms of Hades, but legs astride her husband's bald head, as a trickle of loose earth gently covered her thighs.

Milly fainted.

She slowly opened her eyes to see the narrow beam of a carefully shrouded torch six feet above her woolly nightcap, and to hear a sepulchral voice tiptoeing through the fenland soil into her ears.

'What are you two a-doin' down there like two little old mices in your nothin's?'

The narrow beam of light fluttered around her. Montague's face was protruding from the earth between her splayed thighs, which were almost, but not quite, covered by a pink flannelette nightie.

'Are you all right bor?' said the A.R.P. Warden tremulously, shining his torch upon Montague's quiescent face.

'Is he alive gal?' he whispered tactlessly to Milly, sending her into hysterics.

'Pinch him!' suggested one of the two Home Guards who had arrived.

'That's a great old hole!' exclaimed the other Home Guard. 'That old bomb must have gone down a mile afore she went off!'

Montague suddenly opened his eyes and spat out a mouthful of earth.

'Where am I?'

'In your sprout bed, bor!'

One of the Home Guards lay flat on the rim of the crater and began to haul Milly out.

'Don't you do that 'case they go down out of sight,' ordered the A.R.P. Warden officiously. 'What we want is a rope round them. That bomb must have gone down deep afore she blasted off!'

'Have you got a rope bor?' asked the Warden to Montague who was just beginning to get his senses back.

'Oh, cut my clothes line down,' shrieked Milly. 'And be quick. I don't want to get poomonia on top of all this carry-on!'

'Where am I?' moaned Montague. 'I can't hear anything.'

Milly gazed down at the disembodied head between her thighs.

'Oh, you silly old thing.' She poked a finger in his nearest ear. 'You got your earholes bunged up with muck!'

The Home Guard, who had gone to fetch the clothes line, returned and threw one end down to Milly.

'Get this rope under his arms if you can find them, gal,' he advised.

Milly scrabbled like a broody hen in the soft earth, working the rope over her spouse's head and shoulders and finally succeeded in looping it underneath his armpits.

'Right now!' said the A.R.P. Warden to the Home Guards. 'You help Mrs Box out while I hang on to Mr Box's rope so he don't go down the bottom of the hole.'

So plump Milly, decorously holding her pink nightie around her nether parts, was helped up the side of the crater, to be followed by Montague whose faculties had returned and who was bemoaning the fact that he had lost his favourite pipe.

At that moment P.C. Fox arrived on his unlit bicycle.

'What's a-going on here?'

'Nothing to do with you!' The A.R.P. Warden puffed out his chest. 'Bombs is Warden's department.'

'Well, I represent the law!'

'Ar well now, bor, nobody's broken the law. If you want to talk about breaking laws, it's them old devils up there what's a-breakin' of the law dropping bombs. Do you get on your bike and get after them!'

'And guarding the village against the enemy is our job of nights,' chorused the two Home Guards in unison.

If it had not been for the darkness P.C. Fox's face would have been noticeable for its fiery hue. 'Right then, I'll say good night,' he replied huffily.

The A.R.P. Warden switched his torch on and gazed professionally at Montague, who appeared covered from head to toe in black fen mire looking like a warthog rudely awakened from its mudhole siesta.

'Right then!' he said, when the police constable had disappeared beyond the deep shadows of the privet hedge and the crank-crank of pedals had ceased. 'Let's all go and have a nice cup of tea, Mrs Box. Lots of sugar in it - for the shock!' he added, suddenly remembering a smattering of 'First Aid for bomb victims'.

'I want my cup of cocoa!' mumbled Montague, still in a state of shock, as they all trooped through the front door stepping over Big Ben in the vestibule to find H.M.S. Hood upside-down on the parlour mat, and leaving for daylight the yet unseen sight of Money Box's succulent sprouts festooning the roof.

The following morning, as Frank and Mrs Dutton were having their breakfast, the back door opened to admit an excited Ma Shipham who could hardly contain herself.

'Do you know what?'

Mrs Dutton did not know what, except that her 'help' had burst in without knocking! She raised her eyebrows.

'About what ought I to know?'

'Old Money Box and that wife of his have been bombed in the night!'

She plumped down on the Windsor chair.

'There they were walking peacefully down the garden to their shelter. And do you know what? When they tried to get in it they found the whole lot of them there diddycoys crammed in like sardines. So the old couple started to walk back to the house when a great old bomb dropped smack on their garden. They still ain't found that fluffy cat of theirs!'

'My goodness,' Mrs Dutton interjected with her teacup halfway to her lips. 'Do you know what has happened to Mr and Mrs Box?'

'I don't rightly know about that. All I know is that the Moocher who were out at the time told Big Bertha Pope he'd see'd policeman Fox coming away from the diddycoy camp and there's a great old hole in Money Box's garden, with sprouts all over his roof. I suppose they must have been blowed to smithereens!'

'But how terrible,' said Mrs Dutton turning pale. 'They were such a nice inoffensive old couple.'

Frank was already rushing to the door with his school blazer half on and half off dragging his satchel. 'I'm off to look for shrapnel before the school bus arrives!' he announced, tripping over the ginger cat in his haste.

December 1940
The Skating Party

Clear skies and a waxing moon in December brought a sharp frost and by the second morning the pond was sheeted over with thin ice which gradually thickened until, by the third day, the schoolchildren were sliding confidently around the edges and the ducks had lost their battle to keep the water from freezing beneath the far-side willows and were huddling in disconsolate groups beside the Post Office bridge.

On the fourth day the children descended *en masse* to slide and tumble on the ice, much to the consternation of the Headmaster who stood bleating impotently to his gleefully-deaf class to remove itself henceforth from the ice and return to the school playground, meanwhile ordering Miss Lacy to fetch the ladder from the school bicycle shed. His versatile mind, ever prepared for such eventualities, flashed backwards to stories he had read in his youth in the *Boy's Own Paper* where a ladder was the established method of rescuing skaters falling through thin ice.

But the Headmaster was not of indigenous Fenland stock. He was a 'furriner' from Hampstead, and had no inbred affinity with the magical delight that ice evokes in the true Fensman's breast. Thus Old Daggy Flegg's *'She bears!'* went unheard.

The half-dozen patriarchs, muffled up to their hoary eyebrows and wearing balaclava helmets beneath their caps and long overcoats with corn-sack capes over their shoulders, stood in a huddled group and pronounced it to be well and truly 'fruzz'. For Daggy had arrived with his pattens and had executed a graceful three laps at warm-up speed around the circumference of the pond before giving the traditional cry *'She bears!'*.

Together with Harvest Home, June Feast Day, Wisbech Mart, weddings, funerals and Christmas Day, the day the ice bears is one of the holy days of the Fensman's year.

'She bears' rang across the village like the Hallelujah chorus, with the 'Juniors' taking up the chant as they finally made their way in Miss Lacy's wake towards the school playground.

Soon the Vicar arrived with his 'Norwegians' screwed to a pair of polished black boots in his bicycle basket, followed by the Moocher with his pattens slung round his neck, and as the last faint *'She bears'* vanished behind the closing of the school door Daggy, the Vicar and the Moocher were left in sole command of the virgin ice until the weekend. Then the working community and the schoolchildren would be free to descend on the pond with their 'Fen Runners' and 'Norwegians' to emulate their heroes, the Cutty Sees, the Smarts and the Jim Fishes of past National Championships, as they flashed around the pond. They were '*speed* skaters' holding no brief for effeminate 'figure skaters'; they were the greyhounds, the long lean hunting wolves of the ice goddess.

Olivia awoke to the sound of raised voices coming through her bedroom window. It was barely eight o'clock on a grey winter Saturday morning. She shivered, and pulled the bedclothes higher to cover her ears and tried to sleep through the icy greyness of the freezing room. A few moments later she heard Frank pass her room on his way downstairs and the porch door slam.

A cacophony of high-spirited shouts and rippling laughter appeared to be coming from the pond. For a moment she imagined that the war had ended or some other unforseen happening had occurred during the night. Sliding her legs from the bed, and dragging her dressing-gown over the pullover which she wore over her nightdress, she crossed the room. Frost had made the windows opaque with filigree fern patterns through which moving blobs of colour shimmered and spun out of focus. Olivia breathed on the window making a circular patch of clear glass through which the colours materialized into a multitude of children, yelling, singing, sliding, falling, and rolling on the ice. They wore flapping oversize jackets, macintoshes held together with binder-twine belts, cloth caps, rabbit-skin caps, and jumpers of every hue and fit; girls in pixie-hats or tam o' shanters, with skinny bare legs protruding from thin cotton skirts and ending in heavy boots or Wellingtons. Some wore woollen gloves, while others, not owning a pair of gloves, were wearing old socks over their hands, and all were rosy-cheeked and lost in the ecstasy born of ice.

Olivia watched Frank cross the road carrying his skates and sit on the brick parapet opposite the Ship, where he was joined by China, Ferret, and Podge, who came gliding on their pattens out of the mass of sliding infants to sit beside him as he changed his Wellingtons for his skating boots.

She turned from the window and dressed quickly before making her way downstairs to make herself a cup of tea. Since tea-rationing had been introduced Mrs Dutton had insisted that Olivia must use her own rations, which in practice meant that Olivia had a surplus of all the rationed commodities such as sugar and tea left by the cook-house sergeant. However Mrs Dutton was too proud to share Olivia's extra rations and stoically made do with her four ounces a week of fats and one ounce of cheese.

Having boiled a kettle of water on the oil-stove and made her pot of tea, Olivia pulled another sweater over her head, grey army socks over her stockings, and wound a scarf round her neck, before following Frank across the road to the pond. The Vicar had just arrived and she joined him at the pond railings watching the skaters. He beamed at her and raised his shovel hat. His cheeks, she noticed, glowed even more ruddy than usual beneath his twinkling eyes in the frosty air.

'Morning m'dear. What a truly wonderful sight!...Wonderful sight! Where are your skates, Mrs Vernon?'

His were conspicuously hung across his left shoulder, glinting in the weak winter sunlight as the sun appeared behind the Wesleyan Chapel.

'Bravo!' He waved towards Frank who was skimming past at breakneck speed, closely followed by Ferret and China.

'Skating is not one of my accomplishments, Vicar.'

'Then you have not lived, m'dear! We must put that right.'

'Well,' she laughed, 'at least I have the excuse of being born in India, which was not very conducive to ice skating. Bet you haven't played a chukker at polo, Vicar!' she teased.

He chuckled.

'I may have. I too was an officer and a gentleman in my youth. Anyway you are going to learn to skate now. And that boy and I are going to "larn you".' He glanced fixedly at her feet, before turning to walk towards his bicycle which stood against the lych-gate. 'I shall go home and sort out a pair of Milly's skates for you.'

Frank swerved towards her in a graceful curve holding out his hand.

'Come on the ice,' he called. His eyes danced. 'Oh, come on. It's safe enough. Only the edge cracks!' he added as she placed the toe of a shoe tentatively on the ice, drawing it hastily back as she felt it crack.

'I'm going back to the house before the Vicar returns with a pair of skates,' she said, resolutely turning her back to the pond.

'Cracks she bears: Bends she breaks!' chanted Frank merrily.

'We'll larn you,' said China, who had joined them with Ferret and Podge. 'Won't we bor?'

'Oh no you won't!' she laughed. 'I'm off!'

But she found herself trapped by the combined pincer-movement of the Vicar cycling across the Square bearing a pair of shining 'Norwegians' fitted to a pair of high-sided white boots in his cycle basket and Harnser Flegg, his face wreathed in a broad grin, approaching her from the Ship yard.

'These will fit.' Puffing and blowing after pedalling at speed back from the rectory, he glanced professionally at Olivia's feet, 'Like you, Milly had a well-turned ankle!'

Olivia looked hesitant, glancing hurriedly towards the boys for help but receiving only enthusiastic grins. The Vicar cast a disapproving glance at thin, Goray, tartan skirt with its crisp pleats.

'You really ought to have something with a bit more bounce over your bottom,' he observed.

'Vicar!' she murmured primly, raising her eyebrows.

'I mean for when you fall on it!' he chuckled as he finished tying his boot-laces and skated away.

Olivia, having put on the boots and taken as long as possible in lacing them up, sat on the brick ledge below the pond railings surrounded by a half-circle of grinning faces, realising that she was now expected to stand up.

'Come you on, Ma'am,' said Harnser, holding his arms out towards her from a couple of yards away. 'You haye to just stand up and come to me.'

But the moment she moved, her left leg shot away from her, depositing her with a bump on the ice.

'Oh dear!' exclaimed the Vicar returning from his second circuit, while the bystanders roared their approval as she made a frantic effort to regain her feet. 'Let me help you up.'

If Frank had felt terror at learning to dance, Olivia was petrified. She felt that the slightest movement, even the opening of her mouth to speak, caused the skates to run away with her legs leaving her sprawling on her damp and rapidly freezing rear on the hard ice.

'No!' she shrieked as the Vicar and Frank closed in on her. 'Don't you *dare* come near me!'

She dragged herself up on to her feet with the assistance of the pond railings and gingerly turned to face them. Instantly her feet shot away from under her again and she only avoided disaster by flinging her arms wildly about the Vicar's neck.

'Right,' said the Vicar, after she had been straightened out and was standing upright on the ice, held on either side by Frank and the Vicar. 'You are going to learn to be a 'Fen Runner'. Turn out your toes and keep your ankles stiff and we shall tow you!'

'I thought you taught yourself pushing a chair?' she groaned to Frank with a grimace.

'Ah, yes. But this is a much quicker way to get your confidence,' answered the Vicar innocently, as he signalled with a wink for Frank to take her other hand. 'Now forward with the left foot...and away!'

Olivia found herself accelerating with incredible speed as they sped around the pond dragging her with them until she lost her stride and crouched helpless between them with her feet together. 'Again!' said the Vicar after they had waited for her to regain her breath, and they whirled her round and round passing the willow trunks and the chapel, the Post Office, and the Ship until suddenly she found the rhythm and was off solo, leaning forward in speed-skating fashion with her arms behind her back and her scarf streaming out behind her.

'Good old Miss!' yelled China enthusiastically. 'Go you on round again.'

But Olivia, gliding, as she thought, confidently to join them, misjudged her speed, and crashed once again, knocking the group *en masse* in one great hilarious heap of waving legs and bodies sprawling in all directions. She glanced up from where she lay, revealing an immodest amount of leg wrapped across the Vicar's chest, to see Mrs Dutton, watching from the sitting-room window.

'Gosh!' she exclaimed, after Harnser had gallantly come to her rescue and set her up on her feet. 'I must do that again!' and carried on practising until the church clock chimed twelve-thirty which was the signal for the grown-ups to leave for their lunch, leaving the small children to rush on to the deserted ice to slide in peace.

The freeze continued. Hoar-frost sparkled on the sere reed-stems and whitened the fields beneath a sun which glowed round and red each evening as it fell beyond Ramsey on the horizon. Flocks of immigrant starlings rushed aimlessly about the Fen, settling at dusk in great noisy chatterings in the dense reedbeds, where many died, frozen as they slept. Fieldfares and redwings called mournfully as they flew southwards, and bullocks stood forlornly on the iron-hard ground, coughing huskily in the gateways with their nostrils steaming in the frosty air. At night the waxing moon was past three-quarters. Soon it would be full, riding high across the flat land in a cloudless sky, silvering the waterways, glinting along the waves of sedges rimed with frost.

On Monday morning, after Frank had left the house and caught the school bus, and the workers were back to work in the fields, Olivia crossed the road carrying her skates to continue practising alone on the deserted pond. By mid-morning a weak sun breaking out from a low bank of grey clouds brought the patriarchs hobbling out with their sticks to lean against the hump-back bridge, where they coughed and wheezed in between snippets of conflicting advice which they flung out across the ice to Olivia, harking back to the skating matches of the eighteen-seventies and the skating parties when as young men, arm in arm with their girls, they flew along the lonely rivers between village pubs.

The Vicar crossed the Square to join them on the bridge and Olivia glided towards him coming to a perfectly controlled halt by pressing down on her heels, keeping her feet parallel, and leaning forward.

'How am I doing, Vicar?' she asked, looking up into their faces as they lined the parapet of the bridge.

'Excellent, m'dear.'

'You'll have to take her for a run down the Lode, Vicar,' said one old reprobate with a toothless grin. 'Get her a-goin' proper.'

'Ar that you ought,' broke in another, his eyes misted with fond memories. 'Do you think of them old times, Vicar, skatin' with the mawthers down to the Ship at Creek and up to the Feltwell Anchor. Good old times without a word of a lie. Them young mawthers could run like hares on their pattens!'

Great-grandfather 'Slodger' Chapman gave a sly sideways glance at Olivia. 'I dare say you could give the young 'uns a good old chase the way you're a-goin'. Just you go round again for the Parson to see.'

The Vicar nodded enthusiastically.

'Slodger!' he said, grabbing the patriarch by the lapels of his ancient great-coat and with his blue eyes twinkling. 'You have given me an exceedingly good idea!'

'Ar!' groaned the muttering of patriarchs in unison.

'Slodger, it will be full moon on Thursday,' the Vicar continued. 'So if the frost holds I shall organise a Skating Party down the Lode then up the river to the Black Swan.'

Olivia arrived breathless after completing four circuits.

'Black Swan?'

'Yes, m'dear. All the ladies and lads of the village on an old-time Skating Party and festivities in the warmth of The Dirty Duck.'

'Vicar!' she giggled. 'You shock me!'

But he only laughed, pointing a quivering finger at her skirt slush-sodden from a recent fall. 'Come home to the Rectory with me and we will see if we can find more suitable attire for you.'

The Rectory was a gaunt Georgian building at the far end of the village surrounded by an unkempt shrubbery of laurel bushes. Ragged box edges to long-disappeared garden walks beneath collapsed pergolas were set in an acre of lawn and orchard and enclosed within a high brick wall. Now the wall was mellow and mossy. During spring, flycatchers made their nests in the orchard trees trained against its bricks. Bank voles and shrews lived in crannies where the mortar had crumbled. Grass snakes coiled basking in sensual bliss on the sun-warmed earth at its foot, and winter owls slept in the mass of ivy that cloaked the archway over the back gate.

Olivia followed the Vicar along the gravel drive to enter the front door of the Rectory, crossing the threshold into a hallway devoted to rowing sculls, University caps, umbrella-stands holding sticks of every description, fishing creels, old and stained shooting bags, dog-leads, nets and a bee helmet and veil, all hung on nails. Above all, over a doorway in the facing wall, there stared down through glassy eyes the stuffed head of a red deer stag with 'THETFORD FOREST, 1922' printed in gold lettering on its polished wooden shield.

'My goodness!' exclaimed Olivia stepping over a fallen cricket bat to view a set of polo sticks and a pith helmet. 'You really have played polo, Vicar! Or did they come with this mansion?' she quipped.

His eyes twinkled warmly. In fact his eyes and rubicund cheeks appeared to be the only warm objects in the area as he led her through the door beneath the stuffed stag's head.

'Bit of a mess!' he chuckled. 'My bachelor study.'

A sad-eyed, black, field spaniel raised itself from the hearth of a cheerless fire smouldering in a massive marble fireplace to look up as if querying a woman's presence. Olivia started at the shocking untidiness as she glanced round a large, high room dominated by books, chaotically arranged, covering three walls from floor to ceiling - shooting, fishing, coursing, cricket, and natural history, vied with heavy leather-bound theologies, slim volumes of Greek poetry, fusty tomes of ancient philosophies and occult mysticism. Magazines cascaded in fanned-out heaps on the floor from a walnut desk overflowing with papers, fossils, the bleached skulls of animals and birds, pens, letters, uncompleted sermons and, in the centre of all this confusion, a cut-glass decanter of whisky, a bottle of port, and some glasses.

Above the marble mantelpiece hung a large painting in an ornate gilded frame of a plover-netter waiting in his hideout on the Welney washes beneath a crisp October sky with a flock of peewits strung out in a long irregular line coming into the nets.

'Thomas Dutton's work,' said the Vicar, noticing her glance. 'Wonderful bird artist. I buried him less than six months ago. Not a great Churchman!'

Olivia allowed her eyes to fall down to the mantelpiece. Its centre was dominated by a bronze model of a stag with ivory horns, flanked by photographs in silver frames of a young woman wearing a high-necked blouse frilled with lace, her fair hair piled on top of her head.

'Milly,' he murmured noncommittally. 'Now let us see if we can find a proper skirt for you.'

Olivia followed him out of the room and up a dark wide staircase to a long landing leading to a bedroom at the front of the house. Like the downstairs study, it was thickly coated in black Fen dust, but unlike the study it was neat and tidy with everything in its place. The unmade bedstead, the wardrobe and dressing-table were of bird's-eye maple, its golden patina hidden beneath the dust, and bone china and cut-glass toiletries graced the dressing-table on faded lace mats below begrimed mirrors.

Taking a large handkerchief from his pocket, the Vicar swept the layer of dust from an ottoman standing at the foot of the bed and opened it to reveal Milly's skating outfit neatly folded amidst naphthalene and tissue paper.

'Milly had an eighteen-inch waist when we were married!' he remarked lifting out the skirt. 'But by the time she had this made she had filled out a few inches.' He dropped it across the foot of the bed and turned to go. 'I shall wait for you in the study.'

Olivia lifted the skirt from the bed and held it to her waist as the door closed behind the Vicar. It was dark brown, tailored from heavy linen to fit snug to the hips, gored and box-pleated flaring down to an ankle-length hem.

She stepped out of her bedraggled Goray and dropped the skirt over her head, twisting it round to hook up the side placket and finding that it fitted as if it had been tailored for her. Wiping the dust from the dressing-table mirror she gave a quick pirouette to watch the hem swirl before falling to hang straight and demure from the hips.

On a sudden impulse she bent to take the rest of the outfit from the ottoman, wrinkling her nose to the pungent smell of naphthalene as she removed another layer of brittle tissue to find a wash-silk shirt blouse of cyclamen and white stripes with a black ribbon bow at the neck and, below another layer of tissue, a gilet tailored in the same material as the skirt, a fox-skin boa and muffs.

She smiled to herself, mischievously, like a child, and proceeded to remove her sweater.

Olivia returned down the dark stairs and along the dank passage to find the study much warmer. The Vicar had stirred the fire, kindling it into new life. The coals now burned red beneath blazing logs, their heat reflecting from the marble surround to burnish the leather bindings of the books and the walnut desk with soft luxurious warmth. She found him laid back in one of the deep leather Chesterfield chairs with a glass of whisky balanced on his knee like a benevolent unobtrusive ghost. She also noticed for the first time the Persian rug before the fire, the dog at his feet and grey light falling through the tall windows, an unkempt lawn beyond alive with birds fluttering about a bird-table.

Olivia's skirt rustled as she crossed the room.

'Not exactly what one might call an east-wind-defying outfit,' she said nervously. 'Young ladies must have been tough in your young days, Vicar.'

The Vicar looked up from his chair at the sound of her voice. The young woman who appeared in the doorway was like a shade from the past. Olivia had piled her fair hair high on her head, held by a tortoiseshell comb that left unruly tendrils nestling on her neck. She was wearing the long Edwardian skirt with the gilet over the washed-silk shirt.

The Vicar hastily downed his whisky and regarded her with a reminiscent smile on his lips, casting glances back and forth between the figure coming towards him with a smile on her face and the photographs on the mantel.

'Good gracious, Mrs Vernon!'

She glanced at him enquiringly.

'You do not approve?'

*'By Jingo!...*You must wear the whole outfit for the Skating Party!' he enthused suddenly coming to life and slapping his leg. 'Never expected a celibate old bachelor to be granted such a divine visitation in this earthly life!'

He handed her a glass of port which he had already poured out for her and she blushed as she carried it to the opposite chair to sit gazing self-consciously into the fire. The dog sidled to sit at her feet and laid its head on her knee.

'I simply had to put the complete outfit on. It is so beautiful,' she murmured, absent-mindedly stroking the dog's silky ear.

She had a strange feeling of being taken over by the clothes. She noticed how the Vicar's eyes rested on her face as if time had been arrested and these were once again the salad days of his Edwardian youth.

'It was during the February of 1910 that Milly last wore that outfit,' he said gently. Olivia sat bathed in the firelight as the logs flared and crackled.

'Won't you tell me about Milly?' she asked persuasively.

'It is a long story...or a short one,' he answered, lowering his eyes from her face to gaze into the fire.

'Tell me the long story.' Olivia sank deeper into the armchair, drawing her legs under her like a child.

'I have not always been of the cloth,' he said hesitantly. 'Where's your glass?'

He reached over the dog to pour her another glass of port.

'I came down from Cambridge during 1891 after reading Greek and Latin to embarrass my parents totally by taking a commission in the Army and joining a cavalry regiment. At the start of the second Boer War eight years later I had reached the rank of major, and at the end of the war during '03 relinquished my commission and returned at the age of thirty-five to teach Latin and Greek in a boys' prep school not far from my boyhood home in Cambridgeshire. A year later I met and married Milly who was just eighteen at the time. A lovely girl!' he exclaimed. 'Full of freshness and youth....'

Olivia followed his eyes as he glanced upwards to the photographs. 'This house is haunted by her, although the fact is that she never lived here. She died six years later in childbirth in 1911, a year after she had that dress made.'

'And I suppose that's why you took holy orders,' she murmured, holding out her glass to be refilled.

'Not exactly,' he replied pouring himself a third whisky. 'It happened completely out of the blue shortly after Milly died. One Sports Day the father of one of my boys, who happened to be a bishop, was walking across the grass chatting when he said "Maunsell, have you never considered teaching men instead of boys?" and before the summer was out he had made all the arrangements for me to take up holy orders. Two years later I became curate to an East End vicar, and in 1915 my patron bishop offered me this living in my boyhood Fen.'

Olivia sat circling the stem of her wine glass between finger and thumb waiting for the Vicar to continue, but he sat looking into the heart of the fire in silence.

'I think I had better change and be off,' she said, easing herself up from the chair and stroking the creases from her skirt.

The Vicar started, as if suddenly woken from a sleep, and jumped to his feet. 'You must have some luncheon first!'

She followed him along the bleak flagged passage to a spacious kitchen with a stone sink below a pump, an unlit black kitchen range, scrubbed pine table and dresser, and a double burner oil-stove on which simmered a large cast-iron pan and a kettle.

'Broth!' he said, lifting the pan lid to give a stir to some brown turgid liquid. 'Warm you up m'dear.'

He took a crusty loaf from a bread bin and cut it into thick slices and added a second bowl and spoon to a ready-set silver tray. 'Carry this back to the study and I'll bring the broth.'

'I understood that your sister lived with you!' Olivia said softly, when they were once again sitting opposite each other before the fire with bowls of broth on their laps and the pan still bubbling merrily on the hearth.

'Good gracious, no! Drusilla is a virtuous prune living alone in her own sanctum sanctorum in Front Street between Granny Fallow's cottage and the bakery. Drusilla has got her priorities all mixed up. She believes that cleanliness comes before godliness. She is the upright thurifer dispensing the incense of Mansion polish and Izal. If I allowed her in this lovely, liveable old house everything would be mercilessly swept away into the rubbish pit, the dog would be scrubbed hairless and we'd both be dead in a week!'

Olivia gave an girlish giggle as he leaned across to fill her glass.

'You are incorrigible,' she said, tapping his arm confidentially, 'and I'm feeling quite tipsy!'

'Have some more broth.'

'What's in it?'

'The remains of yesterday's jugged hare.'

'Isn't that cooked in port?'

The Vicar chuckled.

'I'm off!' announced Olivia brightly, her face glowing, and feeling deliciously warm and mellow inside.

'If you must,' sighed the Vicar. 'But it has been very pleasant to have your company.'

She laughed. 'If I stay any longer I won't be able to stagger back to Jubilee House. And what do you think your flock would say to that?'

'They'd have a good old mardle, that's a fact. The old church would be filled for weeks without a word of a lie! I'd be as famous as the old parson of Stiffkey!'

'Oh, go you on bor!' she retorted laughing as she slipped through the study door and ran up the stairs to change her clothes.

The Vicar met her at the bottom of the stairs holding a carpet bag in one hand and a coat across his arm.

'This is the rest of Milly's outfit,' he said, taking the folded skirt and shirt from Olivia and placing them in the bag with the coat and gilet.

Olivia took up the bag and preceded him to the porch.

The Vicar surveyed her anxiously. 'You will be sure to wear Milly's togs for the Skating Party?'

'Of course!' she answered quickly.

'Then I shall write out the notices straight away and have them displayed in the Ship, the Post Office, and the shop. Meet in the Ship 7.30 p.m. on Thursday. Leave for the Black Swan at 8 p.m. when the moon rises.'

'I know someone who won't be allowed to join us if you mention the Ship as a meeting place!' she replied, grinning.

There was a space of silence.

'Over-indulgence in devotion to the spirit, both Holy and aqua vitæ, is destruction to the soul,' he intoned. 'Maybe on second thoughts it would be diplomatic to say "Meet at the Lode staithe at 8 p.m.".'

'See you seven-forty-five in the Ship,' laughed Olivia, giving him a kiss on his rosy cheek and walking away down the gravel path leaving the old Vicar standing alone between the tall white Tuscan columns of the Rectory porch.

'Give me your skates, and I'll get them sharpened.'

Frank banged on Olivia's bedroom door as he passed along the landing.

She opened the door.

'Ready for the Skating Party? I'm off to the smithy with mine.'

She dropped back on the fireside rug where she had been reading a magazine before the fire as Frank entered to collect her skating boots.

'Coming with me?' he asked.

Olivia groaned. 'I'm stiff all over,' she answered, gingerly leaning against a pillow propped against the leg of a chair. 'But I shall be fine by this evening!' she added hastily with a grin, as his face clouded in dismay.

The blacksmith's smithy stood just off a junction of a lane and the Street beyond the Gospel Tree. During the summer months it nestled half-hidden beneath the dense foliage of an aged wych elm, which gave dappled shade to the shires patiently waiting for their turn in the travus, where the horseshoes were heated in the forge and hammered cherry-red on the anvil surrounded by the pungent smell of burning hoof.

In winter when the tree's bare skeleton was silhouetted against leaden skies, and the horses waited with their backs turned towards the slanting rain, the travus became the haven where the patriarchs congregated to gossip their days away in the white-hot glow from the forge which flickered upon their wrinkled, leather-brown faces turning them into grotesque gargoyled shapes shuffling and coughing in the dim shadows.

Aaron Smart looked up as he pared a cob's hoof with a buttrice as Frank entered the travus. He was surrounded by the usual half-dozen patriarchs smoking foul-smelling pipes and Boer Robert who had brought the piebald cob to have its shoes roughed.

'You haven't brought them pattens to be sharped by any chance?' said Aaron, dropping the cob's foot, and shaking the parings from his leather apron.

'Yes please Mr Smart,' answered Frank. 'Ready for tonight's skating party.'

'The mentality of people! They have all the year to think about getting their pattens sharped and what do they do?' He glared at Frank. 'They have to bring 'em in just when I have every hoss in the fen to rough or turn. Chuck 'em down with the rest and bugger off home!' he said testily.

Frank turned and noticed a pile of skates in a heap on the floor beneath the handle to the bellows.

'Like a cart-load of idiots!' continued Aaron, as he furiously pumped the bellows handle causing the furnace to roar and glow white-hot in a swirl of dancing sparks.

At this inopportune moment Ferret arrived with Marsh Farm's trap pony. 'I've bringed the road pony for to be roughed, and Daggy's, and Dad's and my pattens to be sharped!'

'There you are!' Aaron faced his audience drawing a beefy bare arm across his sweating brow. 'Mentality of bloody people!'

Ferret gave him a condescending look as she went to stand beside the bed of cherry-red coke and loosen the binder-twine belt of her mac exposing a thin cotton dress.

'My mentality's alright, Mr Smart. I've earned a bob off Mr Barrett to bring the pony in to you!'

'Ar...and I'll have it off you for sharpening your pattens!' he retorted breaking into a wide grin. 'Cheeky young mawther!'

Frank seated himself on a block of wood beside Boer.

Boer winked at Aaron.

'You make sure that's all he take off you, gal,' said Boer. 'He look rarely full of oats and as frisky as an old goat!'

'Oats! He don't know what oats are. That's old stale beer swilling around what makes him so cantankerous!' She turned to Frank. 'Are you a-comin' tonight?'

'You know why the old parson started up this old lark,' wheezed great-grandfather Roberts from the shadows. 'He have a mind to get the Captain's missus skating down the Lode so's he can hold her hand in the moonlight. I'd rarely have a laugh if she thaws and they all have to walk home!'

'That's twenty mile by road,' chuckled another asthmatic voice.

'Fare to be a rum old bird the Parson!' chimed in old Slodger Chapman shaking his balaclava-shrouded head reminiscently. 'A rum old bird!'

'Half past seven!' Olivia exclaimed raising herself from her fireside chair. 'Time to change for the skating trip.'

Mrs Dutton lifted her eyes from the book she was reading as Olivia left the room.

'I hear that this skating trip will be to a public house.' She turned to peer at Frank over the top of her reading glasses. 'You will wait outside if any of the villagers enter it.'

'I'd be frozen to death,' he giggled.

'In that case you had better stay at home,' she replied decisively.

'The Vicar chose the Black Swan simply as a landmark where we are to turn round. It's about seven miles up river and we can have a little rest in the warm before starting off back. Just like the Sunday School Outings!' he answered brightly.

The reappearance of Olivia, framed in the doorway wearing the Edwardian outfit, caused his mother to raise her eyebrows and drop her book obviously unamused.

'Really, Mrs Vernon! What will the village think if you dress up like that!'

Olivia flushed slightly, glancing at herself in the over-mantel mirror, and laughed.

'The Vicar asked me to wear this outfit for his especial pleasure. He wants to be reminded of his young wife!'

'In that case you should not humour him,' replied Mrs Dutton severely, returning her eyes to the book and dismissing the subject.

'He's a lovable old dear.' Olivia gave the fox boa a flippant swirl around her shoulders. 'I have no idea when we shall be back,' she murmured, picking up her skating boots and following Frank out of the room.

A large full moon rising above the Chapel greeted them as they closed the porch door.

'Perhaps we had better not go to the Ship,' she laughed.

'Ma will have spies?'

'Probably.' The sharp frosty air made her catch her breath.

'Anyway, everyone seems to be heading towards the Lode.'

She took possession of his hand as they turned into the Street, to walk quickly side by side with the moon behind their backs flinging long shadows ahead of them. Shadowy couples and small groups of chattering villagers hurried along the Street, their voices and laughter ringing through the crisp frosty air and firefly-flickers danced at each step from polished pattens swinging on their straps from nebulous shoulders.

Daggy, Harnser, Rosie and Ferret came up from behind riding their bicycles.

'Wotcher bor!' shouted Harnser, evidently well illuminated with the Ship's 'inner-light'. 'Good old night for a trip in the moonlight, Ma'am!' he added as the quartet clanked by.

Daggy in the rear suddenly noticed Olivia's genteel Edwardian look and wobbled alarmingly. 'Gawd!' he croaked hoarsely as he hit the kerb and miraculously managed to keep going. 'I thought you was a ghost!'

Daggy dismounted and proceeded to walk beside Olivia pushing his bicycle.

'That's a fact. Without a word of a lie you look beautiful. Same as them Cambridge young ladies used to look when I were young.'

'Thank you, Daggy!'

Daggy gave her a long sideways glance. 'Don't you let the old Parson see you looking beautiful like that, Ma'am!'

'But it was his idea that I should.'

'Oh my Gawd,' gasped Daggy nearly dropping his bicycle. 'If he see you looking like that he'll be so mazed he won't see the Dirty Duck. He'll hold your hand in the moonlight and take us all the way up to Cambridge!'

Daggy pushed his bicycle in brooding silence for at least thirty seconds. 'I come to the conclusion,' he said at last, 'you'd better be my partner. Just to save the poor old Parson gettin' mazed!' he added hurriedly.

'I really don't know. How am I to know that you won't be mazed?'

'Ar, that I won't. I ain't never been mazed in my life, though I fare to think what it would be like! But that there old Parson, he's always mazed!'

'Then you and I and the Vicar will keep together. How's that, Daggy? Then we shall all be safe!' she murmured sympathetically.

'Ar...I suppose that'll have to do,' he mumbled as they approached shadowy figures standing on the top of the Lode bank.

The one-time landing stage where five tall crack willows had grown from the old groyne posts hummed with the chatter of excited voices as the party clustered in a merry group fixing pattens to boots. The Vicar, wearing a white woolly skating hat with a red bobble, stood on the moonlit ice surrounded by skaters milling around while the laggards finished strapping on their pattens. Madge, holding hands with Granna Fallow's nephew who was on leave from the R.A.F., leisurely circled beyond the dusky fringe of sedges. The whole of Willows End seemed to be congregated on the ice, only the Headmaster and his wife, Mrs Dutton, and any other 'furriners', including the occupants of The Grange and the Methodist Minister, being conspicuous by their absence. Some, including R.S.M.Kingshott, the Postmaster, the Postmistress, Big Bertha Pope, and those patriarchs who were not victims of agues and rheumatics, were there solely to watch the start of the 'Parson's latest foolery'. Farmer Barratt had abandoned the fug of the Ship's taproom for the frosty air to press a ten-shilling note and two half-crowns into the Vicar's hand to buy liquid sustenance for his flock when, or if, they reached the Black Swan.

Olivia seated herself on a plank of wood placed across two buckets and removed her shoes. The moon's brilliance enchanted her. It flung back shadows across a pool of silvered grass from the five willows, their topmost twigs reaching outwards casting inky tracings on grass rimed with frost, glinting like fish-scales. It silvered her white boots with fairy-tale magic, conjuring up childhood visions of ice princesses and swan-maidens.

'Are we all here?'

She heard the Vicar's voice above the babble and finished buckling the belt of Milly's coat before gliding out from the willow's shadow towards him. The coat felt voluptuously warm. It was a short lovat coat, belted like a Norfolk jacket with large patch pockets and a strip of fur on the collar.

Harnser, like a broody hen with her chicks, started ushering the Vicar's flock into some semblance of order on the ice. Frank joined Olivia with a haversack on his shoulder to take her shoes, and the Vicar and Daggy simultaneously arrived at her side.

'Ah! Mrs Vernon,' exclaimed the Vicar. 'You look enchanting.'

'Ar! That's what I say,' rejoined Daggy, hastily slipping round her to take up a position next to her right elbow.

The moon-whitened ribbon of the Lode stretched ahead between its bordering banks high above the sunken fen. Olivia glanced over her shoulder to see the line-up of the figures behind them waiting for the Vicar's signal to start. The brilliant moon cast an opalescent glow from a cloudless sky which reflected back from the ice on to the people's faces, softening them and investing them with the beauty of the old Dutch masters.

Ten Mile Griggs, Fancy Griggs, and Molly made a trio on her left, with Harnser and Rosie, Runner Roberts and Selina, Abel Chapman and Sarah forming a second wave of couples. These in turn were followed by Madge and her airman, China, Chippy, Podge, Ferret, Podge's sister Lucy, and Frank, and, well to the rear, an unexpected duo, consisting of virginal Violet Judd and the Moocher, held hands in the shadow of the willows.

'Ready m'dear?' asked the Vicar. 'By Jingo, this is a wonderful experience, one you will never forget!'

'Ar,' said Daggy, edging closer to Olivia's side. 'And don't you forget to stop at the Swan, Parson. Too much moonlight is really bad for you'.

'Party!' The Vicar had automatically donned his Major's cap from Boer War days with his voice taking on the stentorian timbre of authority. 'We are about to move off.' He glanced over his shoulder. 'Forward!'

And they were off, shrieking, giggling and shouting witticisms to those left standing on the shore as they moved forward. As if by some hidden command the searchlight generator rumbled into life half a mile further along the Lode and the beam came on, meeting the Ten Mile Bank light to form an archway across the ice.

The party settled down as they skated beneath the arch, gathering momentum in effortless gliding strides, lulled by the crisp hiss of skates on ice. Olivia began to feel the true beauty of the Fens. She had entered a realm of infinite space and silence beneath a dome of sky whose only limitation was the circle of the horizon, across which the moon cast its light unhindered by hills. Its only shadows fell from the tall reeds, the isolated windbreak poplars and willows around stark farms, churches and derelict windmills. The silence was broken only by the fugitive pipings of high-flying night birds or the sudden harsh cry from a heron ringing through the crisp frosted air.

After a mile and a half they turned into the main river.

'Thirty-five year since I were on the old river,' said Daggy. 'Proper old winters when I were a boy when they froze regular as clockwork.'

'The years have changed,' sighed the Vicar, glancing at Olivia's long skirt from beneath which the white boots flashed, reflecting the moonlight as the wide hem lifted and fell as she glided over the ice.

The gleaming ribbon of ice stretched ahead, its edges lined with stiff rushes and unkempt sallows rimed with frost. Polled willows cast their shadows across the skaters' path. A team of mallard passed overhead with a whistle of wings, invisible against the velvet night sky until they crossed the face of the moon.

'I hopes them old devils ain't been a-sitting on the river today!' exclaimed Daggy. 'Do someone's in for a cold bath!'

'Why?' asked Olivia. 'Surely a few ducks don't matter!'

'Oh, they certainly can cause accidents to the unwary,' answered the Vicar. 'What happens is that a flock of ducks keep a patch of water open by swimming in it during the day, but then they leave and thin ice forms over it with nothing to show the skater that it is there.'

'Oh dear,' said Olivia. 'And what does one do?'

'Trust in Gawd!' chuckled Daggy. 'That's right isn't it Parson!'

But before the Vicar could form a suitable reply Harnser, Fancy, Ten Mile, and Abel flashed ahead 'speed-skating' for pure joy, followed by Ferret and the four boys.

'Look you out for duck flashes, Harnser!' Daggy bellowed as they passed.

Selina, Rosie, Sarah, Molly and Lucy closed ranks and continued gossiping, sounding like a migrating flock of snow buntings. Madge and Granna Fallow's nephew skated dreamily behind with their arms round each other's waists, followed by Violet having the time of her sheltered life holding hands with the Moocher.

At last a dusky, solid shape appeared on the right bank half a mile ahead which quickly materialized into a stark, low building bathed in silvery-green moonlight and surrounded by bare willows.

'The Dirty Duck,' chuckled the Vicar, steering Olivia towards a shelving landing stage on which a couple of upturned punts glistened with hoar frost.

She flung out her arms to keep her balance as her skates hit the edge of the gravel. Stumbling to lean against the nearest punt she lifted her head to face the brilliance of the moon re-awakening the sheer intoxicating joy of being alive as she sat unlacing her boots waiting for Frank to bring her shoes.

The Black Swan was the domain of Harry Roach, a wizened little man as bright as a weasel. He invariably wore a pair of shiny black trousers and waistcoat over a collarless striped shirt with a brass stud which danced little jigs on his prominent Adam's apple, bobbing and leaping ever higher as he became more and more excited holding forth on some favourite subject. For 'Old Harry's' fame as a living edition of *Whitaker's Almanack, Pears' Encyclopædia*, and the *Sporting Life*, encircled the Fens.

The Willows End contingent burst through the blackout curtain and noisily entered the taproom. Harnser and Fancy, closely followed by the Vicar, made for the bar, pushed and jostled forward by the rest of the party.

Three Land Girls wearing green jerseys and corduroy breeches were standing before a bright fire, their glossy brushed-out hair and fresh pink complexions a world apart from the wind-beaten regulars who crowded against the bar or sat on the rough benches against yellowing plaster walls. On these walls hung fly-spotted sepia photographs of old cricket teams, burly men in the likeness of W. G. Grace, bewhiskered and moustached, and skating teams wearing otter-skin caps and eel-skin garters over thick woollen stockings posing against a backdrop of Welney Wash polled willows. The family names were the same - only the changing fashions marked the generations.

Olivia, ducking beneath the swaying blackout curtain, found herself being propelled towards the Land Girls, who, understandably surprised by this vision of an Edwardian lady with a pair of white kid skating boots hanging from her shoulders, made way for her to collapse on a settle next to the fire. Their eyes continued to widen at the sight of a Pickwickian vicar, also sporting a pair of skates hanging from his shoulder, heading for the bar.

'A good evening to you, Harry,' boomed the Vicar.

The hum of conversation suddenly stopped as the Dirty Duck's regulars stopped in mid-sentence and a ring dropped with a metallic clatter as a quartet of dykers playing bull-ringles turned their heads.

'Ale for the men. Gin, port or whatever they choose for the ladies, and ginger beer for the youngsters!' he announced, raising his gloved hand and nodding benignly towards a gaunt old man sitting quietly on a fireside settle opposite Olivia. A glass of gin had appeared as if by magic in her hand and she smiled warmly in the direction of the Land Army girl. She was a handsome girl, with dark-brown hair gathered loosely beneath her uniform hat, and dark eyes full of easy laughter, chatting with a broad Midland accent to a regular sitting beside Olivia.

'Is that *really* a parson?' asked the girl, lowering her voice. 'In a pub!'

'Ar gal, that's old Patten Parson. Gawd bless you gal, everyone know him! Real old champion skater he were in my old Dad's time,' answered the man. 'And him over the other side of the fire were another old champion. Ronnie Roach he is. Them two together were great old fighters for the sweepstakes years ago.'

Olivia smiled to herself as she gazed into the spluttering heart of the fire and settled back warmly as the tobacco smoke, steaming bodies, and blazing firelight coalesced into an amber fug in the low, blacked-out airless room. The Land Army girl removed her hat, allowing her hair to tumble untidily across her face.

'It's a-goin' to be a regular old booze-up, gal,' grinned the man, sliding an arm possessively round her waist and drawing her down to sit on his knee in anticipatory delight. 'That's if the old Parson's payin'.'

'Parson!' shouted Ronny Roach tipsily. 'You Willows End lot never did learn to skate!'

'Beat you lot any time.'

'Ha! Don't you forget nineteen-o-two.' A gust of derisory laughter swept around the bar from the Black Swan regulars.

'Ha!' The Vicar's face took on the raddled appearance of an apoplectic turkey cock. 'Willows End men were never beaten. They were among the most accomplished speed-skaters in the Fens. In fact in the world of speed skating they were invincible.' He glared balefully at his old rival. 'You could never find a man to match a Willows End man.'

'Then your memory's gone, Parson, that it have! What about nineteen-twenty-nine down at Linley? So don't you go mardling a lot o' squit. Young Billy Judd there could beat any one of your lot any time of the day or night.'

The Vicar thumped the bar in a most irreverent manner.

'I'll lay two pounds that he can't beat my man to the half-mile post and back.'

Young Billy Judd, a powerful man with blond hair and piercing blue eyes who was one of the dykers playing bull-ringles at the far side of the room, raised his hands above his head and grinned.

'He don't have a snowball's chance in hell against Young Billy,' the man sitting next to Olivia murmured gleefully in her ear. 'He were born with a pair of pattens on his feet.'

'Oh dear,' thought Olivia. 'There goes the church fund.'

'Runner,' boomed the Vicar through the fug to Runner Roberts, who was peacefully downing his third pint of best bitter. 'You have just been challenged.'

'Ar,' grinned Runner, slowly finishing his pint before swaggering towards the blackout curtain. 'I had better get my pattens on.'

The hushed silence that had fallen across the room at the falling back of the blackout curtain was rudely shattered by the sound of settles scraping the brick floor and of boots scuffling as the company lurched and jostled in the wake of Young Billy through the door and out into the frosty night air.

Olivia joined the rush carrying her second glass of gin to stand at the edge of the frozen river. She was followed by the Landlord, who came bouncing through the curtain, as if propelled by springs, carrying a shotgun.

'Don't you go yet!' he shouted, beside himself with excitement, to the two contestants who were poised side by side in the centre of the river. 'We'll do this here proper, with a starting gun.'

'Gawd! Don't you shoot Runner,' cried Selina tipsily. 'I don't want to be a widow yet on these cold old nights.'

Bang! The explosion reverberated through the nearby willow carrs and reedbeds setting marsh pheasants crowing and starling flocks leaping blindly into flight. Away went the contestants to a flying start, with Young Billy leading the way as they flew along the silvered strip of river to vanish into the misty night.

'Excuse me....' One of the Land Army girls had crossed the staithe to stand beside Olivia, 'but I'm awfully fascinated by your outfit.'

She spoke with an upper-class accent and had a faintly puzzled expression on her face. 'I have seen very early photographs of my mother wearing similar outfits...but it's so terribly unreal in 1940!' The girl glanced sideways at Olivia as she drank from a half-pint glass of ale. 'I mean...quite spooky out here at the time of the full moon.'

Olivia reflected for a moment. 'You could say that I am a congenial spectre,' she grinned gaily. 'I passed on during 1910. So I suppose I was of your mother's generation!'

The girl blushed. 'I didn't mean to be rude.'

Olivia chuckled with childlike delight. 'Actually I am a bit of the Vicar's nostalgia. His deceased young wife, Milly, wore this outfit over forty years ago, and I am helping to resurrect memories of his youth by wearing it this evening.'

'How jolly!' The girl laughed. 'But, honestly, he doesn't look much like a clergyman to me!'

'He is a jolly fine vicar, a very lovable old vicar, a darling of a vicar,' replied Olivia, merry after her second large gin. 'Out guarding his flock.'

'This is his flock!'

Before Olivia could reply the contestants reappeared as they swept through the greyness into the area of moonlit ice with Young Billy leading, much to the glee of the Dirty Duck regulars.They rushed forward to give a tumultuous cheer - which faded into a moan of disbelief as Runner shot ahead to win by ten lengths.

The Vicar, pushing his way through the Dirty Duck regulars, leapt up and down wildly, voicing his approval. 'That, m'dear, is what Headmaster would call *strategy*,' he whispered in an aside to Olivia. 'He made a calculated use of their man as pacemaker and then, by Jingo, he beat him at the post!'

'At least the church funds are safe for a while,' she laughed.

'Never at risk!' chortled the Vicar. 'Providence has seen that this little trip has paid for itself.' The Land Army girl giggled. 'By Jove! Where did you come from?' he said, noticing her for the first time.

'Originally? The Garden of Eden. Bearsted in Kent.'

'Good gracious! Then come and have a glass of apple juice with me.'

He took her by the hand and turned happily towards the pub door. 'Now, back to the festivities for a last round of drinks on our friend Ronald Roach,' he shouted.

'Ar,' growled the loser truculently. 'If this here fruz holds we'll be up your Lode for a return match afore long,' and, two pounds down, he led the unhappy Dirty Duck regulars back into the homely fug of the taproom.

At 10.45 the Vicar marshalled his boisterous flock through the blackout curtain into the night to overcome the intricacies of buckles and thumbscrews as they clumsily fitted skates to boots sitting on the upturned punts. Finally, after muttered curses and giggles, they tumbled on to their feet and got under way, the long-married couples romantically holding hands as they glided along, veering from side to side in warm, alcoholic bliss.

They sang, beginning with lusty choruses of 'She'll be coming round the mountain when she comes', 'Ten green bottles', and 'Old Macmara had a farm', which sent snipe corkscrewing and mallard quarking high into the night sky. The frosty air tingled on their cheeks. After the oppressive fug of the bar it filled their lungs with a sharpness that was almost a pain, making them catch their breath.

Olivia glided over the ice beside the elderly Vicar with only the hiss of steel skates breaking the silence of the night. The high moon was sinking towards the south-west in a clear sky. Daggy had deserted her. He was somewhere behind, skating three-sheets-in-the-wind following a tacking course and mumbling his risqué ditties of 'Fair Cadilly' who had skated on this stretch of river a century before.

By the time they had reached the junction of the river and the mouth of the Lode the tempo of the singing had slackened. It was the girls alone who sang, the almost pure oxygen in the crystalline air having had its effect on their menfolk's fuddled brains, leaving them bemused but held steady by the capable arms of their spouses.

For Frank, as he skated in a line strung across the Lode with Ferret, Lucy, and the three boys, it was also a night to remember, his introduction to the joyful debauchery of a 'booze-up', a joy further heightened by his share of two bottles of brown ale which China had wheedled from Daggy Flegg.

The party had reached the staithe where they sat, squatted, or lay, on the white frosty grass of the Lode bank in small groups, fumbling and cursing in various states of competence as they faced the task of removing pattens from boots for the short walk home to the village.

Olivia seated herself on an upturned punt and began to unlace Milly's white boots. She paused to look back along the silent Loke, experiencing the moon's mystery drifting like the air of an ancient song, rising and falling among the brittle sere reeds.

'A very satisfactory evening!' chuckled the Vicar. 'Are we all here?'

It was Rosie who answered, for Harnser, who had marshalled the start of the expedition with so much merriment and wit, was now staggering, maudlin and tearful, with his pattens hanging precariously over his shoulder homeward along the drove.

'Ar, I think so, Vicar. Everyone 'cept that slummocking mawther, Lucy, and him what's on leave from the R.A.F. She'll have anything in uniform, she will. Oh, and old Daggy, though he turned off along o' his drain.'

'Excellent. Right, off home now. A truly excellent evening!' And taking Olivia's arm he led his triumphal skating party off the dirt drove and along the village street where they disappeared in ones and twos as they entered their cottage doors.

Mrs Dutton, waiting in the silence of her living room, heard the merry, slurred 'Good nights', followed by gusts of laughter coming from the returning party as they passed the window. She glanced at the clock - *half-past midnight* - then heard Olivia's voice bidding the Vicar goodnight and his reply, her rich warm laughter, then the crunch of her shoes on the gravel path.

Her lips tightened in advance of the door opening, ready to greet the home-comers with her usual stony stare, meanwhile praying with all the conviction of an embittered mother for the shameless woman to leave...a prayer soon to be answered.

Friday 6th of December 1940
Goodbye to the Fen

Olivia overslept on the day following the skating party and it was mid-morning before she left Jubilee House to post a letter to her husband, now stationed in the Dukeries where the regiment was regrouping.

As she closed the door she was greeted by the spectacle of the Postmaster heading towards her, pedalling furiously as he worked up speed to cross the hundred and fifty yards which stretched between the Post Office and Jubilee House, frantically waving a small yellow envelope in his upraised left hand.

'Telegram... Telegram.'

Their paths converged in the centre of the road with the Postmaster's heavy bicycle skidding to a halt on the frozen tarmac as he applied the front brake with his right hand while continuing to wave the bright yellow envelope above his head with the left.

'Telegram for you, Mrs Vernon!' he panted as the bicycle slid sideways beneath him.

Olivia blenched, fearful for her parents' safety in the air raids.

'Not to worry! Excellent news!'

He executed an accomplished *pas ciseaux* by leaping with his legs wide apart in mid-air allowing his still-moving steed to slide to a jangling halt in the gutter. 'It's from the Captain, Ma'am. He wants you to join him immediately!'

Olivia took the envelope from his outstretched hand.

'I shall send an immediate response to say that you are coming,' he said, beaming at her, before bending to pick up his bicycle for the return dash across the Square.

'I think I had better read the message myself before deciding on the reply,' she said coldly, opening the envelope.

'Good! Splendid! Quite right!' he chortled, unabashed.

The message, written on the buff form, was terse. She could imagine Dickie counting the words: 'Have arranged a room. Will meet 7.45 p.m. train Ollerton. Wednesday 19th. Dickie.'

She read the message three times, slowly because of the Postmaster's presumption. Meanwhile he had retrieved his bicycle and was standing, foot poised on pedal, ready to make a flying start back to his telegraph machine.

'Yes,' she replied frowning. 'You may send a reply. Just put "Will arrive 7.45. Wednesday. Olivia."' She turned to retrace her steps to her room carrying the unposted letter.

'I have the reply form here, Mrs Vernon,' said the Postmaster gleefully, holding out another buff form.

'Oh, Mr Howes. Surely you can fill it in for me,' she answered with sugary sweetness. 'After all you know all the particulars *far* better than I!'

Back in her room she flopped down on the bed with irritable resignation.

'This damned war!' she thought. 'Moving, moving, moving!' She glanced out of the window to look down upon the Square. Miss Lacy's junior class was doing P.T. in the schoolyard. Her shrill voice penetrated the casement 'Arms up, stretch, bend. Keep your legs straight Rosie Wright.' Old Slodger Roberts was hobbling towards the warmth of the smithy muffled up to his eyebrows in a great-coat and muffler. A noisy gang of jackdaws squabbled wretchedly over a dropped crust of bread. Bare of leaves, the church limes echoed her resignation as she lifted her suitcases down from the wardrobe.

Presently the white skating boots lying in a corner caught her attention. She sighed restlessly and looked again from the window. Sunlight sparkled on the frosty chancel-roof behind yews silhouetted against a blue sky. Packing could wait until tomorrow! Today she would call on the Vicar and suggest one last skate along the Lode. Magically her spirits lifted as she pulled the long socks over her stockings and changed from her Goray skirt into Millie's brown linen skating outfit.

At half past four Frank burst into the sitting room, where Olivia was sitting in front of the fire toasting a slice of bread on a twisted-wire toasting fork.

'School breaks up for Christmas on Friday!' he said. 'What shall we do for two whole weeks, Mrs Vernon?'

He flung his satchel dismissively across the room spilling homework and text books around the slumbering ginger cat and flopped down on the sofa.

'I have to leave you to join Dickie on Wednesday,' she stated flatly.

'Honest?'

His face clouded.

'Yes. Honest. I had a telegram from Dickie this morning telling me to join him at some outlandish Nottinghamshire address.'

'You *have* to go? Will you be back before Christmas?' She rose from her chair and crossed the room to put her arm round his shoulder.

'I'm afraid it will be to stay,' she replied wistfully. 'I always hate this constant moving following the Unit around. Do you know six months ago I dreaded having to move to the ghastly Fens? Now I don't want to leave them!'

After the British Expeditionary Force had sailed for France Olivia had moved into her parents' Chelsea home, one of the fine houses in Cheyne Row adjacent to Embankment Walk and the river. During that first uneventful winter of the 'phoney war' life in London had been gay and easy-going, with lively tea dances to Joe Loss, Tommy Dorsay, and Victor Silvester's bands at the Dorchester and the Savoy. The night clubs were crowded, and nobody seemed to have a care in the world. Buildings were sand-bagged. Bomb shelters were dug and a blackout was enforced. But the war had seemed a long way away when the telegram arrived from Dickie asking her to join him in a Fenland village. Her friends had sympathized, painting a grim picture of a desolate god-forsaken country of moronic rustics and a perpetual east wind.

She contemplated Frank solemnly.

'I'll tell you what we'll do! We'll go to the cinema tomorrow evening on Ossie's 'Tuesday pictures' bus. That new film is on with Betty Grable and Don Ameche, 'Down Argentina Way' which is supposed to be jolly good. I know you're potty about Betty Grable, Frankie!' she teased.

'Do you *have* to leave?' he reiterated.

' 'Fraid I must.'

'You *want* to go?' he blurted out resentfully.

Olivia remained silent. The great churchyard yews beyond the lych-gate opposite spread funereal gloom through the gathering dusk.

'Oh, Frankie, don't be so dismal!' she protested reprovingly. 'How about lighting the lamp while I put the blackouts up? Your Ma will be home any moment now.'

'I don't suppose *she* will miss you!' he murmured sulkily, flouncing out of the room bearing the Aladdin lamp away to the scullery to trim its wick.

Fen villages possess the finest bush telegraph system in the world, and by tea-time all the inhabitants of Willows End had been informed of the impending departure of the Captain's lady. As always, being prone to embroidery and drama, the 'why' of her sudden departure acquired diverse explanations. Customers of the Shop were led to believe that 'the War Office had been bombed and that poor gal's old father what's one of them generals what works there's been killed, and she's had a telegram to say she got to go home to look after her old mother!' Whereas the version delivered with a nod and a wink by the Postmaster's wife to gossips with an unusual appetite for penny stamps was a relatively true account of the now famous telegram. Therefore it was no surprise to Frank when Mrs Dutton's first words on her arrival home, directed to Olivia with bitter joy, were 'I hear that you will be leaving on Wednesday.'

It had been King Kong who had enlightened the villagers about Olivia's 'pedigree', for the unravelling of every 'furriner's' pedigree was always a source of great cogitation and surmise by fertile fenland brains. R.S.M.Clive Kingshott broke the enigma quite early during Olivia's seven-month stay in the village. They had discovered a common nostalgic for India. They swopped memories of Western Maharashtra. 'I must actually have watched you on the parade ground!' she had said, wide-eyed 'and heard you bellow!'

King Kong had twirled his moustache. 'Ar! I were a fine feller in them days, with a crack regiment, m'dear, second to none!'

'I suppose that would have been about 1923,' Olivia had replied. 'I was nine at the time, just before Mother and the rest of the wives left to spend the hot season in the mountains above Simla, and I was packed off to a prep. school for girls in England.' She contemplated him solemnly. 'One of Father's pet sayings was "The cornerstone of the Regiment is the Regimental Sergeant Major! The whole Regiment would face total disaster without the R.S.M.".'

Mr Kingshott gave his moustache another twirl and thrust out his chest.

'Ar. That's right. We had a colonel in them days, a queer old fellow. Used to spend half his time with the ladies in Bombay and the other half with the other officers on long shooting trips. Left everything to me to manage!'

'I remember! "Squiffy" Johnson!' she giggled. 'Daddy followed him as Colonel when he retired. He was a bit of a dandy and wore a monocle.'

'Major Warburton!' King Kong's steel-blue eyes had become decidedly moist at the recollection. 'He must have been your father. Gawd bless us! It's a rum old world, isn't it, Ma'am?' He mopped his face with a large red handkerchief. 'What's the Major doing now?'

'Oh, he had retired before the war. But he is now back at the War Office as a Brigadier being driven around in a huge Humber staff-car by a glamorous W.A.A.C. driver. Mother is living in Chelsea, just off the Embankment.'

'Well, that's a rummun. To think I must have see'd you as a little gal at the other side of the world. Then to see you back in Willows End - 'tain't believable is it now?'

So the 'pedigree' of Olivia Vernon, née Warburton, had been broadcast abroad to all and sundry from the Ship, the village shop, the Tuesday evening Women's Institute meetings and wherever gossips met, until her fame had spread outwards traversing the droves to reach the most isolated of the fenland smallholdings.

Wednesday the 11th of December...It was raining from a leaden grey sky. A thaw had set in, and Frank lay miserably awake curled up in his narrow bed listening to the monotonous drip of water from the eaves. The front door slammed as Mrs Dutton left the house and he heard the dull rasp of her footsteps on the gravel fade away as she turned to pass up the street.

He burrowed under the bed-clothes to blot out the sound of Olivia as she moved around her room in a last-minute rush collecting her belongings. He did not want to be there when she left. This was to be the second time he had been deserted within seven months. Her footsteps paused outside his bedroom door. Her voice invaded his blankets.

'Aren't you coming to see me off, Frankie?'

He dragged the blankets higher, pretending to sleep.

'Frankie!'

He was aware of the door opening followed by a sudden bounce on his mattress as she sat on the side of his bed.

'Oh Frank! What on earth am I to do with you? Get up and see me off!'

She laughed her bubbling laugh, smacking the bed-clothes, and turned to leave. 'Come on, Frankie. I'll give you five minutes. Then I shall come and drag you out.'

He stared at the ceiling feeling inwardly forlorn before starting to dress. 'How can she laugh when she's leaving us?' he asked himself.

Olivia was sitting in the kitchen wearing an unbuttoned gaberdine trench-coat over a navy suit and pale pink blouse, surrounded by two suitcases and a tin travelling trunk.

'All my worldly goods!' she exclaimed glumly as Frank entered the room.

He flung her a sideways glance, noticing with a pang of jealousy that she had reddened her lips with a bright poppy-red lipstick, darkened her lashes, and pencilled the curve of her eyebrows. She was so beautiful in her sophisticated way that it made his adolescent's heart ache to look at her.

He looked instead at the cases, then, flinching from the sight of the silk-stockinged calf that lay across them, stared glumly up at the ceiling.

'There's fresh tea in the pot. You'd better hurry or you'll miss your bus!'

Olivia shrugged her coat off her shoulders and poured him a cup of tea. 'Mr Rowsell will be here any moment with the taxi, so hurry up and drink it.'

He took the cup from her outstretched hand and avoided looking into her eyes.

'I'm not going to school.'

'Oh, well, in that case you can see me off properly at the station. Mr Rowsell will bring you home.'

'I wish you weren't going!' he mumbled.

She gave him a swift look. 'Don't be silly!' she answered in a hard, flat voice. 'Wish I were not going.' She grimaced. 'That's the story of my life!'

'I'm sorry,' he said bitterly.

'Oh, Frankie!' she laughed. 'Cheer up! It's not the end of the world. You'll be off to join the R.A.F. before the summer is out, flying a Spitfire without a care in the world and the darling of hero-worshipping W.A.A.Fs!'

He blushed crimson and turned to glance through the window as the sound of tyres rolling to a standstill on the gravel outside the front door heralded the arrival of Sam Rowsell's Vauxhall 12 taxi.

Frank's heart plummeted like lead. Everything was finished. He was to return to a life of utter loneliness and misery. Olivia rose from her chair, hurriedly buttoning her coat, before stooping to pick up a suitcase.

'Rough old morning Ma'am,' said Sam Rowsell, appearing in the doorway. 'Wind's changed right round and this old drizzle's a-going to set in till the New Year. Do you see if it don't. Grab you one end of this trunk, bor, and help me get it in the boot. Are you a-coming too?'

Olivia threw a wistful glance round the now familiar living room before closing the door and passing beneath the bare wisteria twigs into the drizzle of a grey morning. The pond was beginning to thaw, and the ducks were standing belly-deep on pools of open water which lay on top of the ice. The village was deserted. The cottage roofs dripped, depressingly grey, without the sun to bring life to their red pantiles, and the gilded church weathervane cock was a dusky silhouette against the overall greyness of sky.

She sat leaning forward on the back seat of the taxi as it followed the flat, featureless road over the rainy, dreary fen, which for the first time revealed to her its Jekyll and Hyde fickleness as a godforsaken, desolate land. It seemed fitting that this grey shroud had been drawn over yesterday's sin in its luminous blue sky, for it eased her leaving, putting away her personal pain at the necessity to submit to yet another move in her life.

Frank sat on the front passenger seat beside Sam Rowsell wrapped in his own grey shroud of self-pity, watching the monotonous sweep of the windscreen wipers.

'Don't you have to go to school today?' asked Sam, trying to make conversation in the silence which hung heavily in the car.

'No.'

'Have you broke up for Christmas?'

'No.'

'Have the Captain found you a nice place to stay?' Sam asked Olivia, changing his tack. 'I believe it's a...'

'I have no idea,' she answered abruptly.

Sam remained diplomatically silent until they crossed over the sluggish grey water of the river by the iron bridge and turned into the station yard.

Downham Market appeared deserted. Looking up the Green a mist of rain was screening the Dial House and Bridge Street beyond in an ashen veil, through which an old sugar-beet lorry came chugging, dark smoke pouring from its rusted exhaust as it headed out towards the bridge. On the platform, half a dozen young soldiers, returning to their units from leave, waited with their kitbags and rifles, accompanied by self-conscious sweethearts or over-possessive mothers. An airman, immaculately groomed from his polished black shoes to his slick Brylcreemed hair, cast an appreciative glance towards Olivia as she took Frank's arm and led him a little way along the platform.

'Thank you for coming to see me off,' she said quietly. 'I would have hated to stand alone on a draughty platform waiting for the train to arrive.'

He managed a smile.

'Will you remember me?' he burst out plaintively, breaking a long silence.

'Of course I shall!' She gave him a whimsical grin. 'When I remember you it will always be as a young elfin Pan showing me a reed-warbler's nest in your secret fen. I shall recall a cloudless blue sky, willow leaves, a brood of young waterhens. I will remember a bejewelled fish, a fabulous creature on a prehistoric log, skating on moonlit ice.... Of course I won't forget you!'

She bent to pick up her cases as the train arrived with a deafening hiss of escaping steam and preceded the airman into the nearest carriage.

'Oh, Frankie!' she called, dropping the door window to lean out towards him. 'Don't forget to return my skates and Milly's togs to the Vicar and thank him. Tell him I shall be writing to him.'

She presented her cheek for a kiss. In desperation he clung to her, burying his face in the wet-smelling material of her scarf until the train began to move.

Olivia turned to wave one last time, and was gone. Frank stood watching the train steam slowly away from the station until it disappeared in the grey drizzle, heading for Ely. He turned right after leaving the station, passing the large corn mill to make his way to the river where he sat on the old staithe looking out over Stow Bardolph Fen.

The rusted ironwork of the bridge above the grey, turgid mud echoed his mood of utter desolation. A solitary gull perched on the rotting hulk of a converted ship's lifeboat uttered a ghoulish laugh, scattering a shower of rain droplets as it shook its feathers and stretched a wing. Frank sat hunched in a bitter torpor. The continuous drizzle misted his hair with droplets of water which dripped from his eyebrows to form tiny rivulets that soaked his scarf and trickled insidiously down the neck of his blazer. A solitary swan ghosted over the centre of the river, the steady oompha-oompha of its stiff pinions gradually fading away through the drizzle following Olivia westwards.

Frank watched the swan, following its flight in a spasm of yearning, the great arched wings cupping the air bringing back the memory of Olivia's full white skirt lifting in the breeze as they ran together down the Lode bank in the October sunshine.

The gull laughed again. He hated the gull's mirthless laughter. Laughter was dead, a thing of the past and not to be tolerated now that Olivia had deserted him. He picked up a half-brick and flung it at the bird, sending it circling overhead screaming abuse before heading upstream towards Denver.

Frank arrived home, having had a lift back from Downham Market in a sugar-beet lorry, to find Jubilee House in the throes of upheaval. He tentatively opened the door to notice that Olivia's round table had been returned to its old place below the sitting room window, while a droning murmur of voices and the scrape of furniture being moved came from the room above.

A pile of bed-clothes and what had been Olivia's mattress piled on the landing blocked his way up the stairs, forcing him to retreat to the back stairs which led up from the dairy to the far side of the landing. The door to Olivia's lately-vacated room was open, propped wide by a mop bucket. Beyond the bucket Ma Shipham was kneeling on the bare floorboards with a tea-towel tied round her hair, perspiring freely as she scrubbed the skirting-boards. His mother, working herself up for one of her 'angina' attacks, sat surrounded by the five empty drawers of the chest, muttering to herself as she scrubbed away the last vestige of musky scent from them with carbolic soap.

Frank looked round the bare room, slowly taking in the scene. Ma Shipham's eyes met his. The recently vacated bedstead's spring frame was standing upright against the far wall, dripping a solution of milky-brown Jeyes Fluid on to the floor. The wardrobe, pulled away from the wall with open doors, awaited purification.

'You are home early!' His mother paused in her scrubbing to throw a hurried look over her shoulder at him.

'I went to see Mrs Vernon off at the station,' he answered, woodenly.

She gave a contemptuous laugh, and resumed her scrubbing.

'I suppose she actually did catch the train?' she asked perversely.

'She did.' His heart hardened against her.

'I'm glad she has gone. Never did trust the woman!' she continued, giving an extra-vindictive twist as she wrung out her floor cloth. 'Thank goodness we are leaving these dreary Fens.'

'We're not *leaving?*' he asked in a forced voice.

Mrs Dutton's face remained expressionless.

'On the last day of January,' she said, with a brittle tang of exultancy in her voice. 'I have accepted a post in my old school on the coast.'

'We're not *leaving?*' he reiterated dumbly.

He felt as if his whole world was breaking away into chaos - his father dead, Olivia gone, now this threatened parting from the Fen - nothing remained.

'You might as well leave school,' she said consolingly. 'No chance of you matriculating!'

'I'm going to apply to Cranwell as a cadet when I'm seventeen. I want to learn to fly,' he said sullenly.

'Huh! With *your* command of maths!' she cried in contempt. 'Pigs might fly.'

He shrank helplessly at her bitter irony. Ma Shipham paused in her scrubbing to give a comforting wink behind Mrs Dutton's back.

It was this disappointment in her son's lack of scholarship that was the deep-down cause of Mrs Dutton's crabbiness. As a young woman her thirst for knowledge led her to graduate as a gold medallist in History, and by her mid-twenties she had reached a distinguished academic position as a historian. But she had given this up to marry the bookish ornithologist and live far away from her urban environment in rural Norfolk.

Thomas Dutton spent his days peering through a brass microscope at dissected specimens of tissue as he worked on his study of the cranial nervous system of birds. Mrs Dutton was equally dedicated to her books, reading far into the night by the light of the Aladdin lamp. They both shunned company, and relations were kept at arm's length.

Each weekday morning Mrs Dutton had walked the two and a half miles to a neighbouring village school where she held the post of Infant teacher, returning home at five o'clock to cook the evening meal before settling down to read. Although outwardly she blamed his school for its failure to bring out the latent talent which she hoped might lie germinating in the sluggish grey cells of her son's brain, subconsciously she realised his backwardness was the result of her lack of ability to show affection, and so he was left to find his own company and develop his interests among the villagers. Thus Mrs Dutton knew little of what her son was doing, or where he was at any one time during the week.

Frank retraced his steps down the back stairs to sit on the high bentwood chair in the study listening to the muted chatter of the zebra finches. The tears began to flow slowly down his cheeks as they had done seven months before on the morning of the funeral. As then, the study with its aviary became his retreat. He sat hunched within a grey fog of disillusionment, overcome with resentment that life could hold so much unendurable pain. Rain dripped drearily from the eaves to gather in droplets on the window-frame before sliding silently down the glass like bars to his prison.

Much later he was roused by a sudden joyous trilling from the African wren. The room was lighter and the grey pall had lifted with the faintest sign of a blue streak in the sky above the church tower. Boer was leading the horses home from the fields. Church Farm's cows were ambling towards the shippen for milking, and a wraggle-taggle girl was walking slowly across the Square.

Frank rushed to open the window.

'Wotcher Ferret. Where are you going?'

Perhaps...perhaps there would be life after Olivia............!